To Marga

Lots os Love

P Bacc

x x x

The Deal

Gemma Christie

DEDICATION

To my husband and boys, who are my everything.

CONTENTS

ACKNOWLEDGMENTS

Thank you to my family, who always believe in me.
Thank you to Hannah, for reading draft after draft at the beginning
and to Joanne, for the help in the end.
And thank you to God, who gives everyone talents to increase on.

Cover Photographer/Designer: Rachel Evans
Cover Models- Phil Bruce & Kate Ball

PROLOGUE

Some girls spent their whole lives imagining their wedding, the flowers, the church, hundreds of guests, the white dress, every smallest detail all planned in their heads. At an alter would stand the picture of perfection, a modern-day Prince Charming, an eagerly anticipating fiancé who was both handsome and devoted. He and the day would both be a dream, perfect and flawless in every way. Their wedding day would be everything they had ever wanted, and more. Their wedding day would be the happiest day of their life. And so it should be.

I sighed.

If I was being vague, sarcastic and completely emotionally unattached, then I guess I could *technically* say that I had everything most girls had dreamt of. It was an utter lie and we all knew it, but it might make this moment more bearable. The reality of my wedding day couldn't have been further from my childhood dreams if I tried. Yet, here I was, walking down the aisle. Everything perfect, yet everything wrong.

The church was a classic, old, stone building that sat remotely in a small, insignificant village of Scotland. It stood picturesque on the edge of a cliff side, overlooking the North Sea. The sky was clear and blue and endless, as if a blessing from above, and the slight breeze gently ruffled the daffodils that lined the path leading to the old church doors. The whole thing was beautiful. More than a bride could ever really wish for. I knew it, but I still couldn't find any joy from it. Inside the church, cute little wooden aisles ran down either side of the room. The stained-glass windows cast an array of multi-coloured patterns on the stone floor and onto the wedding guests, who sat separated on each side. The left of the chapel sat the family of the bride, all dressed and ready for a ceremony, despite the multitude of tissues and tears. My mother was wearing a canary yellow dress with matching hat and looked practically near hyperventilation as she desperately clung to my father. His facial expression screamed, 'how-has-this-happened?'. Their moral support towards each other was a sight I hadn't seen since my childhood but instead of giving me hope, it only seemed to highlight my current loss. On the other side of the chapel, the benches were laden with support for the groom. Front and centre sat my father-in-law to be. His expression was somewhat more difficult to read than my own dad's. Did he hate me for this? Would he welcome me into the family still? He was a shrewd businessman and with this many people around, watching, his face gave nothing away. He sat motionless, showing a calculated blank stare, letting nothing escape him. Time was quickly and uncontrollably flying by and all too soon this moment in my life would be done and my new future would begin. And when this show was over, all cards would be shown and I would know if I was family or not. Not that either of us had any say on what was happening. I glanced around. I knew there were other familiar faces in the crowd, blending into the background, but if I was being selfishly honest, there was only one person in that chapel that I really wanted to see. Only one person that would hold any of my straying attention. Only one person who mattered. I glanced around again over my shoulder, noting that the guests had all come out of the woodwork for the show. To anyone who didn't know any better, it really did seem like a proper wedding, but to those of us who knew what the past held, well, they knew there was a lot more riding on the next few minutes than just remembering our vows. I glanced behind again, skimming past the fascinators and up-do hair styles, until my eyes rested on the line of black suited, soldier-standing men who secured the perimeter. They were an obvious contrast to the rest of the congregation; rigid, cold and dark. Even if their final goal was the same as the rest of the crowd, to witness a marriage, they very much overshadowed the beauty and peace that should have reigned in that old chapel. With arms folded, scowls dawned, and muscles flexed, they were a stark reminder of just how trapped I was, of just how little control I had over what was happening to me. A throat cleared ahead and drew my attention back. To him. Back to the alter, back to the unwavering, loyal, devoted groom. *My* devoted groom. The things this man had given up for me was astounding, it literally left me indebted to him for the rest of my life, maybe even longer. I would never be able to repay him for his love, his kindness, his selflessness. I watched him at the end of the aisle, watching me, and I knew, I *knew,* that I would spend the rest of my living days trying to make amends, guilt-ridden amends. He stood ahead; tall and firm, hair was parted smartly to one side, a flower in his button hole. He was a proper fiancé. A proper gentleman. Even with the shine of sweat glistening on his forehead, he looked gallant and proud. He would, and had, given up everything to look out for me and as I stepped down the aisle towards him, this almighty drowning sensation rose from my stomach to my heart and into my throat. Was I going to be sick? I swallowed it down like poison and looked at my fiancé again to try and find some perspective, some reassurance.

I exhaled. Long and hard.

He was my *fiancé*, for goodness sake. He was the man who had sacrificed everything for me. He was the man who loved me so dearly. He was also the poor man had no idea that I was no longer in love with him. He didn't know that today, my wedding, was literally the worst day of my life and that with each step closer to him, my heart was breaking. Each step towards him brought a surge of doom that settled in the pit of my empty stomach. His eyes locked on mine and I continued to walk, as determined as possible, putting one foot in front of the other. He was getting closer; the pulpit was getting closer and the dread was getting worse. How had it all ended like this? How had something I thought I had always wanted become something so opposite, so incarcerating? My mind started racing backwards in time, grasping at the past and the decisions that led me here.

Step, step.

How had I managed to screw everything up so badly and ruin the lives of everyone I'd ever loved?

Step, step

How was I marrying the wrong person? *By force?*

Step, step.

My breath was coming short and shallow and my mind pounded with painful reruns, with all the memories of the last few months. How had I destroyed my life so royally?

CHAPTER ONE
It was still happening.

I grew up in the middle of a war, albeit a corporate war, but one that had long since spilled onto the streets and split the city apart. It was a war where gangs and terrorists didn't run the game, but two leading companies whose influences ranked number one in the world did. They were founded at the same time almost four generations ago and to this day continued to grow in power and force. It sounded awfully movie-ish, but the truth of it was far from glamorous. It was an unfortunate reality, but one that I lived in, daily. The law enforcement all belonged to one company or the other, the criminals all got their pay loads from one company or the other, all the smaller or independent businesses belonged to one company or the other, and if they didn't, they didn't survive long. It was a world where there was no head that couldn't be turned, no 'accidents' that couldn't be covered and no legislation that couldn't be amended to suit. Of course, all these things could never be traced back to either law-abiding, charity-donating, fair-trade, union-representing company. Such power was supported by the best legal and business minds of the world. Every single dealing was iron tight and flawless, at least near the surface. In fairness, unless you were bought up in the knowledge of it or worked amongst it all, you could quite happily live out your life in complete ignorance, and most did. It was a big world and this was a huge cosmopolitan city. It was completely possible for individual lives and stories to run parallel to reality. It offered a blissful existence and one that I wished for often.

So how had it all begun? The two companies started as one, many, many years ago. They were 'Bain and Rodriguez Incorporated' and they had specialised in property and land development. Now they each spread into almost every market sector available and capitalised on everything possible. The founders were two middle class men, friends from childhood, buddies from school and veterans from the war. They had had dreams and had built a successful business on those dreams. But like all 'so history has it' tales, they fell out, both claiming the other to be greedy and conspiring. Money split them in a bitter and vengeful dispute and divided the company into two. Bernard Bain, of Bain Enterprises, and Miguel Rodriguez, of Rodriguez Ltd. Both companies flourished through hard work, commitment and by doing every possible underhanded deal available in order to screw the other over. The two men grew more and more passionate with their hate towards the other and in turn passed that enmity down to their children, who passed it onto their children, and so on. Two families who would have spent generations growing up together were torn apart in a vicious vendetta. That hatred now fueled a modern-day media circus. The two families filled the airways with everything from stories of connections of brutal murders to glossy photos of high powered socialites living it up in the public eye. But the magazines and newspapers never told the truth, no-one ever told the truth anymore.

I was raised on an upper-class estate, one with a large iron gate, twenty-four-hour security and constant surveillance. I went to a higher league school with CCTV everywhere, a regimented schedule and a strict life plan. I was enrolled, part willingly, into vigilant martial arts classes as soon as I was old enough to walk (*"Just in case you ever need to defend yourself, sweetie."*). I studied Krav Maga as if I was an actual member of the elite Israeli Military Defense Force, being made to squeeze four classes a week into my adolescent schedule, along with all my other extra-curricular activities. Yes, it meant that I could kick almost any boys butt at school, in a very fast, efficient and painful manner, but it also meant I lost a lot of over-achieving childhood opportunities. Then in my teen years I was *gently* pushed into other controlling past times too, ones which aided my self-reliance and ones that could be undertaken from a safe and secure area; gyms, lessons, education, tutoring. I was an accomplished person, but it hardened me to the core and left me untrusting on the outside. I also questioned my street smarts, knowing I was never really left alone to fend for myself. Still, it was what it was, and I knew despite the craziness, I was blessed with a fortunate life. My mum and dad, who used to be so in love, both started out working for Bain Enterprises. My dad climbed quickly through the business hierarchy and for the last thirty years had been Bain Enterprises' Vice President. As I grew an understanding of the business world, my dad's job title always gave me a bitter laugh. "Vice President" came from the Latin 'vice' meaning 'in place of' and boy, did that ring true to its definition in my life. As my dad gained power and influence in Bain Enterprises, he quickly lost his marriage and family. Mum decided she didn't like being second in his life anymore and I could never really blame her. Dad's job took the place of his family; all powerful Mr Bain in place of my mother. It was just one starting place for me to begin my hatred of that damned company, of the ugly business it drew my whole family into to. I grew up on either the floor of my mum's independent Wedding Boutique (ironic really, when you think about where this story ends) styling my own clothes with leftovers, or on the floor at my dad's office, reading reports and highlighting manifests, occasionally helping out with business when I graduated from university. And graduate Uni I did. Due to such a controlled and directed adolescence, I advanced from further education, top of my class with a very motivated high IQ. The Head Education Analysis of my prestigious University attributed it to the 'lucky' young-age at which I was saturated into the business world. His words stung each time I heard them, it didn't ever feel very *lucky*. In truth, I felt like I had lost more than any one person could lose, especially to something that should have been so sidelined in a life; a career. 'Work to live' was not a motto reflected in our house, that was for sure. I left both homes when I was seventeen, unable to stomach hearing about the constant battles of Bain and the dreaded Rodriguez. There was so much hatred and contention between the two rival businesses and so many ruined lives, that I couldn't stay immersed in it any longer. I needed to be free, free of it all. I needed to be completely severed from the toxic influences they inflicted. And so, I cut and run. By the time I moved into my late twenties, I had friends and a social life and things to call my own. It had taken me years to find a place that I felt suited me, that I felt comfortable in, that I felt I could be myself. I had a good job which I loved, teaching Business Studies at a secondary school. It never felt 'beneath me' as the CEO of Goliath, the global marketing company, once told me after I declined a senior position with them. To be honest, I'd been headhunted a few times and each power-grabbing, life-consuming company could never understand why I would waste my talents with teaching. Yet, to me, it seemed only fitting that I should use my time and knowledge to try and save the future generations from the destruction of what I had seen in my life, from the wrongs of everything that had destroyed any free agency industry once owned. To before Bain and Rodriguez consumed the world with their conflict. I loved challenging the young minds of the next generation to see a different path than the one currently set, to think outside the box of what we called 'normal'. The moral rewards that came from being a humble teacher were immense, but sadly, the pay was not, and so I designed clothes on the side for friends, subsidizing my meager income. By my thirty-second birthday my life was this: two modest salaries, a compact apartment with reasonable rent, multiple friends, alive close family, good health and an unbreakable independence that had developed over years of practice. I was now at the point in my life where I was very aware that I could do nothing about the war in which I lived and the scars that it had made, but with humour and hard-work, I could try and better it, one day at a time.

The only connection I had left in Bain and Rodriguez's conflict, was the fact that I was engaged to the almighty Mr Brice Bain's son. Ok, so it was a pretty huge tie, but it was an easily reachable conclusion that Edward and I would end up together at some point. We spent our childhoods together in our father's offices and at the company functions. We were the same age and both dads saw the advantages in the match. I trusted him, and trust was a very guarded trait for me. From a young age we were prepped for each other and at fifteen years old, it eventually happened. It had all been very romantic. At a Bain Enterprises Annual Family Day Edward had bought a ticket for the kissing booth, then after planting a very confident kiss on my young lips, informed me we were now boyfriend and girlfriend. Simple. Sixteen years later, Edward Bain was comfortable, he was reliable, he was safe, he was predictable, he was expected...by both our fathers and to some degree, me. He was all I knew, the only true companion I had ever been with. It made sense to me to stay with him. But despite being a wonderful man, he was also powerful and determined. Just like his father. He was already serving as joint CEO and was set to receive all his father had built up over the last fifty odd years. Edward was next in line to the name, money, company and throne of Bain Enterprises. The one and only heir. There was no doubt that we loved each other, we had been together too long not to, but he was also committed to his dad's company and all that it stood for, including the rivalry. I was committed to hating everything that meant. As you can imagine, relationship tension was something of a given to us on this matter and if I was being brutally honest, that tension was becoming more and more evident the older and wiser we became.

And still, after all the challenges and after all this time, Edward and I were in a chapel, away to tie the knot and say our vows. About to get married. Regardless of everything, it was still happening. And I wished desperately that I could change it.

Maybe my stubborn hatred towards the companies had been the tipping point? As I looked back at it all, it was becoming easier to see that the businesses had been the knife, the dagger that split everything. My mind chased down hundreds of past conversations, looks, exchanges, instances, *everything*, just hunting for a start, an instigator, a single moment that started this all. Then it found it, a memory. Maybe *the* memory? Maybe if on *that* night I had been different with Edward, things would not be where they were now; me being *forced* to marry him. Maybe I could have stopped this all? Maybe I could have changed fates?

.

CHAPTER TWO
Ouch.

'Can we just not talk about this right now, please, Edward? I have twenty-six-papers to mark still.' I sat lounged on my living room floor surrounded by students exam papers. The tiny pile was the marked essays, the somewhat larger stack was the 'pending' pile and the reason I was still up at one a.m. on a Friday night. Working. Edward sighed, stalked to the kitchen and poured himself a drink, no doubt finishing off the last of my grape juice, the juice he didn't even like. He had come straight from the office so was still dressed in his dark blue Armani suit and Gucci shoes and was also charitably sporting the light blue supermarket shirt I had bought him a few months ago. I was definitely the most lower class of the two of us. I knew he only ever wore that shirt for my benefit, as his tastes were somewhat more extravagant. Always the thoughtful gesturer, was Edward. His tie was loosened and the top few buttons of that budget shirt undone. Once upon a time, the sight of his bare chest would have made me think, 'screw the homework' and I would've dragged him off to the bedroom. But now, after so many years together and with the conversation topic he was proposing, *again*, I was, sadly, very much in control of my emotions tonight.

'Eva, we can't just keep ignoring this. At some point, very soon, the business will be mine...be *ours*.' He came back into the living room and sat on the sofa opposite me. My eyes quickly clocked the dark purple juice in his glass.

'I know, Edward, how could I not? It's just that I have all this to do by Monday.' I waved my jewelry-less arm over the papers on the floor as he checked his Bvlgari watch for the time. I was sat in yoga pants and a vest, slippers and my hair in a bobble; no make-up and no decoration. This was the joys of a long-term relationship in full, right? You didn't have to get all dressed up anymore. In reality though, it was actually quite a shame because I used to like looking good for his benefit. He humphed loudly to himself and slouched back in the chair as I tried to not react to the irritating sound of his obvious frustration. I continued to mark poor Tony Richardson's paper, who was not getting even a portion of the attention he deserved, as Ed leaned forward and nosily picked up the only magazine that lay on the coffee table. It was last year's *Cosmo* issue from the Charity Ball that we had attended together. All the A-List celebrities had been there: magazines, press, cameras, expensive clothes, tiny waists, miniature dinners. It was always more about publicity than charity, but Edward had asked me to go along, despite knowing that I hated them. And I had gone, of course, for him. He sat back and ruffled the pages loudly as he flipped to the center spread. I had kept the magazine for the very same reason and I had looked at the center pages many times; the double sheet photograph of Edward and I. He looked so dashing that night and even I hadn't look too shabby in the dress he had bought for me (he hadn't trusted me to choose my own one, probably quite fairly). The crystal-clear picture of us came to the forefront of my mind, knocking poor Tony Richardson's homework into disregard again. I was the same height as Ed, both tall; although he always looked more elegant with it than me. My long and normally pony-tailed hair had been done by some fancy hairdresser man that day (who Ed had also arranged) and he had told me, that despite neglect, I had the richest natural brown locks he had ever seen. I wasn't too sure if it had been a compliment or not, but he had smiled whilst saying it and since that day I'd found myself quite content with my plain straight hair. Following the hairdresser, my make-up had been done by a very non-smiling make-up artist. She too, had offered me another back-handed complimented, but one which hadn't even slightly offended me. She had been scandalized by my omission to never wearing make-up, but had observed that that was obviously the reason I had good skin. And she was right, no make-up in Edwards world was scandalous. But I saw no point in trying to keep up with all the countless women I saw throw themselves at Edward, their skin plastered in colours and shades, their intentions just as obvious. I was and would never be like them (as the media often pointed out). I had clear-skin which darkened nicely in the summer, I had big full lashes that already caught on the lenses of any glasses I wore, let alone lengthening them with mascara, and I had crystal blue eyes that stood out so much they hid my tired bags beneath. I had luckily been blessed with my mother's genes and I felt no need to mask that. But after hours of pampering on that Charity Ball night, I had looked beautiful; a different kind of me, but beautiful none-the-less. Even I could admit it on that one occasion. Edward exhaled as he focused on the picture of us and brought me back to our present. The caption at the bottom of the full page colour spread read

"Famous Childhood Sweethearts still going strong: the chiseled charmer Edward Bain (32) and the most envied natural beauty, Eva Mack (32)".

I tried to refocus on my work again, but made it no more than five seconds before Edwards deliberate heavy breathing and magazine flipping drove me crazy. My concentration was completely shot, and I knew it was pointless to even try to continue with work. I breathed in deeply, centering myself (my martial arts teacher would be so proud) and put my pen down. I turned to him.

'Ed, if it'll make you happy, I can spare ten minutes, we can talk.' He looked up at me with that lop-sided smile I had fallen for so many times before, scratched his smooth chin and sat forward. There was a small look of victory in his eyes that I knew all too well.

'I have to sign the papers soon. We *need* to talk about this. You need to sign them too, Eva. I'm not going to take ownership of the biggest company in the world and have my wife entitled to none of it. I want you to sign for rights and shares. If anything, ever happens to me, I would like to know that you are taken care of.'

'Edward,' I began, sighing in frustration. 'I just have such a big problem with this. I know that you want to look out for me and I appreciate how wonderful you are, it's just that I'm not comfortable with it. How many poor business owners have lost their livelihoods and more, because of Bain Enterprises? I know you think you are doing the right thing for me, but can you see where I'm struggling with this, morally?' He shook his head, angrily, and rubbed his temples. I knew the signs all too well and I prepared myself for the impending '*look*'.

'Eva!' he practically yelled, making me jump. There went the rational adult conversation. 'You have to be realistic. This is *business*. This is how the *real world* operates outside your silly classroom.' And there was the '*look*'. I hated that patronizing, condescending stare and he always did it when he thought I was being unreasonable, or worse, stupid. Just now, I was sure he thought I was being both. No other option could explain his cheap *teacher* insult, which hadn't gone unnoticed.

'That's not fair, Ed. You know fine well that I understand the business world perfectly. I'm just not comfortable with being in-line to that much money when I know how it came about.'

'"*How it came about?*"' he shouted, standing up and clenching his fists. He was exceptionally worked up tonight and I could tell this wasn't going to end well. 'You make it sound like my father's a murdering, masterminded criminal,' he grunted to himself, trying to reign in his temper. 'Why is it so hard for you to just do as I ask for once? I am *telling* you, as the rational adult in our lives, that you *will* sign these papers. I'm sick of your childish views on life and I'm sick of having to be the one who plays the bad guy. You drive me crazy, Eva.' His chest was heaving now and there was no sign of his full-throttle rant ending. 'You'll do as you're told for once, I swear it. I will not have this ridiculous conversation again with you. You'll sign what I tell you to sign and you need to get over this aversion to my, no, to *our*, *main* source of income. Bain Enterprises is my life, which means it will officially be *your* life soon too. You need to find a way to get past your naivety and just deal with it. It's my right to take care of you, even if you don't agree. This discussion is over, Eva, and we're not having it again, so help me!' He ended abruptly and then made to storm out. He must have been more insane tonight than I thought if he reckoned he was going to be allowed to leave after that obscenely sexist and belittling rant. I stood, clumsily, fumbling to my feet. I already knew in my head that I shouldn't rise to the occasion and that the fact Edward was so unexplainably angry about nothing was probably just him blowing off steam…but, the independent, feminist fool in me wouldn't allow my pride to be so dented with no defence.

'Excuse me?' I blurted, incredulously. I got that he was obviously frustrated at something or had just had a long day, but I couldn't believe that he had just, pretty much, told me I was a brain-dead insubordinate who should just *comply*. When had I become an employee? *'Excuse me?'* I repeated, maybe louder than I had planned. I'm sure that the neighbors downstairs must have been rolling their eyes again by now; *'here they go again, another argument.'* If I wasn't so maddened by my bruised ego, I may have cared enough to quieten down slightly. But as it was, my loving fiancé had just to all intents and purposes told me to 'shut up and do as I was told.' When exactly did we move back to the seventeen-hundreds? 'What did you just say?' I asked, advancing towards him. I must have looked more menacing than normal because he backed up, slowly. The messy hair and lack of make-up probably helped. 'Did you just tell me to *obey*? To *conform*? Am I a child now? You must be joking, right, because you've said some crazy stuff before, Ed, but that would be by far the most ridiculous to date.' I waited for an answer, standing in the typical arguing woman position; arms folded and eye brows raised.

'Eva, don't start with me,' he said, firmly. He blatantly knew where the somewhat heated conversation was going; this wasn't our first fight and he knew all too well, if pushed far enough, that I could burn just as hotly as he could. 'I've had a long day and I've got another long day tomorrow, too. *You* are being unreasonable about this *whole* thing. I'm getting *sick* of the same conversations *over and over* again and you-not-listening,' he raised his voice into a full-on, frustrated yell. 'You just do what *you* want, what *you* think is best, with no regards for me or for consequences,' he was completely shouting at me now, pointing at me with a condemning finger.

'Well not-this-time! You hide behind that crappy job of yours, all preachy and self-righteous. When in fact, you know nothing, you haven't got a clue. You blame everything that's gone wrong in your life on my company, my dad. But enough is enough, Eva. So help me, you will sign those papers or else.' He finished with a heaving chest and bulging eyes and I stood stunned, and a little shell-shocked to be honest. The anger in the room quickly dissipated as realization settled in; yes, yes, all of that had just been said. A loud silence now filled the very obvious quiet as we stood, staring at each other. Edward though must have realised he had gone too far and he quickly moved towards me, his hands outstretched. I stood speechless, Edwards previous rant nipping at me from within. I felt his hands rest on my shoulders and rub them gently, the way he'd done so many times before to comfort me. A few cautious seconds passed and I still hadn't mustered a reaction, still hadn't responded to his attempted pacifying. Edward obviously began to panic, and rightly so, as he started whispering to me, calmly and gently. I detected a tone of pleading in his voice, the voice that I knew so well, but his words just ran off of me like water, cold water. We'd argued before and said the odd selfish, unthoughtful thing, what couple hadn't? But in my opinion, which apparently didn't actually count anyway, neither of us had ever gone this far. Neither of us had ever said such unkind things. Was this *too* far? When and what exactly was '*too*' far anyway? Telling me that he was the ruler of us, the dominant male and that I was pretty much just an insecure, blaming, nonpotential, useless, second in place, woman? Was I supposed to blow up and smash things now, like they did in the movies? Should I be yelling and screaming and throwing him out? Would that be the normal reaction? Because right now, I felt nothing.

'Eva?' Edward was repeating my name, as he lifted my chin so he could see my face. I hadn't even realised that I'd been looking down. I don't know what he saw when he looked at me, but my usually composed exterior seemed to give him reason to leave, and leave fast. He let go of me abruptly and headed for his jacket.

'Look, maybe we should just talk about this tomorrow...' he paused, '...after we've both calmed down'. he zipped up his cream Dolci and Gabbana jacket and I watched the shiny 'D&G' logo swinging from the zipper just beneath his stubbly chin. I straightened my cheap supermarket vest, unable to stop my head from thinking. '*Calmed down?*' I thought to myself. I hadn't even spoken a single word yet. I felt my head slowly nod once in agreement as I was becoming vividly aware of a numbing sort of void that was spreading through my body. My thoughts drifted and I tried to identify whether my heart was hurt or if it was just my pride. I watched Ed leave, listening to the front door bang closed. With worrying confusion, I concluded that the only thing hurting in me, was in fact, my pride. Surely it should be more than my feministic values that were offended by his lecture? And if that was the case, that only my dignity was ruffled, what exactly did that mean? Why was my heart not more invested in all of this? I stood in the same place as Ed had left me, frantically thinking. I glanced to the table where my work still lay and my eyes caught the photo of us in the magazine that Ed had left. We stood in each other's arms, both smiling, genuinely happy. We were engrossed in only each other, content and satisfied. I breathed deeply and evenly, then let out a massive, long sigh. Had that picture only been a year ago? Had those warm feelings only been a year ago? We were practically mechanical now; motions, routines, habits, everything was done systematically. But we functioned and we made sense, and that was important, right? I pulled my pony tail tighter on my head, hoping it would somehow help constrict my spiraling thoughts. All it succeeded in doing though, was reminding me of how regimented and mundane my relationship with Ed had become. We had no whirlwinds, no butterflies, no loss of sense and rationality, no extremes of any kind to be honest. Ever. I didn't even know when the last time I had felt any of that was. *Were we even in love anymore?* I started dragging my feet back over to the living room and sat down again in the midst of exam papers, all still unmarked. I stared vacantly at the remnants of the grape juice in Edward's cup, struggling to focus on anything. Was it over? Were *we* over? I sighed deeply, forcing air out from the very depths of my lungs, then lay my head back onto the sofa. What did I do with this new realisation? If I was no longer in love with Edward, and maybe hadn't been in a long time, where did that leave me? The words 'break up' flashed through my mind and my stomach churned. Edward had been all I had known for…for forever. I felt sick, like my life was suddenly crumbling. I forced my eyes closed for relief, but instead was met with vivid images of our lives together. Then images of what our breakup would be like: the press, my parents, Ed's dad, the Company, the media circus, our shared belongings, our childhood memories, my responsibilities…the pictures of the disaster were endless. I had seen many a socialite suffer a public breakup, with the horrors of tasteless and callous media coverage. I quickly realised that despite having stayed out of the media world, that the paparazzi would be unavoidable. It would all be painfully exposed for the world to see. Could I do that? Survive that? I opened my eyes quickly to try stop the sickness from rising further. *Break up?* The words stabbed at me again with an immobilising pain. I focused on my breathing to stop myself from running to the bathroom to throw-up. Inhale. Exhale. Inhale Exhale. A tear leaked from the corner of my eye and ran down my face. Damn it! What the hell had just happened? Had our seventeen-year relationship just ended in seven minutes?

CHAPTER THREE
Something was wrong.

I woke the next morning, disorientated and to the vibration of my phone on the coffee table. Thankfully at some point during my torment last night, I had finally fallen asleep. I reached for the noisy object now buzzing its way across the table in the other direction and jarred my neck. I yelped loudly and my memories of last night's argument came rushing back in with the pain. A groan escaped me, both at my stiff neck and the stinging reality. But, it hadn't been an awful dream, it had been real. With my phone finally in hand, I glanced at the displayed time; ten-forty-six a.m., then registered Tammy's name flashing on the screen.

'Hello?' I asked hoarsely, clearing my throat and sitting up properly. I pulled my somewhat squint hair bobble out and let my hair fall against my back, still damp from the previous night's shower.

'Eva?' Tammy's voice was loud and piercing to my still sleepy ears and I scrunched my eyes in reaction. What day was it again? When had I finally fallen asleep last night? And how had I ever slept in until eleven a.m.? I groaned, dropping my head slowly from side to side to stretch my muscles out.

'Hi, Tammy.' I finally slurred out, rubbing my eyes and yawning loudly.

'Are you still in bed?' she asked, slightly amused. I resented her tone, although let it slide on fear that maybe I was in a more sensitive and touchy mood than normal.

'Yeah.' I stretched my back and began to stand up, glancing at Edward's glass still on the table. Thoughts of it all made me nauseous. 'I'm just up now. It was a rough night last night.' I knew she would assume I meant a 'night out' sort of rough night and that was fine by me for now. I didn't think I could handle any questions before a hot shower. Tammy and I shared everything, so she'd hear the truth soon enough.

'Ahhh, I see,' she replied, a little more sympathetically. I could hear her heels clicking on the pavement, she was obviously out and about, no doubt dressed like she was going to Fashion Week. Tammy Campbell always looked fabulous; shoes, bags, dresses, coats, the works. The girl was a designer Queen and despite having a mediocre job which paid similar to mine, she had the best and most expensive of everything. I always assumed that her parents were loaded and that she drained them, but regardless of the source of her apparently huge and endless income, being around her was like watching something straight out of The Devil Wears Prada; all glamour, make-up and heels...and no tact at all.

'Well, get your cute ass in the shower and don't be late for our lunch. I hate waiting at restaurants alone, men in awful clothes always try and talk to me.' I laughed at her vanity. Only Tammy.

'Oh, it's so hard to have men throwing themselves at you all the time.' I teased, now walking towards the bathroom and rolling my neck. 'I'll be there at twelve, drama queen.'

'You'd better be missy, or I won't show you the new shoes I'm away to buy. They're divine.' I rolled my eyes at her.

'Couldn't possibly miss out on that,' I replied, sarcastically, but she was already hanging up the phone with the sound of a boutique door bell ringing in the background. I quickly jumped into the shower with Tammy's ridiculousness still swirling in my head. She made me smile despite the weight of last night's events. I rinsed the shampoo from my hair remembering, like it was yesterday, the first time I had met her. We had been thirteen and in our first year of senior school. Whist I was self-assured, confident and tall, Tammy had been small, skinny, timid and easily pushed around. I had been going to martial arts classes for years already and as much as I never understood back then why they were so compulsory, I did know that I was confident, self-assured and assertive because of them. They were the reason that when I saw Tammy, like so many times before, cowering fearfully from her latest aggressors one day, across the park after school, that I couldn't just walk by. We were not friends and had never talked, but something in her eyes had reached for me in that situation and it was the same thing that I occasionally still saw in her now. She had been in the kids play area across from the school, surrounded by a group of senior girls, maybe a year or two ahead of us. From where I was walking by, I could hear the catty shouting and taunting of teenage girls. From the corner of my eye, I saw her being shoved backwards to the muddy ground and something had snapped in me. I could still remember, vividly, the blood beginning to pump around my young body as the anger and adrenaline urged me across the soggy grass. I had quickly found myself between a surprised, yet grateful, Tammy, and the group of silly, unassuming bullies. I looked up at the girls with threatening malice, daring them to take another step, to offer another kick. From there, it had all happened rather quickly and after a fast duck then retaliated swing, a winded girl and her friends left sheepishly, never forgetting my face. It was maybe on that day I had realised that I was the type of person who would never back down or step away from a fight. It was definitely on that day though, as I extended my hand out to Tammy, that we had become solid friends. A friendship that survived the tests of time and the changes that brought. Tammy had sworn never to be weak and fragile again, no matter the consequences and sacrifices that took, and I had sworn to always stand by her. And whilst outsiders would look at us and not understand how we could be friends when we were so blatantly different, I would remember the look in her eyes that day we first met and remind myself, that once family, always family, regardless. Drying myself from my speedy shower, I grabbed the pair of jeans she had brought me for my last birthday, the expensive designer ones, and pulled them on. I popped on a pair of pumps, just like you used to wear to gym class, thankful that I was tall enough to pull them off. If I wore a cute top and fancy coat, she would probably just about allow me to be seen with her in public. I pulled my hair into a messy bun, hoping to get that my-hair's-naturally-this-way-even-though-a-hairtsylist-spent-hours-on-it sort of look. I turned my nose up at the reflection of the end product. Ok, so maybe it was more just a messy bun, but it would have to do as I was pressed for time and still needed some makeup on today. Tammy had a strict 'when in public' policy. A few strokes of mascara later and I headed to the car. Oddly enough, to exactly oppose my non-extreme lifestyle, my car was an Aston Martin DB9; black, V12, six litre engine, twin exhaust...oh, she was beautiful. It had been the one gift from Edward I had hardly protested about. It was my pride and joy, and, yes, I felt like an idiot driving it to the local supermarket for some milk or parking it next to the Ford estates in the teacher's car park, but I loved it. It was my one materialistic lust, every other thing in my life, I could take or leave. I loved the purring roar of the engine when I pressed that start button and the power I could yield with the simple touch of a foot. It never got old and the rush never lessened. For some reason, my whole life, I'd loved driving fast, feeling the wind rush on my skin and seeing the world slip past me in a blur. Which it would need to do just now if I was ever going to get to Tammy on time.

I parked up at the indoor lot and beeped the lock, catching the watching eyes of two young men climbing out of their two-door VW Golf. One of them nodded at me with a smile, to which I politely returned and jogged on quickly. If I had been single at any point, this car would have been a miracle worker. It was eleven fifty-five when I arrived at the restaurant. I stood outside catching my breath and congratulating myself for actually making it on time. It was an expensive, bookings only, up-market place, with tinted glass windows and a menu of foods I could hardly pronounce, let alone know what they were. Tammy liked her fancy places though and this was one of her favourites. The well-groomed concierge opened the frosted door for me, wishing me a good afternoon in the process. We always had the same table here, so I made my way straight to our normal place, paying no attention to the watchful eye of the lady at the reservation booth. Tammy was already there, her perfect lipstick-ed lips sipping from a large wine glass. She stood up to greet me, a big smile on her immaculately painted face.

'On time,' she chirped with surprise, eyeballing me up and down quickly and nodding with approval, 'and not looking too shabby either, I'm very impressed.' She hugged me tightly. She smelt like the perfume section in Harrods and matched its prestige too. Her blonde hair was loosely curled around her long narrow face and her brown eyes were outlined with black kohl. Her cheekbones were pink as roses and her nails the colour of blood. She was scarily thin, if you asked me, even for her small height, but perceived looks mattered to Tammy. Today she had on tight, tight, tight skinny black jeans, a plunge-neck emerald green revealing satin top and a large gold D&G chain to finish it all off. She wiggled her feet at me as soon as I had let go of her, obviously directing me to her new shoes. I recognised them instantly as the ones she had shown to me in a magazine last week at lunch. Jimmy Choos, red, loud (hideous in my eyes) and all for the 'super reasonable price of six hundred and seventy-eight pounds', or so she had said to my bulging eyes. They looked fabulous on her, of course, so I played along with my role; gawking, flattering, questioning, doing all the things girlfriends should. Eventually we sat and ordered and began catching up on the week passed. I knew that I would tell Tammy about my fight with Edward eventually, I was just biding my time for now. Tammy always had time to listen to my issues with Edward and the business, despite me knowing that it must have been boring to hear. She was just a good friend like that. As we placed our food orders I was happy to be distracted for a while by her tales and recent antics, which were apparently right now, with an older man from her work.

'Tammy, he's sixty-five and married!' I stated incredulously, smiling at her shamefully.

'I know,' she replied with a guilty smile, 'but he has so much money and power, it's hard to say no to that, and nor do I think I should. He's the married one, not me.' She winked at me and took a sip of her wine. Tammy was ruthless sometimes. She believed in working her way up and getting what she wanted, even when it cost others a great price. We had argued about her ambition before and the things she had done to get her way, but it had been a fruitless mission. She would not change and I would never leave her. Instead we had come to an unspoken truce many years ago; she would only ever tell me the glossy brief details and I would take it with a pinch of salt. This was one of those times.

'Tammy, be careful sweetie, ok?' I eye balled her over my glass. She sighed like I was telling her she had to wear yoga pant for the rest of her life, then nodded dismissively, waving her perfectly manicured hand at me. I had known the girl for forever, we had been best friends all the way through secondary school and had been roommates through half of University. When she gave me her version of that 'look' I knew it meant not to lecture her, and I didn't plan on it.

Dessert was a light milk chocolate mousse and despite its fluffiness, it didn't alleviate the impending weight of what I knew was coming. About half way through its deliciousness, I finally plucked up the courage to drop the bomb of last night's events and hoped that her full belly would aid in keeping her reasonable. It was a tall order.

'WHAT?!' she yelled loudly over the background piano music and the relaxing murmur of lunch-eating rich people. I glanced with embarrassment around at the staring diners, blushing slightly. Tammy couldn't have cared less though, her spoon had been thrown back to the dainty plate and her hands were clenched into fists. 'He said what? He actually said that to you?' I went to reply, but quickly realised that she wasn't actually asking a real question as she immediately ploughed on with rage. 'I can't believe that he said that, how dare he…how dare he! Just wait till I get my hands on him.' Her eyes were practically bulging from her head and her cheeks had turned a shade of red which almost matched her Doir lipstick. She paused for a second to take a rather large gulp of wine and I grasped the opportunity to throw in a few words.

'We left it on pretty bad terms, Tammy. I'm not too sure what to do this time.' It was maybe my exasperated sigh mid-sentence or the genuine look of concern in my eyes, but she lowered her glass and exchanged it for my hand, squeezing it tight.

'Eva, darling, are you ok?' she looked at me, deeply, and I nodded, then shrugged. The whole thing was a bit of a mess to be honest, wasn't it? Tammy must have known that it was more than the argument that was worrying me and she sat back, perfectly still, waiting for me to continue talking. She already knew there was something else I needed to address, something she sensed that I needed to get out. She was great like that; just sitting and waiting and listening to everything I could possibly say on a situation. I remembered last week's coffee, when I had told her about one of Edwards latest business deals with an International company, and how unsure I was about it. She had sat intently listening the whole way through as if storing it all in an important memory bank. She was a long-suffering friend who I treasured dearly. Especially right now. I gave her hand a squeezed back, having a moment of appreciation for her. In my odd cross mix world of fame, media, and mundane, I could always trust Tammy. I inhaled deeply for courage, hoping to get all my thoughts out before crying or breaking down. Voicing the idea that Ed and I might be over was a lot harder than I thought it would be. I stammered and paused a few times, Tammy sitting, waiting, with her perfectly dolled-up eyes looking at me intently.

'The whole argument started, again, because I keep putting off signing these papers. I know he means the best for me, but he just doesn't understand why I don't want to be involved in anything to do with his company.' I closed my eyes and mustered some strength, 'I did some thinking after Ed left last night and I'm not sure that he and I…' My phone began to buzz across the table, my mum's name flashing on the display. I hesitated for a second, debating not answering. Working up the courage to admit that Ed and I were more than likely breaking up was not an easy feat. But my phone kept buzzing and I let go of Tammy's hand to answer it, reluctantly, holding up my figure to say, 'hold that thought'.

'Hi, mum.' I tried to say as chirpily as possible.

'Eva?' My mum's voice was frantic, as she yelled down the phone at me. Her obvious panic made my hairs stand instantly. There was something about that freaked out tone of voice that instinctly drew fear from inside you, like you already knew something was seriously wrong before any real words were spoken. And when your mother's voice sounded like that, it meant that something was wrong, very wrong.

'Mum? Mum, what's wrong?' I could hear her practically hyperventilating at the other end of the phone.

'Eva, it's your dad...I don't know what to do, I tried, I did, I just, I...'

'Mum!' I interrupted loudly, trying to break through her panicking garbles. 'Mum, what's happened to dad?' I was already standing, my heart thumping with worry. I had already started imagining what could have happened to him; the accidents or the illnesses or the worst-case scenarios. When you heard your mother sounding more scared than she had ever done in her entire life, your imagination instantly ran wild.

'I've been up all night trying to talk to him, Eva, but he just won't listen.' Normally the confirmation of hearing the fact that my dad was actually alive and had not been in a horrific accident or something, would have been enough to calm my crackling nerves, but the sheer panic and concern I could still hear in her voice was enough to confirm that everything was very far from being all right.

'Mum, you need to tell me what's happening. Where is dad?' At question of dad's whereabouts, she shrieked like a banshee.

'He's at his office preparing for a meeting at three o'clock, alone, with Cane Rodriguez!' Her words registered with me, but it took a few more moments for the complete understanding to settle in. What? Cane Rodriguez was our sworn enemy, the owner of the opposing company, Rodriguez Ltd. Both businesses hated each other, passionately, and it wasn't like a rivalry of hard glares across a board room table, this rivalry was filled with distain and utter loathing and despise. The amount of disdain that Edwards dad and Rodriguez had towards each other was petrifying and quite frankly, unnerving. Confusion replaced my original panic, but only for a split second. Why would dad ever have a meeting with Cane Rodriguez? Cane would kill him on site, without a single second of hesitation. We all knew that. An out of hours meeting with Rodriguez himself was insanity and it could only mean one thing, that dad was in some kind of trouble. It also meant that his boss, Mr Bain, Ed's dad, knew nothing about it. I couldn't remember a single time where Rodriguez had ever personally met with a member of Bain's council members. They were sworn enemies and that was true for all employees. Dad worked for Brice Bain which made it a simple fact; dad was a foe. Rodriguez was a known recluse, seldom seen out in society and never with opposing business men, even in corporate society. He was a dangerous and vicious man and dad knew this. Why would he ever willingly agree to a meet?

'What?' I heard myself saying, whilst trying to collect my bag from under the table. It didn't make sense. 'Why? Why does Rodriguez want to see dad?' I had my mobile pinned between my ear and shoulder and was pulling on my jacket. I saw Tammy's eyes flicker with interest at the name Rodriguez.

'No, Eva, your dad set up the meeting. He's been working on some secret proposal and wouldn't confide in anyone about it, he wouldn't even let his driver take him to the meeting point. The only reason I know anything about it is because he wanted to borrow my car, and,' she paused, 'to get me to sign a copy of his updated will, in case anything happened'. She began to screech and sob again, something I hadn't heard my mum do over my dad since the days of their divorce. Tammy had stood up now too, obviously seeing that something was very wrong. I covered the bottom of my phone.

'Family stuff.' I explained, apologetically. 'I have to go, Tammy, I'm so sorry. I'll call you later, ok?' She only had time to nod as I turned from the table and ran for the door.

'Eva, he's at the office to pick something up from his safe. You need to get to him there.' It may have seemed odd to an onlooker that mum lay the responsibility of finding my dad on me, but she knew I was the only one who had any chance of talking him around. I was the only one who had any chance of changing his mind and talking him out of this madness. The two of us were oddly similar. We'd developed a strong bond as father and daughter over the years, despite different views on his career. We had the kind of bond where sometimes, the only voice of reason that you would listen to, was that of the other. Hopefully this was one of those times.

'Mum, I'll find him and I'll try and stop him, ok? Don't worry. None of it makes any sense. I'm sure we're just missing something or it's all just a big mistake.' My words said one thing, but my stomach told me otherwise. I flew through the car park walkway and almost knocked over the same guys who had smiled at me earlier. I yelled an apology at them at them and slammed my car door shut, loudly starting the engine.

'Eva,' my mum's voice whispered, now coming through the cars Bluetooth, 'you know as well as I do why your dad has twenty-four-hour security,' she paused, then said very firmly, 'if he goes to that meeting, we both know he won't come back. It's suicide, Eva.' Her words stung, but only because I knew they were true. My dad would never walk away from a face to face with Rodriguez. No matter his intentions or reasons. Dad was too high up in Bain Enterprises for Rodriguez to miss an opportunity, to miss a chance to advance. Rodriguez was a snake and he'd take any shot at gain he could get. I had read enough on him to know that much. I just couldn't for the life of me think why dad would even dare to organise such a ridiculously dangerous meeting. What would possibly make him do something so reckless? This whole thing was insane, uncharacteristically insane. I had to reach him before he left his office. Or he was a dead man.

'Mum, I'll get to him.' I didn't wait for a reply, but hung up, slammed the gear into first and screeched out of the car park, leaving the two boys standing at their VW, looking sheepish.

Dad's office was on the other side of town. As I weaved through the afternoon traffic my mind focused on the clock. A 3-p.m. meeting. It was one-forty. If I could reach the office by two, there was a chance he'd maybe still be there. I reached for my phone and whilst running an amber light at almost fifty miles an hour, called dad. It rang out as I'd expected it to. I quickly selected the GPS app and found dad's name, then pressed 'find current location'. If dad's phone was on it would tell me where he was. The screen went into search mode and I looked up just in time to see a roundabout quickly approaching. I slammed my foot down on the brake, gripping the wheel with both hands. My heart was beating like a sledgehammer, pounding against my chest and I could hear it over the screeching of my brakes. My rational side was sure this was all going to just be a mix up, that when I found my dad he would tell me we'd got it wrong, that there was no meeting. But as I accelerated faster, something inside me knew the worst, knew my mums fear had been justified. I tried to focus my thoughts on the road, but couldn't stop my mind replaying awful scenario after awful scenario, different possibilities of my father's fate. I tried to focus on reason instead. Why would dad do something so stupid and reckless? I cornered a junction in third gear, the car tearing around the bend like something out of The Italian Job. As I shifted up a gear, my brain shifted too and a memory of a conversation I had with my dad a few months ago came speeding back. Like finding the missing piece of a jigsaw, the whole thing started to make sense. I suddenly knew what dad was up to. I knew his plan and I knew why it seemed worth the risk to him. I also knew that it was a desperate mistake. Regardless of the reason, or how brave you were, meeting personally with Rodriguez was a death sentence. How could I have not connected the pieces together sooner? How could I have failed to miss my father's real intentions? A few months ago, he had asked me to pop into his office to read over something for him, something he wanted a private, second opinion on. It was a possible new business venture. It hadn't been until I was half way through reading it and checking financial forecasts that I had begun to understand what the report was actually proposing. Upon questioning, he had admitted that he had been working on it secretly for months, ever since we had both attended the funeral of Mr Geldy, the man who had worked in the office just down the hall. Mr Geldy had died horrifically from 'suspicious circumstances' and to this day, no convictions had been made. Everyone knew, just like all the other unsolved cases, who was responsible for his death. But as per normal, no-one could tie Rodriguez to anything. I had stood by my dad's side that day at the funeral, both dressed in black, and watched the poor man's family bury their loved one. Dad had found his determination then, he had ranted with passion on the car journey home that there had to be a way for the two companies to co-exist, a way that the two businesses could be satisfied, and that the violence and loss could be avoided. A way that everyone could be appeased. I had run with him and let him bounce ideas around, but only because I knew he was grieving and needed a way to cope with it. I had never thought for a second that the conversation we had had that day would end up in a bound business proposal awaiting a face to face meeting with one of the most powerful and dangerous men on this earth. A man that hated my dad and his boss, Brice, even more passionately. After I had read that report and argued with dad that it was ludicrous, he had asked me in a very serious tone, which now, as I sped towards him in desperation, seemed like the nail in the coffin. 'Eva, would it work?' He had pleaded with harrowing seriousness for a genuine, unbiased answer. I had stared at him for a few seconds before finally telling him the truth. 'Dad the proposal's solid, but it can only ever be hypothetical' I had forgotten that whole day. Until now. I had forgotten the look in his eyes as I had confirmed that the venture could be successful. I should have realised that he had continued his research, that he'd used my second opinion to fuel the fire and a motivation to further his cause. I pushed my foot harder to the floor with sickening realisation; if anything happened to my dad, it would be partly my fault. The blame could lie on my shoulders, almost as much as it could Rodriguez's. My mobile beeped as the GPS identified my dad's location, or at least the location of his phone. It showed the office address and I prayed it was true as the towering metal building came into vision in front of me. The huge structure had its own underground parking, but I didn't even bother to put on my hand break as I screeched to a loud stop, practically mounting the pavement directly outside the main entrance. I ran from my car, glancing upwards towards the top floor where I knew dad's office was situated. It was a Saturday afternoon and that meant there was a smaller scale of security on duty. I hopped the ID barriers effortlessly with random people merely glancing my way with curiosity. Had I been in a slightly less, life-on-the-line moment in time, I may have spared a thought to how uncomforting the security measures apparently were. As it was, I was running as fast as I could and I reached the lifts in a few seconds. I began pounding the elevator button with frustration, yet the lift doors seemed to be in no rush to open. I could hear the huge clock hanging in the foyer ticking away, each click matching my erratic heartbeats and loudly pointing out how much time was passing away.

'Please be here, please be here, please be here, ple...'

'Eva?' My pleading was interrupted by a familiar voice. I turned quickly to see the old security guard, looking at me curiously. I tried to smile, but he didn't seem to be buying it. I paused my physical attack on the up-arrow button. 'Eva?' Jackson asked again with raised eyebrows and slight concern.

'Hi, Jackson.' I offered, as calmly as I could muster, but he glanced at my twitching hand and frowned. 'Have you seen my dad today by any chance?' I asked, again hitting the lift button. Why is the stupid thing taking so long?

'You just missed him. He just went to his car a few minutes ago. You might catch him as he comes out the entrance though.' I didn't wait to hear anything else as I ran, my legs going as fast as they could. I jumped the ID barrier again, almost faltering on the landing. My feet slapped off the shiny marble floor as I ran to the glass doors, arms outstretched, and charged through them with such force that it felt like my shoulders had been knocked out of their sockets. I winced, but kept moving towards the car park barriers. As I closed in on the ramp, I saw mum's old estate pulling up to the card reader. The sun shifted, clearing the reflection off the windscreen and dad's face came into view. If I had had any air in me, I may have sighed with relief, but the danger wasn't gone yet and I charged ahead, up to the car at full speed and slammed my hands angrily onto the bonnet. It stung, but made an almighty bang and dad jumped at the noise of impact. His shocked expression quickly changed though to realisation as he registered me. He instantly began shaking his head.

'Eva, it's for the best. Something has to be done, someone has to do something.' He was leaning his head out of the open window, but made no move to get out of the car or even turn off the engine.

'Dad, its suicide. You can't go. What are you thinking?' I yelled at him, exasperatedly. The anxiety of the afternoon was catching up with me now that I had my dad in sight, and I was mad. In fact, I was furious that he had put us through this.

'Eva, you know more than anyone why I have to try. You hate this war more than any of us, you should understand.' His voice was full of plea and his face was heavy with responsibility and duty. My anger lessened a little. He was noble and brave, I'd give him that, but he was also so stupid. I could hear my mother's pleading voice still clear in my head and the promise I'd made her to stop him, no matter what. I set my resolve and determined to not back down, regardless of his all too known persuasive powers. I squared my shoulders and shook my head at him sternly. Dad must have recognised the action through years of childhood stubbornness and he turned his attention back to his wallet.

'I'm sorry, Eva,' he said, putting his card into the reader quickly and shifting into first gear. My eyebrows shot up into my forehead. The man was going to run. My father was going to speed off into the distance, to his death, leaving me here in the dust, with nothing more than 'I'm sorry, Eva.' I couldn't believe it. Quickly, instinct kicked in and I bolted to the passenger's door, jumping into the car as fast as my body would allow it. My foot had hardly managed to leave the ground before he pulled off with a small screech. I slammed the door shut and locked it, as if the lock would make any difference.

'Eva!' he yelled, shaking his head firmly and frantically. 'Get out of this car now!' He stopped at the brim of the ramp, clearly maddened. 'I cannot be late. You will understand this all one day, I promise.' I shook my head defiantly, another childhood trait I hoped he would recognise.

'I'm not getting out of this car dad, so if you want to go to this meeting, you'll just have to take me with you.' I folded my arms and sat still, not daring to move my eyes from his piercing glare. If he could have wrung my neck in that second, I believe his frustration would have led him to do so. He was now genuinely stuck and I knew why. If he didn't go to this meeting, he had lost everything he believed in and had worked towards, but if he kept me in the car, he was endangering my life too. He sat breathing heavily, wrestling with the decision now placed at his suicidal feet. His eyes locked on mine and it felt like we were playing the kids game, where you lost if you were the first person to blink. But this time, the stakes were very real. Either way now, one of us was going to lose and he knew it. But I would not leave his car, no matter how much he stared at me, no matter how much he shouted or yelled. I would not let my dad drive off to his death without doing something. I refused to, I simply refused to. After what felt like an eternity, he finally exhaled, really loudly, putting the car back into gear and pulling off onto the main road.

'You do not leave this car at any point today. No matter what happens,' he yelled firmly, pointing at me. 'You hear me?' I nodded, then turned and put my seat belt on. It should have felt like a victory; I had dad in my sight, he was alive and he was well. But now I was on my way to the meeting too. Dad was still going ahead with everything, he just now also had me in tow with him. How has this solved anything? I thought with sobering defeat. If anything, me being here, I had only succeeded to escalate the potential casualties from one to two. I sank back into the worn seat, sighing deeply. Good job, Eva, I congratulated myself, sarcastically. Now what?

CHAPTER FOUR
This was my worst nightmare.

The car journey was unlike any other I had ever had before in my life; I had never begged with my father to not sentence himself to death, I had never discussed the potential end of the corporate war with any slight reality or potential possibility, and I had also never experienced a period of time that had ever gone so quickly. In what felt like seconds of pleading, my dad pulled the hand brake on and parked mum's old family car on the sand of a small fishing town, fifty-five minutes away from civilisation. I stopped with my latest ambush of attempted reason when I saw that we had stopped. We were here? Already? I wasn't ready, I hadn't talked dad out of it yet, I hadn't come up with any sort of a plan yet. My heart began to beat again with the same panic that had caused it to race ever since my phone call to mum. My mind began swarming with uncontrollable terror, whilst my whole body felt like it was falling from a great height, my insides twisting with the inability to gain control. I looked out of the window past dad who was organising papers. The town consisted of one road. Old fishing cottages faced outwards to, what would normally be, the beautiful sandy beach. Endless waves of sparkling sea stretched out into the horizon, but today, all it was, was one less escape route. The street curved slightly with old street lamps marking the pavement every few paces or so whilst seagulls flew low looking for food. As far as I could see, there was a small shop of some kind just opposite where we had parked, then a couple cafes further down the road. The cafe at the far end of the street had a green awning up over the outdoor tables and chairs and there sat a couple of men, one reading a paper, the others looking outward. As hard as I tried, my eyes couldn't see far enough to identify anything about them. The only other movement was that of two different men, both large in stature, loitering outside the shop close to us. I heard the birds crying out overhead and their squawking grated on me like nails on a chalk board. I was pulled from my observations as dad turned, taking my hands. My head was screaming out, do something, do something, yet as he began to speak, I sat, immbolised with panic.

'Eva,' he started, quietly but surely. 'No matter what happens, do not get out of this car.' He glanced at his watch and quickly picked up the file from the dashboard.

'Dad!' I begged helplessly, drowning in the sensation of goodbye and fighting back tears. He paused and smiled at me like he had done so many times before.

'Sweetheart, I will be back in a while.' He kissed me on my forehead and squeezed my hand. 'Have some faith, precious, sometimes things do work out. I love you and am very proud of you.' He opened the door and stepped outside with determination. The sea air rushed into the car, chilling my skin to the same plunging coldness of my heart. The door slammed, making me jump and the noise echoed through me as if I was empty. He walked the couple steps off the sand and onto the pavement, then crossed the quiet road. I turned on my seat to follow him with my powerless eyes. Is this what it felt like to watch someone you loved, leave? To feel useless? He crossed the street and approached the two bulky men outside the small shop. He handed one of them a small envelope, who quickly looked inside, nodded and slipped it inside his jacket. Dad signaled his head in the direction of the far cafe and began to walk the length of the street. The two men, who were not fishermen by any means, followed him silently. Dad had at least thought it best to not turn up completely unprotected, but two men seemed futile against the army that was Cane Rordriguez. I climbed over to the driver's seat to watch them bravely make their way. My breathing was staggered and my face pressed against the window pane, urging my eyes to focus better. I grabbed dad's driving glasses off the dashboard and shoved them on, just in time to see them reach the end of the road and the café that sat the only other moving people around. The man reading the paper, who I could see now was wearing light colours, did not look up as dad approached them. But one of the big guys, who was dressed in all black, moved towards them, his arms folded. One of them must be Rodriguez, I thought to myself, wiping the condensation from the window. They began to speak for a few moments and I could see dad looking around. I knew he was checking his surroundings, I had been doing the same and scanning for more of Rodriguez's men. So far though, there was no signs.

'Be careful,' I spoke loudly, willing dad to hear my cautioning words. A few more moments passed and I watched him place his brown file on the table in front of the man in cream. I could see the guy's newspaper fluttering in the sea breeze, but as my dad sat opposite him, he failed to even look up. He had to be Rodriguez; only someone that powerful would be so blatantly rude. I glared at him, wishing that the saying "looks could kill" was true. I hated him, I hated what he had done, what he was doing now, I hated everything about his existence. My focus on Rodriguez was quickly interrupted by my dad raising his hands into the air. I knew the motion well from years of being on the receiving end of it: frustration. Were they arguing? My stomach dropped further, arguing couldn't be good. I focused my eyes more, screwing them up into slits. I could see fingers now being pointed and it was obvious, even from here, that the conversation had become heated. The next few seconds happened so quickly that I failed to even react as my air disappeared and my heart stopped beating. This was it. This was my worst nightmare. Rodriguez knocked the envelope off the table in one aggressive movement and it went cascading to the ground, the papers flying everywhere. As the file hit the floor and slid along the sandy road, dad and the two men with him, took off at a run, dad's seat tumbling to the floor as he sprinted from it. They bolted for a side street and from the urgency in their escape, it was easy to see they were running for their lives.

'DAD!' I screamed louder than I had ever done in my life. My hands went numb as I reached for the door handle and hard as I tried, I couldn't hook my fingers over it to pull. Then to my horror, I saw another dozen or so black dressed men appear from nowhere. They emerged like cockroaches from cracks in the street and at a wave of Rodriguez's hand, they followed down the alley after my father. I wanted to yell for help, to draw attention to me instead of my dad, but I couldn't do anything, my body had frozen. I had no voice and was being swallowed by my fear. I carried on helplessly watching as Rodriguez stood up slowly, folding his paper. He tossed a couple coins on the coffee table and began to saunter away in the other direction, his paper tucked casually under his arm like it was an easy Sunday morning. As I watched him, something inside me snapped, something I had never felt before. I was suddenly enraged, furious and I utterly hated him. Why should he walk away so casually, why should he be allowed to take my dad's life, take him from me? My whole body filled with fury as vehemence overtook my breathing. From the very core of me, I loathed him, I wanted him to suffer, I wanted them all to suffer. My pain and panic quickly vanished and were replaced by this overwhelming and consuming anger. My hands shook with it as I threw off dad's glasses, scrambled through the car door and out into the air. I ran towards the alley, exhorting all my focus. I was completely unaware of the wind on my skin or the sand turning to pavement, I was unmoved by the chairs falling over when I charged past them into the alleyway, and I was oblivious of the narrow dark walls now surrounding me. I wanted my dad back, I wanted him to come home with me, I wanted this all to be over, I wanted- my thoughts were quickly snatched from me as I reached the bodies of the two men dad had hired to escort him. I didn't know if they were alive or dead, and selfish as it was, I didn't stop to check. Their bodies on the ground simply made me run faster, praying that it wasn't too late. I rounded a corner and found myself at a small courtyard, the group of black-shirted men gathered in the centre, all cheering and grunting. There on the ground in a heap, was the crumpled, broken body of my dad. His white shirt was blood stained, his face barely recognisable, his limbs lay broken and misplaced. His body gave no reaction at all as a foot ploughed into his side, sliding him back across the floor to hit some stacked wooden crates. Time slowed to a stall and all I could hear was the steady thump of my heart beating. I prayed with everything I had in me that his lifeless body was actually still alive. The anger consumed me again, but with a calming clarity, and in that fraction of a second where time stops and life decisions are made, I made my choice. I could run, I could beg, or I could fight. And I was a fighter. I focused on my dad and ignored the overwhelming odds. A black shirted man moved forward for the next strike, his leg extended back for the kick, and I attacked. My foot met the inside of his calf as I struck back, stepping between my father and the Rodriguez employees. A loud crack echoed amidst the crowd of deep voices and the guy keeled over, screamed in agony as his tibia broke in half and ripped through his skin. His cry was startlingly loud and brought the whole attention of the crowd my way. Everyone and everything paused in an odd freeze-frame moment where nobody seemed quite sure who I was, what I was doing there, or what had just happened. A very loud silence settled on the scene and the only noise now coming from the enclosed alley, was from the man with the broken leg, who now lay on the floor with his face screwed up in pain and sweat. I ignored his display, refusing to even glance in his direction. I didn't care if he bled to death, he was no longer a threat and that was all my head was registering. My eyes took advantage of the pause and scanned the crowd quickly. I had been taught to evaluate, analyse and plan, always and at every possible chance. There was one man down, twelve men left, four big ones and a smaller guy right at the back who stood in the Catta position, meaning he knew martial arts. The majority of the men were strong, but most likely slow, or at least slower than me and that was all I needed. A small glimpse of hope spurred me. There was maybe a chance I could get my dad out of this...maybe get myself out of this. I was brought back to focus when a laugh finally boomed out from the middle of the group and one of the four big men decided to break the silence. Why did the big ones always think they were so much braver?

'Look, sweetheart,' he began, his voice deep and cold. 'This is none of your concern, move along now, before we decide that you look left out.' A ripple of patronising sniggers trickled through the throng of apes. I smirked at him, tunneling all of my confidence to the surface. No matter how I may feel, I didn't want them to see any weakness. My smile though only seemed to agitate the giant buffoon and he pushed forward to the front. I lowered my stance instinctively, raising my hands up in the ready position. He halted a few steps in front of me, seeing my locked fists and instantly began to laugh, loud. He stood maybe six feet off the ground and as I looked up at him I made sure I could still see the perimeter.

'She's a sassy one boys, I'll give her that,' he mocked. As all the men laughed again, some whistling, some panting. Why did men have to be such sexist pigs? 'Look lady, sling it now, or you'll be sorry. I may take it easy on you because I've got a sweet tooth,' an appreciative chuckle waved through the group again, 'but Wyatt here,' he motioned to a dark-haired sleaze, 'doesn't believe in treating women the same as me. In fact, most of the boys here don't.' More laughing echoed off the tall brick walls surrounding us. They were brainless sheep following the lead of the cockiest in their group. I ignored the warning and locked my fists tighter, urging my nerves and trembling to retreat back down inside, away from prying eyes. The spokesman's humour vanished in an instant and his laugh disappeared into the menacing stares of his companions. 'Woman, leave now, this is nothing to do with you,' he threatened, obviously expecting a backdown. I shook my head as calmly as possible.

'No, this has everything to do with me.' I nodded at my dad on the ground behind me. 'If you let me take him to the hospital, this can all end now and I don't have to hurt anyone.' To this, the entire group erupted into laughter. Apparently, my warning was a hilarious joke. They were underestimating me and it gave me courage.

'I'm sorry little lady, but we have our orders,' he exhaled, wiping his stubbly mouth. 'Tell you what, I'll be a sport and give you to the count of three to leave.' His slimy smile vanished quickly and a cold, threatening glare replaced his sarcasm. This was it. 'One...' His hostile voice began and I breathed deeply. 'Two...' I got into position. 'Three!' With the command and absolutely zero hesitation, the men's ambush began, and it came fast. My adrenaline spiked as the first man ran forward. He obviously expected to knock me out with one punch and be the hero, but I ducked quickly and swung into his ribs. My hand burst into pain as my bones made impact with heavy flesh. He was winded, so quickly and forcefully I smashed my elbow up into his face, exploding his nose violently and sending blood in every direction. As his body hit the floor, the second man came at me with no pause, his fists raised and ready. If there had been any shock from the employees, in regard to my now very obvious capabilities, then it didn't show. They continued to come at me in a non-stop phase of attacks, unrelenting and uncompromising. I quickly moved sideways, efficiently anticipating the current man's actions. He swung and missed and I kicked his closest knee, immediately breaking the kneecap. He fell forward towards me, unable to hold himself straight, and I used his weight to knock him out with a knee to the face. His body slumped heavily as the next big guy came running. I jumped into a kick, planting my foot into his throat and he stumbled, grasping his neck and his Adams apple. I kicked again, this time at his chest and his body flung backwards, knocking over the next three attackers. From the side came the man I had seen last kick my dad. He swung powerfully at me, but I ducked and swiped his footing. He landed on his back with a crash and I kicked with all my strength at his crotch, hoping he enjoyed a piece of his own medicine. He let out an uncontrollable scream, cupping himself, all too late to protect his manhood. I reveled in his deserved pain as sweat broke out over his crumpled-up features. The few seconds of focused revenge distracted me and in those fleeting moments of lost concentration, my attention on the rest of the men slipped. Out of nowhere, a fist met my face at full impact. It felt like a bomb had exploded inside my head as my lip burst open under the pressure and my jaw cracked to almost breaking point. Before I could even deal with the pain, another fist instantaneously connected with my ribs, blasting me backwards into an uncontrolled stumble. I lost my footing, I was winded and reeling for air. Thankfully I'd taken many a hit at my Krav Maga lessons, so the pain and shock wasn't as new and as immobilizing as it should have been. My heel struck against my dad's body, still lying broken on the floor behind me and it was the grounding I needed. I had to keep going so I could get him to the hospital, that was what was on the line here. The reminder instantly refocused me, just in time to dodge the next incoming blow and concentrate on finding air for my straining lungs. It felt like eternity was passing by and the never-ending distortion of fighting and defending seemed to smear out before me in a blur. I kept up, giving a thousand percent, knowing in the back of my mind that no more than a few minutes could have passed, that no more than a few minutes stretched between me and freedom. But it seemed like no matter how much I attacked or blocked, more men just kept coming and more hits snuck past my defenses. My knuckles were bloody, the skin ripped from continual impact. The blood from my lip poured into my mouth, down my neck and over my collarbone, soaking across the front of my top. I spat a mouthful of it out onto the floor, the taste of iron making me gag. In the few seconds it took me to spit, another fist caught me across the cheek with such power that my vision blurred and I began to lose consciousness. I staggered, my hands trying to catch my fall, but couldn't react in time. My body crashed into the ground just as I felt the sharp and suffocating blow of a man's boot collide into my ribs. The pain was so intense that I went numb. I wasn't too sure if I had actually passed out or not, but after a few seconds I used all my might and pulled myself from the ground, determined to keep going. As I managed to sit up, the black shirts seemed to have stopped. Things were cloudy and I urged my eyes to focus and my limbs to gain control through the screaming that was ripping through my body. I slowly wiped away the blood that was trickling down from my head and I saw through my watering eyes that the men were using the time to regroup. There wasn't that many of them left and I sighed in relief, holding in my cry from the shooting pain. My ribs were more than likely broken, but they would heal. I only had a few men to go and I just had to push through the pain and ignore the agony. My dad's life depended on me and broken ribs wouldn't be enough to hold me back from saving him. Through sheer willpower and determination, I had to keep going. I forced myself to my feet and centered myself, steadied the only breath that I could muster and wrapped my fists. The broken skin stung as it stretched over my knuckles again and my eyes watered in pain as I watched the men ready themselves. The small martial arts man walked forward and my heart sunk, teetering on defeat. Yes, he was small, but he was far from slow, that I was sure of. He was also still fresh and full of energy…I on the other hand, was struggling. He looked at me as if I was something he'd stepped on as he readied himself before me, hands and feet in structured practiced positions. He stared at me hard and belittlingly; he licked his lips with disgusting suggestion. I spat out another mouthful of blood in front of him, splashing his shoes with it.

'Now we'll see how you do, precious,' he laughed, crouching lower to the ground. My heart stopped as I waited for the fight to start again. Just breathe I urged myself, just breathe. But I knew this guy was going to be a fight for my life, that I was going to hurt more than I ever had before. He growled at me, baring his teeth with warning and sweat began to run down my back, quickly followed by incontrollable chills. Despite trying my hardest not to, I held my breath. He let out a chuckle that the remaining men behind him echoed, rippling through the group like a pack of hyenas. The noise hummed its way backwards, getting progressively louder and more confident. Then suddenly, a loud piercing voice snapped through the enclosed alley and cut above all the standing men. It was firm and powerful like thunder and had the sting of lightning.

'ENOUGH!' it commanded sharply, ripping through the atmosphere. Then as if the plug had been pulled, the remaining men stilled, immediately standing to attention. The whole environment shifted into one of submission and the men suddenly started stepping aside, parting the crowd like the red sea. Instead of Moses though, a man wearing a cream designer suit, casually walked through the centre clearing. He moved forward with confidence and sureness until he came to stand directly in front of me. He was the picture of both ease and formality, of nonchalance and complete control. Both shock and fear coursed through me as I quickly realised who he was. He was standing right in front of me, touching distance away. The man I despised more than anything in the world, the man I abhorred and loathed: Cane Rodriguez.

CHAPTER FIVE
Making a deal with the devil.

Any air I was managing to breath in, was lost and I fought against the rising panic, fought to keep any form of composure. He was looking directly at me now and his eyes hadn't left mine from the second he had come into view. He was taller than pictures made him look and by far stronger. I could see beneath his pressed shirt that he had muscles, all taut and tight. His skin was a deep olive and his hair dark and cut stylishly short to match his Hispanic features. He had thick heavy lashes and deep brown eyes that penetrated to the soul. His jawline and cheekbones were solid and his shoulders broad and square. The media did him no justice, he was undoubtedly the most beautiful man I had ever seen. He was flawless, all male, and easily too perfect to forget just how deadly he was underneath it all. I pushed away the shameful, physical distraction that was spreading through my body and focused on just how much I loathed him...oddly contrasting feelings. He looked at me curiously, glancing around at the men lying on the ground, then placed his gaze back on me, directly in the eyes again. Basic stubbornness would have told me to not shy away from bold eye contact, but if I was telling the truth, I couldn't look away from him even if I wanted to. His eyes were stunning; deep and dark and assessing. He pointed at the broken bodies lying crumpled on the floor, some out cold, others just immobilised by pain.

'You did this?' he asked, quite calmly. His voice was as soothing to hear as his face was to look at, deep and rough and tinged with a Spanish accent. I kept my fists locked trying to remember that as attractive as he may be, he was still Cane Rodriguez. He was still the leader of the rival business. He was still the deadliest man I knew. After years of rivalry, I finally stood face to face with the warlord himself: my enemy. I'd imagined this moment many times while growing up, imagined how I would tell him just what I thought of him, tell him that he was a bad man with a bad business etiquette —obviously with more colourful language. But now that I stood here with the most feared man in my world staring back at me, my words were gone. My planned speeches were gone. My heated preaching, vanished. In fact, I found myself reacting completely opposite to everything I had ever envisioned. With no rational explanation at all, I lowered my hands, relaxed my stance and let my guard down. My mind was screaming at me, questioning its own sanity, but my instincts were stronger and they were loosening in this powerful man's presence. One of his perfectly shaped eyebrows raised slowly in observation. He was obviously as surprised by my reaction as I was.

'You are, valiente…brave, Madam,' he offered in half English and half Spanish, casting another look at the total number of surrounding incapacitated men. His accent was unnerving, it sounded like warmth and music and happiness, not the things you wanted to feel when your life was on the line.

'Brave?' I repeated, finally finding my voice. 'I wouldn't call protecting yourself brave.' Desperate to keep my wits, I held his stare as he smiled, oddly politely, displaying perfect white teeth. He put his hands in his trouser pockets and allowed a few moments of silence to pass between us, presumably to allow me to think and reflect…and panic.

'You know this is a fight,' he waved his finger around in a little circle, making reference to my present situation, 'that you cannot win. Sí?' He glanced at the number of men still standing fresh and eager behind him, the men I, myself, had tallied up just minutes ago. Despite myself, I nodded slowly in agreement.

'Yes. I know.' He inclined his head back to me, seemingly appreciating my candour.

'Yet, if I was to give my men the order to continue, you would keep fighting, wouldn't you? Even if I allowed you to walk away now?' It was more of a statement than a question and he slowly began pacing backwards and forwards in front of me, as if trying to figure me out. It felt like a lion was assessing his prey. But I was no one's victim, I reminded myself, straightening my aching spine. I watched him as he walked, casually and carefully before me, his eyes alight with something. He seemed intrigued, or maybe amused, but whatever it was he was feeling, it was keeping me alive for now.

'Yes, I would keep fighting.' I answered, without hesitation, lifting my chin stubbornly and defiantly. I hated this man so deeply it was unsettling, it was clearly making me lose control of my senses. I followed his pondering paces until suddenly he stopped and locked his eyes onto mine again.

'Do you know who I am?' he asked abruptly. I let a couple seconds pass before I nodded, rebelliously, remembering the brave and passionate person I was. I held his piercing eyes, swallowing for courage and answered with as much resentment as I could muster.

'Cane Rodriguez of Rodriquez Ltd. The man who values no one or nothing. The man who thinks people are replaceable pawns in a game. The man who plays God and ruins people's lives like they are meaningless shells. Yes, I know exactly who you are, Mr Rodriguez.' Yes! Look at me go. I managed to say a fraction of the things I wanted to say since I was fourteen, even if it was more polite and controlled than I had imagined. He nodded in receipt, scratching his smooth chin and letting a slight, annoyingly sexy, smile play on his lips.

'If you know who I am, madam, why are you here...?' His voice trailed off and he paused, raising a finger at me. 'Cómo te llamas?' he asked quickly, seeming to have figured out who I was. 'What's your name?' he repeated in English for me. I wiped the blood still pouring from my burst lip, feeling sick from the taste.

'Eva,' I stated, coldly, to which he nodded with confirmation, glancing at my dad's body still lying on the ground behind me.

'Tu Padre?' he asked plainly, no emotion. 'Your Father?'

'Yes.' I spat, with as much protective venom as possible. My body tensed with anger and my ribs screamed with protest.

'You know,' he began casually, 'I don't think your father would be very happy with the situation you have put yourself in.' My temper flared.

'Don't you dare talk about my dad when you're the reason I might not even have a father anymore.' He raised his hands in acceptance.

'Fair enough,' he said, coolly. I noticed a few of his employees behind him showing hints of surprise and shock. How long had it been since anyone had stood up to this man? 'But you see, we have a problem,' he continued, placing his hands casually in his pockets again and drawing my attention back to him. 'I gave an order, a punishment if you like.' to this I glared, narrowing my eyes to repulsed slits, 'If I let you and your dad leave here, which I am assuming is what you want, then I have lost.' He stopped suddenly and squared his strong shoulders, matching my intense stare. 'And I do-not-like-to-lose, Miss Eva,' he warned, with a firm tone. Then he shrugged, lightening the mood, as if he was torn between a simple decision. His blatant disregard for my father's life made me even more furious. For me, everything was riding on the next few moments and yet he continued in a calm, collected and professional manner, as if he couldn't have cared less.

'So, what do you suggest?' he half mocked as I wiped my lip again, attempting to stop more blood from seeping down. My mind had been reeling whilst he had been talking, knowing where the conversation was going to end up. I needed to bargain, I needed to make keeping my father and me alive seem somehow worthwhile. I swallowed the lump in my throat as my plan formulated.

'A deal.' I answered boldly, standing taller and firmer. To this Rodriguez flashed another one of his striking smiles. I had his full attention. He waited curiously, nodding to inform me that he was listening. I inhaled slowly. This was my only chance at survival. 'I get my dad to a hospital, call my mum and make sure that he is ok. I also get your word that you will never go after anyone in my family or anyone that I love again.' I paused and he laughed audibly.

'And what exactly do I get out of this?' He poked, smirking at my boldness. There was a small murmur of appreciation from the men behind him. I was entertaining at least.

'Me.' I replied, as calmly as possible. My head was screaming again; what was I doing, shut up; shut up and run! This was madness, my head knew it but my heart wouldn't relent. I couldn't back down, even if I had never been so scared in my life. My dad depended on me now and I would not fail him in the final hour. My answer had been obviously unexpected and Rodriguez's reaction showed it. But he composed himself quickly, offering only a small contemplating 'mmmmh'.

'And what exactly do you suggest that I do with you? How do you benefit me at all?' He stood, patiently listening and I was sure he would be able to hear my heart. There was nothing to stop him killing us both once he heard the remainder of my proposal. I needed to stop looking into those eyes of his and start locking my stinging fists again. I couldn't trust this man, he made a living out of lies and deceit, I was just visiting the office for the afternoon.

'You get the daughter of the CEO at Bain Enterprises,' he nodded, he already knew that, especially considering said CEO's body was still lying on the ground behind me, 'and the future daughter-in-law of Brice Bain.' To this Rodriguez stopped pacing. Was his hate for Bain enough to use his son's fiancé as leverage? I was counting on it, for my dad's sake. I would deal with the consequences of all of this later, when my father was safe, but for now, it was the best and only option I had. Rodriguez looked at me, differently, more assessing.

'Engaged to the junior Bain?' he asked, with what sounded like surprise. He obviously had not known that piece of information, which was odd since it was very public knowledge. Maybe he didn't follow the media as much as I would have assumed. Either way, it was to my favour. He smiled slightly. 'I am sure that it was not he that taught you how to fight, Miss Eva,' His eyes continued to scrutinize me. 'Cuántos años tiennes?' he asked in Spanish, making my arm hairs lift with betraying pleasure. That voice and accent was disarming. He translated it into English for me. 'How old are you?' I straightened my back and shoulders instinctively.

'The same age as you,' I replied, playing the defence. He flashed a dangerous smile at my retort, but then quickly composed himself again.

'And I am?...' he asked, with a hint of testing amusement on his lips. 'Treinta y dos.' I spat smugly, recalling the black '32' text from his file. Yes, I had some skills, I knew Spanish. He was not the only smart one here. My answer drew another smile from him, one that was quickly reigned in as he licked his bottom lip. He seemed amused if nothing else and I wasn't quite sure how to react to that. I had expected hate, anger, violence, even disdain, but his intrigue and glimpses of humour were throwing me. He was different to how I imagined him to be and I wasn't prepared for that. He continued to sweep his eyes over me with an analytical squint. I could see his mind working over things, contemplating my offer and its ramifications.

35

Taking me was a very personal attack on the Bain family, on his enemy, but with me here offering myself up on a platter, well, it was now a very easy opportunity. An opportunity I was praying he wouldn't pass it up. My life and my dad's life now both depended on Rodriguez's answer. He knew it and he knew that I knew it And so, the seconds ticked out, torturing me with unnecessary malice. He lingered and took his time, enjoying, as per his cruel character, being in charge of our fates, knowing that he alone was powerful enough to grant us or end our lives. My disgust for him simmered closely to the surface, barely controlled by the seriousness of my situation. It was life or death right now, that simple and that petrifying.

'Do you know what you are doing?' he finally asked, poison and warning lining his layered words. I nodded firmly.

'Hacer un trato con el diablo,' I whispered, with cautious surety. Both his eyes and his mouth reacted, but with what emotion I couldn't be sure. There was no point pretending, I was making a deal with the devil. Plain and simple. He watched me for a few more silent seconds, then ended my torture.

'Fine. You have a deal, young lady,' he confirmed, his eyes staying on me as he suddenly stepped closer to me. Dangerously close. I could smell his divine aftershave and see the crisp lines in his suit. His flawless face was just inches from my bleeding and beaten one and I could feel his warm breath on me. The heat from it stung my open cuts. His smile had faded and he looked intensely into my eyes. His hand lifted and he ran his finger gently across my cheek and then down to my collar bone. I froze in a strange mixture of fear and fascination. His finger traced my skin so gently that it almost seemed tender and as unwelcome as his touch was, it sent a vibration through my already buzzing skin. I turned my head away from him defiantly, trying desperately to disobey my betraying reactions. But despite my insubordination, my breathing came heavy and affected, somehow coming to life at his attention. His warm finger lingered at the base of my neck, drawing my heartbeats into erratic and unsettling thuds.

'Smith, Trentor, Cregar, put the man in the car and drive this little lady to the nearest hospital. Do not let her out of your sight,' he warned, moving a small piece of hair from my face to behind my ear. 'She may be the best business deal I've ever made.' His eyes settled on mine again, then with one last look, he stepped away abruptly, ending the conversation. He clicked his fingers at the black shirts who had been given the orders and they sprung to action. 'I'll see you soon, Miss Eva. Buenas tardes,' Good afternoon, he concluded formally, turning and walking through the parted crowd from which he had entered. The men enclosed behind him as if he had never been there, leaving only the silence he had commanded.

CHAPTER SIX
An interesting turn to the day.

As his men enclosed around him it took all his strength to not turn back and look at her. His pulse raced with excitement and intrigue. Who was this girl? He walked with his employee towards the parked car with his hands in his pockets and listened to the fading scuffle of moving feet behind him. He had never seen a woman fight like that, both physically and spiritedly. He smiled to himself with pleasure and amusement as he replayed her saying his age in Spanish. She had courage, he would give her that.

'An interesting turn to the day, Mr Rodriguez?' his employee said, slowing to meet his side. He looked up to him with a poker face and set eyes, nodding slowly.

'You could say that.' The deal he had just made came back to him, forcing this new girl aside from dominating his thoughts. She was an asset now, that was all. And this new asset was engaged to Edward Bain, the only son of Brice Bain, the man he hated more than anything. He laughed out loud and his employee cast him a side wards glance.

'Happy, Mr Rodriguez?' he asked with a smile. This brought more laughter.

'Scott,' he began in reply, 'if she is the love of Edward Bain's life, then she is a gold mine. Edward will do anything to protect her and to get her back, and Bain himself will do anything to keep his son safe and powerful. That little stick of dynamite, Eva, could essentially be the best deal I have ever made in my whole career. Quite literally.' His companion nodded in agreement as they neared the parked car. 'And she offered it to me.' He shook his head again trying to swallow the sheer vastness of potential this deal presented to him. 'She offered me the deal,' he laughed.

'She's a feisty one, Sir.' his employee added, taking the keys from his pocket and opening the doors. 'Did you see what she did to the men?' This comment drew another loud laugh, surprising even himself.

'I know,' he agreed nodding and taking his hands from his trouser pockets. 'Have you ever seen anything like it?' His employee shook his head and handed over the girl's fathers file.

'Here, Mr Rodriguez,' Scott said, passing it over to him. He took it, tapping the outer sheets with distracted attention. His mind was recalling the first

time he laid eyes on this Eva. She was surrounded, bloody, breathless and losing, yet he had never seen anything so unspoiled.

'Ella eres una luchadora,' he repeated with a smile. She is a feisty one. *His companion opened the car door.*

'I think she might be trouble, Mr Rodriguez.' Scott commented with caution as he reached the door and began to climb into the backseat. 'I think she could also be the most dangerous deal you've ever made, Sir.' Scott closed the door behind him, leaving him in the cool shadows of the black tinted windows. He smiled widely, now alone, and shook his head at himself, Eva's stubborn and defiant face rushing through his mind again. The way she had felt as he had touched her skin still tickled on his fingers and he drummed them off his thigh in distraction.

'Yes,' he said out loud to himself, placing down the file her father had presented him with. He quickly thought of her on her way to the hospital. 'She's definitely going to be something.'

CHAPTER SEVEN
It's not my blood.

Seeing Rodriguez leave and knowing that I was going to get my dad help, that was when I would have thought my heart would start to beat again. But it didn't. The magnitude of my situation was threatening to bear down on me. I could feel it loitering in the depths of me, pressing to escape, forcing my breaths into rapid puffs. I had won nothing. I stood in the alley still, with men all surrounding me, watching me closely. They were either annoyed that I had escaped their hands or shocked by the events that had just taken place, but either way, their faces hid nothing. I drew my attention from them and back to the only thing I could allow my mind to comprehend, getting my dad to the hospital. I knew that I could not allow myself to think or to feel too much just yet. I knew that if I granted myself that luxury, I would never be able to control myself. I would deal and cope with consequences later, once my dad was safe, once my dad was on a hospital bed, once my dad was ok...*if* my dad would ever be ok. The thought made me stumble and I reached out for the wall to steady myself, watching the men roughly grab hold of my dad's beaten and destroyed body. They began to drag him through the alley, his shoes leaving scuff marks on the floor in his wake. I yelled and pushed myself to his side, taking his head in my bloody hands, desperate to soften his transport. One of the three men Rodriguez had ordered to take us to the hospital had gone to get the car. We approached the still abandoned main street where it was sat idle, waiting for us. As we approached, he popped the boot and began to lift the hood.

'He'll go in the *back seat.*" I yelled with boiling blood, staring at the men so fiercely that they didn't argue. With no care at all, they deposited his body in the car and left me to organize him, whilst they congregated at the trunk to discuss what had just happened. I glanced at the keys in the ignition and then impatiently at the employees. I heard one mutter, "*yeah, but have you ever heard* anyone *talk to him like that and get away with it?*". I had no time for this.

'Screw it,' I said, as I closed dad's door and jumped into the driver's seat. The engine on the BMW roared as I slammed my foot down on the accelerator. The three men yelled in panic as the car tore off, all knowing as well as I did, that if they lost me they would have to answer to Rodriguez. I could see them in my rear-view mirror scrambling to get into another car, but whether they caught me or lost me was the least of my concerns. A hospital was my only focus, not the bumbling idiots disappearing behind me as I sped off into the country. If they caught up, they caught up, if they didn't, I didn't care. I glanced at my dad's broken body lying lifeless on the back seat and started praying with all my might. *Please be ok, please!* By mile three, I'd completely lost the other BMW. I had driven as hard and as fast as I could towards medical help all the while talking and reassuring my dad. As I tore up to the entrance of Accident and Emergency, my breaks screeching to a halt. The noise reminded me of how my Aston Martin had done the same thing only hours ago outside dad's office. Had it only been a few hours since this had all started? It was early evening now and dusk would start setting in soon. Time was spiraling away. I jumped from the car, running to the passenger door, screaming for someone to help me. I brushed dad's face carefully with love, quickly undoing his belt.

'We're at the hospital, dad, you're going to be fine, you'll be just fine, dad, just hold on.' I could hear the running of white clogged feet and squeaking of gurney wheels as it left the hospital door mats and met the outside. It was the sound of help. People in green and white pushed passed me into the car and dad was lifted efficiently and professionally from the back seat. He was being examined before they even began to move and someone was holding my arm and pulling me along with them. *Concentrate, Eva*, I urged myself, trying to stay in reality.

'...Ummm, he was beaten up, attacked by a group of men...' I answered, '...he's my dad.' I was trying to listen but could only focus on what was happening in front of me with the doctors. Was he ok? Was he alive? I felt a hand pull on my arm as we crashed through the swinging emergency room doors and into a sterile treatment room. I watched as needles and monitors began to be injected and hooked up into my father's lifeless body and workers rushed around him with urgency.

'No, I'm fine. *I'm fine!*' I yelled firmly, waving the nurse away as he tried to examine me. He protested, but with no success.

'Let's wait outside for a few minutes while the doctors work,' he was saying, edging me towards the doors. I struggled against him, desperate to not lose sight of my dad. What was happening? Why was no one telling me anything?

'Is he ok?' I asked desperately, tears forming in my eyes for the first time today. 'Is he alive?' The nurse took me by the shoulders, glanced at the heart monitor and then looked me in the eyes.

'His heart is beating, he is alive.' His words were simple and firm and relief washed through my aching body. The next forty minutes passed in a blur. I stood outside the room while bodies rushed in and around me. I'd given out mum's contact number and had waited at the window of the operating room, watching, until eventually my legs had begun to give way and I collapsed into a plastic chair. I stayed sat for who knew how long, just focusing on breathing. He was alive! My dad was alive and that was all that mattered. The nurses and doctors kept trying to examine me, but I shooed off their attempts. They needed to help my dad, just focus all their attention on him. My adrenaline was still keeping the majority of my pain at bay, and although I knew it couldn't last, it was enough to sustain me for now. My painful breath was beginning to slow, but I knew that my day was still far from over.

'Eva?!' My mum's voiced screamed over the noise of the hospital as she came sprinting down the cream, cluttered hallway. Her curly brown hair bounced as she ran and her slightly rounded body pushed its way passed random people blocking her path. She had bright eyes similar to mine and right now they were tear stained and heavy with worry. I stood as quickly as I could to embrace her, relieved to have support. Deep down, I knew she couldn't actually help me with anything about to happen, but she was my mum and she was the epitome of comfort. Her arms wrapped me up in a tight and painful embrace, as if she had assumed never to see me again. When she pulled apart, she began to cry even louder as her eyes roamed over my body.

'Oh, Eva, what happened? Are you all right? You look awful, we need a doctor...' She was rattling off panicking questions, desperately holding onto my arms and looking around for a medical help. I loved my mum dearly, but stressful situations were not her thing.

'Mum,' I finally said, with as much firmness as possible. 'I'm fine. It's not my blood.' It was only part of a lie, but I didn't have time for mum's hysteria right now. My time was running out and I could feel it begin to press into me like a physical reminder.

'Oh, Eva,' she whimpered, tears flowing from her red eyes. 'Your dad?' she asked quickly, frantically looking around into the room with panic. Gratitude washed over me to be with someone else who valued the importance of dad's life. I had just made a deal with Lucifer himself to ensure my father's survival. I could see in my mum's eyes, the sheer volume of fear she had at what my response to her question was going to be. She expected the worst, she knew that death should be the only outcome that would merit today's meeting. Being able to give a comforting answer and watching her reaction sweep through her body, well, it made it all worthwhile.

'He'll be ok, mum,' I confirmed. 'The doctor said that he has a lot of swelling, but they managed to repair the rip in his lungs and stop the internal bleeding. He has broken ribs, nose, shoulder, collarbone...' I trailed off as I watched my mum's eyes quickly change from relief to widen with horror. 'He'll heal mum, he'll be fine.' She began to cry again and quickly stood to go find dad. I breathed deeply, pain shooting through my body with piercing agony. I wiped my eyes quickly to hide the tears. At least the pain took the focus off what I knew I had to do next.

'Mum,' I said, taking her hand to stop her. I needed to explain to her somehow just what I had done, the trouble I had actually got myself into, got *everyone* into. She looked at me and for the first time since she had arrived, she saw past the surface war wounds. Her eyes widened instantly, knowing that something was still wrong, maybe something worse. I swallowed to keep my resolve. I knew that in order to keep them safe, I had to stay committed.

'Eva…what's happened?' I glanced down the hall, readying myself, but my eyes caught the nurse who had been dealing with me earlier. He was now standing with two police officers and was pointing in our direction. My heartbeat sped up. My time was up already? I took both of mum's hands and tried to smile through my pain. I couldn't talk to or trust the police; you never who they were actually working for. The last thing I needed was an overly keen cop breaking this deal and putting everyone I loved in more danger. Rodriguez's retribution would be unfathomable.

'Mum, I will be fine. I want you to promise me that you will work on getting dad better and that is it. Just get dad better. Can you promise me that?' I glanced at the police officers again who were now walking towards us with the nurse. My mum squeezed my hands, opening my cuts again and causing me to almost cry out in pain. But her worried face was enough to keep me silent. 'Promise me, mum,' I demanded firmly, 'promise me?'. She reluctantly offered a nod.

'Eva, what's going on?' she whispered, slowly. I hugged her quickly and as tightly as my body would allow.

'I will be fine ok, you know that I am always fine. I don't want you to worry because I will figure things out. I made the choice of my own free will, it was the best way to save dad and keep everyone safe.' I let go of her hands, stood and began to back away slowly. She didn't call out or try to stop me, she knew me better than that. 'Tell them all I'm sorry, but I did what I had to do.' Tears poured down her face and I turned, quickly walking to the exit. I allowed one last glance at my dad's lifeless frame through the window before I pushed through the doors into the night air, completely alone. I drove from the hospital and allowed a few tears to fall. They were not tears of pain or fear, they were tears of relief and thanks. My dad was alive, "he will heal" the doctor had said. My fate was now up in the air, but I had acted to save someone I loved. What was done was done and I would deal with the consequences. Me alone. I had to be brave. I wiped my stinging tears gently from my cheeks trying not to re-open any cuts. The traffic lights turned to green and with a heartbreaking look back, I indicated left and head off towards the outskirts of the city. Towards the Rodriguez land.

CHAPTER EIGHT
Hoooly-crap!

The drive there was a blur. I purposely didn't think about anything, I purposefully kept my emotions closed in. I was scared my fear and pain would get the better of me and force me to turn around and run if I allowed it an audience. I was no coward; my dad had raised me better than that, this was my only option now. Simple. Anyway, the safety of my loved ones now relied on me and my courage. If I tried made a fool out of Rodriguez, he would retaliate with the fury of Hell and make an example out of all of us. This was my path now, I resigned, and I followed it deeper into the country as lifeless greens and browns whirled past me. There were no signs, no indications of anything ahead, yet I knew that there was. Acres upon acres of private, guarded land. After an endless drive, I turned a corner to finally find a small road leading off to the right. A small single white stone sat on the road side, just as the file had described. I indicated out of habit, despite the roads being abandoned, and slowly began my drive into the belly of the beast. I noted the tall security camera poles scattered along the road side, made to look like phone masts. To the untrained eye they would look just that, but for someone who was brought up in the midst of security and technology, they stood out as if they were painted in neon. My presence was known already, there was no turning back now. The road continued for a few more miles in nothing but forest, until the final sharp turn led me directly to two huge iron gates. They looked like the gates from Disney's *Beauty And The Beast* which Belle stumbled upon by accident whilst seeking refuge. I was sure I would find no such thing here...although a beast, well, that was for certain. The gates stood maybe fifteen feet high and by the looks of it, were the only entry point of a marked perimeter. From a booth, which actually looked bigger than my flat, emerged a man almost as tall as the gates themselves, dressed all in black. He had no ID badge, nothing to indicate who he was or for whom he worked, and that was a definite sign I was at the right place. He approached my car with a very intimidating stare. I inhaled quickly, mustering my courage and opening the window. He was a big man and my eyes travelled north to keep his face in view. He stood at the window, his blank expression staring at me. The seconds passed awkwardly and he offered no greeting, nor gave any indication of planning to do so. *Right, then.* I swallowed and broke the silence as confidently as possible.

'I'm here to see Mr Rodriguez.' I didn't blame his skeptical glare, I kept forgetting what a mess I must have looked. He glanced into the back of the car and then around into the forest. After a few more moments he finally spoke.

'Who are you?' he asked abruptly, his accent foreign, maybe German?

'He'll not be expecting me, but he'll want to see me.' The giant's eyebrows perked a little at my assumption. 'Tell him its Eva Mack.' With no further questions, he stood and walked back into the booth. They would have already identified me off the security footage from my drive up the road. He knew who I was, he would now just need to get clearance. I held the steering wheel as tightly as my knuckles would allow. I could feel my heart beating beneath my chest and it quickened every time I looked up at the huge gates in front of me. Would I ever pass through them again once I went in? Deep inside me, I doubted it.

'You can go in,' his deep voice confirmed loudly from the booth. I nodded nervously and rolled my window back up. The gates creaked and slowly opened to let me pass and my car rolled cautiously into the land of untold horrors. The road remained leafy and marked at either side with dense forest for a few more miles until it finally gave way and opened out into a gravel drive way. My mouth dropped open.

'Hoooly-crap!' I said loudly to no one, as my eyes began to soak in the magnitude of the house that now lay before me. The driveway covered the distance of a football field with a huge water fountain in the middle. The brick feature created a roundabout which held the marks of tires and frequent traffic. A stunning old stone staircase led the way up to the gardens that lay at the foot of the house where weathered gargoyles perched at the top of the climb. The castle itself was magnificent in every way. It was Pemberley, Buckingham Palace and the Taj Mahal, and then any other grand, breathtaking house you could think of. It was undoubtedly the most beautiful building I'd ever seen in my life, so much so that for a few moments as I sat there, I forgot where I was. I parked the car and slowly got out, my mouth still open. The wind blew my hair across my face and I pulled it away quickly, wanting nothing to spoil my view. Forget the gates of the Beast's castle, this *was* the Beast's castle, but bigger and better in all the right ways. Belle should have been so lucky. Through the stained glass leaded windows, I could see lights and chandeliers, I could see floor after floor, room after room. I could see it extend backwards into wings and expanded in size, the stone glistening in the twilight. The turrets on either side of the front facing section added to the building's traditional history, while the security cameras that were quickly moving and adjusting their focus on me, gave it that somewhat more contemporary look. The noise of footsteps on gravel quickly snapped me back from my few seconds of blissful escape to heart racing reality. It may have been an exquisite building, but that also made it an exquisite prison and I was condemned inmate number one. I turned to see four men marching towards me, all with dark looks on their faces. If I was looking for a warm welcome, I was definitely in the wrong place. As soon as the first man reached me he spun me around roughly and slammed me back into the car, yanking my hands behind my back and into some form of extremely tight bonds. They felt like plastic tie wraps and they instantly began to dig into my skin. *Great, more cuts.* The next man began to search me, and far from gently. I recognised him from the alley, Wyatt, when the first guy to address me referenced him as not having any respect for women. I could feel his fingers press into my skin with each grip as he made his way over me, pausing, with a smile, over my upper body. The large guy had been right, he was a pig. I glared at him, disgusted, and with a hint of satisfaction on his smug lips, he moved on and reached for my head. Plainly taking no care for my wounds, he forced my face from one side to the other, checking through my hair and behind my ears. His thumb pressed purposefully down on the cut on my cheek and I could feel the sting as the skin broke open again, cracking the first stages of healing. I winced as tears filled my eyes uncontrollably. Thankfully the man was satisfied though and thrust my head aside before any tears could escape.

'Clean,' he informed the others, grabbing my arm and pulling me forward. I passed one of the other men and noticed his swollen black eye. I recognised him too from earlier in the day, he had been at the alley fight also. I smiled at him sarcastically, nodding at his inflated eye. I wanted him to know that I was proud of my work. He took the bait but I quickly paid for my brazen dig as he lunged for me, hard, knocking me to the ground. With my hands tied behind my back, I could do nothing but fall and my face collided with the gravel again, for what seemed like the millionth time today. He obviously didn't enjoy being provoked and quickly went for another shot while I was down. Thankfully the gropey man, Wyatt, held him off.

'Get a grip, Williams.' he yelled, shoving his co-worker away from me. 'She's expected, now! In one piece.' The handsy guy pulled me up using my arms and I could feel my shoulder sockets begin to give out under the strain. I clambered up trying not to cry out. As soon as I was up he released his grip and again shoved me forward. I found my feet quickly somehow and despite my head now bleeding again, I forced another cocky smile at the man with the black eye. His face turned red with frustration and it gave me nothing but pleasure to watch. I was marched to the front doors and into the foyer and even through my pain I was able to appreciate the splendor now surrounding me inside. Old antique furniture decorated as far as the eye could see. Handcrafted and stylish paintings and rugs, breathtaking and unique, intricately carved wooden rails and skirting boards laid out for the eye to behold. The house was like something out of a period movie and yet, I noted with quick eyes, fitted with all the luxuries of the twenty-first century. One of the men pressed a button on the very technical and expensive intercom mounted discretely to the wall and I watched with interest. There were doors as far as I could see, and as I stood waiting to be moved again, I took the opportunity to start scanning for maybe an escape route or an unsecured exit. But the more I looked, the more I realised it was a vain hope. The building was wired like the White House. From where I stood, I could see seven different cameras, all moving and all zooming in and out. I could see six alarm panels and four motion sensors, swipe-card access points and something that looked like an infrared system. And that was just the obvious ones. I sighed heavily, leaning against the oak paneled wall for support as pain shot through my ribs. What the hell was I going to do? My whole body ached and stung, I was so exhausted that I didn't think I could cry now even if I let myself. Thankfully before self-pity was allowed to set in, the pervy man grabbed my arm again and began to pull me down the hall. He pushed me up the most magnificent staircase I had ever seen and if I had had my hands, I would have run them up the smooth wooden banister which ended in a seamless carved twist. With a last glance, the staircase disappeared quickly and I was dragged down another few corridors and passed numerous doors. This place was a maze and I knew I'd never find my own way if the chance arrived. Finally we reached a very nondescript door, but what obviously held our final destination. It was being guarded by another black shirted, bulky man, this time who stood to attention like his life was on the line. Did Rodriguez only advertise jobs for men over six feet tall and eighteen stone? Is this where all ex-marines came once they were disgraced and thrown out of the Navy for bad behaviour or anger issues? It would explain their size and their attitudes. The guy at the final door glanced at me for only a split-second before pressing the intercom button on the wall. The light went green and he swiped a card down the reader on the door handle, opening it. I wasn't too sure what I was expecting to see inside; chains, shackles, dungeons, torture tools…but my heart began to pound as loud as it had when I had first seen my dad run down that alley. What fate awaited for me across this threshold? What horrors? I closed my eyes and thought of why I was here…*my dad!* His image came very clear to my mind. My dad. This was why I was doing this, why I had made this stupid deal in the first place. I opened my eyes again with new resolve. Whatever was waiting for me inside, I was strong enough. I took courage in myself and forced my feet to move, to walk through the doors. My dad was alive and if my life was the price of that, I gave it gladly.

CHAPTER NINE
Well that's because you're a psychopath.

The inside of the room was somewhat different from what I had been expecting. I wasn't standing in a torture chamber as anticipated, I was standing in an office, a very nice office. Directly in front of me was a huge open fire, logs simmering away with a warming red glow. To my left against the wall stood a stunning antique bookcase, full of leather bound books of all heights and sizes. In front of that sat a solid dark oak desk with crafted legs and corners which held a phone, an expensive laptop and some papers. To the right of the table were open balcony doors, with flowing white curtains blowing in the early evening breeze. I noted that it was starting to get dark outside and the sky was turning an eye-catching pink. I loved sunsets and sunrises, although failed to see its beauty just now. My attention was pulled to my right by the sound of movement and then a familiar voice.

'Miss Eva. Bienvenido, welcome.' Rodriguez said brightly, his hand extended outwards as if to welcome me in. I stepped forward slowly, further into the room. It must have been a hard day at the office as he was dressed in a dark suit now, with a blue shirt and dark tie. In the few hours away from him, I had already forgotten just how alluring the man actually was. It was almost staggering to be honest and I had to force myself to look away from his eyes, determined to keep some kind of dignity. His easy words quickly changed as he yelled in anger.

'Get those off her hands, ahorita!' he commanded loudly, pointing at the binds around my wrists and instructing their removal, immediately. The men that had escorted me up from the car park quickly rushed to cut the tight restraints off. As the plastic fell away, pins and needles instantly followed and the blood began to recirculate. I rubbed my wrists and wiggled my fingers to try speed up the process.

'This lady is not a prisoner here, she is a guest and you will treat her so,' he barked at the four men who stood around me. The men lowered their heads like dogs being reprimanded and I watched in fascination as Rodriguez chastised grown, sizable, powerful adults. 'Do you understand me?' he asked again, impatiently. They all nodded, one of them mumbling 'yes, sir'. 'Good. Go,' he ordered, pointing to the door. They obeyed, quickly.

'Miss Eva,' he continued again, addressing me in a somewhat more pleasant tone, 'I am impressed. I do not know many people who if put in your situation would not have run.' He considered me with a slight smile on

47

his perfect lips.

'It doesn't say much for the people you know then, does it?' I replied as boldly as I could. 'We made a deal and in order for you to honour that, *especially the safety of my family,*' I emphasised the most important factor, 'then I have to keep my word.' I looked him dead in the eyes, praying he couldn't see inside me, couldn't see the nerves and doubt and uncertainty. He stared back at me, analysing, deciding, I didn't know what, but a few moments passed before he looked away. I released my held breathe as soon as he did. Looking at his perfect face and deep eyes was not the easiest thing to do when I was determined to hate him. He seemed to have this way of unwillingly calming and loosening me. It was unnerving and scary, like I had little control when he was near me. Was he like this with everyone? Is this why business went so well for him? Movement to my right caught my attention and I glanced sideways to find the three men who I had last seen in the rear-view mirror of the BMW as I sped off to the hospital. They sat on the long cream leather sofa, perched and petrified. I looked at them quickly, all of them with their heads down and their hands folded out of sight. They looked like children getting into trouble and just as the word 'punishment' came to my mind, my eyes caught another thing in the room. On the long oak table next to Rodriguez lay a gun. I tried not to outwardly react, but I was sure my eyes must have widened as I saw it. You would have thought that being brought up around them and having been taught how to handle them, that the sight of a gun wouldn't have scared me so much. But there was a slight difference between the ones at the shooting range and the loaded Glock lying on the expensive table before me. This one was used to shoot people, not paper targets. As if reading my mind, Rodriguez picked up the sleek black weapon and holding it casually in his hand, relaxed his stance against the table. Facing his three men he turned his head and motioned me closer. I walked slowly forward until I stood parallel to him on his right. I was close enough to see his profile perfectly, close enough to see his chest rising and falling casually in complete control. He looked at me with a playful smile and scratched his defined jawline with his free non-life threatening hand.

'Miss Eva,' he began with a small, rueful grin. 'you are just in time to help me out with a problema' He teased with the word, then turned his eyes back to his men on the sofa. 'You recognise these men?' he asked, nodding at them dismissively. I didn't answer. What was he up to? He took my silence as confirmation though and continued. 'Well I gave my well trained, professional and highly competent men a simple order earlier today, you might remember?' He paused and glanced at me sarcastically, obviously I wouldn't forget. 'To escort you and your father to the nearest hospital and then bring you here directly?' He waited for a reaction from me, but he wasn't going to get one. 'Anyway, until a few minutes ago they had failed me and I had lost the best asset I had ever acquired,' he inclined his head at me politely to emphasise that I was indeed that asset, 'needless to say I was desilusionado, disappointed, but...now that you are here, things have changed slightly.' He shrugged casually. 'I was going to punish them for their incompetence, but since you have altered their failure, I will leave their fates in your hands.' He rolled the words off his tongue musically, seemingly enjoying himself. I looked at him in question, my eyebrows high. He was joking, right? But he sat perfectly still, awaiting an answer, blatantly not joking. The men looked up at me quickly, each with a readable mixture of shock, fear and pleading in their eyes. The enmity and coldness I had seen in them earlier in the day was gone and right now they just looked like I felt; confused and scared. I turned away from them, refusing to play this sick little game.

'It's a hard decision, isn't it?' he coaxed. 'I can understand your dilemma, but I would keep in mind that these men here were all involved in el padres *accidente,* earlier today.' He paused awaiting the rise he knew he could get out for me. I glared at him as madly and coldly as I could, but stayed silent as the words, *your father's accident,* stung me. I would not give him the satisfaction of reacting like he wished. I stuck out my chin with defiance and he smiled, repeating a word to himself with amusement. 'Luchadora.' I was sure it meant 'feisty', but he had muttered to himself and then quickly moved on. He shook his head lightly. 'Anything?' he coaxed, that wicked smile playing on his lips. He knew fine well what he was doing here, toying with me and pushing my boundaries. 'Fine then,' he concluded, standing up, 'I'll help you out. If you continue with your silence, I'll assume that you agree with my original form of reward for stupidity and carry out my intended plans...' he narrowed his eyes at me, 'to shoot them in the head.' I felt my air vanish from my chest, but held my ground firm. I wouldn't play his games. He stepped a pace closer to the men, who by the terror in their eyes seemed to already know their awaiting fates. 'I'll give you to the count of three. Un..' He took off the safety with a flick of the finger. My heart began to race. Was he serious? Was this a test? 'Dos...' He cast a quick side-ways glance at me, lifting the gun to aim. My palms were sweating as he squared his shoulders slightly, readying himself for the kick of a fired round, I recognised the position. He was serious. 'Tres!' he said loudly, with a tone of finalisation. He lifted the gun and went to shoot.

'Wait!' I yelled, stretching out instinctively and grabbing his hand. He stopped instantly, a small smile appearing on his face. He looked at our touching hands with consideration and I quickly withdrew as if stung. 'Stop.' I confirmed, knowing he had won. I shook my head, glancing at the three men on the sofa who looked like their lives had literally flashed before them.

'Are you sure, Miss Eva? They all helped to hospitalise your father and

I am sure that not one of them would have hesitated to finish him, or you, off. Be sure about your decision. Mercy will get you nothing from them.' The gun was still locked in his hand and pointing at the men. I breathed, painfully. He was a horrid, heartless man. What gave him the right to play with peoples' lives, even if those people were scum? He spoke to me again, seeking clear confirmation. 'You wish me to let them go, not harmed at all?'.

'Yes.' I spat, spitefully, refusing to look at anyone. What kind of a sick game was this? These were *his* men, surely, they were worth more than my grace, the enemies grace. I heard his cool laugh from beside me and he let out a casual sigh, standing up and flicking the safety back on the gun.

'It's your lucky day guys,' he said happily to the three men, lifting his arms in the air. 'This young lady has just saved your lives...' His mood changed suddenly like a flash fire and he words turned to threats. 'Do-not-make-me-regret-her-decision. Do NOT fail me again. You will not have a beautiful woman here to save you next time.' He glared at them viciously. 'Ahora van!' He yelled, pointing to the door for them to go. 'And order Miele up here, immediately!' They did not need to be told twice, each practically running for the door, none of them looking back. He stood still for a moment until the door lock clicked closed and we were completely alone. From the corner of my eye I watched him put the gun back down on the table and I relaxed slightly, at least he wasn't going to shoot me, not yet anyway. He quickly switched his attention from the gun, back to me, his whole body turning to face mine. I froze, rigid, contemplating the option of actually preferring to be shot. It was probably the safer choice. This man was hypnotising, when *he* focused on me it seemed *I* could not focus on anything else, and for someone who had always had so much self-control, that scared me. I swallowed as he walked slowly over to me, his eyes searching with every pace. When he was mere centimeters away, he stopped. I could smell his divine aftershave again and feel the heat from his body as he leaned in closer.

'You, Miss Eva are just full of surprises. I am impressed, and I do not impress easily. It's been a long time since I've been intrigued by anyone.' He paused, and I could feel him looking directly at me. 'You know, I would have killed them,' he whispered into my ear, his breathe moving my hair.

'Well that's because you're a psychopath.' I said boldly, keeping my eyes locked on the floor and not daring to look up. I knew as soon as the words left my mouth that it was a stupid and dangerous thing to say, but if he thought I was going to bow before him like everyone else did, he was going to be wrong. I could see it through my eyelashes that he had unleashed a smile and was nodding calmly. I heard him scratch his jaw with his perfectly tanned hand.

'I can see why you would think that,' he said placing his finger under my chin and forcing my face up to meet his. He looked deep into my eyes, so intently that had he not had my face held in place, I would have blushed and looked away instantly. 'But it is not always as it seems, Miss Eva. You of all people should know that.' He began stroking my cheek gently with his thumb. 'You and I are not so different.' This received a reaction. I narrowed my eyes at the accusation. How dare he suggest that we were alike; the last time I checked, I wasn't a ruthless, cold blooded murderer- although the impulse to become one was quickly growing inside me.

'We are *nothing* alike!' I spat indignantly, ripping my head from his disgusting hands. Yes, he was flawless and handsome and beautiful, but he also had the ugliest soul I'd ever met.

'Really?' he continued, unfazed by my blatant repulsiveness. He made no action to move or step away. 'We both believe in fighting, to any extent, for what we think is right…regardless of consequences.' My blood began to boil again. The man was infuriating. His insinuations made me livid, I thought of my dad's body laying beaten on the floor and the three men's faces on the couch as he waved a gun in their faces. We were not alike. Not at all.

'So, you think it is right for one person to control peoples lives,' the unfiltered rant came pouring out of me, 'decide whether they live or die, are beaten to death or not? For someone to punish the outspoken and to silence those who get in the way?' I paused for sore breathe, but Rodriguez made no move to argue or defend himself. Instead he stood statue still, watching me intently with an almost smile on his lips. He was apparently amused and that just bugged the hell out of me. Insufferable, disgusting man. 'You're a sadist who thinks its ok to use people with no consequence, to lie, threaten, murder. No. No, we are not alike in anyway, *Mr Rodriguez*.' I said his name with distaste. '*I* don't have a God-complex.' He began to laugh, his head tilting back slightly as he chuckled to himself. His body remained inches from mine and I wished I could push him away, far away from me. How dare he laugh at me! He was the most patronizing, condescending person I'd ever met: rude, selfish and arrogant. 'Don't laugh at me,' I hissed, as firmly as I could, glaring boldly into his dark eyes. 'You know *nothing* about me.' To this he stopped his laugh, raising his hands in submission.

'Okay, Miss Eva,' he said with a small smile still showing on his lips. 'Don't worry, I'm not laughing at you, I am laughing at your interpretation of me. The more you speak of me with such contempt…' he paused, '…and *passion*, the more alike I continue to think we are.' He collected a strand of my hair into his fingers and twisted it slowly. 'You may not see it yet, but maybe one day the likeness will become more evident to you.' *One day?* He was crazy. There would be no one day for us. I wanted nothing to do with the man, nothing more than what was necessary to survive.

'I doubt that very much,' I practically snarled. 'There are only so many similarities between normal and *psychotic*.' His playful smile disappeared in a flash and his hand grabbed my face firmly, my cheeks gripped tightly between his strong fingers. His whole disposition changed in an instant and a temper flared inside his eyes. This was the side of him that did business, this was the side of him I recognized. He was suddenly taller and stronger, and for the first time since being alone with him, I felt fear. Fear for the consequences of taunting him. If you poked a bomb for long enough, it would eventually explode. I knew that, yet hadn't been able to keep my mouth shut.

'Do not push me, Miss Eva. My intrigue for you will only go so far. Ser advertido.' *Be warned*, he threatened quietly. He didn't need to raise his voice to make me understand his threat, the even tone of his controlled voice was enough to intimidate the hell out of anyone. Including me. He held my face in place and kept his eyes locked on mine for what felt like a lifetime, staring into my soul. Then with an exhale, he let me go. 'You cast judgments on things you don't know or understand. You speak of morals and fairness, yet you *judge* me. You preach of opinions being heard, but you only wish to hear the opinion that confirms your own.' He paused, then just as quickly as he had flared up, he relaxed and again lifted his hand to touch my face. This time he gently ran his finger over my broken lips, as if daring me to speak more. My skin tingled with heat beneath his touch. 'You cannot be both people in this world. I am no saint, but neither are you. I gave up trying to please everyone the day I realised it was an impossible task. You can *never* satisfy everyone, at some point in your little dream, Miss Eva, you will have to make a choice that will destroy the people you love. Maybe then, you will see what it is like to walk in my shoes.' His rising and falling chest was the only signs now of the burning anger that had consumed him seconds ago. I controlled my body and its desire to lash out at him, but I couldn't control my mouth.

'Do you not think, *Mr Rodriguez*,' I said his name with as much malice as I could muster, 'that by being *here*, I'm not destroying the people I love? Your forced me to make this ridiculous deal so that I could save my dad's life. I'm in exactly the position you're talking about, yet the difference between you and me is that I still care about the consequences of my actions.' I knocked his finger away from my face, conclusively. 'I haven't yet witnessed any conscience from you.' I narrowed my eyes at him with defiance. 'Did you even look at my dad's proposal before you had the life beaten out of him?' I kept his eyes, determined to not be subdued by his penetrating stare. But instead of his normal glaring, I found another emotion. One I wasn't too sure how to interrupt. He sighed in an almost defeated fashion, then quietly spoke.

'You do not know everything, Miss Eva, despite what daddy and his boss may have told you. And I don't have to do anything I don't want to do, regardless of who is proposing it to me.' Before the conversation could continue, we were distracted by a discrete beep at the door. Quiet as it may have been, it sliced through the atmosphere loudly, reiterating how intense the moment between us had become. The intercom light was flashing, we could both see it from the corner of our eyes. With no more than a finalising glance, Rodriguez stepped away from my body and walked towards his desk, pressing a small button. I exhaled with relief as the distance between us grew and the air became clear again. Rodriguez perched himself down on his desk and latched his ever-watchful eyes back onto me, crossing his arms over his broad chest. The office door opened and in walked a small, grey haired man. He held a small leather bag clutched to his front that was worn and used, a little like its owner's skin. He had an olive complexion and despite expectations, kind blue eyes. He instantly found me in the room and I watched him scan over my body whilst the door shut quietly behind him.

'Cane!' he exclaimed, careful in his reaction. His tone was not reprimanding, but more like a fatherly reproof. I was quickly learning that even here, in this foreign land, no-one actually seemed brave enough to dare disagree with or oppose Rodriguez. Even the old and wise. In his world, *this* world, Rodriguez was God. Everyone seemed to know it, and everyone feared his wrath. The old man tutted in disapproval but remained loitering at the door. He obviously wanted to move but was awaiting the ok.

'Dr Miele, it was not my doing,' Rodriguez replied a little defensively, shrugging his shoulders. 'Would you though? Por favor?' he added, raising his hand in my direction. That was the sign the old man had been waiting for and he rushed over to me. I stepped back slightly, my guard going back up. I normally would have clenched my fists ready for defence, but he was an old man, maybe seventy odd, and a step backwards seemed enough to let him know of my wariness. Was he here to inject me with a lethal dosage or to torture me? His tanned and steady hand reached out for me, the universal sign of attempted comfort.

'Now dear,' he began softly, 'I just want to take a look at you, see if we can *curate*...fix you up.' His accent was Spanish, just like his boss's, but thicker and more pronounced. I glanced over at Rodriguez who remained sat on his desk. He nodded firmly at me.

'This is Dr Miele. He has been our family doctor since before I was born. He is the best of all Spanish doctors and has seen many war wounds, I can assure you. You are in good hands, Miss Eva.' I normally would have needed more convincing than the word of my enemy, but to be honest, between the genuine look of concern in the old doctor's eyes and the now almost unbearable pain I was in, I had little energy left in me to fight. I relaxed my shoulders and nodded towards the doctor who moved quickly before I, or Rodriguez, could change our minds. He gently took my hands into his and looked at my black, clotted ripped skin. Then he moved to my face which was swollen and sticky with setting blood. He began to tut again as he continued to examine me.

'My poor dear, you have been in the wars today,' he spoke softly and gently as if I would break at any moment. 'Where are you sore, except from the obvious?' I touched my side where my ribs were. He nodded and went to his bag. After listening to my chest and heart, which must have been beating faster than a hummingbirds wings, he carefully lifted my top and placed his warm hands on my ribs. I dare not look up at Rodriguez who was still sat on his desk observing me. Something about my bare skin being on show with him watching made me self-conscious. More than it normally should. I tried to focus on the old doctor instead and his audible gasp as his eyes landed on my side.

'Por todod los diablos,' he cursed loudly, 'it is a wonder you are still walking. I have seen many a man much larger than you be crippled by the pain of your injuries.' I glanced down to see my side; black and blue with bruising, red and tender. 'Broken ribs are very painful.' *No kidding.* He continued, pressing into my side and I winced, unable to control it. I wanted to scream out, but Rodriguez's watchful eye was enough to keep me silent. He sat still, not saying a word, ever assessing what was in front of him. Dr Miele continued to examine me for a few more minutes, gently prodding and pushing my body in al the places that hurt. It was taking all my strength to keep my tears at bay. Finally, once he seemed satisfied with his inspection, he turned to Rodriguez.

'She needs stitches and painkillers- strong ones that will numb all the pain.' He closed his bag and gently patting my arm. 'She has at least three broken ribs, a couple broken fingers maybe and extensive bruising. Impressively few injuries considering the beating her body has taken today. In time she will heal fully though,' he paused, 'penosamente…painfully,' he added looking to me. 'But she will heal. I will see to her properly once you are concluded.' He waited for Rodriguez to reply before moving, which he did in the form of a single nod.

'Thank you, Dr Miele,' he offered politely. 'I will send for you once we are done.' At that, the old man left the room without another word nor backward glance. I stood still, pulling my top down straight and feeling Rodriguez's eyes still watching me.

'Ok, then,' he began formally, standing up and putting his hands in his pockets. 'The rules,' he began, and I looked back at him, trying to mask my confusion. *Rules?* 'You do not leave the premises; the gates are your boundaries. Any escape will make our agreement null and void. *Especially* the part regarding your family.' He paused to let the message sink in, but it wasn't needed, I understood perfectly; I escape, he goes for my family.

Simple rule. His formal voice continued. 'You do not snoop around my things, this is my house, you will treat it with respect. You will not look through my effects for information, if you do, our agreement is null and void. You will not use any form of communication. All phones and internets are locked, even the reception is monitored. Any attempt to do so and I will know, and it will count as a breach in our agreement.' He began to pace in front of his desk. I watched him walk, but I didn't quite understand what was happening. I knew he was giving me a set of rules which if broken would cost my family's safety, but I didn't get how the rules he was talking about would apply to me. I would be locked in a small windowless cell, in the middle of nowhere, with a guard and meals passed through a slot in the door, surely? Why would I even need to know about the telephone service? I looked up to see Rodriguez now standing still, watching me.

'You are confundido...confused? Why?' he asked, bluntly. My emotions were now showing very obviously on my face as normal hardened mask was lost. I was tired. I stammered awkwardly, trying to find the words. 'I don't understand how any of this is applicable to me?' I finally got out, exhaustion beginning to take hold. The fight in me was dying. And fast. I could feel my facilities begging for rest, my insides crying for peace. I needed a bed and that old doctor's bag for some drugs. I glanced past Rodriguez to the balcony windows where the curtains were still blowing in the breeze. It was dark out now and I could see the stars in the sky.

'Miss Eva. You are not going to be kept like an animal. You may think that is what I am, a 'psychopath' wasn't it? But I do have some manners. You'll be here for a substantial period of time, at least until I have decided what is the best use for you. But until then, you will be mostly treated as a guest. You will be left to your own time and entertainment. You will not be guarded twenty-four hours a day like a convict. You will have already noticed that security here is tight and I believe that even if you did have the opportunity to run, that your concerns for your family would stop you from doing so.' He paused with a serious stare. 'Which rightly they should.' He cleared his throat. 'Even as we speak, your father will have had an untraceable tracker placed in him, which I will have constant access to. That means I can find him at any point that I so wish. I just have to press a few buttons.' My pulse quickened at the threat.

'What?' I said incredulously, before I could stop myself. An untraceable tracker? Rodriguez's eyes had narrowed at me with what almost looked like entertainment. I hated him.

'Yes, Miss Eva, a tracker. Injected into your dear father's neck whilst he lay sleeping at the West Side Royal Infirmary, south wing, fourth floor, room twenty-three. Don't worry, he wouldn't even have been aware of the prick of the needle.'

'Why would you do that?' I spat, as the full implications of his words began to settle in. It meant that for the rest of my dad's life, this monster standing here in front of me, would know exactly where he was at all times. There could be no running, no escaping or hiding from him and his reach. The understanding scared me to the core. It meant that at any time he wanted, he could find my family. It meant that even if I was ever desperate to, I could *never* break my deal with him.

'Seguro. Call it business insurance if you want, but it ensures compliance on your end-'

'I've already said I will stick to my word, I am here, aren't I?' I interrupted quickly, with a somewhat panicked and agitated voice. Rodriguez simply stood, watching me with his ever-guarded perfect eyes. It infuriated me.

'As much as *you* have, so far, proven surprisingly true, that does not mean you shall stay that way. And as I was away to say, your loved ones will also be informed of *your* tracker, ensuring their compliance also.' My eyes widened, and my hand instantly flew to my neck. 'Rescuing you would be pointless now since I will always be able to find you.' He was bluffing. I knew that, I hadn't been injected with anything. I would have felt it. Seeing my reaction though drew an amused smile from his perfect lips and he began to shake his head. 'No Miss Eva, I didn't *inject* you with anything. Injection is not the only way to implant the device. I have some very clever business friends who have long since figured out how to penetrate a host without the use of an obvious needle.' I shook my head.

'You're bluffing.' I said, forcefully taking my hand away from my imagined punctured skin. To this Rodriguez shrugged slightly with another coy smile.

'If that is what you wish to think, then go ahead, but please do remember that I have big plans for you. The leverage you offer me is unmeasurable and I will not risk losing you. A deal is a deal after all. And as far as you are concerned right now, tracker or no tracker, Miss Eva...' he lowered his eyes and cast them at me with a cold stare, 'I own you.' I swallowed the bile rising in my dry throat as his eyes penetrated deep into my soul. The heavy truth was like a vacuum, sucking my air away and I struggled to keep up my façade of composure. No matter if I or my family ever had the chance to run and escape this mess I'd made, it would be pointless. He would always be able to find us and to bring the justice he would see fit for breaking the deal. I tried to inhale steadily, but it came sharp and staggered, wrought with fear. Rodriguez saw it and his eyes flared for a fraction of a second, something buzzing in him just beneath the surface. Then he coughed, clearing his throat, and getting back to business as if my world wasn't crumbling down in front of him. 'I am a busy man, Miss Eva, I do not want to have to worry about your security and your every move. If you are at least on my property I shall be able to keep an eye on you whilst continuing with my work.' He raised his eyebrows in question indicating he was finished talking and did I understand? I did understand. I was also speechless. How could this man be two completely different people? The hospitable, courteous, gentleman who was going to let me wander free and unchained, yet at the same time; the unforgiving, cold, criminal who would micro-chip me and shoot three men in the head? I nodded quickly in response, my mind reeling with questions. He nodded back and continued. 'You are welcome to use the gym, pool, tennis courts and all other facilities, clothes and other required materials will be provided to you as soon as possible. If you need anything, my employee Scott will correspond with you and he will make you as comfortable as possible.' He finished and waited, watching me for a few seconds, then nodded conclusively and pressed the button on his desk. The door opened almost instantly and a large man with bad skin entered. My escort, I assumed. My head was spinning, and my heart was torn somewhere between being oddly grateful and full of despise.

'Take Miss Eva to her room please and let Dr Miele know that she is ready to be seen.' The man nodded and waited for me to move. I paused awkwardly. I had just learnt that any freedom and safety I had ever had was gone, yet I felt that for some strange reason, I should say thank you. He was going to treat me like a guest. He wasn't going to lock me in a black hole and throw away the key. These were acts of kindness in what was, make no mistake about it, a war. I was an enemy to him, just as he was to me. I hadn't expected kindness from him in any form. Yet, despite his compassion, he was still the very reason all of this had happened in the first place. I could hear time passing by, but I stood internally debating for a few more moments, trying to digest all the new information that was pinging around in my head. Finally, reason won and reminded me that I shouldn't have to thank anyone for basic humanity. And at the end of the day, no matter how different Rodriguez and I were, we were both human. We were level on the field of existence, even if he thought himself superior. I bit my bottom lip and turned to leave the room without any last words.

'Miss Eva?' Rodriguez called after me in his charming voice. His head was now turned down towards the papers on his desk. 'May I suggest that you have a bath before you go to sleep tonight, it will help with the stiffness tomorrow.' He paused looking up at me, his eyes finding mine and locking on. 'Confía en mí,' he added with sincerity. The sound of his words telling me to *trust him* made my heart pound and my breathing quicken. I needed to be away from this man and his straps, away from his tricks. His words pierced me, and his gaze confounded me. Everything about what I knew of him screamed that I could and should not *ever* trust him; he was a clever monster, and that was all. But somewhere amidst all the hate, fear and reservations, something pushed against me and reached out for him. I could feel it inside every time he looked at me. Feel it betraying me and moving towards him. It was unnervingly scary, like I had no self-control. How could you despise a person so passionately, yet feel so drawn to them? Rodriguez was the devil himself, and I knew that. I was playing with fire here, but I couldn't seem to stop myself.

CHAPTER TEN
Unable to shift her.

She left the room and he stayed sat, watching the door close. He couldn't quite control the smile that was playing on his lips. She was a bold and brave thing, that was for sure. His employee's words from earlier in the day came back into his mind and he laughed to himself. Luchadora. Yes, she was definitely feisty. She had not appreciated being forced into playing with his men's lives. Could he recall the last time a woman had been so openly disgusted with him, in his home, while in his element? He tightened his lips in thought, scratching his chin. Had it ever even happened before actually? A female contending with him? The thought made him stir with the challenge and then all too quickly deflate with pathetic realization. Eva may well have been the first person in an age to give him one-hundred percent, undiluted honesty. Were the people in his life ever honest with him at all anymore? Did anyone ever truly say what they thought to him, rather than what he wanted to hear? He exhaled loudly. But that was how he liked it, right? Hearing the things he wanted to hear; getting the results he demanded to get. Yet this girl's ballsy bluntness was somehow refreshing, like new air in a stuffy room. Did she actually think he was a, what was the word she used?...a psychopath? He licked his lips with recall, as the anger that had flashed through him irrationally at the word, resurfaced. Was he a psychopath? He swore to himself loudly, shaking his head and standing up. No, of course he wasn't a maniac...complex maybe, demanding for sure, but he was very aware and in control of who he was. He walked to the balcony doors and let the curtains brush in the breeze against his tensed body. He breathed in the night air and quickly shook off the feelings that this girl had already embedded in him. She had been in his life for mere minutes and he was already questioning himself. People did not get to him. Simple. And neither would this random, if not highly intriguing, woman. But why did her opinion bother him quite so much then? He shook his head, unable to stop the smile from returning. She was under his skin, there was no doubt about it and no point denying it. He had forgotten how it felt to be affect by someone, and he couldn't quite decide if it was a feeling he had missed, or one he would rather do without for the rest of his life. He walked back to his desk and picked up the phone, dialing a number. It was time to get back to business and rid himself of these childish, pointless emotions.

'Yes,' he began on cue to the answer of the phone, 'tell him it's Mr

59

Rodriguez.'

'Oh, hello, Mr Rodriguez. Hope you are well this evening?' the polite and slightly flirty female voice began, waiting silently and expectantly for a reply. He ignored the engaging tone.

'Fine. Thank you.' He offered flatly. And conclusively. After a split second, of obvious disappointment, the females voice returned to polite and efficient, professionally asking him to hold. He had spoken to this assistant a few times now, each and every time she would acknowledge him with a perky invite to converse. Each and every time he would shut her down, despite the fact that she sounded attractive. At the thought of attractive women, Eva came back into mind. He groaned at himself, apparently unable to shift her from his thoughts. Her bare midriff from earlier shot to his foremind. She looked so soft, so smooth. He bit his lower lip with guilty intrigue. She was gorgeous, no real question about it. But was she more attractive than this random assistant on the phone, or any of the model, elitist women he had been with before? Maybe. Maybe not. She wasn't into make-up or hair styles or designer clothes, that was for certain, but she was what his mother would have called a 'natural beauty' and he didn't disagree. There was definitely something in her, something different, and it felt like gravity, disconcertingly pulling him towards her against his better judgment. She had been so obviously uncomfortable at him watching her being examined earlier, watching her lift her up her top and reveal her bare skin. Had he been a better man he may have looked away. But he wasn't a better man and he never made any claim to be. Her flushed cheeks and squared jaw had been the only things to betray her confidence and show how desperate she had been to cover up. Maybe it was that which he found so alluring? The fact that she, so obviously, had no idea how beautiful she really was.

'Mr Rodriguez, he will be with you in just a minute. Would you like to be placed on hold...or stay on the line with me...?' He could almost hear her held, hopeful breath. He rolled his eyes.

'Put me on hold,' he demanded. Yes, it was blunt and unapologetic, but he had no interest in her and the sooner she got that message, the better.

'Oh! Aw Ok,' she stammered, apparently surprised by his disregard. He heard her swallow and then quickly place him back on hold as requested. He shook his head, making a mental note to next time send a direct email rather than call and have to deal with this needy, childish, social climbing girl. Her reaction though did serve one good purpose as his thoughts, again, guiltily, found their way back to Eva Mack. "You're bluffing" she had said to him when he had told her about the tracker. She has said it with such questioning confidence that he had found it hard not to laugh. His lips twitched again at the thought of her *bruised and defiant hand going to her slender neck. Of course it was a bluff, but the threat to perhaps one day follow through was there, if needed. Did the idea of knowing where this woman was all the time increase his heartbeat? Yes. But for what reason he still wasn't quite sure.*

'Cane?' A man's voice began from the telephone, distracting him from his thoughts. The tone was direct and disciplined and took him back to the world he knew and was sure of. Business and politics.

CHAPTER ELEVEN
I shook my head, typical.

Dr Miele attended to my face and dressed my hands. He checked my ribs and gave me handfuls of colourful drugs. I sat now in a white dressing gown having just got out of the bath. My skin was destroyed, my bones were in agony, and my muscles ached. I looked out the window of the five-star quality hotel room I was in and breathed, all the day's events rushing through my mind. Dr Miele had given me sleeping tablets purposely to try and stop the nightmares he had informed me would certainly come. I hadn't disagreed and had taken the two pink capsules along with everything else he had given me, no questions asked. I prayed they would kick in soon, I didn't want to be awake any longer, I didn't want to have to relive everything from today, thinking again and again of how I could have changed things. The tears poured from my eyes, soaking into the sleeve of the white expensive robe. I let myself cry as my heart caught up with me. The guard I had put up all day came crashing down with an almighty bang and I sobbed with the memories and fears, reliving each petrifying moment from the day, making my hands shake uncontrollably. My heart was breaking under the weight of my new burdens. Every sob sent pain through my chest and doubled my agony. How had this all happened? What had I done? I had never felt so alone, so I prayed. I prayed for forgiveness, I prayed for sleep to come and take me. But after what felt like an eternity of anguish had passed, rest did not come. I was apparently to pay for my rash actions first before I was allowed sleep. Pain, fear, worry, guilt, all of it came out. Agonisingly. Finally alone, I was made to face what I had done today and let the startling consequences begin to torture me. This wasn't just *my* punishment. My actions would punish everyone who had ever loved me too, something Mr Rodriguez would be sure to see done. I had quite literally made a deal with the devil, a man with no conscience. I exhaled with a whimper, feeling like I literally had nothing left in me to give. I was empty and void. *God, I'm so sorry, what have I done? Forgive me.*
I awoke on the bed, under the covers, still in the bath robe. For a few split seconds I forgot where I was and what had happened. In the morning blur, I was back home in my flat and my life was still together. But as I stirred, and the room came into focus, everything came rushing back. I closed my eyes again, praying it was all a bad dream, that it would all be gone when I reopened. But it didn't go, not even close. The room only became clearer and clearer the more I awoke. I rubbed my eyes carefully, not wanting to disturb any of the dressings on my hands. I was a fast healer, thankfully,

and that was at least a comforting thought. A couple days and these cuts would no longer hurt. A week or so, and I would be healing nicely. The scars the old doctor said I would be left with, they were not something to celebrate though. I shook my head at myself, there was no point in self-pity now, it would do me no favours, offer me no help. I had cried enough tears last night to last the year and as I looked out the window, I saw blue sky. It was a new day. A walk, some air, some time alone out in the open alone, that was what I needed. I pulled off the covers trying to remember when I had gone to bed last night. My last memories were of me on the sofa, crying. The drugs Dr Miele had given me must have been good if I had no recollections of dragging myself across the room and into bed nor of the time that I did so. I thanked the kind old man in my heart.

The shower was both welcoming and sore as the heat disrupted my cuts and the hot water stung my grazed skin. But fresh hair and clean teeth did wonders for everyone, even me. I opened the cupboard doors to find a few items of clothing hanging, all in my size. Rodriguez was good, I'd give him that. I grabbed a pair of jeans and a simple plain top, reaching for a set of underwear which all still had the expensive shop tags on. There was a warm hoodie on a hanger which I quickly pulled on and headed out. I was expecting to meet a guard or someone outside, but all I found was an envelope stuck to the door. I carefully took the letter down, opening it. Inside was a small packet of drugs and a note from Dr Miele.

Miss Mack

I hope that a good night's sleep finds you feeling better this morning. You need to take these as soon as possible, they will help keep the pain at bay. I will deliver some more sleeping tablets tonight when I come to check on you and your bandages. May I recommend that you eat breakfast to help soak up the medicines in your body. Food will stop you from feeling sick. The breakfast room is on the main floor level, third corridor to the back, seventh room to your left.

Regards,

Dr Miele

I think I was in love with the man. He was a saint. My stomach began to rumble at the thought of food. The last time I had eaten had been yesterday afternoon while at lunch with Tammy. The sudden thought of Tammy made my eyes water. What I wouldn't give now to have her here to confide in. Would I ever see her again? Would I ever see *anyone* again? I slapped myself mentally before I spiraled into self-pity; *food and a walk, Eva, pull yourself together.* I moved on alone, wondering around the house unaccompanied. It was an odd sensation being allowed to look in rooms and examine all the beautiful furniture. I was in the home of Cane Rodriguez...CANE RODRIGUEZ! I kept reminding myself of the fact as

I looked around his stuff and idled through his kingdom. In a million years, I would have never placed myself here. Yet here I was, slowly pottering and quickly beginning to realise the sheer size of his house. So many doors led to other staircases and other hallways. The place was a maze and I was beginning to think I would never find the breakfast room, let alone my bedroom again. Thankfully, I turned a corner and happened upon the top of the beautiful staircase we had climbed yesterday. I smiled at my small success. I had located the first floor. I had my hands unbound this time and as I quietly walked down the steps, I ran my fingers over the polished and smooth old oak. It was cool to my touch and I lost my thoughts in its simple beauty. It was not until I reached the last few steps that I realised I was being watched. I jumped slightly, looking up from the banister to see Rodriguez, standing at the base of the steps, his dark coat on. He was watching me intently, six black clothed men standing around him. He had a briefcase in one hand and a file in the other. I froze. Both from surprise and embarrassment. I must have looked like a complete idiot awe-ing away at a wooden banister like something out of a period drama. I exhaled slowly, praying my cheeks weren't turning red.

'Enjoying the house, are you?' Rodriguez asked, with a small smile creeping onto his lips. I bit my bottom lip, only managing to reply with a tiny nod. He pointed behind me. 'That staircase is an original. It was built with the original house itself and is one of the few remaining natural pieces. Its hundreds of years old.' I glanced at it again, unable to keep my eyes away. Rodriguez went to leave, his men walking towards the doors with him, but he held back for a second and looked at me. 'It's my favourite part of the house, too,' he added quietly, giving me a small conclusive nod and walking out the front door. One of his black shirts closed the heavy frame shut behind them and it slammed, plunging me in silence. I exhaled gently, not wanting to upset my ribs. *A house this size and I still have to bump into him.* I shook my head. *Typical.* With one last look at the staircase, I left it behind in search of the alleged breakfast room, my stomach now louder than my echoing footsteps. A few minutes and maybe thirteen wrong door openings later, I found it, in all its splendour. It was a massive room, long and lined with huge windows. The now almost afternoon sun melted through the colours on the panes and onto the table surfaces that ran down the centre of the room. A chandelier hung from the roof, its hundreds of tiny crystal diamonds sparkling in the beams of sun. Reflections glistened across the old paintings that hung on the wall and they danced over the captured scenes from the past. In the centre of the room at the far end, sat a table full of food. It reminded me a little bit of the main hall in *Harry Potter*, long dining benches and the head table at the top. There were a few people in the room eating, all staff of some kind. A couple looked like maids, a few black shirts, gardeners and two others, maybe chefs? How big exactly was

Rodriguez's work force? Almost completely synchronized, they all turned to me, conversation ceasing. It reminded me of one of those teen movies where the school geek enters the cool kids party and silence settled before the onset of cruel and demeaning remarks. Surely *everyone* could not have known who I was yet, not in a place this big, I'd only been here for a night. But as people began leaning in to each other to whisper, or turning their heads to give me an assessing look, it was obvious that everyone *did* in fact know who I was. My face flushed again, despite my will. I could literally feel the pressure of their gazes weighing down on me like hands forcing me lower. Things weren't bad enough already that I now had to suffer the pain of feeling like a social leper? Thankfully, the room was massive and there were lots of spare seats, so I kept my head down and went straight to the food table, despite it feeling like the green mile to get there. Upon reaching the table, I found a display that greatly resembled a buffet at The Savoy. There were all manners of fruit and cereal, cooked and uncooked breakfast foods, drinks, snacks…the options were endless. I tried to look as confident as possible, taking an apple, a bottle of water and three croissants. I knew I was still being watched as I could feel eyes burning into my back. What had people been told about me? Did they know the circumstances of why I was here? I don't know what I had expected to be honest, I didn't belong here, I was an intruder in their secret, secure world. I kept my head low and quickly headed back for the doors, deciding to just eat my food in the gardens, away from prying eyes. Heads followed as I walked towards the entrance again, murmurs of comments whispering as I passed by. As soon as the door shut behind me, I let out a sigh of relief and listened as the volume of conversation increased again. I stood composing myself quickly. I hated this place. I had been here less than twenty-four hours and if I wasn't scared for my life, I was being treated like an outcast. Maybe it would have been better if I'd been locked away in a room with no-one but myself to point at me and judge…or there was still the option of being shot. The front doors pushed open to a blue-skied day and a brisk fresh wind. I inhaled as deeply as I could, letting the crisp air flow into my lungs and replace all the old, bad stuff. I knew that if I was going to survive in this place that I had to stay positive. I had to somehow keep my hopes up until I made a plan, until I figured things out. Thankfully the gardens were beyond breathtaking, and I quickly noticed that, unsurprisingly, everything was meticulously perfect yet blossoming naturally. I saw a few gardeners as I crossed the main lawns into the flower area. One of them had distinctive messy blonde hair which blew in the breeze and caught my eye. His blue gaze locked onto mine for a few seconds and I could have sworn I saw a small acknowledging smile, that was before another worker ushered him along in reprimand. The trimmed and kept wilderness was an empty haven for me, a sanctuary from prying eyes and judging heads. I walked slowly through the roses and hedges, running my hands along the bushes. I loved nature, things as God made them. Edward had always hated my habit of running my hands over things: walls, fences, trees, whatever was beside me as I walked. It was a childish thing to do and *'not to mention unhygienic'* he would say looking at my fingers with disapproving disgust. I paused my hand over the end of a small branch, the thought of Edward's rebukes so vivid I almost expected him to appear beside me with one eyebrow raised reproachfully. I waited with baited breath, as if he would come, but he did not, nor would he any time soon. I knew that, yet I found myself squeezing the small leaves between my fingers, forcing back my tears. *Hold it together, Eva.* I continued to wander around, investigating the smallest and most insignificant things, anything to take my mind off thinking. I marveled at a water fountain for over twenty minutes, examined the stone sculptures in the far gardens for over two hours, lost myself, quite literally, for what felt like days in the forest on the north side of the house. I kept expecting to finally reach the perimeter gate I had crossed through yesterday, but this place was huge and apparently extended beyond my walking capacities. In the late afternoon I rounded a large hedge and found myself back at the gardens of the main house. I stopped abruptly, totally taken back by my bearings. I was much closer to the house than I had thought, but the sun was falling through the sky and it seemed that another never-ending day was nearing its close. I decided that wandering off again in the dark wasn't the smartest thing to do and since I'd already filled my 'non-smart decisions for the century' quota yesterday, I made my way to the serene pond that lay to the side of the house. There was a small hill and bank that was perfect to sit, so I gently placed myself down and gazed out to the water. The sunset reflected colourfully off the surface and fish appeared every now and then to nibble on the insects, creating hypnotic ripples. I settled into the grass with my legs crossed in front of me, sitting straight backed. After watching the sun turn to red and start to touch the tips of the trees, I lay back and closed my eyes letting the last few rays of daylight heat my skin. I could hear everything around me: the wind, the trees, the quiet noise of voices from behind somewhere in the distance. I could hear the water move, the gentle hum of focusing security cameras, the slowing beat of my heart. I focused on a calling bird, its voice cutting through all the other sounds. It was probably calling out for home. *Calling for home,* I thought to myself...*I wish I could do that.*

I woke to the dark, my eyes focusing on stars and clouds. I lifted my head slightly to see the lights from the house reflecting off the pond. I'd fallen asleep. What time was it? I pulled myself up, yelping at the pain in my ribs. Instantly, cold air came rushing in on me as a blanket fell from my shoulders to my lap. I looked at it curiously. Someone had put a blanket on me? A man cleared his throat behind me and I jumped, immediately crying out loud again. I turned carefully to see a black shirt stood on the hill top, looking down at me.

'I am to escort you to your room,' he said blankly, nodding his head in the direction of the house behind him. I held my ribs, now throbbing. They had been so good all day, but the drugs Dr Miele had given me must have worn off long ago by now. I sighed and gently got to my feet, holding the mysterious blanket under my arm and climbing the hill to where my new escort stood. A couple paces away, I caught a look at his face. He was new to me, I hadn't seen him before. He was a younger guy, maybe my age, give or take, and was far from as stern looking as the others. This employee looked more…blank? Distracted by my thoughts, I stumbled at the top of the bank and put my hand out to catch myself. The black shirt reacted in the same manner, instinctively extending his hand to try and catch me. But just as quickly as he'd responded, he retracted his hand, immediately looking around us. What exactly were their instruction about me?

'I doubt you'll be shot for *almost* helping me,' I uttered sarcastically, getting up, unaided, to my feet. I stood slowly at the top of the hill and sighed with impatience at the young guys uncertain face. *Urgh, honestly*. I needed food, strong drugs and then a bed. And soon. This idiot could happily escort me, untouched, to my room. I was done for the day.

CHAPTER TWELVE
Did I want to die?

I woke the next morning, blissful, still caught in the idea that everything had just been a dream. All too quickly and painfully that illusion vanished, as I glanced at the array of pain killers sitting beside my he bed. I felt the inevitable tears prickle my eyes as the past two days flooded in again and my surroundings took form. I was not in my own bedroom. I was not in my own flat. It was not a dream. Things were not all right. Would I do this same heartbreaking routine every morning? I wiped a tear from my cheek and thought hopelessly of home, of the glass still sitting on my living room table holding the purple remnants of my last carton of grape juice. Ed had put it there the night we had argued, the night I had thought my biggest problem was my relationship. I wiped another tear away, registering the growing pain inside. Did I miss Edward, or did I just wish that the comfort he gave was here with me? Either way, his presence would be appreciated; his arms to hold me and his body to hold onto. I wondered what was going on at home. Did anyone know where I was, if I was alive? Had Rodriguez flashed his ace in Mr Bain's face yet? What would Ed be thinking? He would be so worried and so mad. He would be raging away to himself like he always did when something infuriated him, and he'd be pacing. He paced when he was mad, growling and mumbling to himself, throwing keywords out loudly. He'd no doubt be swearing and promising all the revenge under the sun at Rodriguez. Then dad would step in with his governing and calming way and rationalise everything through procedure. That's how it always played out. Dad always thought good policies and plans could fix anything. But actually, Dad wouldn't be there to help this time, would he? He would still be in the hospital, still hooked up to monitors and machines. Had his bleeding stayed controlled? What if he had taken a turn for the worse? I screwed my eyes up as my head ran away with horrid thoughts. No, no, I couldn't think this way. Maybe he was already home, maybe already in his own bed, maybe being fed chicken soup by mum. These were the thoughts I needed to cling to, to let my mind picture. But despite willing it, my mind couldn't settle on the idea of happy news, not when reality was so bleak just now. It knew that Dad could easily have suffered complications in his state, or his condition could have quickly worsened with no warning. He had been so fragile when I had to leave. The tears began stream and panic set in as I realised that I didn't even know if he was alive. He had been, the doctors had *told* me so, but complications happened with the body all the time, right? If something had gone wrong with dad, they wouldn't even be able to find me to tell me. My mum would be at home all alone dealing with it. I closed my eyes and could still picture dad's broken and lifeless body, being kicked across the ground. I could still feel the terror that raced through me at that second. The tears began to flow, the room began to spin, and sickness rose in my throat. I was on the brink of sinking into the depths of sobbing fear, I could feel it trying to pull me under. Suddenly a loud knock from the door echoed through the silence and made me jump so hard I almost fully left the bed. My tears of despair instantly switched to those of pain as I cried out loud, my hand flying to hold my ribs. To this the door opened and, thankfully, Dr Miele's head appeared in the room. Once he saw my recognition, he quickly entered and rushed to my side, his magic leather bag in hand.

'My dear girl, there, there,' he whispered soothingly, placing a doctoring hand on my very clammy and hot forehead. He wiped tears from my cheeks and graciously did not mention them again. 'I did not mean to startle you, I came to check up, but fear I may have caused more damage.' He spoke quickly and calmly, with his Spanish accent tinting each word. He gently took my protective hand away from my side and lifted my top. 'Let me see, querido.' He called me *dear* just as a grandparent would, touching my skin gently. Hearing affection, even from an affiliate of the enemy, was somehow soothing. 'Have you been taking the pain killers and other pills I have been leaving for you?' I glanced at the small pile sat by the bed and nodded.

'Yes, I have.'

'Buena chica,' he muttered to himself, as he fixed my bandages and passed me over my next round of drugs. He moved his attention to my cuts and bruises, which stung, but didn't make me cry uncontrollably. 'You are healing quickly, Miss Mack,' he offered, while examining some unsightly scabs. The black and blues were already turning into yellowy-greens and I knew that within days, all my bruises would be gone and no trace of the scariest moment in my life would be found.

'Thanks,' I replied as chirpily as I could, giving the kind old man a genuine smile. He observed me for a second, as I rounded my fists and tested my healing knuckles, then he slowly sat down on the bed.

'You are beautiful young woman,' he began, somewhat to my surprise. I laughed, despite the pain.

'Especially just now,' I joked, waving my hand over my messed-up face. He chuckled kindly, appreciating my light heartedness.

'You are strong, and you are…valiente, Miss Mack.' He finished putting a large plaster on my knuckles and I looked up to him in doubt. Despite his words, I didn't feel very *brave* right now. 'You must hold onto these. I know you have bad few days and I fear you will shed many tears before it is over, but you must stay strong.' He looked me square in the eyes; his steady and sure, mine wavering and tear stained. He patted my hand gently then shook off the intensity of the moment. 'And you know,' he began, much louder and happier, 'Mr Rodriguez, he is a fair man, no? He is not so much of the…animales, he is made out to be.' I looked at the kind doctor with 'really?' eyes and he smiled, standing up and beginning to pack his bag. 'He is hard because leader must be hard, but he is good man, at heart, and he will be as fair to you as he will be able.' I didn't reply nor change my unbelieving expression. Dr Miele just offered a wider grin and walked towards the door, ignoring my obvious skepticism. He paused with his hand on the handle, looking back my way. 'My papa always say to me, "El verdadero corazón de un hombre es visto cuando todo lo importante para él está en riesgo."' He translated it into English for me. 'A man's true heart is seen when everything important to him is at stake.' I rolled my eyes with clear cynicism, far from convinced.

'The man has to have a heart to start with,' I replied, sounding very jaded. Dr Miele laughed lightly, even though it was obvious he disagreed.

'Adiós,' he nodded, leaving my room and closing the heavy door behind him. I lay there for a second contemplating his words and trying to relax. I quickly realised that when I woke up in the mornings and lay in bed, that was when I let myself think, and that was when I lost control of my thoughts and emotions. What if it hadn't been Dr Miele that had come in this morning, but a black shirt, or worse, Rodriguez? And I would have been lying here, shaking and crying. No, this couldn't happen again. From now on, when I woke, I had to get up. There could be no self-pity, no lapse in my defense. I knew how to hide things from people, I was sure that doing it from someone I hated, would be easy. If I was going to be stuck here, in this world, in this house, then I would do something productive. Something distracting. I got out of bed carefully and got into the shower. I was on day three. I decided it was time for an update on my dad. I needed to know if he was ok, despite the uncertainty making me nauseous. I also wanted an update on me and my prison sentence. I was surely entitled to know what my fate was, even if I could do nothing to alter it. As I stood in front of the limited wardrobe, I decided I wanted some clothes too, more than the three outfits that hung before me. I put on a pair of yoga pants and a vest thinking maybe I would go to the gym. Given, I wouldn't be able to do much, but the focus and the time involved would be a good distraction. Then, after the gym, I'd go see Rodriguez and demand answers. Waiting around was killing me. Plus, going to see him when I looked awful was probably a good idea...the way that man stared at me gave me the shivers.

After half an hour of roaming I found the gym and it was far from a small room. It was larger than the gym back home I held paid membership for, and that establishment was a second home to more than a few hundred people. I was quickly discovering that Rodriguez did nothing small. A black shirt employee had let me in from his guard at the door and I guessed that if Rodriguez had been here, no one else would have been allowed entry. I felt slightly strange as the door closed and I found myself reflecting off floor to roof sized mirrors that covered the entire room. I glanced at my messy face and then quickly looked away again, happier not knowing what I currently looked like. There were towels and a fully stocked fridge just at the entrance and a stereo system with what looked like thousands of MP3 songs stored on it. There was every type of athletic equipment available and every form of exercise on offer. I swallowed. How much money did this man have? I knew Edward was in-line for all of his dad's money, all of Brice Bain's empire and wealth, but maybe I'd underestimated just how *much* money that was. I exhaled loudly at the thought, a slight smile touching my lips. Being here was like living in another world. Yes, Ed had fancy stuff and expensive taste and an extravagant lifestyle, but this was a whole other level. My smile vanished quickly though as I recalled with pity how Rodriguez's house was inherited; from his dead parents. Not the best way to receive something so spectacular and I wouldn't wish being orphaned on anyone, not even my worst enemy. I exhaled away the oddly empathetic feelings towards him, and walked over to the stereo to look through it. There was a playlist still loaded up, probably from the last person in the gym. My hand paused as I saw Rodriguez's name slowly feed across the LED screen. He had been the last person in here? Shivers tickled my neck. How long had I missed him by? I knew I planned to speak to the man later, but the idea of seeing him made me feel strange; unprepared and vulnerable. My finger was still paused over the play button and curiosity got the better of me. I hit the green triangle and track one began to play. It was slow-ish Latino music, actually quite perfect for a warm-up. I walked into the centre of the room onto the blue mats and stood in front of the mirrors. I carefully began to stretch, looking at myself in reflection. I had lost weight, I could see it instantly. I guessed three days of hardly any food and insane amounts of stress would do that to anyone. My jawline was more defined, and my collarbones stuck out more predominately than before. Although my face was still colourful and slightly swollen, it actually looked worse now than it felt. My legs and arms had a lot of scrapes and bruises, but unless I bashed them, they didn't bother me too much. I stretched my calf muscles and registered that, considering it all, my broken ribs were the only thing causing me actual pain and at least Rodriguez was allowing me to deal with that through medicine. The emotional pain on the other hand, well that was the killer that kept getting the better of me. The next song began, and it was an upbeat remix of a classical piece. I couldn't decide if it was Mozart or Baroque, but it was easy to match in tempo and strangely catchy. The next six songs were all just as random; upbeat remixes of Latino music, classical, country, opera, each making me smile with surprise. Rodriguez was an eclectic man, I'd give him that, if nothing else. About an hour later and I was done. I hadn't really been able to do much at all to be honest, I did have broken ribs after all, but I had wondered around a bit, stupidly attempted a few things, and had killed some time. Now, I was sweaty, red and most importantly, hungry. As I turned off the stereo, I debated showering and eating before going to see Rodriguez, but I knew that I was just stalling. The idea of voluntarily going to see him was like choosing to jump into an artic plunge pool: chilling and reckless. I dropped a towel into the basket on top of the only other used one from today, probably Rodriguez's, and opened the door. The black shirt was still there, motionless as a statue, only his eyes registering me. I cleared my throat, the universal sign of wishing to engage in communication.

'Could you point me to the direction of Mr Rodriguez's office, please?' I asked as confidently as possible. The man looked at me, reactionless. 'Or at least tell me where I'd find him. I need to speak to him.' Still blank. I tried again, with a frustrated sigh. 'He did say to just find him when I needed him and that some guy called Scott would help me, but I don't know where he is either.' This seemed to work and the man lifted his radio and asked for a 'four-one-one on Mr Rodriguez'. The reply came, informing him that he was in his office all morning with appointments. The man put his radio back to his belt.

'Left down the hall, one floor up, third right, third right.' His eyes assessed me one more time then moved back to the hallway as if I was transparent and no longer standing there. I repeated his directions in my head.

'Thank you,' I muttered quietly, not sure if manners were really required when someone was pretending you weren't even there. I walked the labyrinth until I found the stairs and then paused, my foot on the bottom step. Maybe this was the reason all of Rodriguez's men were so fit, there were stairs everywhere. I finally reached the top, three breaks later, and was met by a large mirror mounted to the facing wall. I sighed as I looked at myself, uncontrollably panting. My hair had fly-aways everywhere, my face was flushed, and my vest was damp from exertion. I looked like I'd run ten miles in peak of a summer's day. I tilted my jaw. Just as well I couldn't care less what Rodriguez thought of me then. I head off towards the first set of third rights and quickly realised that my hands had begun straightening some of my flyaway hairs subconsciously. Traitors. Reaching Rodriguez's office was easy to tell, as two black shirts stood either side of the door, erect and alert like sentinels. They both clocked me at the same time, and I swallowed through my dry throat, approaching them with purpose.

'Is Mr Rodriguez in?' I asked, nodding towards the office behind them. I had butterflies, damn butterflies erupting everywhere in my stomach and I could feel them starting to make their tingling way to the rest of my body. This was a bad idea. My body was already betraying me, and Rodriguez wasn't even in sight. I lost my nerve and instantly began to regret coming here. *Say he's busy, say he's busy, say he's busy...*

'He's expecting you,' one of them replied, mechanically. *Damn it!* The bigger of the two black shirts pressed the buzzer and awaited acceptance. The light went green and the black shirt swiped a card and opened the door. I breathed as deeply as I could, knowing I couldn't back out now, and took a step forward.

'Thanks,' I muttered to the man, as I passed by him. He nodded, then closed the door. Had it only been two days ago that I'd first walked into this room? Two days ago since my whole word fell upside down? It felt like longer. Much longer. The office was still the same as that first visit, this time with the mid-morning sun pouring through the open balcony windows. The satin curtains danced in the breeze like they hadn't a single care in the world. I instantly clocked the oak table looking for the gun, but it was empty of everything except some papers. Rodriguez was at his desk on the phone. He was wearing a navy-blue suit that clung to all the right places. His light blue shirt sat against his chest with the first two buttons opened, exposing just enough of his tanned body for me to notice and then instantly hate myself for it. I exhaled. Holy-hell, the man was hot. There was almost no other suitable words for it; he was *hot*, plain and simple. I didn't use that term often in my life and so the fact that my mind plucked it out of nowhere for descriptive uses now, did nothing but set off internal alarm bells. I needed to get myself together here. I wasn't a teenage girl, for goodness sake. I was a grown-ass woman, being held captive by the man I hated more than anyone in the world. I just needed to get my body to remember those facts now and we'd be fine. As if hearing my thoughts, he lifted his head and acknowledged me. He nodded for me to take a seat and held up a finger to indicate that he'd be just one minute. His eyes lingered on me, no doubt thinking what a state I looked, but then went back to the papers in front of him. He was speaking very firmly, his Spanish accent touching each word. He was obviously talking business due to his heightened tone and so I chose not to sit, awkwardly prying. Instead I went to the fireplace and ran my fingers across the white marble. It was cool to the touch and felt nice against my heated skin.

'Eso no es aceptable.' Rodriguez was saying very firmly into the phone. I glanced over to him to see him throw his pen to the desk and run his hand across his forehead, angrily. Business apparently wasn't good. I knew I shouldn't take so much satisfaction from that. 'That is not acceptable. The order was given three days ago.' He was yelling down the phone now, his eyes narrowed with rage. 'I am not running a day care centre here and I don't want pathetic excuses. That file will be on my desk by this evening or there will be hell to pay. I want results, and I want them today. O vas a ver!' I felt awkward standing listening to him and being reminded of his temper, a temper I knew would be frequently coming my way. Instead I quickly and quietly made my way passed him out onto the balcony. The silk curtains swept over me like clouds as I passed through and opened up to a breathtaking view of the lake I'd fallen asleep at the previous night and then all the land that lay behind it. I looked down at my personal haven with question. Had Rodriguez seen me there yesterday? Seen me sleeping? The idea made me defensively nervous and yet filled me with a guilty thrill. The latter of the two emotions troubled me. I was rapidly becoming highly aware of my subconscious, seemingly uncontrollable draw to Rodriguez. It wasn't healthy, and I knew for sure it was far from safe. I looked up from the lake, out to the surroundings. There were acres of forest and garden as far as the eye could see. The sun was climbing into the blue sky and the morning breeze chilled my damp back. It felt good to inhale the clean crisp air, good to have a moment of solitude.

'Miss Eva,' Rodriguez's voice spoke quietly, now directly behind me. I turned quickly, finding him standing inches away. How long had he been there? I hadn't even heard him approach. 'I did not mean to keep you waiting, I apologise.' I noticed that he now had buttoned up and secured a tie around his handsome neck. He was standing uncomfortably close and I was yet to decide if it was an intimidation thing or if he just didn't believe in personal boundaries. Either way, he always felt too close to me. He wasn't smiling, but the anger I had seen on his face a few minutes ago was gone too. I stepped aside slightly, moving away from him.

'That's okay,' I began quietly, 'I didn't mean to interrupt. I erm…maybe should have made an appointment or something.' *Made an appointment?* What was wrong with me? *Oh my goodness, you're an idiot, shut up, Eva.* His face cracked a smile, not a full smile, but enough to lift the corners of his eyes. He stepped in beside me and placed his hands on the balcony, finally looking away from my flushed face and out into the gardens. I rolled my eyes at myself, chastising my vocal clumsiness.

'You do not need an appointment, Miss Eva,' he replied simply, still hinting a smile. I watched him from the corner of my eye. The sun shining directly on him made him look even more like a Greek God, reflecting off his golden skin. He had small lines around his eyes and some unshaven stubble. His eyelashes turned up at the ends and his lips were a soft pink colour that were slightly dry. As much as I hated him, he was flawlessly stunning. 'I am sorry you had to hear that earlier,' he said, breaking my detailed study of him and the silence that had begun to stretch out. He nodded back towards his office. 'It was unprofessional of me to have had you brought in here while I was still conducting calls.' I kept my side stare of him.

'Business bad?' I asked optimistically, a slight smile unable to stay hidden. He appreciated the humour and shook his head, the corner of his lips turning up also.

'Nothing you need to worry about, luchadora,' he replied, with a small incline of his head. 'I aplogise for my lack of thought.' If I had not been physically trying to control my emotions, I feared my heart could quite easily have run away from me here…towards him. That suggestion of a smile and promise of attention made it very hard to hate him, the way he spoke and addressed me made it difficult to remain steadfast in my anger. Edward was a gentleman in my eyes, thoughtful and caring. But Rodriguez embodies old school manners, old school politeness. It was hard to stay mad at *anyone* who resembled any form of Mr Darcy. Chivalry was such an outright appealing quality and so uncommon these days. It was every girls Kryptonite, even cold hearted me. I distracted myself by focusing on his words. I wasn't sure what 'luchadora' meant, despite having heard him say it before. I made a note to ask Dr Miele, the closest thing I had to a friend, what it meant. The way Rodriguez said it to me, with slightly amused features, made me sure it was something worth asking about. As if knowing my thoughts were about him, he turned abruptly, catching my eye. He assessed me very openly, then smiled again. I had never met anyone who made me feel so exposed. I had also never met anyone who felt that it was socially acceptable to so blatantly stare at people. I swallowed with the pressure of being under the microscope.

'How was the gym?' he asked, still looking my whole body up and down. His finger tapped the railing in an almost playful manner and I shifted my weight uncomfortably, beginning to, for some reason, wish I'd showered and changed. I tucked a strand of loose hair behind my ear self-consciously. He smiled again at this and nodded. 'Don't worry, Miss Eva,' he continued, still watching me, 'you look perfect to me.' I turned to him with raised eyebrows.

'Excuse me?' I choked, incredulously.

'You were feeling self-conscious about how you looked, I was just reassuring you that even after the gym, you still look fine.' He waved his finger at my skin. 'Bruises and all. You needn't be concerned.' The simplicity of his tone and the way he stood, still smiling slightly, made me lose all form of words. My mouth had actually fallen open, I could feel it, but I couldn't close it. Firstly, he was developing an uncanny knack of knowing what I was thinking. It worried me. Secondly, how did I react to a comment like that? Was it a compliment or an insult? And when it came from the mouth of the devil himself, Cane Rodriguez, surely it merited a smack to the face.

'Um cumplido,' he added, looking away out to the gardens again 'It's a compliment, Miss Eva,' he answered. I was glad I was already red in the face, because I couldn't actually have stopped my reaction now, even if the world had depended on it. I blushed. Red and hot. Shamefully transparent. The now deafening silence stretched out between us and as much as I wanted to regain the upper hand with a smart, witty retort, I couldn't think of anything. Literally no words would form in my head. I felt like an idiot. "A compliment" his words replayed inside me. Really? Was he making fun of me? Was this whole thing a way to amuse himself? Why did I even care what he thought? In fact, I reminded myself…I didn't. I didn't care. At. All. He was an animal, a dangerous manipulator with no compassion. It was that simple. I tore my gaze away from him. I didn't like playing games and I reminded myself, I didn't like him. Full stop. He must have sensed the shift in my attitude as he straightened up and put his hands into his trouser pockets.

'How can I help you then, Miss Eva? You came here for a reason I assume?' I latched onto the focus; *yes, I had come here with a purpose, good point.* I turned to look at him again, hoping to project some kind of fake confidence and push past the mixed feelings of hate and awkwardness.

'Yes,' I began, gathering my wits, 'yes, I was hoping you would let me check on my dad's progress.' I raced on quickly not wanting to give him any time to protest. 'I know it's not part of our deal and that it breaks the rules you set, but I was hoping if you or one of your men was in the room or monitoring the call, that maybe I could just …'

'Miss Eva,' he interrupted firmly, holding one of his hands up. I stopped in defeat. In his defence, he had been more than fair so far and I had never negotiated for any such rights. But it didn't mean I wasn't gutted. I wanted desperately to know how my dad was doing, to squash my worst fear and know that he was still alive. I lowered my eyes as he continued. 'I checked on your father's progress this morning and there has been no changes since yesterday. He is mending well in hospital and they hope to release him in a few days. Your mother has been there the entire time and he is set to make a full recovery.' His hands stayed in his pockets and his eyes stayed locked on mine. 'I knew you would be concerned.' He added plainly, as if he needed to explain his actions. A powerful mixture of emotions flooded my body. I barely knew which ones to process first. My dad was okay? He was still okay. Everything had been worth it so far. My mum was with him and he was going to be fine. I held onto the railing to steady myself as relief swept through all of me. It was the warmest and most releasing feeling I had had since this whole thing started. I breathed in deeply, letting the assurance extend to all my body. Dad was all right. As the knowledge began to settle, Rodriguez's face came back into focus. He was watching me with an analytical stare, almost as if trying to understand something. I held his gaze consciously whilst both gratitude and relief filled my insides. He had called the hospital each day to check up on my father. For me? Cane Rodrigiez had done that. For me. He was utterly perplexing and confusing in every single possible way. Nothing inside of me understood him or anything he did. I never knew that I could feel such disdain and hate towards a single person, yet at the same time, think he was one of the most gentlemanly, thoughtful souls I had ever come across. The latter being more prominent, especially at this moment. But he could not be both people, I knew that. No one could be *both* people. One side had to be real and the other an act. I just didn't know which was which yet. Everything I'd read and ever known about Rodriguez told me that *this*, this nice side, was the act. He was actually a lying, ambitious cheat, who cared for no one but himself and his business. But the man who stood in front of me and who was showing nothing but compassion and thought, he was the Rodriguez that seemed real, that seemed genuine. It was beyond confusing and I was becoming less and less sure how to act around him.

'Thank you,' I finally said, a little flustered with sincerity. For a split second I went to touch his arm or hug him, as I would to anyone who had just done something nice for me. But my head quickly made the correction, sobering me with reason. This wasn't a friend or a long-term acquaintance. He was Cane Rodriguez. I retracted my hand quickly, but not before he had seen it. He watched me inquisitively for a few moments. I could see the thoughts going on behind his gorgeous eyes and could feel the depth his gaze was reaching for. The relieved and grateful side of me lingered, but everything else in me yearned to look away. To break whatever trick he was playing.

'De nada. *You're welcome.* I knew you would be worried,' he finally replied, quietly, whilst his eyes danced unapologetically across my face and exposed neck. Slowly he lifted his hand, bridging the space between us, and moved a strand of my hair from my cheek. My body began to traitorously lean towards him, I could feel it moving without permission. His fingers touched my skin the way they had done the first time I had come face-to-face with him. It sent my arm hairs to standing and quickened my breath, a zing shooting through me to every part of my body. I thought of him leaning in to kiss me and suddenly every neck hair stood on end and alarm bells began to sound. What the hell was I doing? They were right. I was engaged. Forgetting even that; I detested this man, he almost killed my dad. My relief over my father was obviously clouding my judgment. I snapped backwards, pulling away, suddenly flushing with guilt and shame. Rodriguez did not move though, he just watched, his emotions as tight as a vault.

'I should go.' I said abruptly, making for the inside office again.
'Not so fast, Miss Eva,' he said loudly, before I ran through the silk curtains to safety. I stopped and turned back to him, my yoga pants holding tight to my shaking legs. 'I had planned to speak to you today anyway.' His hands

went into his pockets again and his eyes tightened up. 'Your presence will be required in the next few hours.'

'For what?' I asked, still standing a few paces away.

'It seems, despite being told so, your fiancée wants proof of life. He wants to know that you are with me, alive and unharmed.' He sneered sarcastically, his gentle face changing in an instant. 'Very gallant. And I guess before we move ahead, *dear Eddie* should start the way he means to continue, by not trusting me when I say you're safe.' He shrugged. 'I may have been a little loose with the terms 'safe and alive', but it's good for the game if he worries about you.' It was odd how quickly my feelings could change, almost as quickly as his mood. I looked at him with disgust. Very real disgust. This was the other man, the other Rodriguez, the one Brice Bain's files described perfectly.

'Game?' I repeated with disgust. 'This is a game to you?' Guilt for Edward's worry and pain was flooding into me. Rodriguez was right, Edward would be desperately concerned about me. I had brought all this on him and he had only ever wanted to look out for me. Now I was standing on a balcony, making googley-eyes with his arch nemesis? *My* arch nemesis. I made myself sick! I was selfish and thoughtless and totally self-absorbed. 'Have you ever even cared enough about anyone in this world to know what *concern* feels like?' I was suddenly mad at him. Really mad and fueled quite nicely by my guilt. Not a great combination to have around an already volatile, dangerous man. 'Have you ever cared for *anyone* but yourself?' I stared at him with hard disgust. He did not react as boldly as I did, but I had apparently touched a nerve and his cool and collected hands left his pockets, whilst his clear eyes narrowed in response. Still, I stupidly pushed on. 'You play games with people because no one will ever love you enough to care if *you're* safe.' I pointed directly at him. 'You're pathetic.' To this he suddenly advanced on me, grabbing my arm and pulling me back into his office. He was mad.

'¡no me busques las cosquillas!' he ranted firmly, '...*do not push your luck*! I swear to you. My patience only goes so far, and you seem all too happy to try me.' He pushed me passed his desk. 'You speak with such dignity considering you are the reason the Bain family are in this situation anyway.' I pulled my arm free, defiantly, and spun to face him. I refused to be dragged like a little child across his office.

'Me?' I yelled back, angrily, spinning around to face him. 'Am I the one who tried to murder my father for proposing a peaceful truce? Am I the one who uses fear and pain to get everything I want? Am I the one who won't let go of a petty family feud?' To this he let out a cold, evil laugh.

'Oh, you rant and preach about things you don't even understand. You are a little princess, fed off Edward's money and status, thinking you are entitled to more than you own. Don't you tell me who I am or what I am responsible for doing.' His fists were clenched now. 'No sabes nada,' he spat venomously. *You know nothing.* My blood boiled.

'I know more than enough to judge you.' I yelled back, refusing to back down.' I know what you do, I know what your company does.' I was so mad I could feel my palms sweating with anger and my temperature rising. I pointed at him, advancing, fueled by rage-filled courage. 'You ruined my life.' I screamed. 'You ruined my childhood. You've ruined my illusion of good and justice. You are the reason I go to so many funerals. You are the reason I don't trust people to ever do the right thing.'

'ENOUGH!' he screamed loudly, slamming his hands down on the desk with such force it sounded like it had broken. The main office door burst open and the two black shirts from outside ran in with guns armed and very quickly aimed at me. It was enough to break the tension, to break the anger…to knock some scary sense back into me. What was wrong with me? Did I want to die? I looked up at Rodriguez who was staring straight back at me, his jaw tensed and his chest rising and falling. He waved his hand dismissively at the two black shirts, who quickly backed out of the room and closed the door again. We stood in silence for the next few moments, both breathing, both calming. After what felt like forever, he crossed the room to my side and stopped centimeters from my face, his body touching mine. I could feel his heat and his breath against me but I daren't move from my defiant stand. When he spoke this time, his voice was quiet and empty.

'Miss Eva, I am sorry you feel that I am responsible for all those things. I am sorry that your hate for me is so…arraigado…' he paused for the translation through his deep breathing, '…deep-routed.' He was talking slowly, but I could feel his heart beating quickly against my arm. I understood all of a sudden why people said it was a fine line between love and hate. I hated him, it was true, but when he stood this close to me, I wanted him to stay close, I liked the feeling it stirred inside me. 'You do not know me though,' he continued, pausing and inhaling deeply as if he wanted to say more, but couldn't. I dropped my head slightly, feeling somewhat reined in and defeated. 'You will do as you're told, Miss Eva.' He stated plainly. 'Please do not make me ask you again. You will be collected from your room later.' And with that he crossed the office, opened the door and nodded for one of the men to escort me. I let myself be pushed by my back towards the exit and dared not look at Rodriguez as I left.

The black shirt allowed me to stop by the canteen on the way back, probably just to silence my grumbling stomach. I was thankful though when he put me in my room, closed the door and left. I wanted to be alone, to think, to reflect, to panic. I took a bite of the bread roll and lay down on the bed. That had been a slightly more heated conversation than I had planned for. I thought over Rodriguez's words. The fact that he called me a 'princess' drove me crazy, I hated people thinking I was some kind of social climber or money grabber. But when Rodriguez thought it, for some reason, it stung more. I thought of the things I had said to him, or shouted at him, as it was. Now that I was alone, my hands began to shake. I had seen the faces of the two men who burst into the room. I didn't think many people lived long enough to raise their voice at Rodriguez, let alone say some of the things I did. If I wasn't such an asset, I had a very real feeling that one of those bullets may have been embedded in my head. I shook my hands to try and stop them trembling, my fear catching up with me. Adrenaline and anger were a strange thing, strong enough to overpower sanity and sense, at least for a little while. I took another bite of my roll hoping it would ease my queasy stomach. I chased it quickly with some of Dr Miele's wonder drugs. If ever I needed their enforced effects, it was right now.

CHAPTER THIRTEEN
Dramatic effect.

The bedroom door flew open and black shirts started pushing in. I jumped from my sleep, the bread roll from earlier still sitting, half eaten, in my hand. I had no idea what was going on, but the men seemed in no mood to explain. One of them ripped me up off the bed by my arms and I yelled out in surprise. He forced me to my feet, pushing me forwards. I fell clumsily and could feel my pang in protest.

'What's going on?' I begged, feeling the familiar swell of panic.

'Get up,' one of the men shouted, grabbing my hair and pulling me to my feet. I screamed and scrambled up, steadying myself quickly and holding onto my side. I looked at them, quickly realizing, that what had originally felt like a group of black shirt employees, was in fact only two men. I recognised them instantly from the day I'd arrived; the feely pervert, Wyatt, and the man still sporting a black eye, Williams. Williams was the one standing closest to me now and I quickly recalled that on the last time we'd met, he'd tried to kick the life out of me whilst my hands were tied behind my back. That should have been the first sign that the two of us were never going to be best friends.

'What are you looking at?' he snapped viciously, baring his teeth. My hands began to tremble, betraying me, and I clasped them to hide it. Whatever the men were here for, I already knew that it wasn't going to end well. For some reason, they were so much more aggressive than any other employee and they seemed to be looking for an outlet for their anger. To hell if it would be me, though. If Rodriguez wasn't allowed to push me around, these two goons definitely wouldn't get to either. I glared back at Williams, as belittlingly as possible, casting a raised eyebrow towards his eye.

'What do all the boys say when you tell them a girl gave you that black eye?' He growled angrily. It was just as well I had already taken painkillers today because as he lunged himself at me, I already knew it was going to hurt. His hand whipped across my face in a hard, stinging slap which instantly brought tears to my eyes. I could feel my skin begin to burn where his handprint would be etching itself on my cheek.

'You think you're so important, don't you?' Williams asked, licking his lips. I pulled my hair from my eyes and forced a smile. The waterworks wouldn't show me as weak, not while I could help it.

'Well, more important than you.' I spat, encouraging him to launch himself at me again. I dodged quickly this time, moving aside, but I only landed in the grasp of the man who liked to touch. Wyatt held my arms together with one of his big hands and leaned into my hair.

'Aww, she smells nice,' he announced with delight, taking a long inhale. I wriggled, trying to free myself, but he spun me and pinned me against the wardrobe. The handle cut into my back I could feel warm blood begin to leak out, trailing towards my waist band. I was sure seeing the results of their handiwork would just fuel them even more and despite the pain, I was mad at myself for bleeding so obviously.

'Get off me,' I shouted, struggling against him. His hand clamped down around my neck and he licked my face, making pleasurable noises. Ok, enough was enough. That was disgusting. I slammed my knee up into his groin as hard as I could, and the black shirt crumbled to the ground with a high-pitched squeal. His grip loosened, and I ripped myself free, sprinting to the door as fast as my shaky legs would take me. Just shy of crossing the threshold, I felt hands on my back and I was suddenly shoved with such force that I flew forward, crashing into the ground. I skid across the wooden floor and into the hallway wall. I was aware of my ribs throbbing, but the buzzing in my head was stopping me from focusing. Was I about to pass out? I had hit my head on the ground and I could feel it pulsing loudly, consuming all my sound. I groaned, loudly, trying to get myself back together. I was beginning to learn, from my past few days experience, that after a certain amount of inflicted pain, the body stopped registering individual blows. Thankfully too. I'd already proven this morning with Rodriguez that adrenaline trumped pain and fear. But, while lying in a heap on the floor, still partially blinded by unconsciousness and knowing that somewhere in close vicinity was a very angry man coming my way, well, that knowledge just didn't seem to instill much comfort. I heard the footsteps before my vision cleared and a large hand grabbed me by my hair again. I yelled out trying to find my feet. What had I done to make these guys hate me so much, to be so violent and aggressive? Was this how all Rodriguez's men were? My eyes began to clear through the tears, just in time to see a hand slap across my face again. This whole being beaten up thing was starting to get old and my poor body surely couldn't take much more of it. I raised my hands up in defeat, yelling loudly through my panting.

'Okay, okay.' The black shirt didn't hit again, but he didn't let go of my hair either. I used the pause to try catch my breath. 'All right,' I begged, feeling a new cut on my lip. Why was I always bleeding for goodness sake? I was sick of the taste of iron. 'I'm sorry.' I repeated, my upheld hands still shaking with shock. I looked the black shirt in the eyes. 'I'm sorry.' He tightened his grip on my hair and began to smile. *What a slime.* He tilted my head backwards, smugly.

'Say it again,' he demanded, his body pushing mine hard into the wall.

I could feel the blood from the cut on my back smearing, warm and slick. I looked closely at the man, Wyatt, who was holding me. He was strong and muscular, but stupid and cowardly. He was a bully, plain and simple, and I knew, all too well, how I did with bullies. It wasn't in me to back down, to let them be, or to steer clear. A bully needed taken down a few pegs, needed someone to stand up to them. That was naturally going to be me. I parted my lips to speak again and he leaned closer, practically squashing all my air out. He was desperate to hear me beg, like all predictable predators. He smiled to himself, victoriously.

'I'm sorry,' I whispered, 'that you're so damn ugly and hit like a girl and tha....' I would have kept going, if I'd have had the time, but he growled, lifting me up and slamming my back against the wall again. My air whooshed from me as my feet dangled out beneath and he threw me to the ground with a grunt. I prepared myself for the piercing pain of a foot in the face, but it never came.

'WHAT THE HELL IS GOING ON?' bellowed a new man's voice. I opened my eyes, cautiously, to blurrily see another black shirt marching down the hallway towards us. He was the guy who I was supposed to liaise with, Scott. He seemed to be the highest up in command and right now he looked mad. Really mad. He reached me and, considering the past few minutes, gently lifted me to my feet. 'Rodriguez has been waiting for her for ten minutes.' He glanced me over, quickly. 'You were told not to lay a finger on her.' He waved his large hand at me. 'Look at her.' Williams lowered his head.

'Collection didn't go quite as planned,' he muttered. There was a grumble from the bedroom and the newest addition to our party looked in to the see Wyatt, still lying on the floor and cupping himself. He flashed a quick glance at me and I could have sworn I saw the corner of his mouth twitch with a smile. 'Get out of my sight,' he barked loudly. 'I'll deal with you both later.' He quickly turned and marched me off down the hall from where he'd come. I stumbled slightly as my body began to start processing the new assault of pain. The guy holding onto me must have felt me falter and he kindly tightened his supporting grip. My head was definitely bleeding, I could feel the blood starting to ooze its way down my eyebrow. My slapped cheek was no doubt beetroot red still and my lip stung with each lick. That wasn't even including the very real nagging from my ribs as the pain tried to push through the barrier of the pain killers. I tried to ignore the aches and used our destination as a distraction. I looked around...where *was* I going? I had never seen this part of the house before. We walked, well, he walked, and I leaned, for another few hallways and turns, until we reached our obvious destination; a well-guarded door. My heart did the same thing it had done the first time I'd entered into Rodriguez's office a few days ago; almost stopped beating with fear. Every securely monitored door elevated my heart rate and made my head run rampant. Rodriguez needed to send Edward proof of life, but that could be done by sending a few thousand vaults through my body and holding up a phone while I screamed…or worse, chopping off a finger! People loved to chop off fingers in all the gangster movies. I started breathing heavily, my shakes moving from my hands into my legs. I liked my fingers, all of them. The door guards stepped aside and let us pass through without words, although I noticed their exchanged glances at my appearance. Why was I always covered in blood and beaten whenever I was taken to see Rodriguez? And just at that thought, the devil himself entered the room. He looked over to me and stalled in his step, his eyebrows suddenly raising with shock. But despite the momentary lapse in emotions, he quickly composed himself and swallowed.

'Miss Eva, why is it every time I see you, you look like you've been in the wars?' His tone was light, but his eyes were not. I could see fire and wrath boiling in them just beneath their beautiful surface. He looked to Scott, who was pretty much just holding me up now. 'What happened?' he asked firmly, putting his hands into his dark suit pockets. He had on a crisp white shirt with no tie and the contrast of colour on his dark skin made him look even more striking.

'Wyatt and Williams.' The black shirt replied, repeating their disgusting names. 'They're out of control,' he added, with a small tightening of his lips. I listened in silence, whilst watching Rodriguez intently. In my mind, I could still hear myself, just hours ago, accusing him of everything under the sun. We had parted on very thin ice. Despite that though, there seemed to be no lingering trace of those heightened emotions. The anger behind his clear expression right now was glaringly obvious, but it was definitely not aimed at me this time. His two, apparently 'out of control', employees were currently monopolizing that reaction. I guessed disobedience was not one of Rodriguez's favourite characteristics.

'Deal with them for now, Scott, until I can, por favor,' he said calmly. But something in the way he said it, made my arm hairs stand up. What did 'deal with them' mean? I didn't exactly care if either of them disappeared to be honest, at least then I wouldn't have to worry about bumping into them alone again, but I was far from easy with the idea of being involved in anything to do with torture, or worse…death. And surely when it came to Rodriguez, it was always safe to assume it would always be worse. The memory of the three men and the gun from the other day came to my mind. Rodriguez had been quite happy at ending three lives there. What were another disobedient two? A surge of panic swept through my body and I was sure the black shirt holding me up must have felt a sudden weight as my legs began to fail. This was a whole new dangerous world for me and I knew nothing about surviving in it. I had been reckless and lucky so far, but at some point, I was beginning to understand, that I would probably, more than likely, end up dead if I kept pushing my luck. And that was a sobering thought. 'Miss Eva,' Rodriguez began, turning his attention to me.

'Please, sit.' He motioned to a chair in the middle of the small, windowless, beige room we were now in. I began to look around at my surroundings. There was a small table and a cold plastic seat. In front of that was a camera, set up on a tripod and a tablet attached to it. I eyed the camera anxiously, dreading what physical horrors it would soon be recording. The black shirt dragged me over to the chair and sat me down facing the lens, and despite my fears I collapsed into the chair, thankful to not be relying on my legs anymore. Rodriguez walked over and perched himself on the table in front of me. He smelt divine. Through my damn torment and fear I still managed to clock his smell. I was broken, it was simple. There was no other good reason for my physical reactions. I kept a straight face and hid my feelings, but quickly clocked his consistent closeness again. He was *always* too close. He looked at me and shook his head. 'Are you in much pain?' he asked, showing no facial expression. *Yes, I was in complete agony.*

'No, I'm fine,' I replied, bluntly. To this he smiled a little. I was amusing him again.

'As soon as we are done here I will send for Dr Miele,' he paused, 'who will be very upset with me again.' He crossed his arms and leaned forward slightly. 'You don't exactly look like I had planned, but I think you will probably get more of a reaction like this.' He smiled again, but this time in a more ruthless, vindictive way. tI made me nervous, very nervous. He looked at the camera behind me. 'In a few minutes we will open a conference call with your dear Edward and his weasel of a dad. The feed has been bounced around the world and encrypted enough times for your...cariño...*sweetheart*, to think you are anywhere from China to the Amazon. Not to mention all the plane and train tickets purchased to multiple locations over the past couple days. Or my armoured vans transporting goods with guards to secure holding places, or the enclosed and protected buildings and warehouses guarded as if a very precious item was being stashed inside...' he paused to let the fact that he was very clever and the fact I was never going to be found, settle in properly. It was working. He was doing a fine job. I suddenly felt suffocated. I could be being held anywhere in the world as far as Edward would know. I was an hour away and it might as well have been another planet. I desperately tried to calm my breathing as the realisation settled in. I had been holding on deep inside, not really dealing with the situation, because I had thought or believed that I'd be found and that everything would work out. But Rodriguez was right, which he knew...I was never going to be rescued. I had been a fool to hold onto such a hope. A heavy weight constricted my breathing and forced air from my body. I gasped slightly dropping my head. Holy crap this was all such a mess! I was too wrapped up in my plunging despair to notice Rodriguez still watching me. *Just breathe Eva, keep breathing.*

'Miss Eva?' Rodriguez's voice came calmly, cutting through my thoughts and panic. He was waiting for my composure to return, I could see it in his watchful gaze. I mustered all my strength, pulling on every fiber of my courage and after a few seconds, I was able to look him back in the eyes. The intensity of his stare was almost too much. It always felt like he was trying to read me, trying to see straight into me. And the more he did it, the more it was beginning to seem like he could. But not now, not this time, not while I was on the verge of panic and breakdown. I could feel the despair inside me trying to get a firm grip, trying to pull me under. But it wouldn't win, it couldn't win. Not yet anyway. I held Rodriguez's gaze as boldly as I could, focusing all my efforts on this moment and not my sudden understanding of my situation. He nodded slowly, as if satisfied I was where he needed me to be. 'I'll be in the room over there,' he pointed to an adjoining room behind him, 'and you'll be able to see me. You will also be able to see on the tablet here, Edward darling and his serpiente…snake, of a father,' he paused, 'but until this red light,' he tapped the camera, 'has turned on, they will not be able to see you. Understand?' I nodded slowly, taking one thing at a time. He stood up and straightened his dark suit trousers. 'I just thought it would be nice for you to see the future family of yours at work.' He considered me for a second longer, then nodded to the black shirt standing at the side. The black shirt came forward, clinking, and quietly began to handcuff me to my seat. My mouth dropped.

'What the hell?' I argued, already knowing it was pointless. I lifted my hands as far as they could now go, which was maybe two inches.

'Efecto dramático…dramatic effect.' Rodriguez answered with a smile. 'I'm afraid you're going to be gagged too, and I *know* you're not going to like that at all.'

'What?' I yelled loudly. 'This is insane.' I shot daggers at him whilst he stood in front of me and the black shirt advanced with an ominous white piece of material.

'Anything you would like to say before we start?' Rodriguez asked, stepping away towards the next room, a small playful smile dancing on his lips. I glanced at my cuffs and compose myself quickly. How dare he enjoy himself over this.

'Yes.' I replied boldly, catching his attention again. He stopped walking and turned back towards me, an eyebrow raised inquisitively. He held his hand up to the black shirt to wait and inclined his head for me to continue. 'I have an itchy nose, if you would be so kind as to scratch it?' I held his eyes, which were turned up with amusement. He let out a small, sincere sounding laugh, the kind that made your stomach flip.

'You are one of a kind, luchadora, I'll give you that.' He shook his head at me, chuckling.

'What does that mean?' I asked a little firmer than I intended, my temper a little on the short side. I didn't like that he was calling me something I couldn't understand, let alone counter or react.

'It means fighter, mostly, but in your case the better word would probably be, feisty, Miss Eva. Which you most definitely are.' He offered a small last nod, before walking off into the next room and quickly calling over his shoulder for my nose to be scratched before being gagged. I snatched my face away from the awkwardly approaching finger of the employee and once the material was securely in my mouth and I could no longer get any words to form, I turned my attention to watching Rodriguez in the next room. He was preparing himself and conversing with another suited man. I guessed the companion was a solicitor or advisor of some sorts. He looked like a clever yet devious man and was dressed to match his sharp unforgiving features. I assumed quite quickly that he was strictly a business man, and the type of business that could be followed with a paper trail. The lines on his suit were pressed far too perfectly for someone who got their own hands dirty and the fact that he didn't look in my direction even once, was another indicator. After a few minutes of observing, the lights in my room dimmed and all men, minus the biggest one, left. The remaining black shirt stood behind me, not speaking, but breathing loudly and making his massive presence very known. I rolled my eyes to myself, feeling somewhat frustrated. What exactly did he think I was going to do; Houdini my way out of the handcuffs, Volcon-pinch his neck and make a quick escape? I jingled the handcuffs with aggravation, causing Rodriguez to cast me a side-wards glance from his on-camera position in the other room. I lifted my hands as far as they would go and shrugged sarcastically at him at him as if to say, 'What? I'm still here'. He smiled again, discretely, then looked back to the camera. I was so happy that I was a continuous source of entertainment for him in what I'm sure would otherwise have been a very run-of-the-mill day. I growled to myself. If I was being honest, amidst the outwardly display of cheek and flamboyance, there were definite stabs of panic. Given, I wasn't getting electrocuted or any of my appendages being cut off as previously concerned, but in just a few moments I would see Edward and Brice, my future father-in-law, and the idea of that scared me almost more than anything. Firstly, I didn't want to see how Ed was handling it, I didn't want to see the pain I had caused. Secondly, I didn't want to feel the guilt that I knew was going to follow this call, nor the self-pitying that I would sink into for who knows how long afterwards. Thirdly, I didn't want to see the messy chaos I had thrown everything into by giving myself over to our enemy. And fourthly, the scariest thought of them all; I didn't want to admit to myself yet, that this small tablet mounted in front of me, might offer me the last time I would ever see the people I loved again. Once this call ended, I would be alone again and maybe forever. Yet, like everything else from the last few days, I was handcuffed to a stinking chair and had no control over anything. I was pulled from my thoughts as everything fell silent and my tablet suddenly lit up with a feed I recognised well. It was from Brice's conference room three, the room I'd played hide and seek with Edward in many times whilst we were young. I pushed past the emotional memories and found Brice, sat at the center of the table with his lawyers and advisors surrounding him; they were the backbone of a very complex man. My eyes quickly scanned passed them, searching for Ed, and they finally found him standing at the back, behind his dad. He looked tired and stressed and I could see the lines around his eyes. He had his hands folded across his chest, like he did when he was feeling pressure from something. My eyes began to tear at the sight of him. My Edward, trying to play the brave solider. Before I knew it, I felt drops fall from my eyes. What had I done to him? I used my shoulder to wipe away the tears, hating having no free hands to hide my weakness. I saw Rodriguez glance at me quickly from the other room, and through my blurry eyes, I could have sworn I saw a hint of pity linger in his stare. But the moment passed in a second and he turned his focus back to the screen, back to business.

'Brice Bain,' he began with a somewhat chirpy tone and inclining his head towards the camera. 'It's been a while since we've last spoken face to face.' Rodriguez had chosen not to sit in a fancy conference room surrounded by intimidating business men, like Bain had opted for. Instead, he sat just like he had a few moments ago when talking to me, perched on the end of a small table, hands casually in his pockets. Alone. This man was no fool. He was clever and calculated in everything he did, and he was good at games.

'Rodriguez, you have gone too far this time, you have crossed a line and you will reap the consequences of it.' Bain was mad, his face was red and was darkening by the second as he yelled out his threats. He had that same look on that he always had when he spoke about Rodriguez.

'Well that's a bit hypocritical, Brice. Let's not talk about going *too far,* shall we? We both know you are the king of that.' Rodriguez paused to let his words sink in. Whatever they meant, Bain's face tightened and he quickly silenced. 'But there's no point in bringing up the dirty past right now, is there?' Rodriguez continued, taking his hands from his pockets. And just like that, I watched as one sentence gave Rodriguez power over the room, control over the conversation. If this had been a case study at University, I would have been impressed, but as it was, my livelihood was in the noose and it didn't seem quite so magical right now. 'I'll at least do you the courtesy of saving you time and tell you that there's no point trying to get Jackson to track this feed. It's untraceable.' He scratched his chin casually. 'Isn't that right, Jackson?' Rodriguez asked out loud, as a man slowly and sheepishly entered the screen next to Bain and nodded in defeat, removing a set of headphones.

'He's right, Mr Bain. Not even I can trace this one, he's jumping and re-routing all over the world.' I recognised the man instantly. I knew him as Jack and he was Brice's leading computer nerd. A really, nice guy, actually, and it was sad to see him looking like he had failed his boss, especially when I knew that all of this was really my fault.

'So, shall we just get down to business then, now that that is all cleared up?' Rodriguez clapped his hands together like he was ready to go fire up a BBQ for the family picnic. 'I hold the ventaja, the Ace here Bain, and I *will* be playing this card. Can I assume that you will be complying with all my requests, question free?' Rodriguez was obviously delighted, smugly playing and tormenting him. Brice pushed his chair back and stood up angrily.

'I will never bow down to you, Rodriguez. You do not call the shots, you immigrant,' he was bellowing, his fists clenched and waved at the screen. 'You think you can take from me with no consequences, then you have another thing coming.'

'Like how you took from me with no consequences, Bain?' Cane snapped back, his voice edged with sharp, vicious implication. Whatever Rodriguez was talking about, he again instantly silenced Brice, who returned to his seat suddenly quiet. 'Actually, that is a perfect place to start.' Rodriguez continued, his manner returning to normal; cool and collected. 'First on my list; you will pull out of the Shanks Builder's Campaign and let me have the rights.' He paused to let his words settle in. How did he even know about the Shanks deal? It was still in complete secrecy. Ed had told me, obviously, and the handful of other people involved, knew about it. But that was all. It was a massive project that had been in the running for a couple years now. I knew how much time, effort and money had gone into securing that deal, so the fact that Rodriguez knew about it, well it meant only one thing; Bane had a mole. Someone on Bane's team was leaking information out to our enemy. It was the only possible way that Rodriguez could have that knowledge when I knew how tight security had been. I quickly realised that Brice and Ed would assume I had given Rodriguez the scoop, that I gave him the information. The thought didn't sit well with me at all. I knew which side I was on and where my loyalties lay. That devotion being questioned made me nauseous. I watched through the sickness as conference room three's eyes all began to instantly roam around, looking at each other knowingly. The Shanks Building Campaign was worth billions and they had just lost it at the demand of their nemesis. I watched Edward with dedicated eyes. He hadn't moved a muscle yet, not even at Rodriguez's first request. 'Secondly,' the devil himself continued, 'you will release your annual financial spend reviews to the press by the end of the financial year...the real ones this time.' This demand raised more than just eyebrows, voices pitched up in protest and a full-scale debate kicked off in the conference suite. I would have liked to have been naive enough to think that it was just the loss of business edge and privacy which was creating the concern amongst the Bain employees, but I knew, as well as every man in that conference room did, that the main problem with that information release was all the illegal and criminal deals would be exposed. All of them. And there were a lot of them. I looked away from my stone-cold fiancé to the loose and confident Rodriguez in the other room. He was good. Scarily good. And that made me panic in a way I hadn't let myself do yet. This man could manipulate anything...so just how far would he go with leverage like me? His first two requests would already stand to practically cripple Ed's business, so how many more deals would Bane Enterprises have to comply with because of me? For the first time, I started properly thinking about my options. My outs. I looked back to Edward, who stood motionless and still. I was holding out for a miracle, for an act of God to make this all right. I had made this deal for good reasons, with good intentions, and maybe I was hoping the universe would acknowledge that and help me correct it all, but it was not going to happen, was it? This whole mess was just going to get worse and worse. I had a created a catastrophe that would ruin not just lives, but businesses, industries, economies...all of a sudden, my breathing was harder than it had ever been and a realisation engulfed me. My head fell to the desk as I tried to get air into my lungs. Despite how much I kept a brave face or hoped for a happy ending, the decision I made in that alley a few days ago would literally destroy people; Edward, his dad, Brice, his company, its employees and their families, my dad, any business related to Bain Enterprises and their employees and their families...vomit rose in my throat and I began to swim out of consciousness. I was the tiny pebble causing the immeasurable ripple effect. What had I done? All of the endless lists of destruction and pain caused by a desperate and snap decision, swirled sickeningly in my head. It would all happen because I was in Rodriguez's hands, stuck here captive and useless. Responsibility dawned on me with eye watering weight and I began to shake. I could only let this all go so far before I would have to take responsibility and rectify as much as I could. In any hostage situation, the key play was always to remove the leverage. It was straightforward sound business. I was the leverage. If I was not around, neither party had any demands to make or leverage to use. Simple. I gulped with fear. If I died, all this would end, and life would go back to the chaotic, messy way of before. But at least it would be functioning. To stop all of this, could I kill myself? If needed, I could do that? Right? It would be the first selfless thing I'd done in days. If I was gone, this whole nightmare ended instantly. Rodriguez had no ace and Brice had no reason to comply. The world as we knew it would stay intact. When worst came to very worst at the end of all this, and I had hung on as long as I could, I knew now what my plan had to be. I knew now what my escape route was. It was my way out of the deal. I inhaled slowly lifting my head, my eyes going back to Edward. I felt sick. Just the knowledge of that being my possible end was enough to make bile rise in my throat. But I still had some form of control left, I still had time to act and try change things. I swallowed the sickness down. Business was not a fast world, this I knew. I had time to change things still. I just had to keep my head up and eyes open. I could do this, couldn't I? I refocused back on the conversation as Rodriguez silenced yells from the conference room.

'And finally, to end *today's* list of demands...' he paused here, a long pause, and I turned my head to look at him in the other room. He breathed deeply and said quietly a simple statement that made no sense to anyone apparently, except Brice, who looked appalled. 'Before the end of all this, you'll tell the world...la verdad...the truth.' Rodriguez's eyes flashed an emotion I had never dreamt I would see from him. It disappeared so quickly that it may never have even been there, but I was becoming an expert at staring at him and reading his tells. Sadness, the emotion was definitely sadness. It shocked me so much that I zoned out on everything around me except the strange alien man standing in the next room. He felt sadness? Who was he? What was this 'truth' he was speaking about? It was something deep enough to provoke a genuine human response from him, that was for sure. A shuffle from the black shirt behind me brought me back to the conversation, which was now more heated than before. Brice was standing and yelling with sheer despise at the camera. I had never heard him scream so angrily before, nor with such venom or colourful language. The 'truth' was apparently worth a lot.

'You will never get away with this Rodriguez, you are a rat and an imposter, you deserve nothing from this life or me. You will rot alone in your private estate with no-one to care for you and about you, you pathetic son of a...'

'Sit down, Bain.' Rodriguez interrupted firmly, his tone flaring with anger. His voice commanded so much control that even Brice Bain himself, silenced and slowly sat down. 'There are ladies present after all, let us watch our language, shall we?' He said it calmly, with a small smile on his lips. He knew what he was he taunting with. His words finally forced a movement from Edward, who stepped forward. I saw Rodriguez's smile increase, as if Edward had finally come out to play. 'Ahhh, Edward. So nice of you to decide to eventually join us. I'm surprised you've not had more to say so far.' I glared at Rodriguez, he was a horrid man and was going to enjoy torturing Ed more than Brice, simply for the fact that he knew how much

Ed meant to his father. Ed was his sole heir, his sole love. I watched Rodriguez and Ed, suddenly realising how strange it was that they were the same age. They seemed years apart, in so many ways.

'Where is she, Rodriguez?' Edward finally asked, loudly and confidently. 'She's my responsibility, *you* cannot have her,' he threatened viciously. To this Rodriguez just laughed, I could hear the echo delay on the camera from the other room. My chained fists clenched as I tried to steady myself. The gag in my mouth was wet and stifling and stopped me saying anything of any help to Edward. The madder I got, the more the gag infuriated me. All I could do was sit and watch, like a useless spectator. I hated Rodriguez, I hated the wretched man so much that it made every muscle in my restrained body tense.

'You know,' Rodriguez continued with a smug smile, 'she's a feisty one, isn't she?' He glanced at me with a discrete smile, as if we had some kind of in-joke now with the word feisty. I didn't retaliate. ' She does put up a good fight; I can see why you've kept her around for so long.' To this Edward blew, slamming his fist onto the desk in front of him.

'Damn you, Rodriguez. I swear on my mother's grave, that if you lay even one finger on her, I'll kill you myself.' Rodriguez laughed casually, completely unfazed by Ed's threat. I could see and hear the anger in Edward's eyes and it made tears pour uncontrollably from mine. Rodriguez cast a glance at me and saw the tears, he paused for a second then turned back to his audience.

'Now, now Edward. Such loyal and noble intentions. Bain family qualities, I am sure.' He let the sarcasm linger, then placed his hands back into his pockets, business mode. 'She's been with you now for how many years?' he pushed, 'and do you want to bet that you've not made her grito…scream, quite like I have in the last three days? Muy impresionate!' *Very impressive!* He whistled shaking his head suggestively. Edward threw his mug off the conference wall while cursing Rodriguez. I jumped as it smashed, and Edward screamed into the camera.

'I am going to KILL you, Rodriguez, I swear, I'm going to wring the life out of your pathetic body with a smile on my face. Leave her alone, you maniac. She's better than you and you know it, you don't deserve to be able to even touch her.' Edward was pointing his finger at Rodriguez, his eyes shiny and red with resentment. Rodriguez laughed.

'You say that *I* don't deserve her, Edward?' He paused and quickly turned his head to me, casting me an odd, almost apologetic look. I held his eyes with confusion, tears still sliding down my face. As the fleeting look past and he went back to the camera, I was left feeling unnerved. Why would even a slightly remorseful look leave the devil himself's eyes…unless something bad was coming? His confident voice continued boldly though, paying no heed to my inner anxiety. 'I don't deserve her, that's interesting.

But *I* wouldn't have been sleeping around with other women at the same time as *supposedly* being in love with her, Eddie. Especially that ongoing thing you have with her best friend…cómo se llama ella…' he clicked his fingers in pretend thought, 'what's her name…oh yes, Tammy.' He cleared his throat. 'At least I don't *pretend* to treat her well, Edward.' Rodriguez's eyes flashed back to me. I must have looked quite shell shocked. What a cheap, ridiculous thing to say. It also showed how little Rodriguez knew. Ed didn't even like Tammy, he avoided her, quite literally, like she had the plague. *Go on Ed, tell him where to go.* I waited for the fight of honour and the loud confirming denial. But it didn't come. I kept waiting, and it kept not coming. Rodriguez was still looking at me and I him, but I left his stare and turned my focus back to Edward, who was now standing dead straight, glaring at Rodriguez. Seconds passed in silence, but they felt like an eternity. Why was Edward just standing there? Why wasn't he calling Rodriguez a liar and a cheat? Why did the look on Ed's face resemble shame and fear, rather than injustice? In my haze of confusion, I heard Rodriguez's voice carry on, his deep tone producing words like deadly silk. 'I'll admit that at least this Tammy, in comparison to the others, has a certain something. Although she's a little too plastic for my liking. And the whole sneaking around behind everyone's backs and faking work trips away when you're actually meeting up in hotels…' He stopped for a melodramatic sigh. 'It's all a bit too clichéd for me. But each to their own right, Bain?' Rodriguez concluded, a smirk cast at the silent father who sat still on his chair, listening. Rodriguez had stopped casting side-wards glances at me now, thankfully, because I was struggling to blink and breathe let alone hold any composure. It couldn't be true. It couldn't. It actually couldn't be true, of course not. Of course, it wasn't. But Rodriquez's words, coupled with instant recalls of Edward awkwardly refusing to be around Tammy, all started shooting through my spiraling mind. With painful confirmation. *Deny it Ed, deny it now. Please!* Yes, we weren't perfect, and we'd been arguing a lot lately, but this accusation was ludicrous. It had to be. Tammy was my best friend; my confidant, my go-to for relationship conversations, my trusted and devoted investor…the sister I never had. And Edward was my longest friend, my loving partner, my knows-my-past and all of me. He was Ed, *my* Ed; trustworthy and reliable. It was a lie. It *had* to be a lie. But Ed's face was the sealing deal. He looked disgusted, with himself. *HOLY* CRAP! Just when I thought life couldn't get worse, when minutes ago I was analyzing suicide, when I thought I was at rock bottom, the walls crumbled down even more. I was an idiot. I was and am an absolute first-class idiot. Loyal, old boring me, sitting at home waiting for my A-Lister fiancé to come back home, faithfully, to come back to his nobody. I struggled to swallow whilst looking at Ed's eyes. The betrayal tasted so vividly bitter that it caught in my throat and make me gag. How could they? How could they do this? Had I been that naive and blind? How long had it been going on? I choked, spluttering. Did they laugh at me as they snuck away together? Questions consumed me with shocking speed and the sudden need to know *everything* I'd stupidly not seen. Ed and Tammy? Tammy and Ed? Sleeping together? Sneaking around? I kept saying it over and over again in my head, trying to register the full implications. A numbing feeling was burning its way through my body, not anger. Despite all that was going on with this crazy thoughtless deal I had made with Rodriguez and the situation I had put us all into, it was Ed's affair that now seemed the most sharp and painful. The deceit was quickly hammering its way heavily into my heart, denting it in an irreparable way. But worse than the numb feeling of shock and deceit, was this feeling of stupidity and blame. Yes, blame of all things, sat heavy in my stomach. I never made things easy for Edward and I knew it. He was a good man, or had been once upon a time, but I never joined the life he led. I knew that girls threw themselves at him all the time, but I just thought that our past made us solid. Tammy was beautiful, ambitious, glamorous, so...so different to me. To boring me. Could I blame him for wanting more than a school teacher with yoga pants and her hair pulled up into a pony tail, when daily, beautiful and young passionate girls offered themselves to him free on a plate? I looked at his eyes and it broke my heart. YES. Yes, damn it. I bloody well could blame him! An utter feeling of loss flooded through me with pulsing anger. I may have been a bit lower market and a bit less glittery than the women he mixed with frequently, but I damned well didn't deserve for him to be fiddling with my best friend behind my back. How could he do this? How could he do this to me? Frustratingly, I knew that he loved me, I *knew* that. But it didn't stop the mix of painful sadness and humiliation from coursing through me. Would I ever trust him again, would I ever respect him again, the man I had loved for so much of my life? I looked at his face through blurred and tear flooded eyes. Maybe, in a long time from now. But I knew, as I watched his tense and tortured body though, that I didn't hate him. I was putting him through a worse hell just now, being dangled and threatened by Rodriguez, than a broken heart could inflict. I was mad, hurt and extremely disappointed...but maybe in a twisted way, I almost felt like we were slightly even. Maybe his treachery was lessened by my deal with Rodriguez. The deal I had put him in too. If I was brutally honest, despite the betrayal, I was maybe even deep down inside a little relived at him having messed up royally too. Tammy now, on the other hand, I could hate her. I needed someone to vent it on and for some strange reason the betrayal of a sister was beginning to edge ahead in the hate-race. Tammy was probably somewhere, fawning around, having her nails done, getting off Scott-free. And that made me mad, tense-my-fists-and-want-to-scream-out-loud, mad. All the times I had gone to her with relationship problems, trusted her without a shadow of a doubt. All the years we had been best friends…wasted, gone. I wanted to sob and scream all at the same time.

'You told her this already?' Came Edward's quiet voice through the tablet speakers as he avoided his father's eyes.

'*You* never told her, did you? You know, she's surprisingly forgiving, she may have forgiven you the first time, but la segunda…y la tercera…y la cuarta, *the second…then the third…and then the forth*…and then the fact that it's been with her best friend, over and over and over again.' He tutted with a sigh. 'I just don't know if even a woman like Eva could get over that. I don't blame you for lying though, I'd want to keep that package around for as long as possible too, especially when she's full of so much energy…you know what I mean Edward, don't you?' Edward's shameful demeanor changed quickly, and he growled with anger.

'They meant nothing, Rodriguez. Don't you dare ruin her through this.' Edward yelled at Rodriguez's smile. 'She deserves better than this. I swear, let her go and take me instead.' To this, Brice stepped in with his business voice on. Losing Edward was definitely not an option, me maybe, but not Edward.

'Look Rodriguez, before we all go ruining our lives on your orders, how about you prove that you even have Eva. And saying that you've injected her with some weird tracking device means nothing but fear mongering and dirty tactics. The words of a liar and a cheat mean nothing to us. If you have her, like you say, show her to us now or we are gone.' Brice had finally pulled me into the game, what I had been gagged and chained to a chair for in the first place. I was somewhat in a different disposition to what I had thought I would be when this moment arrived, but nonetheless, I was dreading seeing the stares of their faces and the knowledge in their eyes that I had brought this all upon them. And worse, seeing Edward look at me with his sad eyes that no longer belonged to me.

'Fine, as you wish.' Rodriguez said, nodding casually and signaling the camera man to open the feed. I freaked out. I didn't want them to see me, not all beaten, tear stained and now dealing with a heartbreak. I didn't want Rodriguez to have the pleasure. If I could only get away from the camera's view, then an empty room would be enough for Bain to think Rodriguez was bluffing. He would call the whole thing off in a rage and cut the feed before they could get me back in place. I didn't care what happened to me anymore, I couldn't do this to Edward, despite everything I'd learned. I panicked and as forcefully as possible, I jumped up from the ground and head butt the black shirt behind me. I felt the crack of his nose on the back of my head and he yelled, stumbling down to the ground in sudden pain and surprise. I was cuffed to the seat still, but escape wasn't my plan. I just had to get a couple feet to the left, so I was out of view. I stood up and began to run, rattling like a demented criminal with a chair attached to my rear. Between the yelling and swearing from the black shirt, and the scuffling and scraping of my chair, it was loud enough to be heard in the conference room and Edward began yelling.

What are you doing to her, Rodriguez, I swear if you're hurting her...' But Rodriguez was already on his feet, composing himself and quickly covering the commotion.

'What can I say, Edward, I did say she was spirited.' The camera feed cut into my room and I saw the red light burst into colour just as the recovered black shirt's strong body knocked me hard back into the camera view, crashing into the wall. My head whiplashed back, and I yelled as we both fell to the floor, the chair still attached to me. It crashed down on top of me dramatically, in an epic disastrous failure. In my dazed state I could hear Edward screaming and swearing and was vaguely aware of being hauled back up to a sitting position. Things seemed fuzzy. Had I passed out? I wondered how many knocks to the brain could someone sustain before getting brain damage? I would have to ask Dr Miele next time I saw him. Disgusting images of Ed and Tammy kissing, swam past my eyes as my vision began to come back. They made me recoil and quickly aim my focus back to reality. Then the camera in front of me began to sharpen and knew that I had royally failed. In fact, judging by the pulsing in my head, I may have just made the whole situation look worse. Maybe my 'act first, think later' trait was becoming old and just dangerously stupid. It had done me well so far in life, but maybe now, here in this world, there was a bit more at stake. Instead of me sitting here, beaten-yet-composed for the world to see, I had just given the whole conference room a front row viewing of me *being* beaten, live, and with no composure in it at all. I really was an idiot, wasn't I? And I never felt it quite so vividly as I did now. I went to wipe the tears from my cheek, but found my hands still cuffed to the chair. I whimpered, accidently letting it slip out of me. When I looked up, I found Rodriguez staring at me from the other room, with as always, an odd mixture of expressions on his face. He had gotten to his feet and although I was still blurry eyed, I could have sworn he was smiling again. I hated him so much, the smug, confident, arrogant, evil pig. Let's see him find out his fiancé was cheating on him with his best friend, then get his butt kicked on camera and see how well *he* handled it.

'Eva? Eva baby, can you hear me? Eva, are you okay sweetie? Talk to me.' Edward was yelling desperately into the camera and as my focus came back, I could see the sheen in his eyes. It was never fun to be rugby tackled by the black shirts, but I knew that it must have been harder to sit and watch. 'I am going to kill you, Rodriguez, I swear it, I will kill you. What kind of a man are you?' Edward was bellowing, anger and rage pouring off him. 'You beat a woman tied to a chair? You are disgusting.' Seeing his obvious and very real pain broke my heart and tears began to fill my eyes again. Yes, he'd lied and broken my own heart, but I would never wish *this* on him as penance. *Please turn the camera off, please turn it off.* I didn't want him to see me cry, for him to think that I was being defeated or broken. I didn't want him to have to watch me break down, but I couldn't hold it in much longer. I could feel the collapse inside of me, tunneling up and trying to claim reign. *Please turn it off, please.* The tears were beginning to totally fill my eyes and my vision of Edward was blurring into watery shades.

'Oh, stop yelling, Edward. She can't hear you. And you talk with such dignity for someone who's been sleeping around as if she means nothing to you.' Edward kicked a chair, sending it crashing off a wall. He ran his hands through his hair with helpless frustration. Rodriguez was thankfully done though, and his hands went back into his pockets. 'Gentleman, as requested, you've seen that she is still alive...' he paused displaying a perfect sarcastic smile, 'and well enough. My demands will be addressed within this month or she will suffer the penalty...' he paused again, leaning closely to the camera, 'I do not normally like to do all the work myself, but with this one, I will take great pleasure in getting my hands dirty. Do not make me wait or she will pay las consecuencias.' With his last threatening glare, the camera feed went dead and the red light went off. As soon as I saw the light go out, I fell apart. I didn't care who saw me, I didn't care if I looked weak. I had just witnessed the utter ruin of my life and the guilt and pain and confusion and betrayal was all finally too much. The tears flooded and poured from my eyes as I began to sob. Uncontrollably sob with my whole body. It was all such an utter mess. I was an utter mess.

'Todo el mundo salir ahora!' Rodriguez's voice commanded loudly, telling everyone in the room to get out now. I heard it above my gasps for air, but I didn't care about my punishment now. I had nothing left in me to care for. I could hear the rooms empty and the doors close, then I could hear a single echo of footsteps walk my way and pause in front of the table. Rodriguez was looking down at me and I dropped my head. I didn't want to be watched, judged as being weak. I felt the cuffs being opened and removed. He lifted my head from the table and held my chin with his hand, so I couldn't move away. He looked at me deeply for a few seconds before gently taking the gag from my mouth. As soon as it left my lips, I began to sob harder and my hands went to my face, trying to cover my shame. I wanted to be alone. Alone in a dark and windowless room. Alone with my pathetic self from now until the end of the world.

'Levantarse.' Rodriguez requested, telling me to stand and pulling the table from beneath my head. I forced myself up to my feet, feeling them shake under the pressure. He pulled my seat away and put them both in the other room. I backed against the wall and watched him lock the door and pocket the key. My legs gave way and I slid down to the floor, tears still flooding from my stinging eyes. I knew punishment was coming, I had disobeyed his orders and he had just promised Bain of the consequences. I was trembling, but not with fear. I could still see the pain in Edward's eyes, the genuine worry and fear. I could still feel the stab of unfaithfulness and cheating. I understood very clearly what it must have been like to have watched his arch-nemisis have me bound, beaten and my life threatened. I knew Ed and I would never be the same. I knew that I would never be the same. My head fell to the floor and my body followed, crumpling into a heap. I continued to weep, for I don't know how long. It felt like an eternity was passing and I was completely alone in the world, no salvation and no comfort. Was this hell? Was this everlasting torment and torture? Being forced to survive in the mess you had made, drowning slowly? Suddenly, at the depths of my pain, I felt a warm hand touch my bare shoulder. I knew it was Rodriguez, I knew it was his soft fingers that were gripping me and holding me in consciousness, and as much as I hated everything he had done to me, right now, I hurt too much to care. He knelt down next to me and rather than inflict his torture, he gently lifted my head from the ground and placed it on his lap. He didn't speak, he simply stroked my hair and just watched my tears fall. Time passed. How much time I don't know, but I know it passed. I ached inside from crying and my head rung with tension. Then finally, Rodriguez whispered something, breaking the silence. He leant closely to my face and his breath warmed my wet skin.

'I've been where you are, Eva. You cannot stay there too long, or you will never make it back.' He gently wiped tears from my face with his thumb. 'Trust me, you need to claw your way back.' With no explanation at all, except that he was right, and I knew it, I sat up and wrapped my arms around his neck and drew my body into his. Instantly I felt his warmth and pressed into him, praying for an end. I needed to know there was more out there still, that I hadn't lost everything. There was a hesitant delay, but after a few seconds, Rodriguez's arms encompassed me, holding me close to him as I continued to cry. I could feel a sudden shift in him, as if an urgency inside him had risen to the surface. Did he feel the same need as me to feel something too? To feel anything that wasn't pain? I had seen the split-second sadness in his eyes before and it was that, I assumed that, led him to the floor in a dark, locked, windowless room, to hold me. I cried into him for what felt like hours. He made no effort to speak or to get back to his work, he just sat with me, occasionally running his fingers down my shoulders and hair. It felt like two worlds had collided, two entirely different entities meeting somewhere in the middle, in a space that had never before existed. Finally, after my body could sob no more, the crying began to retreat and then eventually stop. I knew I would hate myself for all of this tomorrow. I knew the rational side of me would remember this night with a fraction of its pain but all of its humiliation and as I pulled slowly away from Rodriguez, my head still hung low, I couldn't bring myself to care. I began to breathe deeply, aware that the odd neutral moment for the two of us was coming to an end. I cautiously looked up at him, wiping my eyes with my clammy, shaking hands. He held my gaze nobly, no hint of smug satisfaction or judgement. We both breathed, letting the unexplainable phenomenon fade off into the dark surrounding night. Would I ever be able to explain this side of Rodriguez, where charity and sympathy overruled all his other traits? When he promised torture and vengeance, he gave me unrelenting compassion and care. I nodded slowly, taking my final composing breath. I was ready when he was. Rodriguez kept my focus and gently traced my face with his thumb, his eyes soft and deep like I had never seen them before. As he reached my chin, he nodded slowly back and let his hand drop. He stood up abruptly and brushed off his trousers, and that was the moment done. He held his hand out for me and I took it gratefully, not sure I would actually be able to stand alone anyway. It was a painful climb to get back up and all of today's knocks started to throb and ache. My mind and body were exhausted and wanted to sleep, I could feel it coming in for me, desperate to claim it's time. I needed to switch off and re-energise, to go somewhere where there were no thoughts or painful reminders. I knew once I woke up in the morning everything would seem different, maybe better, maybe worse, but at least different.

'I'll send Dr Miele to your room, then I suggest you get some rest.' Rodriguez walked to the door and opened it quickly, nodding to the guard to collect me and take me away. The black shirt did so, practically carrying me passed Rodriguez, who caught my eyes one last time. I smiled slightly at him and he inclined his head gently, as he did so often, then turned his back and closed the door.

Dr Miele had told me that the head could stand a good many knocks, but statistically, the more I bashed it around the higher the chances were that one fatal blow would find its way home. I took the comment to mean, start being more careful. He had tut-ed a lot while examining me and had given me those magical sleeping tablets, double dosage, and put me to bed. It was turning to twilight by the time I started drifting, drugged up and spaced, and everything was starting to seem just fine again. Maybe if I could stay in this moment just now, then life would be ok again. If I never slept or woke or existed again, apart from in this blurry, dazed state, then maybe my life would be fine again. But as much as I fought it, sleep came for me, claiming what was his, and took me away, took me closer to waking.

CHAPTER FOURTEEN
Oddly charitable.

He locked the door behind Eva after watching her broken body and spirit being carried away by Cliff. Cliff was a big, strong man and beside him, she looked so frail and small. Despite her defiant and bold personality, she was just that; delicate and slight. It was surprisingly hard, for him, to watch her looking so vulnerable, especially when he knew her heart longed to fight. He leaned against the stark wall, allowing its coolness to soak into his heated and clammy body. It had been countless years since he had connected like that with anyone, since he had let anyone close enough to share anything. He had forgotten what it felt like to have a genuine moment with someone, something not tainted with doubt and laced with deceit or second guessing. He hadn't expected it and it had thrown him. The wall was a solid place to lean while he breathed deeply looking for answers.
What was this feeling and this curiosity Eva was stirring in him? He had sworn off intimacy and trust as weaknesses years ago. Now he found them stealing back into his heart, inching at his judgment. He ran his hands through his hair, instantly thinking of Eva's falling easily and gently through his fingers. He shook his head to get a grip of himself. Yes, she was utterly different to anyone he had ever met before, yes she was likely the most beautiful woman he had ever laid eyes on, and yes she made something burn inside him that he had never felt before, but, she was practically a Bain. Maybe she had been sent to infiltrate him, to make him think and feel and begin to trust again? Maybe this was all part of a plan? Bains were masters at deception after all. How could he know that she wasn't a fake? His head demanded reason and his jaw tensed with compliance. Yes, she was a fake. Women were naturally better at trickery and deception. He had learned that the hard way in the past. He stood off the wall and resolved to keep it together. He was a professional after all, he'd been dealing with cheats and shams his whole life. People lied and tricked to get what they wanted, and that was just a fact. He walked back into the room where he had sat watching Bain and his crew fumble like children, floundering with no line to cling to. He smiled. He had the best upper hand possible to man. He already knew that Edward, and thus Bain, would roll over and comply rather than lose Eva. He would give Edward that. Despite his actions with Tammy, he genuinely seemed to care for Eva. But that care would consequently be the reason he would lose everything. Those feelings would ruin him and that was something the whole of Rodriguez

Ltd was betting on. Right there was the reason to not ever have any personal vulnerabilities. They could be exploited and taken from you. A knock at the door distracted his from his thoughts and he looked up to see Scott and Cliff loitering at the threshold.

'Entrar,' he beckoned, allowing them both entrance. Cliff spoke first, his tone respectful and careful. Rodriguez clocked his employees bear sized hands held submissively behind his back, the way he always did when talking with people. Cane remembered finding him cage fighting in Cuba; a puppy forced into being a wolf. Good loyal men always had colourful and dark pasts, in his opinion anyway. They just needed someone to take a chance on them. Cliff had been working with Cane now for five years and despite being ferociously loyal, he had never seen Cliff raise a voice, let alone a fist, to anyone. Puppy, Cane thought to himself with a small inner smile, definitely still a puppy.

'That is the girl in her room with the doctor, Sir.' Cane re-perched himself back on the table where he had sat during the camera feed. He smiled at Cliff in thanks.

'Brilliant, Cliff, por favor,' he paused, glancing at Scott discretely, then back to Cliff. 'I take it she seemed...all right?' Cliff shrugged and nodded.

'She's surprisingly tough for a small thing, if you ask me. I've seen some battle scars in my time and I'd say she'll live.'

'Great.' Cane concluded, letting Cliff know he was free to leave. He headed for the door but paused at the handle, lingering.

'Sir?' he asked, quietly. Both Cane and Scott looked over to him, his frame filling the height and width of the frame. Cane nodded, acknowledging his request to further speak.

'Si?'

'The new guy, Pete, he's pretty torn up about earlier. He says he just panicked when she began to move from the camera and he hadn't planned to knock her over. He's a big guy you know, I reckon he just misjudged his strength.' Cliff cleared his throat. 'Think he's pretty worried, Sir, since you so specifically instructed no further harm to come to the lady...and well, I guess he knows what happens to failure here.' His words hung suggestively in the air. Yes, people were punished for failure, but where in the business world were they not? Scott stepped towards Cliff to usher him from the room.

'Cliff, what Mr Rodriguez does with Pete is none of your concern.' He turned the door handle and held his hand out towards the hall, signaling that it was time for Cliff to leave. Cane stayed sat, but called after his giant employee.

'Will you vouch for him, big man?' Cliff turned to look at his boss with question. 'If you'll watch him and keep him right and there are no other incidents,

I'll let this one slide.' Cane paused with realisation. 'I'm feeling oddly charitable tonight.' Cliff's smile appeared and then quickly was retracted back to professionalism.

'Yes Sir, I'll take that responsibility. I'm a fan of second chances, Sir.' To this Cane let out a small laugh of appreciation.

'Yes, you are Cliff, aren't you my man?' There was a small reciprocal twinkle in his eye as Cliff left and Scott closed the door.

'Oddly charitable?' Scott repeated with a straight face, despite the tone of his voice. Cane gave him a knowing stare and turned his attention back to the now blank screen, indicating that the conversation was not to be pursued. He sighed to himself as Scott unplugged cables and he glanced through to the other room where he had sat embracing Eva so tenderly and privately. That feeling of want and heat rushed through him again and he loosened his shirt buttons silently. His traitorous mind replayed the scenes from the alley where his eyes had first met Eva's. He could remember the smell of blood and sweat in the air, the noise of pain from his men and then there, in front of him, a slender and defiant women, her chest heaving and her knuckles raw. She was so strong in mind and yet so aware of her weakness. She was undoubtedly the most beautiful thing he had ever seen, before he even knew how attractive her spirit was. The way she had held his eyes as he had read into her heart. He buried a smile as he recalled her bold retort to him, 'I wouldn't call protecting yourself brave.' Naturally she was correct, but such strength and valor had to be admired, even if she was a Bain. The heat from her body as it pressed into his still burned on his bones as he thought of the shared silent moment earlier. It caused such unnerving in him he barely knew how to keep it under the control of his sensibility.

'Sir?' Scott's voice seemed louder than it should have been, and it brought Cane back to reality.

'Si, Scott?' he asked, trying to shake the feelings.

'You OK?' Scott was Cane's most trusted employee, maybe even the closest thing he had to a friend. Scott had spent years working at his side, observing and deliberating. Their relationship was deep routed, and unlike some of Cane's other workers who were honorably loyal, Scott went beyond that role, to the point of devotion. There was history between them, an act of faith and kindness that had led to a brotherly steadfastness. Scott was not as easily fooled as others in Cane's life. He may not have seen all of Cane's cards, but he had seen enough of them to call him out when he saw a bluff. And he was seeing a bluff now. Cane reprimanded himself, sternly, for letting his feelings get to him. His thoughts quickly rebuked his head and heart. Despite how much he may 'trust' Scott, some things about himself he would never divulge to anyone and this included the

irrational and unexplainable drag he felt toward a strange girl he met only days ago.

'Yes, of course I'm OK. Por qué? Why?' Cane lied, turning to face him and knowing that his face and eyes would show nothing. He had spent years perfecting his defence mechanisms. He was now flawlessly unreadable when he wanted to be, which was almost every minute he was awake. Scott held his blank face for a couple seconds, then either seemingly satisfied or sensible enough not to pursue, he nodded with a small shrug.

'You just seem slightly off your game. It's a strange situation having this girl here and all, maybe it's just that.' He waited for a response. He was off his game. Scott's words were shamefully true. Things inside him that had been put to rest were awakening with no conscious invitation and they needed to go back to the bench where they had been sent to wait out the match years ago.

'I know it's an odd hand to play Scott, having this woman here, but she is too precious to leave anywhere else. She could be the turning point to a very long-awaited win. Lo entiendes? You understand?' Scott nodded, once.

'I understand. I wasn't questioning your motives, Sir.' Cane smiled to lighten the mood.

'I know you weren't, Scott. And I know having her here is a strain and difficulty for all the staff, so I will do my best to move swiftly. She must be quite disconcerting for everyone to be around whilst under such strict instructions.'

'The incident earlier with Wyatt and Williams Sir,' Scott began, referring to the state in which Eva had arrived tonight; beaten and bleeding, 'I'll deal with them, harshly. It was unwise of me to have sent them in the first place. They've been a growing problem, but tonight was just a blatant disregard of orders.'

'Gracias, Scott.' Cane said, knowing he didn't need to add anything to confirm how maddened he'd been by the situation, even if it did work to his advantage for the camera. He would have never let it happen to her purposely, despite the fear-mongering threats. He thought about her time spent in his custody so far and his conscience, what little part that was allowed to feel, panged with self-reproach. Was that the third time she had been attacked and beaten since in his custody? He may be portrayed as a vicious monster to the outside world, and this façade may be a welcome barrier, but he would never actually hurt a woman. His mother had taught him better than that and he knew she would be ashamed of him right now.

'If it helps at all Sir, she got a good few hits in before I arrived.' Cane looked back to Scott, who was now heading towards the door with a handful of cable. He was smiling, despite himself. Cane's eyebrows raised in question. 'I'm pretty sure Wyatt will never have children.' To this Cane smiled and Scott took

the sign as a good time to leave. As the door closed, that smile lingered on his lips and he shook his head slightly. She was a unique one, that was for sure. The door shut fully and once he was alone, he found his smile fading quickly. Her face when he had revealed Edward's indiscretions had been almost too much to watch, and now alone in that same room, he couldn't stop the replay of it etching itself into his memory. Utter heartbreak and betrayal. The tears of sheer loss had fallen from her perfect eyes. He knew the feelings all too well. He was aware that every day he did despicable things, unpardonable actions, but they were the price of business. This was all business, he reminded himself. No matter how beautiful she was, how good at deception she may be, this was in the end, a simple, straightforward business deal. He glanced towards the spot where he had held her needing, yearning body earlier and that heat instantly returned to his chest. He swallowed and closed his eyes from the empty room and its recently made confusing memories. Many had thought to break him in the past and had been disappointed by his severe, uncompromising will. This girl would be the same, whoever's side she was truly on. He would not be used, tricked, played, fooled, any of it. His heart would never win against his mind. He forced the heat from his chest, pushing it away with determination. He was Cane Rodriguez. He had a muti-billion, world-wide industry to run and feelings were an irrational and unprofitable luxury.

CHAPTER FIFTEEN
I must have looked a little surprised.

The next day had been dreadfully slow and unbearable. Surprisingly, the intimate experience with Cane was not as shameful as expected. Instead, those unexplainable moments from the night before were totally overshadowed by a different thought, one that consumed my every minute of the day. I agonized over the information about Edward and Tammy like a fanatic, letting it devour all my emotions and sensations. The day began with rage and temper; ranting and raving to myself as more and more seemingly innocent memories began to come to me. By lunchtime, the thoughts had turned into images of disgusting things; stolen kisses while I was at the bathroom, hot passionate sex in his bed, private gifts and secret moments. From there it was an easy slope to self-pity and blame accompanied by tears and sobbing. By dinner I had become an expert at repeating the cycle. Not being able to address the situation; not being able to hash it out or scream about it all to Ed, was driving me insane. Why had he done it? How long had it been going on? Where had it happened and how many times, how many girls? The questions that would never be answered were running wild in my brain. I was sickened to the point of frenzy, to the point of beginning to look like a crazy woman. It was not relevant that I was no longer in love with Edward. I knew my heart wasn't broken with love-loss, but it was betrayal that was ripping my insides to pieces. By late evening, when Dr Miele came to see me, I was verging on insanity and exhaustion. I hurt all over from being tense and from crying and from the rigid anger. I welcomed the escape of sleep and downed the colourful tables, eagerly awaiting their release.

Day five found me waking to the same repeating crush of emotions. I quickly realised, as I held in the flood of tears, that like all painful things in my life just now, they had to go into the vault. I had to get past this if I hoped to survive here. So, with a few inhales and exhales, my mind took control and shut away all the vivid and conjured up images of Edward and Tammy. The vault that already housed the intricacies and implications of this whole insane deal that I made with Rodriguez, now became home also, to all of Ed and my best friend's lies, cheating and the deceit. It all went to the tomb, every last painful piece of thought or emotion, and it was locked away tightly. As the impenetrable door shut in my head, instant relief swept through me. I knew they would resurface at some point and would be just as unbearable then, but at least for now, I could leave my room and pretend that I was unbreakable and bullet proof again. And that was what I needed right now, more than anything.

The next few days in the house flew away surprisingly fast. The gym and dog walks filled a lot of time, mixed with exploring the house and the gardens. I was in a strange twilight world, one where I existed, but had no effect on the reality around me. Time was beginning to hold no meaning, along with the importance of the day and date. I had no plans, nowhere to be, no one to meet, no job to get to, no appointments to keep. I was vacationing in life, drifting aimlessly from hour to hour, and day to day. What I did have was time though, seemingly endless amounts of empty time. And in that empty time, I thought. Only about safe things, but I thought of the things I had seen and witnessed so far, here in Rodriguez's land. I had not seen my favourite two black shirts since the episode in my bedroom a few days ago. I prayed I would never have to see them again. I could still remember their harsh hands and cold eyes and how much they hated me. I shuddered at the thought of what they may have done to me if Scott hadn't arrived when he did. Rodriguez's words still echoed in my mind, 'deal with them, please'. I still wasn't sure what that had meant, but the lead in my stomach reminded me that Rodriguez was a killer, no matter how handsome and honorable he could seem. And these terrifying thoughts were a good thing, they kept reminding me that despite his normal human side, there was a dark, forbidding shadow lurking ever nearby. He was capable of anything and he had no limits.

It was late afternoon and I had so far today been to the gym and taken the three dogs for a walk. I was becoming very attached to Rosetta, Lilly and Zeus. We spent good quality time together and they were always happy to see me. I had caught Rodriguez watching me from the house sometimes while swimming or walking, but we hadn't spoken, not since the camera day. Despite its outweighing, the thought of what happened between us in that room, still roused feelings I couldn't explain. We had both been so vulnerable for those minutes together, no masks or pretenses. It was odd to have experienced such an intimate moment with someone who was so closed and complex and intimidating...and deadly. It was something I would remember my whole life, but it was also something I didn't want to keep reliving in my thoughts, especially when those thoughts both embarrassed me and made me feel things I shouldn't. Those bizarre moments alone with Rodriguez, probably should have been locked away into the vault with the other painful experiences from that night, but for some reason, they had been allowed to stay free, roaming my mind like a predator.

I wandered down a new hallway, looking at the old pictures and tapestries hung on the walls. I was studying a particularly detailed piece, when my eyes caught an open door to my right. From the small crack, I could see it was a library. Curiosity got the better of me and slowly, I pushed the door open.

It creaked, and I winced.

'Hello?' I called out, timidly, praying Rodriguez was not in here. Thankfully no answer came, and I pushed the door fully open. As I entered the room, my mouth dropped open. It was huge. The floor to roof was jam packed with books; old leather-bound covers, new shiny laminated ones, history books, modern books, fact, fiction, shelves upon shelves of novels and authors. It was a classic monastic library, with rolling ladders, various levels, old oak shelving. It reminded me, like so many other aspects of this place did, of the library in *The Beauty and The Beast*. The thought brought me back to the first day I had arrived at Rodriguez's gates. I had been trying so hard to be brave at that moment, that I had hid the look of awe on my face. Little had I known what lay behind them. I had not seen those gates again, nor any gate or exit since, no matter how far I walked. The estate was huge, and I was very much locked in the middle of it. Coming back to reality, I glanced around to my left where I found a huge old fireplace and a fluffy welcoming rug lying at its hearth. By that, was a beautiful old desk with an organized chaos of books and papers laying on it. As I walked closer, I noticed the different letter heads on some of the papers. Cautiously, I paused to flick through them and confirm my surprise suspicion. They were charity letters to Rodriguez Ltd. I leaned down on the old worn leather seat and began flicking through them. As far as I could tell, the ones with a highlighted tick were the ones that were either being considered or accepted, the rest with no ticks were sat on a separate pile. I glanced at the accepted letters: cancer research, autism, school PTAs, AIDS, homeless, fallen heros, personal plea letters, there were hundreds of them. Whose job was it to go through all this mail? It hadn't even crossed my mind that in the normal world, Rodriguez's company was just that: a normal, thriving, multi-billion-pound company. Of course, they got charity mail, it was one of the biggest and most successful businesses in the world, they of all people had money to give away. My eyes caught a letter with a picture of a high school boy attached to it and I nudged it out slightly. I was pretty sure this would classify as 'snooping', but I wasn't exactly doing any harm or learning anything consequential. With my inner encouragement, I sat, perching on the worn, comfortable seat. The letter was addressed directly to Rodriguez and was written by a woman with joined and loopy handwriting. The word 'thank you' seemed to appear a lot, along with the word 'grateful', and for some reason, they stood out to me more than anything. I had, surprisingly, found myself feeling those same emotions towards Rodriguez on a couple of occasions now and even just thinking about how weird that was, was disconcerting. The letter was catching Rodriguez up on the life of the boy in the photo. He was apparently due to graduate high school this year, he had a place in University and a good job to help him learn values. *'I owe you everything, Mr Rodriguez, you saved my little boy and I shall never be able to thank you enough. I thank God for you every night in my prayers'.* I read that last sentence again. Then again. And again. People *thanked* God for Rodriguez? Was I in an alternate universe? I thought how bizarre it was, that Rodriguez could qualify for such praise and love and yet be wholly eligible for hate and despise also. He must live a confusing life. My mind was turning with thoughts as I lay the letter back down on the desk with a sigh, and while doing so, I instantly realised that I was no longer alone. I jumped up quickly out of the old leather chair as if it had stung me, whipping my head towards the presence watching me. My heart pounded with guilt and fear and if I was being honest, embarrassment. Rodriguez stood just beside the fire place, his hands in his light grey trousers. How had I not heard him arrive? The heat rose in my cheeks with impending dread. Of all people to catch me.

'I'm so sorry,' I began, my hand on my heart. I was talking quickly like a busted school girl and despite being able to hear myself, I couldn't shut up. 'I never meant to snoop, the door was open, and I love libraries and I was just going to take a look around and smell the room, then I saw the photo and I never meant to read it...it just...I just...' I stammered a few times and then finally stopped, quickly realising that Rodriguez hadn't yet said a word. Nor did he make to do so. I sighed in defeat. 'I am sorry. I wasn't doing it maliciously, I swear.' I stood for a couple awkward seconds, awaiting a reaction, but as the seconds ticked on and no flames of wrath engulfed me, I decided to try and make a getaway. Upon my third step towards the door, his deep voice spoke, halting me.

'Miss Eva,' he said gently, taking his hands from his pockets and turning to look at me. His voice was relaxed and calm and showed no sign of anger. I exhaled with relief, not even aware I'd been holding my breath. I turned around, allowing him to address me and as I did, I was able to take him in. He had on a loose white shirt to go with his light suit bottoms. I noted mentally, that light colours always made his skin seem darker and his features even more defined. I liked it. He walked towards the desk and cast a glance at the papers I had been ruffling through, the photo of the teenage boy still lying damningly on the top. He looked back up at me. 'You came in here to,' he paused and rubbed his day-old stubble, *'smell the room?'* He repeated my words with a smile lingering on his lips and his eyes sparkling with amusement. He was apparently in a good mood. I shuffled a little, trying to look away from his searching eyes. I had said that, hadn't I, whilst I was rambling on and trying to talk myself out of trouble. His smiled increased ever so slightly, as if he knew my embarrassed thoughts. I tried to glance away, he was almost unbearable to look at when his lips turned up at the sides and his eyes lit up with interest. I was no longer in denial. A few days ago, I had come to terms with the fact that I was physically attracted to Rodriguez. I had seen him step out of the swimming pool and I had dropped my glass of water to the floor by accident. The glass had knocked against the window, two floors above him and he had looked up to find me standing there, staring. Rather than *me* be the self-conscious one though, he had quickly covered up with a towel and, almost timidly, disappeared into the main house. His reaction to being watched had sealed the deal for me. I had agonised about my attraction to him for the next few days, finally settling on the fact that I *knew* I had been attracted to him from the first moment I had laid eyes on him in the alley. But physical attraction meant nothing. I was physically attracted to George Clooney for goodness sake, but that didn't mean anything was ever going to happen. You could admire a wolf's beauty, but you still wouldn't have one as a pet, right? I just had to continually remind myself of who Rodriguez was, and of what he was capable. Normally, this was easy to do, because at the end of the day, ninety-nine percent of the time, I hated him. When he was in his normal, standoffish, cold manner, I could simply deal with it, if not forget it even existed. It was moments like now though, when he was unusually relaxed and playful, that this lustful, physical attraction of mine was dangerous. And almost impossible to ignore.

'Ummm,' I stammered a little, trying not to look up at him as he awaited a response. 'I like the smell of libraries.' I muttered, seeing another one of his small grins. I wondered what this man looked like when he truly smiled, no inhibitions or reserves. I imagined it to be one of the most deadly, natural phenomenon's to ever exist. He inhaled deeply, closing his eyes, as if putting my statement to the test. I watched him with fascination. He mumbled in his chest with a satisfying noise and my stomach reacted to the sound.

'Sí,' he confirmed, nodding his head. 'you are right, Miss Eva, they do smell good, don't they?' He inhaled again. 'Like leather and wo...'
'Wood,' I interrupted, before he could finish the same word. I had never had anyone else explain the smell with the same words as me before. My eyes found his with surprise. Again, that hint of a grin touched his lips. He pulled the seat out in front of the desk and I took it as my signal to leave, beginning to head for the door.

'Would you like to join me for a while, Miss Eva? I think you would enjoy my afternoon's activity.' His eyebrows were raised at me, invitingly. My head replied in a bellow, shouting 'NO' from the depths of my every thought, yet my adulterous body answered the very opposite. His eyes sparkled again, as if knowing my dilemma. He seemed to enjoy observing them, my dilemmas, the obvious and internal ones. I swallowed. This was not a good idea, yet before I could stop myself, I was walking over to the desk and he was pulling the leather seat out for me to again sit upon. Once down, he pushed me in and dragged a small stool up next to me. His legs were now close enough for me to feel the heat from and as he leaned into the piles of papers, I could have sworn that he knew exactly what he was doing and that he was enjoying doing it. It was torture, make no mistake about it; torture by constant close proximity. 'You already know now,' he paused offering me a knowing look, 'that these are charity letters.' I blushed again. 'I need to sort through them and choose which we can help.' He picked up a pile and handed me some. I must have looked a little surprised.

'You do this *yourself*?' I asked astounded, gawking at the massive piles and then at him. He smiled slightly again.

'It may surprise you, Miss Eva, but I actually enjoy doing this myself. It is one of the very few things that reminds me of the good dinero, the good *money*, can still do.' He handed me a highlighter. 'Tick it if you think it deserves a better look.' I took the luminescent pen, speechless. I looked over to the boxes on the floor with wide eyes.

'Are those all letters to be looked through, too?' Rodriguez glanced at the hundreds of letters and then at me, nodding. 'How do you get through them all?' I asked, shaking my head in disbelief.

'I don't sleep very much,' he offered simply, beginning to read a small letter written on pink paper. I followed his lead and opened an envelope, starting to read. One letter at a time, and with the sun moving across the sky, I began to form three piles- yes, no, and maybe. Rodriguez had no maybe pile, which didn't surprise me at all. I had soon forgot who I was sitting next to, as I immersed myself in people's lives and pleads. There were some funny stories which made me laugh out loud and received an appreciative look from Rodriguez each time. Then there were ones that brought tears and I would sniff as discretely as I could. On those occasions, Rodriguez would cast a sidewards glance at me, sliding the tissue box gently my way. Hours must have passed, and I looked out of the window to see dusk sweeping in. I sat back and yawned. If the afternoon activity had done anything, it had reminded me that I was lucky, no matter what situation I may be in right now. It was only money at stake at the end of the day, right? Ok, well maybe a bit more than just that, but still. I cast my mind back to the day in the camera room where such despair and guilt had taken hold of me, that killing myself seemed the only way to end this whole mess. Now, as I sat here reading about the lives of people who suffered worse, daily, I felt a whole new level of gratitude and positivity. The current letter lying at the top of the pile, was a plea from a father who could not afford to pay for his son's leukemia treatment bills. The treatment would be stopped without further credit. The man had mortgaged his home twice, worked three jobs and used his own bedroom as a guest room to generate rent. He had lost his wife three years previous and now had to balance work, bills, two children and medical demands. I sat dumbfounded in my own thoughts. Money. Money would save this boy's life and fix their whole lives. Surely, that was the importance of having it? To be able to give it away to help others? If Rodriguez was obviously so happy to give his profits away, why then, did he care so much about taking Bain's company. If he was such an open-minded man, in regard to fortune, and cared nothing of power and status, what cause did he have to hate and pursue Bain's livelihood so unyieldingly?

'Es tarde,' Rodriguez said, breaking the silence. I jumped, snapping from my thoughts. 'Sorry, I didn't mean to startle you.' His mouth turned up slightly again. He was a smiler today. I shook my head dismissively, looking to the darkening sky outside. He was right, it was getting late.

'Not at all, I was in my own world.' I replied, internally allocating out my new feelings of gratitude. He looked at me like he knew exactly what my mind had just journeyed through. I wondered whether that had been why he had asked me to join him in the first place. I watched him watching me, realising that his spontaneous invite to stay and help him, might not have been so innocent. Did he mean for me to regain my clarity and perspective, to be able to finally put away the events of the camera night? Was it maybe even to give him the chance to prove that he wasn't all monster? Either way, I was quickly learning that *nothing* was ever as simple as it first seemed with Rodriguez. He began tidying his desk area and I followed suit, watching the letter from the dad slide onto the top of the yes pile. Regardless of his intentions, it felt like kindness, and kindness was not something I was seeing much of these days. Despite all the complicated layers, I had spent the afternoon with the *other* Rodriguez; thoughtful and humble, loose and relaxed. I glanced at his profile and watched his long dark eyelashes as he blinked. I swallowed to myself with realization. This version of Rodriguez was by far more dangerous to me than the cold, ruthless, business version. I could lose my life with one side of him, but with this side, I reckoned I could all too easily lose my heart. And that was a petrifying thought.

'Te gustaría cenar conmigo, Miss Eva?' Rodriguez voice spoke, suddenly and rather boldly. I widened my eyes in response, blatantly showing my shock.

'Me?' I replied, surprise causing my voice to rise a few octaves higher than normal. 'Have dinner with *you?*' I repeated, still holding onto that squeaky pitch. He hinted that smile again. I was like butter when he did that.

'Yes, Miss Eva, if you would do me the honour?' He sat quite patiently, as if he had just asked me to pass him the stapler. There were no tells on his face, except composure. My head, on the other hand, had launched into a full-blown debate, and I mildly recognised that this inner battle was becoming a frequent event. *No Eva, no you do not want to have dinner with this man. You do not want to be alone with him anymore. You do not want his company for an evening. You do not want to get to know him any better. Just say no. It's simple…N.O. Say it now…No, no, no, no…*

'Yes.' I replied, loudly. My rational mind slapped itself in the face, sighing and rolling its eyes. My gut, on the other hand, began to tingle with butterflies, and despite the circus happening inside, I managed to keep a straight face for Rodriguez. I glanced down at the letters of pain and despair and swallowed. *Trust your gut, Eva,* I told myself as he nodded, happily.

'Bien. Good. Dinner is served at six, on the second floor, south wing, room thirty-two.' I looked at him blankly and he twitched his smile again, scratching his chin. 'Do you know that massive old oak cabinet with the squirrels carved into the wood on the legs?'

'The one with the china set from the seventeen-hundreds in it?' I asked, and he nodded, with an impressed raise of the eyebrows.

'Yes, that's the one. Second door passed that, and you'll find my dining room.'

'Ok,' I said, standing up, suddenly very aware again of whom I was sitting next to. 'Six o'clock?' I repeated, awkwardly. *His dining room?* Maybe this wasn't the best idea.

'Sie. Las seis en punto,' he confirmed, with a hint of humour in his eyes. 'And thanks for your help today,' he added, as I backed out towards the door. I smiled and shrugged, feeling pathetically like a goofy teenage girl.

'Had nothing better to do.' I half waved, clumsily stumping my foot off the door frame with a bang and then quickly sliding through it back into the hallway. I leant with my back against the wall, breathing heavily. I rubbed the butterflies in my tummy, ignoring the throbbing in my heel. Why did this feel like a date? And why was I, all of a sudden, panicking about what to wear?

CHAPTER SIXTEEN
Now in a dilemma.

Five-fifty-five found me standing next to the gorgeous, vintage cabinet on the second floor. I looked at my reflection in the glass. I'd found a pair of very expensive, black trousers in my limited cupboard. Normally, they would have been borderline too tight for me, but now, they lay loosely on my hips and dropped to the floor with wide legged turn ups. They made me look tall and shapely, and if I was being honest, I had every intention of taking them with me when…or *if*, I ever left. I looked over my exposed skin for bruises, but they were all practically gone now. Make-up hid the yellowish remnants of, what were originally, shocking abrasions and the only outer proof of bodily damage now was found on my ribs. I had on a loose v-neck, satin top which covered the remaining bruises and I had absolutely no intentions whatsoever of taking that off tonight. The thought of Rodriguez, removing clothing, made me flush and I self-consciously pulled the hem of my top down, ensuring there was no viewable midriff. The pulling down action though, made my v-neck plunge lower at the front and reveal cleavage. I quickly jerked it back up again, embarrassed and blushing all at the same time. I stood for a few seconds looking in the glass, locked in a massive in a dilemma; my top could not go up and come down at the same time. That was it, I just needed to go back and change. That was the only solution. I went to turn around and leave, but I was quickly interrupted by the door, two down from the cabinet, opening. I jumped to attention, trying to stand as un-awkwardly as I physically could. Thankfully, it was only a waiter, dressed in a waistcoat and a white cloth draped over his arm. He cleared his throat and looked at me.

'Mr Rodriguez asked me to tell you, to either, *'go back and change now'*, or…' he paused slightly and cleared his throat, 'or to *'hurry up and come in, as you look just perfect'*. My face couldn't hide my mortification. It burst out of me in a deep, hot red and the waiter lowered his head politely, although I was sure I saw a smile as he did. Could Rodriguez see me? I looked around as if expecting to uncover some hidden camera, pointed directly at me. Naturally, I couldn't see anything. My life was one big string of embarrassing moments, leading up to the next humiliation. I groaned at myself and quickly turned, following after the waiter. I yanked my top straight contemplating what was worse; the fact that I looked like the vainest person in the world, or that fact that I looked like the most nervous. We passed through the door and entered in to just what I should have expected- a huge room. It was empty, except for a massive, long dining table. A big old fire place sat to the side and weathered historical pictures hung on the walls. Stood at the open burning logs, was Rodriguez. His back was to me and he had one hand resting on the sill of the blazing fire pit. I could see by the way his dark shirt sat on his body, just how muscular he was, and I felt my stomach tighten in response. The fire embers glowed on him, turning him into a glorious, golden statue. I flushed, despite myself, and then quickly tried to get control of my emotions before he turned around. The door closed loudly behind me and Rodriguez spun instantly to find me standing, timidly, at the entrance. He eyed me, very obviously, and I could see and feel his deep stare rolling over each part of my body. It was the most uncomfortable feeling, knowing that he was analysing me, but not knowing what his conclusions were. Not that I cared, of course.

'Te ves hermosa,' he said, with a small head incline. 'I am not too sure what all the fuss what about.' My face deepened its colour in response and I was grateful for the dimmed lighting. Normally when someone called me beautiful, or ever paid me a compliment, I would knock it away and joke it off, but for some reason, when Rodriguez uttered anything close to flattery, I melted. It was pathetic, but uncontrollable. I swallowed passed my dry throat, quickly composing myself and began to walk towards the table.

'Well, if someone wasn't so obviously judgmental, maybe I would have had less to worry about.' I shot back, calling him out on his staring. I stopped a few feet away from him, holding my head high. 'Not that I actually care what you think of me, of course.' I smiled politely and offering him a small head incline in hello. To my utter surprise, his already gorgeous face broke out into a full, wholehearted smile. It filled his whole countenance and displayed his perfect white teeth. Even more surprisingly, dimples appeared on his slightly stubbled cheeks and changed his entire appearance. He had dimples? He shook his head with a laugh.

'Miss Eva, you are the most intriguing person I think I have ever come across.' He laughed to himself a little more, before walking over to meet me at the table. 'And its maybe time that you started calling me Cane.' I must have morphed into looking dumfounded or appalled, but whatever he saw, it made him laugh again. I'd had nothing more than a hint of human emotion from the man in days, and already within three minutes of tonight, he had laughed twice, sincerely. He was an enigma, a complete paradox to me, and one that I was sure I'd never fully understand. But he was the mystery, who now wanted me to call him by his first name, his *actual* name. Not the last name I'd grown to hate, or the name that preceded the legend. His correct, birth-given, human name. I stood, torn, watching him. Was I ready to admit that he was a real-life boy with feelings?

'Now who's staring?' he asked playfully, pulling out a seat for me at the corner of the table and signaling for me to join him. 'It's just a name, Miss Eva,' he added, as he held out his hand towards my chair. I walked to the seat and sat down, still silent. I was unsure what the implications of a proper name were…but they felt very personal, too personal for me to be using. Yes, he was attractive and sexy and confident and rich and powerful and lustfully handsome…*but*, he was still a cold, hardened, criminal, regardless of what he wanted me to call him. You could call a shark a cute little kitten if you wanted for goodness sake, but it's always going to be a shark, which would bite you as soon as it was hungry with no hesitations. I sat down in the luxuriously, padded chair and he sat down in the seat at the other side of the corner. If I stretched my legs beneath the table, even slightly, I would be touching him. Naturally, I locked my ankles together and slotted them underneath my seat, as far away as possible. As soon as he was sat, a waiter appeared and poured his drink for him, then did the same for me. Before the drinks had even finished being served, another waiter appeared with soups and placed them down gently before us. I felt like I was royalty, everything brought before I even knew I wanted it.

'Do you eat like this every night?' I asked, incredulously, looking hungrily at the soup and newly appearing bread rolls. Rodriguez smiled again, placing his napkin on his lap. I followed suit.

'Certain people believe that it is my…*responsabilidad*, to be seen eating this way every night. I am an influential person with people watching me all the time.' I didn't miss that he waited for me to start before he picked up his cutlery. It was just another sneak peek at his impeccable manners. I dipped my polished spoon into the smooth and divinely smelling liquid and put it to my mouth as elegantly as possible. It was heavenly, of course.

'Seriously, every night?' I asked again, still trying to process that someone could eat like this seven days a week. 'You never just fancy sitting on the sofa in your lounge pants with a bag of popcorn?' Maybe it was my tone, or my bluntness, but my question sent Rodriguez into full laughter mode. He put his spoon down and titled his head backward to let a full, healthy laugh out. It was so strange to see, that it made me laugh too. The sound was like waves and sunshine and candy floss, all rolled together. My arm hairs began to lift from my skin in response to it and I felt its boom reverberate deep inside me.

'Miss Eva, of everything that you have seen me do, *this*…' he waved his hands around at the table, 'is the thing that surprises you the most?' He laughed again and then turned his body to face me. 'Is there anything else that you find surprising, that you wish to address me about?' His chuckle faded, but his smile lingered, and his dark eyes danced with complete interest. I cleared my throat.

'Well, I've only seen you laugh three times since I've been here, and you don't exactly smile much more than that. That surprises me.' It was maybe more of a personal question than he had been anticipating, because his aforementioned smile faded rather quickly whilst his eyes clouded.

'Well, Miss Eva, it is a lonely life and one that requires a lot of sacrifices. I do not always have a lot to smile or laugh about.' He took another sip of soup and I watched him with an odd feeling. Was it pity? Was I feeling *pity* for the man who tried to murder my father and who was trying to ruin my fiancé's family? I studied him as he took another mouthful. Damn it, yes, annoyingly it was pity and maybe even some sadness too. For goodness sake, what was wrong with me? Where was my hate and my loathing when I needed it? I slowly took another mouthful of soup and decided, that since he seemed to be in such an open and frank mood tonight, I'd push my luck with some more questions.

'Why are you single, Mr Rodriguez?' I posed, as nonchalantly as possible. He had obviously not expected that question and he almost choked on his soup. It brought the faded smile back to his face though and his eyes met mine. They lingered as if searching me for something, honesty maybe?

'Call me Cane, please? And if I am being truthful, Miss Eva, I simply just have not met the right one. And finding someone who is genuine in my life is… *no es fácil*, not easy.' He took a drink from his glass and watched me over the rim.

'But you have plenty of offers and opportunities, right?' He smiled, deeply, starting to enjoy himself.

'If you are asking me whether I do ok with women, then the answer to that strangely personal question, is sí, yes. If, you are asking me whether I have lots of women who throw themselves at me with money signs and diamond rings flashing in their eyes, then the answer would still be, si.'

'What about before you were who you are now, though?' I continued, feeling the curiosity grow inside of me. I took a bite of bread to try mellow myself out.

'I had to step into this role at a very young age. When my parents died, I was left to run a business that came with many layers and complexities and with very few people I could trust. There was no time to develop relationships or to continue with the ones from my previous life.' Rodriguez finished his soup and very quickly the bowls were taken away.

'You don't think it's a waste, that you have so many opportunities in this life, and yet, you have no one to do them with?' I took a drink and watched him sit back in his chair, locking his fingers together. I was bordering on too personal here now and I knew it, yet I couldn't help but push my luck.

'If by opportunities, you mean *dinero*, well money means nothing to me at all.'

'Money means nothing to you because you have it.' I countered, 'but, no, I meant more like opportunities *created* by having money.' I sipped my drink and watched him for his reactions. 'Some people will never even know some of the things you are able to do in your life.' He nodded in agreement and sat up, his eyes fixing onto mine intently.

'What about you then, you are practically in the same position as me, what do you feel are suitable opportunities?' He kept his stare, obviously now trying to push my buttons back.

'I don't know what you mean by 'the same position'?' I asked, sensing a slight shift in the tone of the conversation.

'You have all of Edward-dear's money. What do you do with it?' If he had been angling for a reaction, then he got one. I *hated* being called a money grabber. Ed and I had argued more over money than anything else in our whole relationship. He wanted to give it to me, and I didn't want to take it.

'If you did your homework properly, Mr Rodriguez, you would know that my bank accounts do not hold any of the money from Bain Enterprises. Nor really any money at all in fact. I don't take any of Ed's wealth, because I know where the profits are coming from. I have a *job*, one I work hard at.' I paused. 'Onc I've probably lost by now, actually.' By my last comment, I was a little louder and firmer than I had planned to be, but Rodriguez seemed unruffled by my tone.

'What do you mean, do my homework properly?' he questioned, repeating my words with raised, inquisitive eyebrows. Watching him closely, I was beginning to realise that he was actually enjoying himself. I sighed with frustration.

'I knew who you were the second I laid eyes on you. I know who your brothers are, I know who your parents were. I know where you were born and your most preferred business strategies. I know that you studied martial arts for nineteen years and took boxing for seven. I know what Spanish village you come from and where you like to holiday. I know it all, because I was made to learn it all when I was young.' I was a little mad now as I recited the drilled-in education of Cane Rodriguez, all the wasted years spent studying our enemy. I stared at him, crossing my arms defensively. 'Yet, you didn't know who I was in that alley. You didn't know I was my dad's daughter or Ed's fiancé. You didn't know I was a fighter, that I trained in martial arts for longer than you, or that I'm a teacher, or that I've never leeched off Ed, not in the whole time we've been together. How have you managed to make it so far in this world and not even know anything about the people you supposedly hate so much?' Rodriguez nodded with a slight firmness and then shrugged, and I could see a sharpness developing in his dark eyes.

'I pay other people to know it for me,' he replied, a chill creeping into the room. I watched him, and he watched me, both now waiting for the other to say something that would blow the whole night up in a flame of arguments and disputes. The tension was now there, palpable, it just needed a spark to ignite it. I held my hard stare at him; the infuriating, confident, smug ass. Rodriguez sat forward slowly and took another sip from his glass, then placed it back down again. I caught a glimpse in his eye, just as he began to speak, and it sparkled like a schoolboy up to mischief. 'And I do actually know some things about you, Miss Eva...' he offered, pausing. I raised my eyebrows in questioning challenge, awaiting his almighty knowledge. 'I knew that your fiancé was cheating on you.' My mouth dropped open, literally, fully open as if my jaw had snapped. I was stunned into silence, something that didn't happen often. Had he just said the words I thought he had? Surely my mind was playing tricks? Of all the selfish, hurtful and manipulative things to say...I glared at him, straight in his arrogant eyes, and just as I was about to erupt with anger, I saw the flash of humour blaze behind his pupils. He was teasing me! The world renowned, soulless and immoral warlord was *teasing* me like a child. Something about that knowledge instantly took the sting from his words and I shook my head slowly, my eyebrows still halfway up my forehead. I picked up my napkin, which was all I could find quickly, and threw it at him.

'I-can't-believe-you-just-said-that!' I yelled through my laughing. I was still shaking my head in disbelief and Rodriguez burst, apparently unable to contain himself anymore. He erupted into a howling laughter that filled the whole room. The napkin I had thrown at him lay on his place mat and he put his head on it as he continued to roar with amusement. My mouth was still wide open, but was finding it very hard to not smile. He so obviously found the situation hilarious. For some reason, when he spoke about Ed's transgressions, they seemed...less, easier, somehow even comical? I continued to watch him as he shook his head at himself. Where were these supposed manners of his now? Every time I thought he was going to stop, he looked at me, saw my mouth still hanging open and began to laugh harder. The whole room filled with the sound of his addictive and beautiful laugh and despite the inappropriateness of words, I soaked up the feeling of his joy, storing it somewhere deep inside me, like I would somehow, unbeknownst to me, need it later. He wiped his eyes with his napkin and handed mine back to me. I snatched it playfully and shook my head at him

'*Lo siento*,' he finally pushed out, holding his hands up in surrender. 'I'm sorry. That was *awful* taste, but you just kept going on and on about how I knew nothing of you and I just couldn't help myself, luchadora.' He smiled again, amused by his wit. 'I really am sorry.'

'You're not forgiven that easily, Mr Rodriguez.' I replied, noting the use of my apparent new nickname. I placed my napkin back on my lap.

'*Por favor llámeme Cane*,' he repeated gently, his accent turning me to putty. 'It's Cane, please?' I slowly nodded, reluctantly, to which he half smiled. 'How about we make a deal?' he proposed, leaning forward towards me. He moved his feet and I felt the brush of his knee against mine. 'How about for tonight, we don't talk about anything to do with business, nothing at all to do with our history. We are just two strangers out for dinner?' He held my eyes, reading me. He was always reading me, and it made me feel like whenever he spoke, he had an underlying meaning. A meaning that only he understood, only he got.

'That sounds like a good idea...Cane?' I replied carefully, holding out my hand as if newly introducing ourselves. He shook it without hesitation and I tried to not pay any attention to the feel of him on my fingers. He nodded in confirmation.

'Eva?' he questioned in reply, to which I gave a small nod.

'*Es un placer conocerte, Cane.*' I said, in my atrociously broken and unpracticed Spanish, hoping I was actually saying 'it is a pleasure to meet you, Cane.'

'*Usted* habla español muy bien,' he replied, with a nod and raised glass towards me. I laughed in embarrassment.

'I got, 'Spanish' and 'good' from that I'm afraid.' His smile stayed put.

'I said that you speak Spanish very well.' To this I laughed, shaking my head in disagreement. Obviously not.

'If by *very well* you mean, asking for the bill and where the toilet is, then I am practically a native.' He chuckled and took a drink from his expensive glass.

Three courses later found us at nine-forty-five p.m. The night had flown past. If we both pretended that we were strangers and avoided any topics that led back to our reality, then three hours could disappear in an enjoyable night. And all too easily. Cane was a funny man. Confident and sharp, yet humble and gentle when required. He was attentive and encouraging, whilst managing to seem like he was really listening. We talked about family, pasts, memories, embarrassing stories, holidays and future hopes. We talked through dessert and coffee and passed our far too many drinks. By the time the clock chimed eleven-thirty, we were relaxed and comfortable at the table, as if we had been friends our whole lives. I hadn't thought about my top in hours and Cane's first two buttons of his shirt were undone, the most casual I had seen him since I arrived. We both knew that it had to end at some point and that we couldn't stay locked away in this room forever. Our ceasefire was going to end, and it was rolling towards us with more speed than I liked. I yawned, placing my hand over my mouth and Cane copied subconsciously. I smiled at him and eventually uttered the words neither of us wanted to say.

'It's late, hey?' I whispered, with almost feelings of remorse. I actually didn't want this to end. Limbo land had been kind of nice. Not only had I been able to socialise again, but I also didn't want to have to go back to hating him and fighting with him. I didn't want to have to wake up tomorrow and pretend none of this had happened. But the man I had got to know tonight didn't actually exist, not in my world anyway, and we both knew it. Cane nodded, slowly.

'Yes, I am afraid it is, and I have meetings all day tomorrow.' I exhaled and shuffled my seat back with reluctance. Cane quickly got to his feet and pulled my chair out the rest of the way for me. I stood up and straightened myself, thanking him and turning towards the door. He walked with me, close enough to know that he could touch my hand any second. We reached the door, and both paused. What an odd time-stopping night it had been. I had found pleasure and common ground in a place where I would never have thought it possible.

'Well, thank you for dinner.' I said, slightly awkwardly. I was very aware that if this had been a real date, in the real world, it had gone so well that I would have been expecting a *real* goodnight kiss. That was a strange and unnerving feeling to have.

'Thank *you,* for dinner, Eva. It's been a long time since I've enjoyed my evening so much. And laughed so much, too.' He looked me in my eyes and my breathing began to slow. He was so stunning and so charming, and it was easy to pretend that this attraction was fine, when he was staring at you with those dark and penetrating pools. It was easy to ignore the fact that the floor was moving...or that Cane was moving, of the fact that we were definitely getting closer. What was happening? My mind began to register an impending option...was he going to kiss me? His hand reached up and moved a piece of hair from my face. The touch of his finger, like each time before, felt like fire lingering on my skin even after it had gone. He was breathing slowly, and his full lips were moving towards mine. I knew that if they touched me, there would be no going back. I knew that if his mouth came anywhere near mine, I would never be able to reverse it. My traitorous body yearned for him though, and despite my head screaming its caution, I was moving closer too, moving forward. His hand slipped around the base of my neck and his thumb began to gently hold my face. I felt on alight, like my whole body was burning. He was inches away and his eyes were still locked firmly onto mine like I was the only thing in the universe. Surely, if he could read me so well, he could see my panic? Was I showing any panic though? Maybe my eyes looked exactly like his did right now; full of lust, desire, want, all centimeters away. I could feel his breath on my lips now, the heat from his skin beginning to prickle my face. He was so close. *What was I doing? What was I doing?* His eyes danced to my mouth and then back to my face as the distance between us vanished. I stood paralysed, torn between my head and my heart. *WHAT WAS I DOING?* Time ran out, and his lips grazed mine, releasing a spark like I had never felt before. It slammed wildly through my entire body, just like an electric shock, then threw me backward, breaking the connection and bringing reality back in with a crack. My hand flew to my lips where they had touched his. I didn't break my stare from his, despite the million emotions coursing through my body, and I watched as his eyes filled with the same mixture of conflicting reactions; anger, frustration, excitement, curiosity and I was sure I could somewhere inside him, disappointment, lingering there in the back.

'I can't,' I whispered, half appalled, half apologetic. 'I can't do *this*.' I pulled my eyes away from his and reached for the door handle.

'Eva,' his voice was soft and laced with a new emotion. It stopped me dead. 'Quedarnos un poco más Eva, *stay longer*,' he pleaded, quiet and sincere. I dared a look back at him and his deep, intoxicating eyes. His hand was reaching for me and as much as I wished this could all be easy and fun, it was far from. This was no one night stand where I could do the naughty and then sneak out the next morning never to see or hear from the stranger again. He was Cane Rodriguez, for crying out loud. Edward's face appeared in my mind and my eyes began to fill. Yes, he'd betrayed me, but it didn't mean I had to do it back, and with the man he hated more than anyone in the world. I glanced at his outstretched hand again and wondered briefly what it would be like to know that it was genuine, to know that was it safe and real and that the brewing I felt inside, he felt too. I bit- my lip hard and then shook my head, opening the door.

'I'm sorry, I just can't,' I breathed, and practically ran from the room, as fast as my shaking legs would take me. I sped passed the oak cabinets and its judging squirrels, through the labyrinth of stairs and halls, until I was at last at my room. I needed privacy, I needed to sort things out, I needed to figure out what the hell had just happened. The door slammed behind me with relief and I flopped onto the bed, picking up the blanket I had inherited the night I had fallen asleep at the lake. I pulled it over me and kicked off my shoes. I knew that I was attracted to Cane. I *knew* that. But now I knew that I got on with him, that we could laugh and connect in a way I hadn't done with anyone in years. I ran my hand through my hair in confused frustration. But I was an idiot if I thought Cane wasn't playing a game. To sleep with Edward Bain's fiancé, willingly, now that would be a cheap shot, wouldn't it? It would be the ultimate sting in revenge. The thought made me instantly mad at myself. I was obviously being manipulated, played. Yet...I couldn't quite shift the look I'd seen in his eyes as he'd asked me to stay. I couldn't shift the image of his hand held out for me to take, the invitation to take a chance. It hadn't seemed an act. I lay back, growling at myself. *Wise up, Eva.* I shook my head vigorously. *He is a master manipulator,* I lectured myself, *he eats girls like you for breakfast.* I rolled over and looked at the clock, it was just after midnight. *Never again,* I promised, closing my eyes to etch the thought firmly into my brain. *Guard up, girl, just like dad taught you.*

CHAPTER SEVENTEEN
No bankable odds.

The slam of the door echoed around the now very empty room, and made the loneliness seem more entire. The fire crackled behind him, dancing for an audience that was no longer there. He stood facing the old oak door as if still hoping it would reopen and her beautiful smile would appear through it again. But the seconds passed, and it stayed shut. It was another closure on yet another missed opportunity in his life. He exhaled and slowly dragged himself back to the table to collect the remainders of his drink. He carried it over to the fireplace, where he stood watching the distracting colours stretch and reach for the air. This was a dangerous game to be playing, he told himself firmly. She was the means to an end, not the path to lasting happiness. He swallowed the final dregs of liquid and with a flare of rage, threw the crystal into the fire place, smashing it to a million shards. The flames reared and roared with the disturbance, echoing what he felt internally. Exhausted, he stumbled to the arm chair and dropped into its soft, cushioned embrace. The grandfather clock began to chime twelve-fifteen and he knew that he should go to bed, that he had early meetings tomorrow, but he was paralysed by the feelings in his body. He had wanted her to stay with him so badly that it concerned him, greatly. When had he last allowed himself to want something so strongly, something that he had no actual way of ensuring? She may be the centre of a business deal, but with Eva, the woman, there were no bankable odds; no computer-generated statistics of success verses failure, no predictable outcome. As a matter of heart, she couldn't be further from a business transaction if she tried. It was madness to invest anything in her with no guarantee of return. Basic business. He rubbed his tired and heavy eyes, instantly seeing her face behind his lids; her soft skin, deep consuming blue eyes, her full lips...his lips barely touching hers. His finger went to his mouth, the sensation of her on him still lingering there. He sighed loudly, letting his head drop back to the chair. She was perfeccion... perfection. He didn't need to say it out loud, he had already lost himself to her and he knew it. He could fight it, he could hide it, he could deny it, but the burning and longing that was consuming his every waking minute, would not be silenced anymore. He had tried that angle and it wasn't working. He glanced over to the table where her place setting still lay. Echos of her laughing at his jokes and playing with strands of her hair as she talked to him, loitered in his forethoughts.

'*No te dejes llevar por las emociones, Cane!*...get a grip on yourself!' *he yelled to no-one, shaking his head hard.* You are a monster and she will never trust you. *Yet, his mind countered, replaying her nerves and self-consciousness at the start of the night, her smile and engaging eyes and the way she breathed as he tried to kiss her. It all shouted otherwise to him, all chipped away at his bitter certainty. Maybe, was the word that was torturing him, over and over like a broken record of hope. Maybe it wasn't all a game. Maybe, just maybe is was real. And that 'maybe', was what he couldn't let go of.*

CHAPTER EIGHTEEN
It was harmless fun.

I got back to the house with Rosetta, Lilly and Zeus after a long walk in the warm, morning sun. It was close to two p.m. already and my gym clothes were still damp. Parked in the driveway was a movers-van, not a huge one, just big enough for a few things. Boxes were being shifted inside by black shirts and I walked casually past, instantly noting the writing marked on every lid, 'Room 27'. I squinted to check I'd read it right. Yes, room twenty-seven. *My* room, was room twenty-seven. I followed the boxes at a faster pace, heading closer to my door. I got there at the same time as a black shirt who was dropping off a smaller package. He acknowledged me with a slight nod, then left the room. Once inside, I saw five other boxes already on the ground, all marked up with the same. I bent down to open one with curiosity and was interrupted by Canes second in command, clearing his throat by the door. He passed me an envelope.

'What is all this, Scott?' I asked him, taking the letter and looking around with confusion. He smiled slightly and shrugged, leaving the room in silence. I quickly opened the letter and found a folded, single sheet of paper with neat and perfect handwriting on it. There were only a few words on the page, but it might have well been a sonnet, the way my heart reacted.

Eva,
I figured that you may want some of your clothes and belongings if we are to avoid you standing outside the dining room for so long next time.
Cane

My eyes widened, and my pupils dilated with initial excitement. Was Cane flirting? I kind of shamefully liked it, acknowledging what it did to my insides. Quickly though, that emotion was replaced with guilt and confusion, and for all the same old reasons. I ripped opened the nearest box, which happened to be the small one I'd seen the black shirt put down. As the card tore away, the contents of a familiar make-up drawer came into view. I picked up a mascara, convinced it couldn't be mine, only for my fingers to feel the teeth marks at the bottom of the tube from where I constantly placed it in my mouth to hold. It was mine. Tops, bottoms, shoes, jackets, hats, cosmetics, books, DVDs. It was all mine and my whole flat was pretty much here. The smell of home had begun to spread into the room the more things I opened and my stomach both panged for delighted in its scent. The mess began to increase also, and the empty and bare space that was room number twenty-seven, began to look just like home. I put my hand over my mouth with a strange sensation of happiness, I had familiar and safe things around me and it spread a warm comfort into my bones. Yet, as always, my joy was short lived, and my head kicked in. All too quickly, a sense of foreboding began to push away the snug and homely ease. This felt permanent now. Room twenty-seven suddenly felt much more long-term. I swallowed, trying to ignore my brain and its constant nagging. I picked up the single sheet of paper again and read through Cane's note again, more slowly and carefully, registering the final few words, 'next time'. *Next time* I joined him for dinner? There wasn't to be a next time. I'd decided that already. Still, Cane did not give up easily, I could imagine him conquering me in record days would be an impressive feat, even for him. I put his letter down. It concerned me how quickly this man could draw such strong feelings from me, mostly against my will too. With a quick thought, I grabbed the box of books and began pulling them out. Surely it would be here? As I thought it, the glossy cover of the magazine that lay on my coffee table came into view. I grabbed it with both hands and pulled it out towards my body, as if it was the answer to everything. My fingers had begun to tremble slightly, knowing that the last person to hold this magazine would have been Edward...his cheating, yet comfortable and familiar hands. I instantly flicked to the centre pages, desperate to see something that felt like steady, something that felt normal and right. And there we were, I saw Ed's face immediately. I opened the pages fully and a note dropped out onto my lap. I put the magazine down and opened the paper up, recognising the handwriting instantly.

My dear sweet Eva,
If for some reason you make it back here, I'm hoping this is one thing you will take with
you or look at. Seeing you on camera yesterday broke my heart. I am so sorry that my life
has put you in this position. I never meant for you to ever be hurt by any of it, I only ever
wanted to look after you. What you've been told, the things about the other girls, Eva,
they meant nothing, and it was a long time ago. I'm sorry I hurt you. Rodriguez is a
snake and a liar, do not trust him at all. I will get you out of this, I'll make it all better,
I'll do anything it takes. Just know that I have always loved you and you are my family.
Be strong my baby, I will find you. Always yours,
Edward.

Not quite the same reaction the previous letter I'd just read got, but it received a reaction all the same. Tears dripped from my eyes and my nose began to run. When I thought of Ed, all these feelings flooded into me that I couldn't process: love, guilt, sorrow, sadness. I wished so desperately that none of this had happened. But if it hadn't, my dad would probably be dead. And what would I do with my previous life now anyway, I thought to myself with sobering reason? Be with Edward and play house? Plan our wedding? So much had changed and I suddenly realised, that despite everything, I was already on my way to forgiving Edward. I felt a lot of strong things toward him still, but hurt and anger didn't really seem to be in the mix anymore. That truth spoke volumes to me. Surely, I should still be livid at him, should still be heart-brokenly gutted? But, I wasn't. Simple. I had no real heightened emotions at all, actually. I realised that the whole cheating situation was now almost just a fuzz of mediocre feelings. I dropped Ed's letter to the floor next to Cane's. They were polar opposites in everything to me, yet I was somehow so deeply attached to both of them. I exhaled loudly looking through the window to the blue sky. A swim, that's what I needed, and in my own costume too.

The rush of the water and the concentration required for me to breathe properly with my healing ribs, was just perfect to distract me from my confusing thoughts. I stood at the side of the pool holding my towel, my chest still rising and falling from the laps. There were no answers to be had for my achy heart, nothing decisive or conclusive, just more questions and unknowns. I felt like a sitting duck, helplessly awaiting whatever oncoming fate loomed ahead and with no idea where it would lead me. How was I supposed to deal with everything when I didn't know where I would be in even an hour's time, let alone any kind of future? Cane had just delivered all my clothes, that felt like a pretty permanent gesture. Was I to be here that long? I slipped my bottoms on over my almost dry suit then I pulled my vest over my shoulders. As I did, I suddenly noticed Cane standing at the windows a few floors up. How long had he been there? He made no attempt to hide that he had been watching me, nor any move to stop doing so. He inclined his head at me though, just enough to be seen. My first reaction was a smile, but I quickly retracted it, my mind schooling me into sense. I pulled my vest down and tied my bottoms, slipping my feet into my flip flops and I could feel him still watching me. I wondered if I'd ever get used to it, the feeling of his eyes on me. I cast one more, quick glance at him before I clicked out of the pool room, quickly saying hello to the maid that I often saw there. She smiled at me and carried on folding towels, unaware of my urgency to leave. Cane stood erect and unmoving, his statue crystal clear in my mind as I left the pool area. The sun was beating through the glass and landing on him like fire. He looked strong and powerful and immortal and his eyes burned dark and deep. I walked from the west wing towards my room to get showered and unpacked, trying to shrug off Cane's annoyingly lingering silhouette. The idea of setting up my room like it was home, was a little exciting, but also a little weird. The same question repeated in my head, how long was I going to be living here? I knew exactly, to the hour, how long I had *already* been here, that tally was constant and apparently never ending. Two weeks, five days and seventeen hours, had come and gone in a whirlwind of fear and pain…and other confusing emotions. My feet had already touched the first step before I heard their voices. I had been so lost in thought that I hadn't seen them talking at the top of the staircase. I tried to back away unnoticed, but it was too late, and I felt the surge of panic and adrenaline rush through my blood as I quickly began to retreat. I'd made it two and a half weeks without meeting Cane's notorious brothers, but my run of good luck was about to end, and they bound down the stairs, two at a time, after me. I commenced a walk-run in the other direction, aware that it wasn't very brave or confident looking, but if I could make it to the next hallway then I could sprint flat out and try make it the other way around to my room, the only safe haven I felt I had. I could feel my palms begin to sweat as I heard them closing in and before I was even near escape, I was grabbed roughly from behind and placed with some force against the wall. It knocked the wind out of me with sharp pain and I looked desperately each way for company. With dismay, I quickly realised we were totally alone. *Get in control, Eva*, I slapped myself, trying to slow my breathing. *At least don't look like a scared little girl.* I instantly put my brave face on and locked my jaw.

'Well, look what we have here,' Elias began, moving in to sniff me. I backed up further into the wall, away from his prying nose. I think it was the first time I'd been so casually sniffed by a human being. 'We have been desperate to bump into you for weeks now,' he smiled, widening his eyes with delight.

'Are we in a rush for something, tesoro?' Andreas asked cockily, calling me 'treasure' and looking me up and down with a playful grin. I kept silent as he surveyed me, trying to hold my head high. 'Well at least now I can understand why he's kept you around for so long. The staff talk said you were pretty, but they did you no justice.' He was smiling mischievously and glancing at Elias for confirmation.

'She is a stunner,' he agreed to his brother, as if I wasn't even there. 'Do you know who we are, princesa?' he asked, leaning closer to my face and inhaling deeply. What was it with the smelling? Andreas laughed.

'Of course, she knows who we are, Elias, all ladies know who we are…especially the hot ones.' They both laughed, apparently finding each other hilarious. I tried to stand up off the wall, despite feeling very boxed in. I needed my feet securely on the ground if I was going to survive this encounter. Cane was one ball game, but his younger brothers were renowned for being boisterous, flirtatious, reckless, and rash. All muscle and looks, no brains or discipline. Seeing them now, up close for the first time, their descriptions were not far off. Elias was the middle child, two years younger than Cane, making him thirty. He was built big and solid, the product of great genes and endless hours in a gym. He had dark hair and dark eyes like Cane, but with straight, bushy thick black eyebrows which gave him a sterner appearance. His features were nowhere near as striking as Cane's, but he was an attractive man still, so much so, that if I saw him on the street, I, and most other girls, would turn around to watch him. But he was the type of guy that would take you on a whirlwind ride and then leave you high and dry for the next better thing, constantly seeking the next buzz. They were both thrill seekers with too much money and not enough restraint. Elias was the ring leader of the two brothers and that was obvious. He always got his way and had grown accustomed to that in life, rarely accepting 'no' as an answer. And I'm sure some found this an admirable quality, if you were say, a charity fundraiser or a person determined to fulfill his dreams, but this trait in a man who had no real morals or prudent judgment was more frightening. I wasn't especially scared of him, but I was sensibly hesitant when it came to playing his games. He believed in following no rules, unless they were set by his eldest brother. I remembered his file always said, 'do not approach alone' and listed multiple brawls he and Brice's men had been involved in. The caution had stuck with me my whole life, and yet now, here I was, completely alone, with him and his evil partner in crime. I turned my attention to Andreas, the youngest of the Rodriguez brothers, aged twenty-eight. He was the least handsome of them all, but that only meant he was just more human looking. He had the same dark hair and eyes, but fashioned a more Spanish-pop-singer look and a very out-there fashion sense. Like his brother, Elias, he was successful with the ladies and always had a tiny woman attached to his arm wherever you saw him in pictures. His tight, grey v-neck bulged over his biceps and his thigh muscles pulled at his skinny jeans. He was currently the least strong of the three men, but his youngest child syndrome made him overcompensate with daring. He would do almost anything Elias told him, and Elias would do everything Cane told him. The two were definitely more the 'face' of Rodriquez Ltd than their elder brother and were consistently photographed and spotted in magazines and social media. I was unclear on just how much work they were actually involved in and how close they were with Cane, but I knew for sure, that despite their family charm and looks, their rowdy and unruly attitudes were not to be underestimated. Cane was one kettle of fish; he was clever and dangerous and calculated, but these two were in another league of unrestrained and unbridled impulsiveness. They did not have the business politics to deal with or the stress of success weighing them down. They had bottomless pockets, no limited restrictions and zero parents for guidance. Thus, they were free to amuse themselves in any way they pleased.

'Where are you off to so quickly then?' Andreas asked, running his finger down my arm. I pushed it away quickly and he laughed, enjoying the new game. 'She *is* a feisty one,' he said, obviously agreeing with what he'd been told, no doubt by Cane and his stupid nickname.

'Since you're here with us, Miss Mack,' Elias began, moving very closely in front of me, 'podemos llamarte, Eva?' He lifted my head with his hand, so I was looking at him. I pulled away.

'Call me what you want.' I replied as defiantly as I could, to his request to call me Eva. Elias's eyes flashed with challenge.

'I like this one,' he yelled eagerly, a big smile of mischievousness spreading across his face. Andreas laughed like a kid at Christmas. 'And she does speak Spanish, like the staff said.' Andreas's smile increased. 'Well since we have run into each other, *Eva*, maybe we should have a talk, get to know each other, you know? Come have a drink with us.' He wrapped my arm through his and began to pull me along with him, Andreas following closely behind. His grip was an iron-vice and I knew I stood no chance of running. There was no point struggling against these two, they were built like brick houses and faster than me any day, forget the fact that I was wearing flip flops and was mending broken ribs. I would just have to bide my time and wait for my chance to escape. They led me down some stairs and toward the south of the estate. I had never been to this part of the house before because it required finger print access, but the dial instantly turned green upon Andreas's touch. The doors into the new wing swung open and the unknown suddenly drained away my confidence. After a few more turns and twists, we burst through a door into what looked like an entertainment room. There was a pool table, a bar, a massive TV, random mix-match couches and a huge shaggy rug in the centre. The fire place was lit, and the TV was playing on mute. I glanced through one of the two only other doors in the room, to see a huge unmade bed sat in the centre of a red and black room. I quickly clocked the massive mirror fixed to the roof. It made me shudder. Urgh! This must have been where the two boys stayed when they were here. It was a far cry from Cane's dining room. They closed the door firmly behind us and as it banged, they enjoyed the look it drew on my face. It felt like snack time in the lion's den. First course: me.

'Sentar, por favor,' Elias commanded, pointing to a stool in front of the bar. I slowly perched myself on it and leaned away from him. Andreas went behind the bar and began to make drinks whilst Elias sat down next to me, much closer than I would like. What was it with proximity in this family? He ran his finger up my arm and it left unwelcome goosebumps. I wasn't intimidated easily, but these two, when together, were a daunting pair, playful and restless. 'Maybe we should get to know each other,' Elias continued with a dashingly, dangerous smile. 'Our dear big brother has given you a 'stay clear' card, especially when it came to us,' he shrugged across the bar at Andreas, who was grinning with delight, 'although I have no idea what or why he thinks that would be necessary?'

'I think it's our past record with attractive women, Elias,' Andreas teased, winking at me, 'and them being so easily seduced by us.' He seemed to be having a ball and that was concerning. 'Although, I'm not sure how we are held accountable if all the *women* throw themselves at us.' He smiled with a dismissive shrug and continued to make, who-knows-what, behind the bar.

'True brother, true. But I don't see anything wrong with a few get-to-know-you drinks, do you? You know, develop a special relación?' He turned to me as if he was actually expecting an answer, like I had a choice about us developing a 'special relationship'. Andreas was now shaking a mixer and I got a whiff of something strong.

'I'd rather not get to know you, to be honest,' I replied, boldly. 'I don't plan on being here long enough to *develop* anything. Especially bad habits.' I held my jaw strong and defiant as Elias's eyes flashed with challenge and his mouth twitched with pleasure.

'She's got spirit.' Andreas laughed, pouring out the green coloured liquid into the three glasses sitting on the bar top. Elias slapped his thigh with humour.

'Oh, I like this one,' he laughed with animation, the thrill of a fight clearly enthusing him. 'I can see why Cane seems so whipped by her.' He took a glass from Andreas and slid it in front of me.

'I'm not much of a drinker.' I stated coolly, sliding the glass I'd been given back across the bar. Andreas laughed loudly and pushed it into my hand.

'Today you are, missy,' he enforced, leaving no room to mistake the fact of having any choice. 'Beber.' *Drink*, he demanded and held up his glass, waiting. Andreas had raised his crystal tumbler too, the light dancing off its patterns. They both hung in mid-air, awaiting my chink. I sat still, not sure what to do. What were my options? Keep making excuses and try to escape, or drink and hope it wasn't poisoned? Neither option was appealing, but I slowly picked up the glass, the green liquor swishing around like a potion. The two brothers began to cheer like a high school football team, delighted I was joining them. I tried to take some security in that knowledge, that they wouldn't kill me, because they weren't allowed to, but as I lifted the glass to my lips and smelt the fumes burning at my nostrils, it gave me little comfort. I took a tiny sip and instantly began to cough. What was this? They both began to laugh, Elias slapping my back for me like a concerned friend would do. Hopefully the sip would satisfy them for now and I put the lethal stuff back down on the bar top.

'Rumour has it that you fight like an *hombre*, but apparently you don't drink like one,' Elias teased, with raised eyebrows. 'This is imported and expensive, you should be flattered we've broken out the big guns to celebrate with you.' He finished his whole glass in one gulp. 'Now drink,' he commanded, nodding his head at the still very full contents of my cup. I winced looking at it, positive my stomach would throw it back up in seconds. I was being honest when I had said, that I was not a great drinker.

'Beber!' Elias encouraged again, slamming his empty glass onto the bar top. The noise made me jump and Andreas laughed. 'Drink now!' I inhaled deeply and closed my eyes, pouring the liquid down my throat. I could feel every inch of it burn, as it travelled down into my stomach. As soon as it hit the bottom, my lungs convulsed, and I began to cough hard, and my poor ribs strained with the pressure. The boys broke into hearty laughter, delighted with the reaction. I was mid cough as the glass was taken from my hand and refilled. Were they serious? The same process happened five more times before they seemed satisfied and moved onto conversation. Though I was now no longer in any safe and secure state to talk and as my body temperature rose and the feeling in my fingers began to numb, I panicked that I would say something I shouldn't, reveal something I wasn't supposed to. Like Brice Bain's top secrets. I rubbed my eyes with what I was pretty sure were my hands, vaguely confirming to myself that I didn't know any of Brice's top secrets and to stop being an idiot.

'Now, Eva,' Elias began, sitting down again on his stool, seemingly untouched by the volume of alcohol. 'We have a slight issue I think we should address.' Andreas had leaned forward to join the conversation and sat with a full glass in hand, smiling cheerily. The room felt like it was moving. 'For some reason our brother, Cane, seems to have a thing for you, a soft spot I think would be the right word to use, don't you, Andreas?' Andreas gulped and burped.

'Oh yeah,' he confirmed. 'I've never seen him so protective over a chica before.' I put my finger in the air clumsily, to display I had a point to make. They both watched me and waited. For some reason though, words were taking longer to form than they should. Surely being on prescribed medication, strong ones, and this green alcohol stuff all at the same time, couldn't be a good idea.

'I am important in some deal he is hoping to make.' I finally voiced. It sounded slow and sluggish in my head. The brothers were nodding and shrugging in agreement.

'Sí, correct.' Elias continued, motioning for Andreas to make more drinks. 'Still, why treat you like… realeza, like royalty? Why bring you to his house? Why take you on like he has?' He was tapping his fingers on the bar with thought. I inhaled. Even through my fuzzy state, the crazy man did have a point. Why had he done all that? Why hadn't I just ended up in that windowless room, like I had expected?

'Because he has manners?' I offered blunderingly, trying to keep control of myself. Andreas and Elias both erupted into laughter. I wasn't sure what was so funny.

'He does have good manners,' Elias agreed, patting my arm. 'But it's not that.'

'You *are* crazy hot,' Andreas offered, lifting his glass to me as if he had just paid me the highest of compliments. I watched him pour two more drinks and pass them to Andreas. This whole situation was very strange. I felt very strange. Elias shook his head.

'You are that, to your credit, Eva,' he inclined his head towards me, 'but I've seen him around muejeres calientes and pretty girls before and this is different.' He put another drink in my hand and lifted it to my mouth, making sure the fluid made its way into me. 'Andreas and I reckon that he has feelings for you.' He lifted his eyebrows awaiting a response. Quite frankly though, I was becoming pretty detached from what was going on around me. What were they saying? Hot women? Cane has *feelings* for me? That he *liked* me? I must have been drunk, as I was sure that couldn't be what was said. My blank face answered any question they were awaiting, and Elias continued. 'So, Eva, this is where you come in and can earn yourself a regular drinking spot with us boys.' The thought made my stomach turn, or the alcohol did, one of the two. He put his hand on my leg and gave it a small squeeze. I blurred in and out while looking at him. He was handsome enough I concluded examining him, but I wished he'd stop swaying. 'All you need to do is behave yourself and make sure you remember that this whole thing is *strictly business*. Don't get any ideas into your head if Cane shows you any more of his *manners*.' Why was he talking about manners? I was confused. Andreas had started laughing again. My head was beginning to buzz, and I felt like I didn't have legs anymore. Where was I? I glanced around and didn't recognise anything…was that a mirror on the roof over that bed? Gross! A clicking noise brought me back to face the brother's grins, as Andreas snapped his fingers to get my attention.

'I think she's pretty done, man,' he was saying to Elias, with utter amusement. Elias was nodding with a wickedly entertained smile plastered across his face, his dark eyebrows high with hilarity.

'Eva?' he shouted, taking me by the shoulders so we were face to face. I wobbled on my seat and felt his hands hold me straight. 'Remember, don't be getting into Cane's head. You are a business deal and that is it. Don't you mess this up, all right?' He was nodding at me and awaiting a response. I nodded heavily back, copying him, with no idea what I was actually nodding for.

'You have very big eyebrows.' I said matter-of-factly before I could stop myself. My hand was moving towards him, determined to feel them. 'They are like black caterpillars.' His brother erupted with laughter, literally howling with utter delight and his eyes began to water with hysterics. Elias swatted my hands away like a fly, his mouth turning up at the sides slightly, despite himself.

'Callarse…*shut up*!' he yelled over to Andreas, 'I don't know what you are laughing at, boy-band-wannabe.' He punched his brother from across the bar. 'At least I don't have *tweezed* eyebrows.' Andreas swung back at him with a macho grunt and amidst the kerfuffle, I lifted my hand again to try touch the eyebrows. Elias smacked me away with an amused grin.

'Elias, she is wasted,' Andreas snorted, as he leaned over the bar to nudge me slightly. I began to keel sideways until hands caught me. The laughter only got louder.

'Crap!' Elias announced with lacing amusement, followed by more hysterics. 'She wasn't lying when she said she wasn't a drinker.' Andreas had come out from behind the bar and was now beside me putting his arm around my waist. They wanted me to stand? They just had to ask, I wasn't a doll.

'I can stand.' I said testily, trying to push Andreas away. Delight spread across his face and Andreas backed up, bowing at the space between us, making way for me to prove it.

'I think you've had too much to drink to stand, Eva.' Elias was saying with such delight, it annoyed me. I'd show them. It was harder than that to beat me. My legs felt like lead though as I attempted to move them off the bar stool, but it was only standing up for goodness sake. *It's hardly a big task, Eva. Just stand up and walk out of the room.* I willed my body to comply, but the lines of communication were distorted, and everything seemed disjointed. I pushed myself forward and landed on my feet with smug satisfaction.

'I'm leaving,' I announced to the brothers, who were literally snorting with stifled laughter. 'Don't try and stop me or else,' I threatened as forcefully as possible, pointing a menacing finger at them, or at what I thought was them. There seemed to be a few versions of them floating around. I turned to leave and was pretty sure I made it a few steps before the floor was suddenly rushing up towards me. I outstretched my hands and felt soft fuzzy carpet. Why was there carpet in the air? There was a massive thud from close by and I was vaguely aware of the idea that it might have been me, hitting the ground. I waited for pain, but none came. It couldn't have been me then, I thought to myself rationally. I moved my fingers and felt the warm material beneath them, confusion clouding my understanding. It was foggy, and I couldn't quite see where that laughing was now coming from anymore. My ears had begun to ring, and my vision was turning into a dull black and grey kaleidoscope. Then suddenly, I was aware the laughing had stopped, and that a new, familiar voice had joined the group. I hoped they wouldn't make me toast the newbie, I wasn't sure I'd actually manage it.

'Qué demonios esta passando aqui?' The voice was yelling with anger, asking what the hell was happening. My hearing buzzed out and the next few shouts were missed. I willed myself to focus and not follow the temptation of inviting silence that was now beckoning me.

'It was harmless fun.' Elias was defending loudly. 'We didn't realise she'd get so drunk so fast.'

'What is the point of me setting rules, if my own brothers won't follow them? Did you not hear what I did to the last two that disobeyed? You want that fate also?' The voice was irritable and angry. Was it Cane? It sounded like a hot bath and a summers day all mixed together…it had to be Cane, only he made me feel like that. My throat was burning, and everything felt too heavy to focus. But I had now managed to get away from the carpet and was sure I was sitting. Doors swam in and out of view ahead of me and I had a vague memory of wanting to leave via them earlier. Maybe now was the best time, I could slip out while the commotion was going on and escape the brothers with their deadly drinks. I attempted to stand, but quickly realised it was not an option. Obviously, the next best thing to do was to quietly crawl to the sanctuary of my bedroom. I began with one arm and then a leg. Unfortunately, the carpet was louder than I would have liked, and each movement sounded like a pair of maracas were attached to my limbs.

'Shhhh, Eva,' I whispered, ushering myself to be silent and stealthy, I didn't want the brothers to notice me leaving. 'Eyebrows will see you.' I quietly reminded myself. Laughing literally exploded from what sounded like right next to me, deep and booming hysterics bursting into the air, making me jump.

'Oh, bloody hell.' The newcomer's voice growled testily, as the howls continued to escalate. I heard mutterings of 'eyebrows' as if it was the funniest word in the world and all I could fathom was, that it was all very strange. My ears began to ring again, and the carpet found its way to my cheeks once more. This was an odd room and unexplainable things were happening. I glanced down to see my swimming costume straps and remembered that I had been swimming earlier today. It felt like forever ago. The grey was encroaching into my eyes again and I could see it making its way in from every direction. The next sensation I was aware of, was being lifted and carried. It felt like I was floating, and I rolled into the warmth on my left. The person holding me was strong and solid, and smelt good. I inhaled deeply and let out a 'mmmmm' sound of appreciation, just as my vision slipped away into complete blackness and utter silence. Had I just passed out?

CHAPTER NINETEEN.
Play the damsel card, quick.

I woke up with my body telling me it was about to throw up. I had no idea where I was or what was going on, but my mouth was watering with no control. Where was the bathroom? It was dark and quiet, and I felt like I'd been hit by a car. All I knew was, that I needed to be sick, and *right now*. I went to stand and fell to the floor. What was happening to me? A pair of warm hands took hold of my shoulders and lifted me up. I struggled against them.

'Get off me,' I yelled, trying to push free.

'The bathroom's this way,' a familiar voice said gently, guiding and lifting me through the dark into the adjoining room. I recognised the toilet bowl and instantly released, the vomit burning everything as it came up. I felt a pair of hands pull my hair back from my face and put it into a ponytail, letting air into my streaming eyes. It felt like I was being sick continually for hours, with no breaks, burning and retching constantly. I may have been passing out between episodes, but I wasn't sure. I was completely lost from the world, except when I had to release the bile that rose too quickly to contain. Then finally, after what seemed like eternity, I stirred and woke to find myself on my bed with my blanket wrapped over me. It was dark, and I guessed it was probably close to midnight. I groaned, and my head pounded. I felt awful. And drunk still. How could that be possible? I lay still and all too quickly, the memories started coming back. I groaned again.

'Crap,' I mumbled to myself, rubbing my face with my hand. Movement in the dark from the bottom of my bed, made me jump. I squinted into the black to see a body sitting on the windowsill cushions.

'I didn't mean to startle you.' It was Cane's voice. Just when I thought things couldn't get any worse. I moaned again and pulled a pillow over my head. I could hear Cane laugh through the feathers.

'Tell me it wasn't you here the whole time?' I pleaded, lifting the pillow from my face enough to be heard. I was suddenly so grateful that it was dark, and I could hide my shame.

'I'm afraid it was,' he replied gently, while still chuckling. I felt the effects of the drink, floaty and hazy, move through my body again.

'Couldn't you have just left me to it in my room?' I sighed, raising my hands into the air.

'And let you choke on your own vomit?' he asked, politely. I grumbled again in self-disgust, which only made him laugh louder.

'It's not funny,' I tried to snap, sliding very ungracefully out of my bed and into the bathroom through the dusky light. My head pulsed as soon as I stood, and my stomach turned with threats of sickness again. Cane sat still as I washed my face and brushed my teeth with enough toothpaste to sink a battle ship. I quickly followed it with half a bottle of mouthwash. The flavour was enough to cover the disgusting taste of puke, but not enough to cover the constantly returning memories. I dragged myself back into my bed and slumped onto my pillow, hearing Cane's smile from under the covers. I repeated it louder this time. 'It's. Not. Funny. Stop. Laughing.'

'No, it's not funny. Perdón,' Cane agreed apologetically, but even through his attempt to appear sincere, I could hear the edge in his voice.

'Could you not have had someone else hold my hair and witness my embarrassment? You could have just given them a big Christmas bonus.' To this Cane let a slip of laughter out again, but covered it with a cough.

'I'm not sure Christmas bonuses come big enough for that.' I could sense him grinning from across the room still.

'Very funny,' I replied, feeling my pajamas scrunch up under the duvet. My mind registered them quickly. Where was my swimming costume and day clothes? I had been *changed* into pajamas. I sat back up immediately and began to look down at Cane with stern eyes. 'Who changed me?' I demanded loudly, feeling around my body for underwear. I could see by the moon's light, that Canes lips suppressed a smile. 'I haven't got a bra on!' I exclaimed, cupping my chest. Cane coughed, either with amusement or discomfort, but I was too preoccupied to care which. 'Cane Rodriguez?' I threatened, slightly slurred and pointing an accusing finger at him. 'If you undressed me and saw things you shouldn't, so help me…' I exhaled loudly, 'I don't care how big and handsome and powerful you are,' I was waving my fist at him now, 'a girl has lines, boundaries.' I flopped back down to the bed, overcome with embarrassment at the thought of Cane seeing me naked. 'Oh, my goodness, he's seen me naked.' I muttered to myself, not nearly quietly enough. Cane coughed again, obviously trying to remind me that he was still there, but even his sexy thoughtfulness wasn't enough to stop the drunken trail of thoughts happening in my head. 'Did you see *everything*?' I could hear myself asking, despite knowing I should shut up. 'I swear, I'm normally tidier down there, but my situation lately hasn't really…' To this Cane did react, quickly sitting up straight and interrupting me.

'Eva,' he began, to which I ignored, now totally lost to myself in a drunken ramble.

'And push-up bras,' I continued, 'they deceive everyone, even us women.' I was waving my hands around my body and suddenly Cane's loud voice pierced my blathering. Why was he shouting?

'Eva!' he repeated firmly, yet with a smile 'A maid changed you.' He cleared his throat, seemingly a little uncomfortable. 'Yo no.' he reiterated in Spanish, *not me*. It went dead silent and I became awkwardly aware that not only had I just been speaking about my lady parts, but that I was still holding one of my breasts. I let go of it instantly as if it had just bitten me. I closed my eyes and could hear my mind chanting loudly in my ears, *I told you to shut-up, you idiot*.

'Oh.' Was the only reply I could muster, whilst simultaneously trying to sink further under the shelter of the covers. I could feel the heat from my skin, bounce off the duvet and come right back at me, heating my body to an unbearable temperature. Cane shifted his position on the seat and crossed his legs. He coughed again, clearing his throat and gracefully decided to change the subject.

'So, do you want to tell me what happened with Elias and Andreas?' I could still see through the half dark that he was smiling, despite the neutral tone of his voice. I rolled my eyes and exhaled, feeling my stomach turn and my body begin to sweat from the heat beneath the covers. I pulled them off me and enjoyed the cool air that rushed in.

'Well, I met your brothers.' I announced, putting my thumbs up in the air. '*Great* guys by the way.' My tone was noted.

'Drunk and sick and you still have the energy for sarcasm.' He shifted position on the seat with an odd look creeping onto his face. 'Can you remember what you were talking about down there?' I squinted, trying to clear the fog in my mind. I could recall being made to drink far too much, chinking of glasses, laughing, the odd snippet of conversations, but it was all still very vague and misplaced.

'No, not really.' I answered truthfully, pulling myself up to a sitting position. The room spun, and my tummy threatened another sickness episode, but I swallowed it down with disgust, feeling a tad too drunk still to be holding any form of a conversation, let alone one with Cane.

'Ok,' he nodded, rubbing his hand through his hair. 'The boys swore they never hurt you or said anything out of place. Can you remember if *that* much is true?' I looked over at him, his face set with seriousness and concern. My eyes blurred as I tried to focus on fragments of the conversations I'd had with the brothers; Elias asking me why I thought Cane was so nice to me, the brothers warning me to not mess the deal up, Andreas calling me hot. I shuddered at that least recall. Some things could stay lost in the alcohol black hole, now I thought about it.

'No, they were perfect gentlemen,' I replied, exhaling with exhaustion. 'They drink too much though.' I added, shaking my finger at him as if it was his fault. I burped silently, and remainders of the green liquid travelled up the back of my throat again.

'That they do.' Cane replied, in agreement. 'Too much money and no focus.' He took his hands from his pockets and looked at me from across the room. 'I'm sorry if they scared you.' To that I laughed loudly, and my vision began to swim in and out.

'I don't scare that easily.' I taunted, pointing at him with a wobbling finger. He sat quiet in the shadows with no answer and a few seconds passed. Shivers suddenly crept over my body and I became aware of how ridiculously cold I felt. I waved a dismissive hand towards him. 'Even you don't scare me, you know that? Your dramaticness...thing and stuff. Your looking into my eyes and coming really close. It's all wasted on me. You're just a boy at the end of the day, Mr Cane Rodriguez...' I trailed off and pulled my blanket up over me again, chattering slightly. I heard Cane stand up and walk slowly until he stood at my bedside. The moon was now illuminating his face enough to see that he was just as attractive through drunk eyes. He sat down on my bed gently, then after a few seconds he touched my blanket.

'Yo no te asuste?' he asked, with a small smile. *I don't scare you?* I shook my head, feeling that buzz begin to thrum under my skin from whenever he got too close.

'No.' I answered, watching him. Silence stretched out for a few moments and I noticed that Cane was looking at my blanket. I pulled it up closer and tighter around my body. 'I like this blanket.' I announced, forgetting whatever we were previously talking about and patting the warm material with my hand. 'We've seen some tough times together.' To this he suddenly looked up at me and a strange intensity came over his eyes.

'It's a good blanket,' he agreed with an off voice. If I hadn't been such a mess, I may have picked up on some underlying sentimentality, but annoyingly, I *was* still drunk, and my normal perceptiveness was somewhat off. My stomach began to grumble with hunger and I realised I was starving, yet the very thought of food made me queasy. The day hadn't ended as planned that was for sure, but at least I had survived my first encounter with the brothers, even if that did mean that I missed dinner.

'Not much of a drinker are you, Eva?' he asked, gently brushing hair from my face and bringing my attention back to him and away from food. I tilted my head into his palm, enjoying the feeling of his warmth against my cheeks. He paused for a few seconds and let me lean into him. Everything was becoming sluggish and blurry.

'No, I am not a drinker,' I answered plainly. 'As you can see.' I waved my hand down at myself. He smiled again, and I watched it, feeling like that smile might be only ever for me. 'Drink gets you into all kinds of trouble and I don't like not being in control.' Cane nodded, graciously.

'Plus, you're an awful drunk, who divulges far too much personal information,' he added with a playful grin. I felt his thumb stroke my cheek and I grinned back at him like the Cheshire cat.

'That also.' I rolled onto my side so that I was facing him and vaguely acknowledged that I never wanted to lose sight of his face and attention.

'In your defence though, you were *made* to drink enough to knock out a body builder.'

'So rude.' I mumbled to myself, starting to slip back into blackness. Cane let out another exhaled smile.

'Yes, it was rude.' He brushed my hair off my face again, leaving my skin exposed to the cool, night air. I was looking at him, but he was fading, and I knew I was falling asleep. 'Ir a dormir,' he whispered ever so gently, telling me to sleep. I felt his warm hand on my face still, stroking my skin softly and it felt so nice, so safe.

'I think I'm sleeping,' I managed to murmur, as Cane ran his fingers through my hair one more time. Then, despite my will, it was dark, and everything was gone.

Week three rolled on and then it finally happened. I was once again exploring the gardens to fill time, when I pushed back a beautiful green bush and was met by the huge iron fence I had first laid eyes on, on the day I had arrived. I had *finally* found the perimeter! My mouth dropped open. It had taken me miles and miles of walking, but I had eventually located it. I had forgotten the sheer size of it, standing maybe fifteen feet in the air, but it was just as black and solid as I remembered. I walked slowly up to it and placed my hands on the cold painted metal. Had it really been three weeks since I had first seen the gates? Had it really taken me three weeks to find them again? It was early afternoon, so I decided to follow it as far as my feet would allow me to walk. I hoped that it would eventually take me back to the entrance and that from there on, I would be able to always pinpoint the exits, just in case I ever needed it. I walked steadily with my hands trailing on the bars beside me, thinking of Ed as I did. I smiled slightly at the thought of him and then walked with him in my mind for miles. It was a pleasant journey and Ed was quickly becoming happy company for me again. Finally, after a couple of hours, I began to hear voices ahead and I slowed to a stop, like a deer catching the sniff of its hunter. As the voices got louder, I crouched into the bushes gently, until I was sure they were just steps ahead of me. I slowly pulled aside a branch for a clear view of what was going on ahead and smiled victoriously. I had found the entrance gates. Directly in front of me was a parked black BMW, just like the one I had driven here. Two men stood speaking to each other, both on my side of the massive looming metal bars. Both had black shirts on and both were talking thickly in and out of what seemed like English and German. One of them I recognised as the gate guard and the other I didn't know at all. They were speaking enthusiastically to each other, retelling a story as far as I could hear. My eyes quickly noticed the open car door and the keys still in the ignition. They were no more than two paces away from me. My heart beat quickened with possibility. I could be in the car and away before either man had seen me coming. Not that I had anywhere to escape to when both my dad and I had tracers imbedded in us. But it wasn't the grand theft auto possibility that had me still crouched behind the bushes, it was the sight of the mobile phone lying on the car seat. I knew from weeks of watching and being around the security, that every half an hour the men all checked in with the central command room. I had concluded that central command moved around daily, from being based in the house to different locations across the property. Genius, but annoying if you actually wanted to see inside for any information. The number the staff all had to dial into to contact that centre, was programmed into speed dial in each of the standard issued phones they carried. Button number one. I knew that the other buttons had speed dials assigned also, but the only two I had figured out so far were, the security check-in and the front gate where I now was. Numbers one and six. I looked at my watch quickly, it was three fifty-seven. I glanced at the men, neither of them paying any attention to the car behind them nor the phone in it. I knew I couldn't steal the phone, I knew I couldn't have a conversation with anyone, I knew I couldn't send a text, I knew I couldn't do anything that could be traced back to me in any way. But I knew I needed to do something. Cane had quite clearly stated the "null and void" terms of our contract and as far on in the healing process that I was sure my dad would be by now, I was also pretty sure that, he couldn't take another beating, or worse. I'd done this deal to secure his safety in the first place, it would be pointless to ruin it all now. But my heart yearned, despite the stupidity of it. My mind was working fast and with two minutes to go, I acted quickly. I quietly crept from the bush until I was squatting at the open door. Picking up the phone I quickly navigated to the options menu and to the speed dial settings. I typed as fast as I could, covering the small clicking of the buttons with my sleeve and replacing the programmed number with Edward's mobile. I glanced at the car clock as it turned to four p.m. I hit save quickly and exited to the main menu again, locking the phone and placing it back on the seat. Then as gently as I could, I backed up into the trees. Just as I did, the black shirts watches both beeped and they stopped the conversation so one of them could return to the car. Had he been looking, he would have seen the bushes next to the open door still moving from my disturbance. Thankfully he had no need to be suspicious of the bushes around him and was totally unaware of any other presence nearby. He quickly picked up the phone and stood beside the car with his legs and feet so close to me I could have touched them. He began his check-in call and I relied on the familiar sounds of an unlocking keypad to guide me through the call pattern. He held down a button, hopefully number one, and waited. It rang and then someone picked up.

'Hello?' Came the wonderfully, familiar sounding tone. Edward! I closed my eyes and dwelt on the reassurance of his voice. It felt like home and it filled my soul with warmth. Right then, as Ed's all so known and recognised voice sunk into my skin and heart, I knew that forgiveness had come. Yes, he had done some awful things, but hearing his voice melted everything away and instantly replaced it with love and hope. I missed him, despite it all, I missed him so much.

'Command?' the black shirt asked, questioningly. He shuffled his stand, obviously unsure what was going on.

'Who is this?' Edwards voices echoed back, demandingly. The black shirt didn't wait much longer, before I heard the beep of the phone call being ended. Just like that, Edward was gone, and I was alone again. He had been so close. I had heard him speak and I was pretty sure that that was something I never thought I'd hear again. I sat deadly still, not daring to move. I could hear my heart pounding and my pulse thumping through my body. I had heard from home. It was that simple. A sound that was old, comforting and safe. A sound I could put into the memory bank and keep close to the surface, to be replayed at any time reassurance was needed. Which right now, was often.

'Have you called into command today?' the black shirt was now asking the man on the other side of the gates. He dropped the phone back to the car seat and headed back off to look at the other employee's mobile, obviously concerned with the odd circumstances. As quickly as possible, I picked up the phone again, deleted Ed's number from speed dial and the recent calls list. I watched as the black shirt dialed into command on the other man's phone but didn't wait around any longer after that. As quickly and quietly as possible, I made my way back from where I'd come, starting slowly until there was enough distance between us for me to start running, which I did, with a victorious bound in my step. As I found my way back to the house a few hours later, my excitement had calmed down and my annoying rational side had already begun to expect that Edward would have thought nothing of the phone call, let alone rush it off to some expert to analyse every last detail of it, with the possibility that it might be connected to me. Still, I had given myself a boost of much needed hope and I at least now, strangely, felt like I had tried to help myself out. Surely this was some degree of victory and I was allowed to have some small amount of celebration? At the end of *this* day, unlike so many others that had passed, I had done more than kill time. I had heard the voice of someone who loved me, glimpsed my real life, and reminded myself that somewhere out there, people I loved still existed. I headed towards the dinner hall to get take-out, which was simply taking my food back to my room. Once back in my haven, I changed into my small comfy shorts and my worn-in, loved vest. I turned the TV on and slid in the DVD I had begun to watch a few nights ago. I was alone and victorious with comfortable clothes and good food and with fresh memories of Edward's voice in my head. Tonight, life was ok.

Halfway through my second DVD there was a knock at my door. I had only ever had Dr Miele knock at my door this late in the evening, but his knocks were normally much more friendly sounding. These were loud and firm, and they made my heart stammer. I paused the DVD and cautiously opened the door. Scott stood tall and square in front of me. He cast a quick glance at my body, which I quickly remembered was pretty uncovered, then cleared his throat and continued with the business he had obviously come to do.

'Mr Rodriguez wants to see you now, in his office.' I swallowed nervously, my mind instantly flashing to my stealthy commando-style phone operation earlier today. I tried to look as guiltless as possible.

'Me? Really? Why?' I tried to speak with the most innocent sounding voice I had, but the tone was falling short on Scott. He ignored my questions and repeated his order.

'Now,' he prompted, outstretching his arm in the direction of the corridor.

'Can I at least change?' I asked, all of a sudden very aware of the fact that I had on hardly any clothes. He pointed down the hall again and reached for the door to pull it open.

'Now,' he said again, with the same straight edge. With little choice, I left my room and stepped off in the direction I was led, the door of my little safe haven closing loudly behind me. I felt suddenly very exposed with so much skin on display. I had lost a bit of weight and had, surprisingly, toned up since being here and I had never been self-conscious about my body before, but for some reason now, I felt more insecure than ever. My shorts barely covered my bum cheeks and my vest was skimpy and tight and thin. I felt practically naked and was pretty certain, that once in front of Cane's assessing eyes, my level of discomfort was going to increase dramatically. I pulled my shorts down lower on my hips and pulled my hair out of its ponytail to try cover some more skin. This outfit was never worn outside of my flat in my normal life, never seen by anyone, let alone wearing it in a house full of assessing strangers. I might as well have been in my underwear. I continued to yank my vest up to hide some cleavage and looked away from Scott, who was displaying a degree of obvious discomfort. *Try being me,* I thought in response to his uneasiness. He was going to be the least of my worries soon, I knew that for a fact. *How many nights have I spent undisturbed in my room wearing full pajamas,* I thought to myself, rolling my eyes and again trying to lengthen my clothes. Cane's office door loomed ahead with the guards standing ever watchful. I wasn't sure if I was just paranoid now or if both the men cast longer looks at me, but I wished it had been enough to distract me from my concerns of what was coming. Any out of office hour biddings were never going to be for hot milk and biscuits, no matter what I was wearing for it. The door lock flashed green and I was ushered through the threshold efficiently, my heart rising to my throat with embarrassing dread. Cane was on the phone, facing his ever-open balcony doors. He had one hand in his cream trouser bottoms and a loose floating white shirt on. The night wind ruffled his clothes around his body and highlighted his broad frame. Why was his flawless, chiseled, hard, masculine body always one of the first things I noticed? I stood for a few seconds watching him, waiting. He was concluding a firm conversation in a strange language and I listened for a second, trying to place the accent; Polish, or maybe Russian? I didn't know that he spoke Russian, I'd never read that in his file. But I guessed that he ran a world-wide corporation, and being fluent enough to converse in different languages was handy. His words were hard and firm, a little like his personality, I thought to myself...and his body. I glanced in the mirror above the fire place and shook my head, reprimanding myself for my thoughts. I was a disgrace. I pulled my shorts down again, as Cane wrapped up the call with what sounded like the word 'duh-svee-dah-nee-ye', definitely a Slavic language, and turned to put the phone back on the desk.

'Miss Eva,' he began, back to his tinted English, docking the wireless receiver next to his computer, 'I have some informa...' He looked up and stopped his sentence instantly. Maybe it was the sight of me looking so uncomfortable or the fact that I was wearing practically nothing, but either way, his expression changed. Annoyingly with Cane, he was powerful enough and confident enough that if he didn't want to talk, he simply didn't. We could have stood there for hours, and if he had nothing he wished to say to me, then we would have stayed in silence. He moved his eyes very slowly and very obviously from my head, down my body to my feet, and then back up again. I felt like I was being scanned by an x-ray machine. His eyes did not leave me for what felt like forever and I could literally feel the weight of them running across my bare skin. I was uncontrollably blushing, and his stare gave me goosebumps.

'You called for me?' I asked sheepishly, trying to break the silence. I should have known better than to try though, as Cane continued to ignore me, analysing everything in his own mind. He moved out across the room and to the other side of the table, next to me. I wanted to back up and keep the table between us, but it would have been beyond obvious. As much as I was openly uncomfortable with the whole situation, I wasn't going to make it any more blatant. I tried again, crossing my arms in front of me like it would form some kind of defence barrier. 'Cane?' I said as firmly as I could, while his eyes continued to linger over me. He inclined his head towards me to show he was listening and smiled slightly, but he didn't answer. 'Cane!!' I snapped, loudly this time. He kept his smile and slowly, eventually, looked up at me, into my eyes.

'Eva,' he answered, still lingering the odd look away from my face. Another few seconds strung out before he turned back to his desk, releasing me. I sighed as quietly as I could, feeling like I had just had a brush with death. I quickly moved to behind the table and began to brace myself for whatever was coming, slightly less confident than normal. I pulled my shorts down again, as he tapped a few buttons on his computer and it burst into volume.

'Hello?' It was Edward's voice. The same voice I heard through the bushes today on the phone. I tried to look innocent and longing. Cane had always read me so well up to now, but he had no evidence this time, just obvious suspicion. I looked over to him, looking at me with skepticism. I put on my best, 'what's going on eyes' and hoped I would pass the test. The call continued, just as I knew it would, with the black shirt asking if it was command. I tried to look like I was confused, thinking that Edward had just been on the phone. Cane finally stopped the recording.

'I don't understand,' I said quietly, hoping to play the confused damsel card, quickly.

'Es verdad?' Cane asked, with both hands in his pockets now and watching every move I made. I held my place, my skin now the only thing between my inner distress and Cane's sought-after confirmation.

'Really.' I repeated his same word. 'What's going on? Why was Edward on the phone? What's happened?' I threw some frantic panic eyes in at the end and waited with baited breath. Cane stood for a minute, with what looked like a hint of a smile on his lips, then he walked the length of the room towards me ever so slowly. His eyes locked on mine with each pace closer and I desperately wanted to back away, but knew that I was being tested. Cane knew I was responsible for that call, he just couldn't *prove* it was me and that was obviously driving him mad. He reached inches away from me and finally stopped, again, ignoring all social etiquettes of personal space. I instantly noticed that he smelt divine and had a slight stubble on his lower face. His white shirt danced slightly from the breeze still coming in from the window. He leaned closer and then inhaled deeply, keeping his eyes locked on mine. I tried to look as confused as possible still, like I had no idea what was happening, but underneath, I was a whirlwind of anxiety and emotion. *He doesn't know,* I told myself, at the same time as trying not to focus on the fact that his lips were just centimetres away from mine and that his body heat was now warming my vest. *He can't prove anything,* I repeated, trying to not get sucked into the vortex of his deep seductive eyes or notice just how much of his chest I could see through his opened buttons.

'Did you have anything to do with that call, Eva?' he asked calmly, watching my pupils for a response. I steadied my breath and held his penetrating stare.

'I don't understand, what call? What's going on?' I avoided the question and chose to try and not lie straight out. Cane was in an oddly dangerous mood tonight and I couldn't decide if he was in business or human mode. Suddenly, he stepped towards me in such a fashion, that I instinctively began backing up. The wall rushed up and hit my back, blocking my escape. He kept his advance until his body met mine fully, pinning me up against the cold wood. His whole frame was now pushed against mine and I could feel his chest rising and falling as he breathed. His hand went to my neck and gently encompassed around it, spreading into a powerful and electric hold. I was breathing heavily, uncontrollably, both scared and excited in a way I couldn't explain or control. I was being held to the wall by my throat, which at that second felt significantly more fragile than it ever had before. It was a warning and I was not stupid enough to misconstrue the intentions behind it. This was both as threatening as it could be without him holding a gun to my head, but it was also as personal as he was allowed to get without crossing any boundaries. I could feel every inch of him against me, so close to being skin on skin. His fingers burned into me like fire and my blood pulsed through my body faster than it had ever done before. He was breathing deeply, and his fingers moved slightly across my skin, his grip staying firm and tight. His eyes never left mine, both deadly with coldness and alive with curiosity. I had long since accepted my physical feelings towards Cane, as shameful and exciting as they were, but not until now had I really, truly questioned his feelings. His eyes were such a confusion of emotions; inquisitiveness, apprehension, want, guarding, they did nothing but stir questions in me. I'd assumed previously that he wanted to bed me for the cheap victory, that he'd wanted to slap Edward in the face, but I'd never allowed myself to think anything else about those intentions. The other possibilities, the ones that included real feelings and emotions, well they were impossible to fathom. But now, with his body pressed against mine like this and his lips so close, it was hard to not question everything. It felt so real, so personal and intimate. He kept me locked in place and amidst the threatening warning of his hand grasped around my neck; I could feel something from him. His eyes searched mine and I recognised the same look on his face that I had seen the night of the camera room. A split moment of truth, and despite the silence between us, the air was weighed heavy with unsaid words. My palms were clamming up and my breathing deepened behind his body weight. The contrast of the cold wood on my back only heightened the heat from him, scorching into me like a blaze. My hands pressed against the wall behind, searching for something to ground myself with, something to keep me pinned in reality as the world began to burn around me. My mind was racing with panic and lust and warning. What was happening? I needed to move, to get free, to breathe normal cold non-Cane air, to fight back, but he was so close, and it felt like he was everywhere. Then through his deep breaths and piercing eyes, his lips parted, and he finally spoke. His hand was still holding the base of my neck firmly, his strong fingers pressing slightly into my skin.

'Do not push me, Eva,' he said firmly and heavily, still reading my eyes like they were the windows to the world's truths. I shook my head as slightly as I could; both fear and heat beginning to trickle down my back. He leaned in closer to my lips and paused as he breathed. His air was now my air and I could feel a need growing in my stomach. My whole body was alive, trying to get enough oxygen to keep functioning. His gaze moved down to my lips and then back to my eyes and with a final piercing glare, he removed his hand and stepped away from me. I was too weak to move instantly, so I swallowed, my hand touching the skin where his had just been. I stayed pinned against the wall as I watched Cane walk back to his desk, his shoulders rising and falling as he steadied his breathing. I inhaled as deeply as possible, not too sure what to feel…concern that Cane had just had me pinned to the wall by my throat, relief that I had got away with the phone call, or alarm that I had never been so turned on in my life. This attraction I had for him was becoming alarmingly dangerous.

'I apologise for interrupting your night.' Cane finally spoke, back in his business tone and turning to face me with one more, full look of my body. I nodded breathlessly, peeling myself off the wood and assuming that that was my cue to leave. I'd long since forgotten about pulling my shorts down and instead focused on crossing the room as collectively as I could. I got to the door and was about to turn the handle when Cane called out my name from behind his desk. 'Eva.' I turned to look at him, his head lowered, and his eyes fixed on me like I was his prey. 'I am always watching you.' He warned, with a split-second flare in his eyes. I didn't linger to contemplate the meaning of his parting comment, instead I yanked the door open and a flood of fresh air whooshed in past me. I raced for my room, paying no attention to any employees still working and walking around. As soon as I closed my door behind me, I pulled my shorts off and threw them across the room as if they had stung me. They fell against the cream wall and slid to the soft carpet. I quickly pulled on pajamas, panting for breath while my mind raced with thoughts; lust, fear, panic…What the hell had just happened? Was I supposed to be scared or was this other feeling of want normal, allowed? I sank into the bed and cast judgmental looks at the abandoned shorts, *stupid things, it was all their fault.*

CHAPTER TWENTY
Business was business, surely?

The office door closed, and he stayed sat at his desk. His hands were flush against the cool oak, his fingers spread apart for balance. He felt off centered, uneasy in his own body and he had never experienced that before. His heart was beating hard against his traitorous chest and his lungs were having trouble keeping up with the demand being placed on his breathing. What was this? His mind bellowed with contradictory frustration and thrill. Glancing up to the other side of the room, he could still see his and Eva's bodies pressed together, etching themselves into each other. He put a hand to his chest and felt his racing heart. Flashes of their lips almost touching and her breaths rising and falling rapidly, flared through his spiraling mind. He was losing control. Maybe his brothers were right, he was getting soft when it came to her. He shook his head and cleared his throat for composure, beginning to feel the breeze on his skin again. A smile grew on his lips despite himself though. She was good, he thought, as he replayed her innocent and confused eyes when he had confronted her regarding the phone call to Edward Bain. He knew it was her, she knew he knew it was her, but yet, her defiance and daring were relentless. He laughed to himself slightly, knowing that the two of them could have argued their case till the end of time and neither would have backed down. Was that what he found so appealing in her? Her unfaltering bravery? Her outright audacity? The fact that she reminded him of how he used to be before this life took everything pure? He leant back in his chair, exhaling with heavy confusion, and locking his strong arms behind his dark hair. Naturally getting her to have sex with him of her own free will was a tempting challenge and one that had danced around his mind since the day this whole deal started. It would be a massive blow to Edward, and thus Bain himself. Some would say it would be the most priceless thing he could ever take from them. But now…? His mind brought Eva back, as she so self-consciously stood across from him in his office. Her body, her face, her stance, they all yelled defiance, yet her insecurities were obvious to him. His heart began to increase its speed again as he closed his eyes and relived running his sight up her long slender legs, her curvy body, her flawlessly set jaw and clear yet hesitant eyes. He exhaled with frustration at himself, straightening back up. What was it with this one? He had met and been with many beautiful women in his time, but none that provoked and enticed such strong and deep feelings, feelings he was struggling to keep control of. He closed his hands into fists as the heat of her skin and the pulse from her neck echoed on his fingertips. She had been so close, he had had her locked in his hold, yet he had never been so out of control. He had wanted to kiss her with such intensity that it had literally taken everything in him not to. It confused him. Why had he held back when the plan had been to bed her, to secure that added bonus? Business was business, plain and simple. She was here so that he could wreak revenge on the Bains. That was it, her sole purpose in his life. Yet something inside him, somewhere, turned with defiance and disgust at the idea of using Eva in such a way, in taking something like that from her without the purest of intents. He glanced back at the wall and searched himself to discover which parts of him were objecting to the idea the most. Was it his head, or his heart? Either way, the appalled pit in his stomach knew that he couldn't do it. His brothers would have to live without the cheap dig and suffice with whatever deal was finalised within office hours. He wouldn't and couldn't *take Eva, not for malice. But his head still posed the heated and loaded question; demanding clarity of itself. Did he* want *to sleep with Eva? His brow creased with the hard truth, and the desire he'd had to kiss her resurfaced again. He'd had this same argument with himself the night they had had dinner together. It was a simple question that he needed to answer, if for nothing else but his sanity. Did he want to sleep with her? He repeated the same question to himself, sternly, commanding a damned answer. It only took him seconds to allow the truth to burn up inside him, undeniable. Yes. Yes, he wanted to sleep with her. Very much so. But he wanted to know her, wanted to understand her, wanted her time and her focus, wanted her attention and affection. He wanted it all for himself. He wanted her to be constantly around in his sight and in his mind. He wanted the purity and simplicity she made him believe in again. He wanted to have her, really have her, so that he could stop his incessant and relentless thoughts of her. His breathing came heavy as the truth tore through him, but the simplicity of his want was short lived.* NO, *he rebuked himself. Being with Eva was not an option, not even a mere possibility. He had seen and heard how she looked and spoke to him, with hate and disgust. She could never trust him nor care for a monster like him, surely…and who could blame her? Not he. No, she was a business deal and would eventually be gone. He would be left with all the power and revenge he had ever wanted and life would return to normal. Simple. Until then, he just needed to control himself. She would never reciprocate such maddening affection, he needed to get that into his head. Yet…as the reprimanding lecture continued in his head, her eyes made his doubt burn. He had seen, whilst she had been pressed against him, her pupils blaze with something. It was something he had never seen in her before, something she had never displayed. The picture of it simmered a small relentless flame in his heart that even the strictest part of him could not extinguish. He rubbed his hands through his hair with frustration. She was just a woman, he reminded himself. No different from any other. This had to stop, for both their sakes.*

CHAPTER TWENTY-ONE.
I had something to look forward to.

Over the last couple days, I'd seen suitcases being moved around and things seemed to be preparing for a break. I assumed that Cane was out of town a lot on business with his line of work, but this seemed like someone, I was assuming him, was going on a longer trip. The idea of being left here alone, was both freeing and worrying. Not to have to bump into Cane or see him was a relaxing thought, but then, the idea of bumping into his brothers and not having Cane here for help, was far from relaxing. Either way, it was not like I had any say about anything in my life anymore, that luxury had long since been forgotten about. I sat by the lake at the side of the house, enjoying the last remnants of the evening sun and thinking about how long I had been in this place now. I must have been into my fourth week. Four weeks! They had both confusingly flown past and yet, dragged painfully slow. I had now though, at least, become a person to the staff, with a name and a personality. I had even, to a degree, made a form of friendship with some, holding conversations and chatting. It was not entirely true to say that I enjoyed my time here now, but it was fair to admit that it was not as awful as it had begun. I was still besotted with the manor itself and the endlessly maintained gardens, soaking up the beauty that lay at my fingertips, but I was still a prisoner here, held against my will, with no say in my fate, and no real friends to confide in. There were some very lonely days and today was one of them. I watched the sun begin to lower in the cloudless sky and registered the onset of evening. I stood and slowly began to make my way back to the house for dinner, alone. As I rounded a corner I bumped into one of those employees I had just previously been pondering on, the few who I had begun to form attachments to. He was a gardener and I had had a few encounters with him whilst I wondered aimlessly and pointlessly around the grounds. He smiled as he saw me approaching and put his wheelbarrow down to talk. His grin was big and welcoming, just like an old friend's. It was happily infectious and drew my first smile of the day in return.

'Eva,' he yelled, as I walked over to him, sheltering my eyes from the bright setting sun.

'Gideon,' I acknowledged, stopping next to his side and admiring his wheelbarrow full of plants. 'How are you?' I began with genuine sincerity, hoping we would stay a while and chat. It was always nice to hear about other's lives when yours was so empty and alone. He rubbed the dirt from his hands on his dark and soiled work trousers, smiling. He was a fit man, roughly my age, with very defined arm muscles. His short-sleeved shirt rose up his biceps as he cleaned off his palms and revealed a line of succeeding white where his farmers tan began and ended. His scraggly, blonde hair, which was bleached from the outdoors and sunshine, sat touching his ears. Every time I saw him, he had some form of bush tangled in his mane, and today was no different. I likened him to a scarecrow, kind and gentle, despite his outer messy appearance. His eyes were bright blue, almost similar to mine, with white laugh lines creasing the corners. He scrunched those sky coloured eyes up now as he focused back on me through the fading sun.

'I'm good,' he sang, his voice merry with content. In our past times together, Gideon and I had talked about the gardens and the plants and he had shown me a few more untouched areas of the estate. We had spoken of family and friends and of things that existed outside the house's perimeter. Gideon was one of two kids and originally came from a part of the country further south. I had visited his home town before, and so we had struck up many a conversation about where I had been that he knew. He had told me about his brother and his parents and what his home life had been like. It made me homesick, but it also made me determined to one day get back to mine. I liked being around him, he was a breath of fresh air, quite literally, and it was always easier to forget my woes when I was around him. 'Where you off to this evening?' he asked, glancing around him quickly. I followed his eyes to our surroundings, we were alone except for the trees and birds.

'I was just going to walk the long way back to the house for dinner. You? Are you just finishing up?' He nodded, extending his hand out in front of him.

'Yeah, I'm actually heading your way if you wouldn't mind the company?' I smiled at his thoughtfulness and took a step forward, allowing him to lift his loaded wheelbarrow again. It creaked under the weight as it rolled along beside us.

'You doing anything tonight, since it's the weekend?' he asked chirpily, squinting at me. I shrugged politely, with a shake of the head.

'I didn't even know it was the weekend to be honest.' I laughed as easily as I could, trying not to get too dragged down by the depressing thought. Gideon's face quickly turned to appalled shame and he lowered his eyes from me, with a fading smile.

'Oh my goodness, I'm so sorry, Eva. That was a pretty insensitive thing to say.' I laughed, waving my hand like I was sweeping away a fly. I didn't want nor need pity.

'Don't worry,' I settled, 'it's my fourth weekend here and I'm not going to start getting upset about having no Saturday night plans now.' Gideon's eyes clouded over slightly, and he fell silent.

'Fourth week?' he repeated in question, with a hint of sympathy. I shrugged as he shook his head. 'That blows.' I nodded in agreement, trying to keep my carefree smile.

'Hey, Gideon?' I continued, walking around a rose bed with him. 'What do the staff say about me?' He stopped walking with surprise and swallowed awkwardly.

'What do you mean?' came his mutter, pushing the wheelbarrow off again so it began to creak once more and echo off into the grounds.

'I just wondered. I remember when I first got here no one would even look at me, let alone talk to me. Now, people seem nicer, people speak to me...people like you.' He smiled at the recognition, but then looked around us again, this time more thoroughly, as we approached the side of the house.

'Well...' he began, much more quietly than before. 'I guess people seem to be on the fence. When you arrived Mr Rodriguez held an urgent staff meeting for all to attend. He told us there would be a lady staying in the house and that you were a guest *of sorts*. We were told to keep our distance but to treat you respectfully. He emphasied that you were important to some business he had going on and that under no circumstances was I allowed off the land or near any communication devices.' Gideon laughed slightly. 'You can imagine the intrigue that stirred.' I smiled at his attempted humour. 'You said some staff still don't speak to you?' he checked, coming to our parting point in the garden. I nodded.

'Yeah.'

'I reckon that the staff who are old school, will be sticking by the original rule from that meeting. The rest of us, well...' he paused, looking around again nervously, as if spilling a top secret. A few seconds past and I waited silently, hoping he would divulge the information tittering on his cracked lips. 'Well, word travels that Mr Rodriguez, erm, erm...' he stopped again, searching for careful words, '...that he has a soft spot for you and that he...' he paused again with awkward indecisiveness, following it with a slight blush of his cheeks. The blushing only made me want to know more and I had to stop myself from shouting at him to hurry up. '...they say that Mr Rodriguez has changed since you arrived.' Suddenly, I was glad that he was blushing as it hoped it would be deterring him from noticing my reddening cheeks. I glanced down away from his face as he composed himself quickly, clearing his throat and lightening the tone. 'Talk is that he is nicer, some of the maids say he's...happier?' he smiled, trying to alleviate some of my blatant embarrassment. 'Either way, I think people got curious and brave and wanted to know what this woman, who tamed Mr Rodriguez, was like.' I quickly recalled Cane's disposition flare in his office last night and his hand clutch threateningly around my fragile neck. *Tamed?* I knew that part was definitely fabricated. 'Anyway,' Gideon carried on, much louder, and with a parting tone, 'that's just an opinion and probably not true anyway, right?' He left the sentence open, as if there was a chance I would confirm or deny it all for him. I didn't, and I couldn't. *Did* I think Cane had changed? *Did* I think he was happier? Again, the heated encounter from last night crossed my mind...he didn't *seem* happier, despite a few turn ups on the corners of his luscious lips.

'Well, I am glad *you* talk to me, Gideon,' I concluded with a big smile. He grinned back, adjusting his grip on the handles.

'As am I,' he replied with a small nod of confirmation. I began to walk towards the front of the house, leaving Gideon to make his way to the rear where the gardeners and caretakers were based.

'Hey, Eva,' he called out after a few paces and I turned back round to his beckon.

'Yes?'

'I'm off for the weekend but do you want to take a tour of the east side forestry one-day next week? I have to go to check on some fencing there. It's really pretty, you'd appreciate it.' I smiled warmly, full of excitement. Plans? Actual plans? Something to *look forward to*? Did I ever.

'I'd *love* to Gideon.' I replied with glee and he nodded back with delight.

'It's a date then,' came his wink and turned back to his duties. I had to stop myself from practically skipping back to the house with joy. I had plans! It was a strange sensation, having something penciled in to do. The last time I had willingly gone somewhere was the day I met Tammy for lunch. I had got out of bed, or as it was that morning, off the sofa, showered in *my* bathroom, got in *my* car, drove *myself* to a car park, walked *alone* to the restaurant and met *my* friend for lunch, in an open and social environment. No gates or black shirts to be seen anywhere. I sighed, my pleasure quickly fading back into reality and towards the loneliness that had been engulfing me all day. Had it really been four weeks since my last free act, since my last day of normality? The staff seemed to think something different of my time here than I did. Changing Cane? A happier Cane? I bit the inside of my lip with thought. Four weeks and nothing had actually happened to *me* though. I had never guessed I would be still in limbo a month on, being analysed by Cane's staff and work force. Spending hours upon hours alone, aimlessly filling time. Why had nothing happened with me? Why was I even still here? What was going on back home? What was taking so long? I assumed that Cane was waiting for Bain to meet all his initial demands before continuing, but how long could that take? I was assuming also that Bain would be stalling, which wouldn't help the time. Did this 'truth' Bain had to come clean about have something to do with the delay? I mulled all the options over in my head. Some days, I didn't want to know my fate or have to deal with the Bain family, and other days, where time seemed like it had stopped, and I had nothing to fill the voids, I just wanted to do something, to do *anything*. Today had definitely been one of the latter days for the most part, and frustrated anger lingered behind my every thought. Gideon had been my only ray of sunshine in an otherwise dark and dreary wilderness. As the sun finally set behind the trees and dusk set in, I decided to call it a night. My desire for dinner had disappeared with my mood and now that my ribs and bruises were all but healed, I had no need to eat for tablets. I trailed up the wooden steep staircase and into my room. I opened the magazine of Edward and I and stared at it blankly. Bitterness continued to occupy my insides and I acknowledged that I was most unattractive in this mood. Edward would surely have told me so. I stroked his smiling face and tried to remember how he smelled and the last nice thing he had said to me. But each time my mind played tricks on me and replaced his aftershave with Cane's, or his words with my captors. I tossed the magazine across the room with a frustrated growl and threw myself back on the bed. I hated this place. I hated Cane and his pig-headedness. I hated life and this prison. I hated never having answers. Why hadn't I been rescued or shot or something? This life, if that's what you could call it anymore, was becoming a never-ending nightmare of nothingness. I was *so* mad. My life had ceased, and I now lived to walk from forest to lake to bed with no-one to talk to and no-one to tell me anything. Tears of anger trickled down my cheek as I lay still. I quickly wiped them away, even more angry that I was so weak. I sat there for hours, listening to nothing and focusing on nothing, until it was late outside. Then, and only then, my favourite time of day came and I finally fell asleep.

I was aware something was happening even before I fully awoke. I heard the noises and the alarms going off in my half sleep, but it wasn't until I completely opened my eyes and got my bearings, that I realised there were actual, multiple alarms sounding and men running around everywhere. The dogs were barking, and I could hear Rosette, Lilly and Zeus clearly from the others. What was going on? I got up, pulling a hoody on over my pajama vest and sliding my feet into my trainers. Just as I headed for the door, it burst open and Scott stood inches from my face, gun in hand. I jumped out of my skin and yelped, holding my pounding heart.

'What's going on?' I asked, watching his gun intently and breathing deeply. He was one-hundred percent focused on everything around us, and so ignored me. He made his way into my room and began searching around in the cupboard and bathroom, talking quickly into a mouth piece.

'The prize is still here, and the room is clear.' My heart stopped. If he was checking to see that I was still here, and intruder alarms were going off, that could only mean one thing. Rescue! The phone call had worked, surely? Edward had figured it out and had come. Edward was on the grounds somewhere, near me, he had to be. I began backing up towards the door, not wanting to waste a second, and as soon as I was clear of Scott, I turned and ran as fast as I could for the staircase. There were people everywhere with radios and dogs and the lights were flashing in the hallways. I could hear Scott from my room yelling at me and for someone to grab me, but in all the commotion, I managed to slip past all the arms and hurtle down the stairs. I was close to the front door when a new set of hands suddenly managed to make contact and pulled me backwards. I screamed at the obstruction as my feet left the ground and were placed back down with a new, tight grip around my waist. I was caught. The black shirt was yelling that he had me, but I was moments from the door and wasn't away to let a no-named, employee stop me from seeing Edward and from being rescued. I slammed my elbow backwards into his chest and winded him, then wriggled free from his hands while he was reeling for air. I took off again towards the front doors my hands outstretched for the handle. I pulled it open, half hoping to see Edward and an army of men standing on the other side ready to take me away, but all that met me was the dark night air and the same scene I knew all too well; the car park and the front gardens. The only difference in tonight's viewing, was that black shirts were scattered everywhere, and security lights were sweeping and searching all over the grounds. Dogs kept barking as I ran down the steps towards the fountain, hell bent on finding Edward maybe somewhere in the woods or at the main gates. I hadn't heard the black shirt come up behind me again and as soon as he clamped his strong arms around me I began to scream frantically, struggling with all my might.

'Let me go.' I yelled, fighting against him. 'I want to go home.' I screamed, trying to push him away, but he was stronger than I would ever be, and he held me tightly, pulling me to the ground into a lock. I continued to struggle in vain, his vice just tightening and my hope diminishing with it. Then, just as it had all started, the alarms stopped, and the courtyard lights returned to normal. The black shirts radio went off in his ear and I heard the words 'all clear'. I stopped my fight instantly, hope fleeing my body as quickly as it had arrived. I had missed them, Edward had been here, and I had missed him. Despite everything he had done, Edward was still family. I still wanted and needed him. Seeing that I had ceased my struggle, the black shirt released his grip on me and stepped back a couple paces. I sat unmoving, looking out into the dark driveway towards freedom. I had a strange sense of emptiness and loss filling inside me, like I had missed my only chance or something. I was suddenly exhausted. The black shirt began to talk into his radio and I was vaguely aware of him being told to leave me.

'Leave her here?' he asked, confused.

'Leave her,' his orders were confirmed. The perimeter was now secure again.

'Mr Rodriguez says, she has nowhere to go'. That was the line that stung the most, as all the people surrounding me began to disperse back into the night. Workers stepped by and walked past me, giving me no attention. I sat with my white sneakers nestled into the dark stones and sighed deeply with self-pity. I began to feel the cold, night air brush over me with no consequence, as if even it thought I didn't exist. I wasn't sure how much time had passed, it couldn't have been long, but I became aware of someone sitting down next to me. My head was resting on my knee looking out into the darkness and I couldn't see his face, but from his smell, I knew who it was instantly.

'He wasn't with them, Eva.' Cane's voice said calmly, with his ever-knowing comments. I didn't look up nor reply. I knew he was right. Edward had no stealthy skills at all, his Special Op's experience was limited to outdoor team building days with the office, and even then, his team always lost. Still, he had found me, right? 'The small group didn't even confirm that you were here, let alone get close enough to the front gates to do that. That's *if* it was even Edward darling. Anyway,' he continued, coolly, 'I'm surprised after all you've found about him lately and the fact that you two do nothing but fight these days, that you would even be happy to see him.' I rolled my head over to face him and his hope crushing comments. They were true and harsh to hear. Yes, Edward had cheated and broken my heart, but despite that, I still wanted to see him, to feel warmth and love again.

'Why are you here?' I asked, emotionlessly. If it was to make sure any of my remaining optimism was crushed, then he was doing a fine job. Despite feeling drained, I managed to clock how annoyingly flawless Cane looked right now, the moon dancing off his golden skin. If I'd have had the energy to chastise myself, I would have, but I didn't, I had no fight left in me right now. And what was he talking about mine and Edwards arguments for? How could he even know something like that? I had surely never mentioned it. If it was to add sting to the injury just caused, he was succeeding with flying colours. 'Why am I still here?' I continued, weak of energy. 'What is happening with this deal of yours? With me?' He seemed to be ignoring me, letting the silence linger on longer than any normal person would. Then, he finally spoke, his tone tight and direct.

'When I have information about the deal that you need to know, I will tell you.' He put his hands into his trouser pockets. 'I am leaving for Spain tomorrow for a few days on personal business. Until tonight, because of *someone's* reckless phone call tricks the other day,' he cast a knowing stare at me, to which I didn't even try to respond, 'I felt pretty safe about leaving you here. Now I have changed my mind. If they are searching for you, I'll give you very noble of them,' he added with sarcasm, 'and they suspect you to be here still, they may well try again, and this is a risk I am not prepared to take.' I watched him intently with no arguments or back-biting. What was he saying? I was the reason he was going to have to cancel his holiday? If he wanted me to feel guilty at all, then he was barking up the wrong tree tonight, that was for sure. I couldn't have cared less right now that he was going to miss out on topping up his already flawless tan. 'You will need to be packed by eight a.m. sharp or you will be leaving with no clothes.' This made me lift my head. What? I was going *with* him?

'Pardon?' I asked, loudly, hearing my voice echo in the empty grounds around us. He stood up and brushed his bottoms off.

'You heard me, Eva,' he confirmed, as he walked off back into the house. Tears welled up in my eyes. I was going to Spain? I glanced at my watch, its dials illuminating in the clear moonlight. In five hours? To do what, to stay where? To be even further away from people who loved and cared about me. I wiped my tears, sighing loudly. What I wouldn't give now to be battling out the betrayals and my pains with Edward. Even that sounded more appealing than being kidnapped off to a foreign country. Total, complete forgiveness was coming faster for Ed than any ray of hope was for me. I exhaled with shaky breath and another tear rolled down my cheek.

'Great.' I lay my head back down on my knees, looking out at the long, dark empty drive way. Alone.

CHAPTER TWENTY-TWO
You're a business woman, right?

I hadn't slept that night at all. I had finally dragged myself back upstairs at five-thirty a.m. as the sun began to light the morning sky. Normally, the sunrise would have brought clarity, but not today. Spain? What did a prisoner take to Spain anyway? In fact, though, what did I actually care? There was a suitcase waiting for me in my room on my bed when I finally arrived back there, and I glared at it like everything was its fault, kicking it as hard as I could and stubbing my toe. Then after another half an hour of moping, I had finally flung random clothes into it, paying no heed to matching colours or styles or anything. I had no idea where I would be held 'safely' in Spain, but I was pretty sure I wasn't going to need a bikini and daisy dukes. When the eight-a.m. door knock came, and Scott opened it to collect me, I was sitting on the end of my bed waiting, the case at my feet. I hadn't slept, and I no doubt looked like it. I had a book in one hand and a cardigan in the other. I had no purse, phone or passport to carry on with me and so, once the door opened and I was given the head nod indicating 'it's time', I stood and dragged my case to the door. Scott took it from me as soon as I reached him like a proper gentleman, and then closed my door behind me. I was put into one of the few black cars that sat waiting out the front, and my case was tossed into the boot. The door was closed, and I was left on my own, amidst the smell of leather. The car eventually pulled away, but unlike the rest of the cars, mine drove off towards the rear of the house, passing the stables and onto a small road that I had never paid any attention to before. We drove through thick forest for a good while before coming to a main road and headed off towards the country. I closed my eyes against the morning sun and everything around me. They stung and were heavy and matched exactly how my heart was feeling.

A short nap later found us pulling up to an air field with high fencing and barbed wire. I stretched groggily, noting that the entrance gate had a security guard positioned at the lock and surprisingly, he sported a black shirt and no name badge. The sign mounted to the fencing simply read, "Private Property, No Trespassing". We were granted entry quickly and the car rolled out onto the tarmac smoothly. Apparently, Cane had his own air field, although why I thought this was surprising was beyond me now. We pulled up to the only plane on the track, a medium sized private jet with no logo or sign and my door was opened for me. I climbed out, squinting in the morning sun and looking around into the distance. There was nothing that could be identified for miles, nothing I recognized. Where was I? I couldn't have been more than three to four hours from home and I couldn't distinguish a single landmark. Scott took my case from the boot and held his hand out towards the plane. I sighed and walked forward, too tired to bother asking questions. Inside the plane was just what I had come to expect from Cane, sleek and stylish, updated with all the mod-cons and yet tasteful at the same time. There were four sets of seats available each centered around a middle table. It reminded me a little of train seating, but with leather recliners and enough room to play a little football. I could see a bathroom at the back, a bar and an eating area with a couple tables and chairs. On the wall hung a massive plasma TV and to its side, a few shelves of books. It smelt of new car and citrus and was naturally immaculate. The curtains on the windows ran the length of the cabin and were a stylish deep burgundy, heavy enough to block out any light if so desired. Cane was sitting in the middle set of seats, facing the front of the plane. He put his papers down when he saw me come aboard, standing like only he, or Mr Darcy, would when a woman entered the room. It was annoyingly thoughtful.

'Eva,' he greeted, inclining his head at me with a morning welcome. 'Please feel free to sit and make yourself comfortable.' He motioned to the seat opposite him, but if he thought I was going to spend the whole flight avoiding his penetrating gaze or attempting to make small talk, he had another thing coming. I walked passed him to the last set of seats and sat down in one facing the opposite direction. He smiled with what looked exasperation, his eyes watching me pass him.

'It's like *that* today then, is it?' he said to himself, shaking his head slightly. Scott paused next to him to pass on some papers and flight information. I heard him speak quietly to Cane.

'She's not said a word all morning,' he mumbled gently, turning to face away from me. I rolled my eyes at them. They moaned when I was loud, and they moaned when I was quiet. You couldn't please some people. I watched them over my shoulder as they exchanged a few more words and then Scott shook Cane's hand, quickly turning and walking back out of the plane. He closed the cabin door, apparently not coming with us. It surprised me slightly to see him leave, he seemed to go everywhere that Cane did. I guessed that even employees were allowed time off at some point, even if that seemed far too fair a thought towards Cane at this moment. I pulled my cardigan on to combat the chill from the air conditioning and sat looking out of the window and the annoyingly bright morning sun. Would I make it back to my country again? The uncertainty drove me nuts and I sighed, pulling my hood up to cover my face. I could feel Cane's eyes watching me, but even he was more sensible than to try and talk to me this morning. I knew that I was in a mood, I knew that I was having one of the those off days when everything just built up on me, but that didn't smoother the fact that I felt like a time bomb, ready to explode at any minute. Normally, on these days, I was left to my own devices and could sulk it all out in solitude. Today though, I was being forced into close confinement with the instigator of all my problems. I yanked the thick curtain closed, blocking the sun out, then hunkered down into the soft leather seat, feeling it begin to mold to my shape. Maybe once I'd slept things would seem better and my normal optimistic self would return? Hopefully anyway, as I was pretty sure I was going to need it. By the time the plane took off I was already, thankfully, asleep and I was vaguely aware of my ears popping as we climbed higher into the atmosphere.

I woke up about two hours later, still on my own. I stretched and heard Cane look my way as the tapping on his tablet paused. A blanket had been covering me and it fell to the floor as I reached up into the air. I considered it for a second, quickly realising that Cane must have put it over me as I slept. Damn his thoughtfulness. I cracked the dark curtain open and was met with an outside of crystal blue sky and fluffy white flooring. The sun shone brightly, casting rectangular patterns on the fancy carpet and I glanced around, feeling somewhat more social and refreshed. I had been right, life did seem more manageable now that I had slept a little. Or maybe it was just that while we were so high up in the sky and away from the world, literally, my troubles felt suspended in an intermediate state. I stood, stretching and made my way to the bathroom, thankfully not having to pass Cane, who had kept his head down and moved onto some papers. Naturally it was no normal plane toilet. There was a shower which was bigger than my whole bathroom back home, a massive wall to wall mirror and a cupboard full of all the personal cosmetics you could dream of. I shook my head. This man did nothing by halves. I used the cupboard full of goodies to freshen up and by the time I emerged back out into the cabin, I was feeling more and more like myself; uselessly confident and pointlessly optimistic. I watched Cane as I walked back towards my seat and then paused, before sitting down. Against my better judgment, I continued forward towards his seating area. He looked up at me as I approached, and I could see the remaining hint of a smile on his lips.

'Buenos días,' he began politely, wishing me a good morning and raising slightly from his chair. He gestured his hand to the opposite set of seats and I sat slowly. He placed his papers on the table in front of him and considered me for a moment, waiting for me to start the conversation and no doubt see what type of mood I was now in. He looked fresh and shaven, pressed and clean like he was in his Sunday best. I thought he had said he was going away for personal reasons, yet he still looked like he was facing another day in the office.

'Where are we going?' I asked, quite calmly, looking out of the window with a casual exhale. He followed my gaze to the striking sunshine and replied in the same tone I offered him.

'Spain.' I glanced back at him with a raised eyebrow.

'It's a pretty big country, Cane. Are you able to narrow it down?' He smiled a little playfully and shrugged.

'Why is it important? Did you want to send a postcard once we get there?' I eyeballed him with sarcastic amusement, not sure if I was fully ready for his humour yet, which was apparently out to play today.

'Very funny,' I replied dryly, glancing down at his papers. 'Am I at least allowed to know why you, and now *we*, are going to Spain?' I could only imagine what 'personal reasons' would actually be to Cane; acquisitions, hostile take overs, negotiations, business sabotage, bribery, corruption.

'It's my grandmothers ninetieth Birthday,' he replied, simply. 'And we are going to attend her party.' I turned my head to him, eyebrows raised. I wasn't expecting that answer. A *normal* answer. I felt a little pang of guilt for being so quick to assume the worst, despite his past track-record. I replayed his words in my head, 'we are going to attend her party' and began to consider them for second. *We? We* are going to attend? I was going with him, to his grandmother's party? How exactly was he going to explain that? Then as if reading my thoughts, he said, 'Good question.' My eyes shot to his and narrowed.

'I didn't say anything.' I protested, with slight aggravation. I had no idea how he always managed to preempt what I was thinking, but it had long since become an uneasy accurate habit.

'You were wondering how I was going to explain you.' He gave me a second to argue in, but I let it slide, now more curious about his next words than I was about being predictable. He licked that full bottom lip of his and proceeded. 'That would have no doubt led you on to wondering about whether my ninety-year old grandmother knows about the kind of life I lead, if she knows about you, if she knows about this deal we are brokering.' I creased my brow, I wouldn't have said *we* were brokering anything, but still. He ignored my face and continued. 'And the answers are all, no. No, she does not know about my business life and nor shall she ever. When my parents died she wanted nothing more to do with the family business and vowed never to get involved in any of it again. This is something we have all honoured over the years. She has been kept from all the company harm and influence and we go out of our way to maintain that lifestyle. But having you with me was not something I had planned for and she is not the kind of woman you can esconde, hide, things from.' He paused and scratched his smooth chin as the sun shone across his face, making his eyes glow. His shirt pulled against his chest as he inhaled deeply, and the thin material did little to hide the broad expanse that lay beneath it. I watched his firm frame with an unsettling lust, taunting me inside. I swallowed and returned my gaze to his face, where he sat watching me. His eyes were dancing with thought and his mouth tickled a mischievous smile. It made me nervous.

'What?' I began, full of wary suspicion. 'Depressing as it is to admit, I know that look.' He stopped, taken aback and then smiled slightly at me. It was an odd smile, one I was pretty sure even he didn't quite know what to make of, yet he kept my eyes locked on his for a few seconds longer. It was like he was trying to decide just how he felt about me knowing *his* tells, and knowing them well enough that I could start to read *him* for a change. Finally, silent on his conclusions, he cleared his throat.

'I've been pondering my predicament since dawn,' he began, an edge in his voice. 'You are a business woman, sí?' he leaned forward on his chair, a glint of something new in his eyes. I shook my head.

'You know I'm not,' I stated bluntly, to which he shook his head in disagreement.

'You may hate *this* business world, but you know the business industry probably better than most men on my payroll. And you *teach* business for goodness sake, Eva.' I wasn't sure if he was complimenting me or prepping me, so I sat still and allowed him to continue. At least he had obviously, finally, done some research on me and I liked that he now knew I wasn't just an air-headed leech. For some strange reason, it made me feel like he viewed me slightly more as an equal and less like a brainless pawn, even if his view was only an illusion. 'I have two options that I can see. One,' he raised his first finger, 'I store you away somewhere with twenty-four-hour security, and then all I will do is wonder how long it will take for you to get into trouble,' he paused and gave me a, you-know-its-true, look. I attempted to suppress a smug smile, but knew that I was failing. He narrowed his eyes at me. 'With option one, all I'll end up doing is having to continually make excuses in order to check in on you and my grandmother is old, but she is not estúpido.' He raised a second finger. 'Or two, you come along under the pretenses of *accompanying* me.' Until this last line was spoken, I had sat perfectly still, quietly listening. But upon hearing the words 'accompanying' fall from his lips, I couldn't do anything to hold in the barking laugh that erupted from me. Was he mad? Surely, he was joking? I leant over as my outburst increased in animation. He couldn't be serious? There was no way in hell he had the gall to even *suggest* something like that, let alone mean it. Surely? Yet, despite offering a slight smile at my reaction, he held his hand up to allow himself to continue. I stifled my volume, but could feel the absurdity of it all still bubbling inside, right beneath the surface. 'If we pull the week off and my grandmother suspects nothing...' he paused here, ignoring my still shaking head and awe-struck smile. Never in a million years would I play happy families with him. '...And she celebrates her birthday none the wiser...' here we go, I heard myself utter, '...then I will allow you to see your parents.' My smile vanished immediately. I went from being unbelievably positive that there was nothing he could offer me that would ever tempt me to accept his ludicrous proposal, to all of a sudden holding myself back from shouting out 'DEAL' at the top of my lungs. We all knew where making deals without thought got me. Instead, I sat frozen with consideration. My parents? I tumbled into silent turmoil, unmoving as I contemplated, weighed up options and desires, and battled out my head and heart. Cane waited quietly, ever watching, ever knowing what was going on inside me. Could I do this, to see my family, to hold and talk to them again? Could I pretend to care for Cane in order to hear news from home and find out plans for saving me? Time ticked away as I deliberated every little detail, weighing up the pros and cons, until I was finally sure of my decision. I looked up at him, locking eyes.

'Terms?' I began, moving forward on my seat. He nodded, knowing he had pretty much won.

'My grandmother has to believe by the end of our time in Spain, that we are a genuine pareja, a genuine couple.' He stopped, maybe seeing the look on my face. I was in internal chaos, thrown at the idea of being a lovey-dovey couple with Cane. I began to doubt my decision, I couldn't ever do this. It was too much. I pushed away the 'other' unexplainable feelings that were floating around in the background, not even sure what they were doing here in the first place. How could I do this? I would never be able to convince someone that I liked Cane, let alone was in a sustaining relationship with him. I swallowed, with a refusal on the tip of my tongue, but just as I was away to turn down the deal, I thought of my parents. I saw their faces, felt their warm hugs, touched my dad's healed skin, let them see that I was ok and that they didn't need to worry…I buckled again. I *could* do this, and I *would* do it, if I got to see my mum and dad. It was that simple

.   'Fair.' I finally replied, coming to terms with the fact that I was actually doing this, that I was actually going ahead with this ridiculous scheme. He nodded, looking a little relieved, then continued.

'All the previous communication and snooping rules still apply.' I nodded, expecting this one already.

'Fair.'

'You get to see your parents in a location that I choose and organise and for an hour only, supervised.' An hour? I went to argue but realised by his firm jaw that this was already pushing him past his limits. I nodded, reluctantly.

'Fine.' I agreed. 'Although, every time I am forced to do something beyond the basics of this agreement, I receive an additional half an hour of visiting time.' To this he smiled, shaking his head.

'My grandmother is very traditional, very old fashioned. She will have us in separate bedrooms Eva, don't worry about your morals.' I returned his sarcastic smile and kept my eyes firm.

'Bedrooms? I was meaning more like just having to *touch* you.' I raised my eyebrows in challenge and awaited an answer. His smile widened to *almost* showing dimples, he was seemingly enjoying himself. I watched his cheeks for the enticing indents to show and was glad that they didn't quite break through. If Cane smiled properly, I feared I would have lost all resolve and done the whole damn thing for free.

'Fifteen minutes, luchadora,' he offered. I was no idiot, I knew when to take a proposition that was sure to get no better.

'Deal.'

'Fine. We have an agreement. You comply, and don't cause any issues, then you can see your parents when we are back.' He eye-balled me suspiciously. 'Sin mal comportamiento..." he added, pointing his firm finger at me. 'No misbehaving.' I nodded once and sat back, smiling at him like butter wouldn't melt. I felt like I had just won the lottery. I could totally fake this, a few days of yucky, uncomfortable hell and I would be hugging my parents before I knew it. I could finally replace the image of my dad's broken body with one of health and normality. Of one with him standing and smiling at me again. I couldn't contain the smile as I thought of what my future now held, of the opportunity that now brightened my horizon. Cane continued to watch me from his seat and observed my obvious delight. He shook his head to himself. 'Why do I feel like I just made a deal with the *diablo*?' He asked himself, emphasizing the word 'devil' and smiling. I shrugged with excitement and cast my innocent angelic eyes at him, batting my lashes. He laughed through his nose and picked up his papers again. 'If you want anything to eat or drink, there's food in the fridge up there. We should be landing in a while.' He pointed towards the bar area at the front of the plane and began to mark things on his report again, his eyes gone from me. I stood barely able to contain my bounce. I hadn't felt this light in weeks and I practically skipped over to the fridge to collect a glass.

'Would you like anything, *honey-bun*?' I called over my shoulder to Cane, whose pen stopped moving abruptly and his shoulders raised in a cringe. His over-exaggerated reaction drew a bigger smile from me.

'Speaking of honey-buns though, actually,' he began, his shoulders back to normal and his tone suddenly dry and serious, 'should I be concerned about your relationship with Gideon Christie?' The question took me by surprise and I dropped the glass from my hand, my eyes darting back to him. The cup bounced slightly, and I grabbed it quickly before it rolled away and smashed. Cane kept his head in his papers, but his pen was still motionless, awaiting.

'What do you mean?' I asked, genuinely.

'Word is you two see each other a fair bit. Should I be concerned?' *Word is*? My mind flashed through Gideon's and I's so little encounters, that the thought was over in seconds. *A fair bit of each other?* People did like to talk, didn't they?

'I like him, if that's what you mean? He's nice to me and spends a bit of time with me, talks to me, unlike others...' I watched his back with nerves playing in my stomach, although I wasn't sure why. Had I broken rules? Was I getting Gideon in trouble? The last two employees who had disobeyed Cane, had vanished, never to be seen again.

'Mmmm,' was the noise that left Cane's lips, as his pen returned to his papers and continued to write. I stood with uncertainty.

'I didn't realise you were the jealous type, *honey.*' I half joked, sweetly trying to lift the odd mood that had settled. To this Cane placed his pen down again and actually turned to face me, his eyes finding me in an instant.

'Eva, I only get jealous when I have something important to lose.' His eyes danced over me, as his sentence was left open for interpretation. I swallowed away the potential of his words quickly, exhaling, and attempting to keep cool. 'And I'll have a drink, por favor...*sweetie-pie,*' he added, with sickeningly false emphasis. I exhaled silently and ran with the lightened humour. I made a gagging noise and his shoulders briefly shook with laughter as he returned to his work. I made a mental note to be careful with Gideon. The last thing I wanted was my only friend to end up on the wrong side of Cane Rodriguez's temper.

Upon touch-down, I was surprisingly more nervous than I should have been. I knew this wasn't my real potential in-law and that I didn't *need* her to like me, but still, the butterflies were in my stomach. I looked over at Cane and wondered if I would be able to pull this off with him. I knew we had had our moments when there was *something* there between us, but faking continual affection for days at a time, well that was a whole other challenge. I was also slightly concerned that trying to convince everyone else of our devotion was only going to unearth and expose things I had been trying to keep buried. I watched Cane whilst he waited at the plane door, his hand holding the handle and his arm muscles tensed against the bumpy landing. I would get to hold my mum and dad in my arms and tell them I was sorry and that I was all right, if I could pull this off. I had been covering my real feelings for years as I grew up in the limelight of Edwards fame, this would be no different. I could pretend to like someone I thought I still hated if it got me what I wanted. It was just patience, biting my tongue and breathing. Simple. The plane door opened, and the smell of dust and heat encompassed the dry, stiff air-conditioned cabin. It smelled like holidays and I breathed it in deeply. Cane glanced at me quickly, with a curious look at my flared nostrils, before stepping outside and disappearing. I ignored him and reminded myself that it was something I would need to learn to perfect over the next few days; seeing and hearing what he did, then letting it all wash off me with no consequence. How hard could that be? I

165

collected my book and followed him out into the beating midday sun. Holy crap, it was hot. I quickly peeled my cardigan off my arms and instantly felt the prickling pressure of a high temperature push into my chilled skin. I exhaled loudly, whistling exclamation and fanning my face with my hand. It was *really* hot. Cane laughed at me.

'I hope you packed better than that.' He remarked, casting a glance at my jeans and cardigan. I stopped dead, half down the steps. I *hadn't* packed better than this. Firstly, I was in the mood from hell last night, and secondly, I thought I was going to be held in a dirty, dark motel room somewhere in a desert whilst Cane conducted some shady business. I wasn't expecting to be attending a birthday party. 'Está bien, it's fine.' Cane continued, holding his arm out to direct me off the plane, 'we'll get you some clothes while we're here.' I carried on walking down the steps, trying to ignore the fact that he had once again read my mind and finished my sentences. He walked towards the black car and opened the door, holding it for me to get in. I smiled slightly at his propriety, still surprised by it. He shook his head, the sun beating off his already more golden glow. 'Even monsters have manners,' he stated, giving me a stern look. I quickly got in the car as the door was closed behind me rather firmly. *Door slamming*, I thought to myself as the car shook slightly, t*he perfect start to any normal relationship.*

We drove for an hour or so through some of the most beautiful Spanish countryside I had ever seen. Groves as far as the eye could focus swept past us in an array of colours; lemons, olives, oranges, all the sweet smells the senses could wish for. I sat, glued to the window admiring the breathtaking views and quaint old buildings. Cane sat opposite watching me, a small, subtle smile on his lips.

'Have you ever been to Spain?' he asked casually, still staring at me as I stared out the window. I dragged my eyes from the scenery to him, and nodded.

'Si señor.' I replied in my best Spanish accent, which wasn't very good at all. It made him laugh though. 'Then why do you look like you have never seen any of this before?' He waved his hand towards the window and I shrugged.

'Just because I have seen it all before, doesn't mean it's any less...' I paused searching for the correct word, 'hermosa...beautiful?...' I waited for Cane's confirming nod before continuing, 'any less *hermosa* to look at each time.' I switched back to the window just in time to see children playing in the passing field of yellow. 'You're just desensitized to it all.' I added over my shoulder to him. Cane made no attempt to argue and I happily went back to my viewing.

CHAPTER TWENTY-THREE
Yes, it was worth every inch of risk.

He watched her as they drove, her eyes lighting up with each turn of a corner. Her hand was pressed against the window pane and her lips curved up every now and then. He glanced past her out into the scenery and found that he couldn't suppress the small smile tugging at his own mouth. Seeing everything through her eyes did seem to make it all beautiful again. He watched the yellow fields fly by for a few seconds, before returning his gaze to Eva's face. He exhaled slowly and then quickly felt his face hardening. He realised that he was doing it again, he was fascinated by Eva. This was nothing but crazy and he was getting sick of the same constant battle. His mind switched to the latest deal they had just struck. He was noticing a trend when it came to making deals with Eva, that they always seemed to be more lucrative for him. And this latest one was no different, even if only for personal reasons. It was reckless and uncalculated, true. He also knew that his brothers were going to kill him. He had just sent them a memo, updating them on the situation and informing them of the new arrangement with Eva. He knew what they would say if they were here. He could hear in his head, their reprimanding voices, as clear as his own. This was madness, the whole entire thing was utter insanity. What was he thinking? Why had he even proposed such a ridiculous idea, when off the top of his head, even in this second, he could come up with a million other better ones. He swallowed, as Eva's face lit up into an intoxicating smile and he watched her, feeling his shoulder begin to relax slightly. He knew fine well why he had suggested what he had, why he had gone with a fantasy rather than a cold, cut strategy, and he was done trying to kid himself anymore. The idea of being with Eva, like a normal, happy couple, was just too good a chance to miss...even if it was all just pretend. He also knew, that it was most likely, the closest chance he would ever have to taste happiness...happiness with her. He had to cease it, he had to give himself the one small window of hope, even if it was only for a few days. Already, he could feel the impending end of Eva in his life, feel it slowly gnawing at him and robbing him of the little light he could identify inside. He wasn't ready to let go of that spark yet, to lose that growing feeling of peace. And he knew that those feelings were directly related to Eva, completely attached to her. Something about that made him panic slightly, like he was going to lose a precious commodity. And, he reminded himself, he knew all too well how much he hated to lose. He cleared his throat and shifted his weight, still gazing at her intoxicating face. Was this risk worth it, he asked himself, already feeling the doubtful weight from seconds ago begin to ease with each of Eva's smiles? He lowered his head to try and hide the elation he was sure must be showing in his eyes…yes, yes it was worth every inch of the risk. Even the slightest chance that she would look at him affectionately, walk by his side in the evening air, place her gentle hand in is, address him as if he was hers…yes, if even in only the make-believe world, it was a risk worth taking.

'We'll be there soon,' he spoke, breaking both the silence and the spiraling thoughts inside his head. She glanced over her shoulder at him, from viewing the window, and threw out an easy grin, as if it was the most natural thing in the world to do.

'That's ok,' she sung, 'I'm in no rush for this ride to be over.' A small knowing laugh escaped Cane's lips and he felt his heart physically expand within. He knew exactly what she meant.

CHAPTER TWENTY-FOUR
Had I just passed the first test??

We pulled up to a large set of wooden gates, not long after four p.m. Up the stony driveway, I could see a beautiful old Spanish villa set into the side of the mountain and overlooking the valley. It was a postcard, even down to the big, deep blue, Spanish flowers that grew along the side of the driveway. They reminded me of the bluebells I was used to back home and I pressed my face against the window, my mouth opened slightly. It was breathtaking, quite literally. Cane laughed at me from across the car as the gates opened and we drove through.

The house was a stunning, yellow stone villa that occupied a very large portion of the cliff side. Set at the top of a hill, with stunning green vines climbing their way up its sides, it was charming and enchanting and captivating. It was the place you would dream of coming to for your honeymoon and then each and every anniversary after that. The drive led up to the white front doors, passing through a garden full of every colour under the sun. A swing chair sat undisturbed to one side of the drive, surrounded by lush green grass. The sun shone down on the paintwork and highlighted the aged cracks in its surfaces, only adding to its majestic splendor. I inhaled deeply, trying to identify the smell that was tickling my nose, and then exhaled loudly again, trying to wrap my head around the fact that places like this did apparently exist outside of the movies…and that apparently, they all belonged to the Rodriguez's family.

'Here we go,' Cane said, breathing deeply and casting me a warning look. I ignored his caution and continued to enjoy the house. As we stepped out of the car, the Spanish sun instantly began to burn down on us and I could feel my skin begin to bristle again with delightful welcome. The front door opened and the most adorable old lady I had ever seen in my life drifted out. She was old school Spanish, through and through, down to her sandals, looking just the way everyone else in the world imagined old, Spanish people to. She pottered slowly towards Cane with the smile of the century on her face and her darkened, tanned arms outstretched, for what was obviously a very eagerly awaited embrace.

'*Cane, comas das?*' she was singing in her thick and poetic Spanish accent, kissing his forehead as he bent down to embrace her. Watching him with her was a strange thing for me. He seemed so genuine and caring, which was hard to believe when I had seen him be so cold and calculated.

'Bien abuelita. I'm good Grandma,' Cane was replying, gently holding her arm. She studied his face deeply, holding his cheeks locked between her two old hands. I could hear her talking to him in fast, animated Spanish that was too quick for me to keep up with. He nodded and smiled, as she pulled him lower and kissed his head again with glee. As she did, she caught sight of me, standing in her drive way. I was in scruffy jeans and a baggy top, looking about as sheepish as I would have been, if I had been meeting my real grandmother-in-law for the first time. What if she hated me? I thought quickly, as she looked back to Cane and asked him something in Spanish. He pointed at me and replied, then eventually turned to English.

'This is Eva, grandma.' The old lady turned her eyes on me and began to give me, an all too familiar, assessing stare. I now knew where Cane got it from. Although, when he did it, it was unnerving for all the wrong reasons. Grandma here, still gave the sense of being sized up and read right down to the soul, but at least it was that straightforward. I held still and awaited her reaction, like a dog sniffing out its new owner. Finally, she must have seen something she liked, my nerves maybe, and she smiled, reaching out for me. I sighed with relief and walked to her quickly, taking her withered and tough old hands. She gripped on tight and pulled me down to her height. She was strong for an old woman. From the corner of my eye, I could see Cane tense slightly with concern. Grandma here was maybe the only *real* care in his life.

'*Hola Sra Rodriguez. Como estas?*' I offered, hoping I was saying, *Hello Mrs Rodriguez, how are you*, and not, *I would like my bill now*. She smiled warmly at me, which I guessed was a good start.

'*Muy bien*. Hello my dear. It is lovely to meet you,' she replied, in her thickly accented English. I smiled back at her, mostly with relief that she could talk my language. We all knew my Spanish wasn't exactly top notch.

'Thank you so much for having me on your special Birthday.' I put my hand on my heart with a genuine head nod, 'significa mucho para mi...it means a lot to me,' I continued, with what was only partly lies. She patted my hand, beaming with sheer delight, then suddenly let off a small squeal, and began pulling me off towards the house.

'No, no,' she began, waving at Cane to follow, as an afterthought. 'Thank *you*. Cane has never taken woman back to meet me before, this must mean you very important to him.' She said, casting a smile at a truthfully nodding Cane.

'Sí, this one is very important to me indeed, Grandma.' He had a smug smile on his lips and I cast him a snide glare, while Grandma was looking away. He shrugged back at me as if to say, 'what, it's true'. The inside of the house was just as striking as the outside, with white ceramic walls, bare, yellow, stone roofs and beautiful, dark, wooden beams supporting the whole home. Plants and old furniture stood everywhere, mixed in with wonderful old paintings of Spanish villages and scenery. It was the most adorable house I had ever been in and as we entered, my senses were overloaded by the smell of home cooking and love. Grandma let go of my hand and pottered ahead to the bottom of a stone stair case. For ninety, she was doing amazingly and practically floated from foot to foot as if she hardly touched the ground. She turned and looked at us both, standing quite comfortably far apart from each other.

'I only have the, habitación principal...' she waved her hand around looking for the translation for me, '...master room, made up for Cane, as I not expected more company until the week. But you two share, until the maid is back on Monday to make other room up.' Her words must have caused a simultaneous look of shock from us, and she laughed at our reactions.

'Grandma, we are fine with separate rooms, we know and respect your rules in your house,' Cane said quickly, before it was too late. I nodded, quite intently, to back up his words. She smiled at us both.

'I am old enough now to know, that things are no longer what they used to be. I have no doubt that you have been living under one roof for quite some time now, no?' Well, she hit the nail on the head, didn't she? I looked over to Cane with a hint of humour in my eyes. At least this answer wouldn't be a lie. But the pause was confirmation enough and Grandma continued, obviously mistaking our exchanged look for one of affection. Little did the poor, old woman know. 'A couple nights together will not cause any more daño...anymore harm. I'm ninety in three days, there's nothing I not seen or heard of now.' I glanced at Cane again with 'want to bet' eyes and he pointed his finger at me, warningly.

'Grandma, we do not wish to go against your house rules,' he tried again, but Grandma was done, and her mind was made, apparently a Rodriguez family trait.

'No digo más...Cane stop fussing, it is settled. Take hermoso...' she smiled at me, 'beautiful, Eva here, upstairs and let her freshen up. Enough on subject.' She began to walk off to the kitchen, leaving Cane having been told. I couldn't contain my smile, delighted to have witnessed Cane being reprimanded by an old woman. He glared at me, probably already knowing my thoughts, and this time I was quite happy with that.

'Venir,' he said quietly, holding his hand out to the upstairs and inviting me to come. Upon entering the upper level, it was easy to see that the house was massive. Grandma obviously no longer came up stairs and maids were employed to keep the place tidy. All the bedrooms were left with unmade beds, except the main master room, which had white cotton sheets and towels laid out for us. At the far side of the room was a balcony that opened up onto the most breathtaking views of the valley beneath. The glass doors were hooked open and the net curtains danced in the early evening breeze. The roof fan spun with a gentle purr and cast an odd, relaxing hum into the atmosphere. Magnificent wardrobes lined the perimeter of the peach painted, stone walls and a desk sat at the far end of the room housing an antique looking mirror. A hand-woven rug lay on the tiled floor and my feet registered its thick softness as I stepped onto the fabric. It was just exquisite; the whole place was just charming. Then I noticed the bed. It was a stunning, wooden, four poster, with net curtains falling down the sides. It was the perfect bed, if you had been sharing it with someone you didn't despise. Cane reached my side and stood looking upon its troublesome duvet.

'This is going to cost you a lot of fifteen-minute extras, Mr Rodriguez.' I informed him, sarcastically, to which he threw me a look. I smiled and perched on the end of the large soft mattress, waiting for his new arrangement to be revealed. I kept waiting. He didn't talk. 'Cane?' I prompted, slowly beginning to catch on to where his train of thought was heading. 'I was joking.' I announced, loudly. 'We are *not* sharing this bed together, not under any circumstances, do you hear me?' He looked across with those eyes of his and I stood up, crossing my arms firmly and shaking my head. 'No. No chance.' I repeated, louder, and glaring at him. 'I'll even say it in Spanish for you, so you understand me fully. No hay manera en el infierno!'

'No chance in hell?' he repeated with a straight face, yet a slight twinkle in his eye. He considered me for a minute, probably trying to decide if I could be influenced otherwise, but my glare stayed strong in his direction. The last time I had done something he hadn't agreed with it, it had ended up with his hand around my neck. But this time he was not the king of the palace, his dear, sweet, old grandmother was, and she was not to be upset. A confrontation here would be unacceptable.

'Bien,' he eventually concluded, *fine*. 'I'll sleep on one of the unmade beds and come back through in the mornings.' I nodded at him with acceptance, walking towards the balcony to shake off the unnerving feeling I had just experienced. 'She better not notice,' he threw out after me, as I brushed past the net curtains. I rolled my eyes at him, even though I knew he couldn't see my defiance. The view was stunning, and the sun beat its rejuvenating rays into my skin as the warm breeze blew my hair across my face. If this had been under different circumstances, this would have been close to perfect. Cane appeared at my side, breathing in deeply and resting his hands on the old railings. 'Do you want to change before dinner?' he asked, with what was not really a question. I ignored his tone and simply nodded. 'You can go shopping tomorrow,' he added, glancing sideways at me. I turned to face him with a sweet smile, batting my make-up-less eyelashes.

'With your credit card, *darling*?' Cane shook his head at me.

'Yes, with my credit card, *darling*.' he replied, smiling slightly and looking out to the view before us. I watched him, slyly, from the corner of my eye. It was easy while standing here in Spain, making easy-going jokes and easy-going conversation, to forget just who he actually was. I had to keep reminding myself of the times I had seen the other him in action; the gun on the table, our fight in his office, the time we first met in the alley...the cool, casual Cane standing next to me, in the setting Spanish sun, was not the full Cane. He was merely the fluffy kid's version of the whole man. I needed to remember that, even *if* his Grandmother was adorable. As I thought of his family, the thought suddenly hit me- his brothers. A wave of anxiousness rolled through my stomach. The ever-seeing Cane, noticed my change in disposition and turned to face me with an almost concerned look on his face. I was mad at myself for the moment of weakness and quickly exhaled, toughening my tells. I swallowed slowly, as if doing so would make my words seem more casual.

'Are your brothers coming to the party?" I began, as passively possible, still gazing out to the scenery. Cane looked back out to the valley with me, nodding, understanding my manner. He slid his hands into his pockets with slight hesitation. That meant yes. I turned my head further, looking a compete one-eighty away from him. I didn't want him to see my concern. I had learned to cope around Cane, we had developed an understanding of sorts. But his brothers and I were not so harmonised. I couldn't imagine being forced to get drunk again, or goodness knew what else they could make me do when in their holiday-mode. I quickly recalled the last time we had met and the events that unfolded in their entertainment room. My stomach turned with just the memory of how sick I had been the day after that horrid green drink. There *was* something appealing about his brothers, and I had to admit that to myself. I could see why they were so enticing and appealing to others. But, for me, as prisoner who they deemed as a threat, their reckless actions scared me. Things seemed to have a tendency to go wrong when they were around, and I just didn't want to be the one who it all went wrong with...again.

Sí, they are coming," Cane replied, firmly. "They arrive tomorrow evening." I nodded, nonchalantly, still looking away from him. My head was racing with concerns. It was bad enough being imprisoned in Cane's house, but in another country, where I knew noone, didn't know the house and didn't have even a room that was a refuge, well, it made me feel more insecure and unsafe than ever. "They are under strict rules," he continued, in what seemed like, an almost encouraging voice. I finally turned my head back to him and caught his eyes. "They know the drill with Grandma too," he counseled, inclining his flawless head towards me.

'Well, if they know the drill, then that's ok then," I muttered sarcastically, turning again to the escape of the scenery. I sighed silently, gathering my strength and suffocating down my reserve. Apprehension wasn't going to keep me safe or help me deal with them. That was up to me. I took some comfort in the knowledge that they *still* weren't allowed to kill me…not yet anyway. I cleared my throat, wiping any trace of real emotion from my face as turned back to Cane again. "Did you mention dinner?" I asked chirpily, letting him gaze over me with assessment. He stood silent for a second, then nodded.

"Sí, cena, dinner," he repeated, taking his hands from his pockets and directing me back inside. I felt the fan instantly begin to cool my heated skin as I stepped in to the bedroom. "Shall I just turn around while you change?" Cane asked, his small smile increasing in size. I marched across the room and opened the door into the hallway, tightening my lips and nodding him out.

'You can wait in the hall.' I warned, dryly, watching his amused grin as it passed me. I shook my head at him. Once he was gone, I changed into the only thing I really had that was suitable for the warm Spanish nights; linen trousers and a halter neck top. I slid my feet into flip flops and tied my hair back into a pony tail. If Ed didn't get make-up anymore, there was no chance I was going to do it for Cane, and so I opened the door to let him come in. He hung at the entrance, looking me up and down.

'Ready?' he commented coolly, signaling me out of the room. I nodded and followed him out, not knowing what his appraising look had concluded. Did I look ok for dinner? Was I suitable? I hated when he didn't share what he so obviously thought. He was undoubtedly, still, the most infuriating man I'd ever met.

We ate dinner outside on this adorable dining area, just Cane, Grandma and I. There was a chef and a server constantly loitering by, but they were the only other people on the estate with us and once they had finished up, they said their goodnights and left. We talked of Spain and history, of my family and Cane's past, and all the things I was sure Cane did not want me to hear about. Whenever the conversation touched on something he wanted to avoid, he'd step in and lead it in another direction. And to be honest, that was fine. I was finding that the more I knew of Cane, the more confusingly complex he became.

'Cane, you get some more drink, por favor?' Grandma asked, smiling and patting him on the hand. He paused for a split second, obviously hesitant to leave us alone. After a split second though, he quickly stood up, nodding.

'Excuse me ladies, I'll just be a couple of minutes,' he spoke politely, but cast a hard stare towards me. I wasn't sure what his concern was for, it was *me* being left to the wolves. This adorable old lady held more of the Rodriguez gene than appeared on her surface and I was pretty sure I was about to be in the firing line. Alone. I returned his stare with the most reassuring, yet, hurry-up-eyes that I could muster. Cane pushed his seat back and quickly rushed off inside. This was it, my first alone test with

Grandma. I focused on being able to get my time with my parents and prepared myself.

'So, Eva,' she began in her thick Spanish accent, turning her focus onto me. I swallowed and smiled, sipping the remnants of my drink. 'How did you two meet?' she asked, as sweetly as possible, but with her gaze reading my every move. She was definitely related to Cane, there was no doubt about it, as I felt her eyes begin to bore into mine. I fidgeted slightly, trying to decide what to say. I remembered my dad telling me once that the best way to lie was to stick to as much truth as possible. Obviously, the truth parts here are massively important to the situation that Cane and I were currently in, but still, I guessed I could adapt the tale slightly. I placed my glass back down and turned my body to face her more, hoping that it would read as an open and honest gesture.

'Well,' I began shrugging shyly. 'It was actually in a little beach village. He was doing business and I was there with my dad and our paths just crossed.' I kept my smile as she nodded. Why hadn't Cane planned all this story out for me? He was the evil genius mastermind, not me. Obviously, at some point, his Grandma was going to have asked these questions.

'*Eso es buenp,*' she began, running her old fingers through her white hair. 'That's nice. You know Cane has never had much luck with the ladies,' she continued, with something I wasn't sure that I wanted to hear. 'His life changed when his parents died, and the dating became thing of the past. He had to grow up very fast. He has seen many girls over last few years, but they are always after wrong thing, his name or su dinero…his money…' she paused, and watched me as if expecting to see some flash of guilt. Thankfully, I could answer this question with complete utter honestly.

'I can hand on heart tell you, Mrs Rodriguez, that names mean nothing to me and I am very much, *not* after his money. Those are things I don't rate highly.' Grandma settled back into her chair, obviously happy with my answer. Had I just passed the first test?

'¿Cuál fue su primera impresión de él…' she continued, then quickly changed back to English. 'What was your first impression of him? What did you think of him when you first met?' She was smiling in a childish way and her eyes had lit up. 'You can always tell what kind of a relationship you will be having by the first few thoughts and feelings.' She sat peering at me with eager eyes, waiting to see if her Grandson had found someone who thought as much of him as she obviously did. I swallowed again and decided to keep relying on this near truth thing, which seemed to be working all right so far.

'Well, to be honest,' I began, 'I was a little intimidated by him. He had all these men with him, who all obeyed him to the letter. I knew who he was instantly, but powerful people have never really impressed me.' I recalled the moment Cane had first walked down the sea of men in that back alley, to stand in front of me. I remembered thinking how much I hated him, but I couldn't exactly tell Grandma that part. I remembered how confident and powerful he looked, pacing back and forth in front of me like he had no cares in the world.

'And?...' Grandma prodded me, pulling me from my thoughts and back to the dinner table. She could clearly see there was more that I was not saying.

'Ummm,' I stammered, slightly. 'He had on this cream suit and I remember thinking that not everyone could pull off a cream suit as well as he did.' I smiled as she awww'd vocally, obviously happy with my words. 'I remember watching his face get clearer as he walked up, and then when he was standing directly in front of me, I remember thinking he was taller in real life and much more...*handsome*.' I said the word cautiously, quietly still caught in my memories. Without the thoughts of my dad and the pain, I could quite clearly recall being stricken by how handsome Cane was. Grandma smiled deeply, clasping her hands together with glee. 'He has these dark eyes that can penetrate through you and read your very soul, and when he *properly* smiles, his whole face changes and these dimples appear that you never knew he had. He's firm, but fair when he can be, and he has these old school manners which just remind you of how men *can* be. He's closed and he's quiet, but at moments of intimacy, you can almost see all of him.' I remembered the library, the dinner when we had almost kissed, the camera night. I was pulled from my memories and stopped speaking abruptly as I registered the noise of Cane returning with the bottle. He hadn't heard us, but I instantly realised that I had gone too far. That I had said things I hadn't meant to. I bite my bottom lip in realization as a disconcerting shock thrummed through me. Was that what I *actually* thought of about Cane, how I *really* felt about him? Were these emotions mixed in me somewhere along with my anger and my frustration? Because I was pretty sure, up until now, that I just simply hated the man. Right? Grandma was staring at me, as if lost in my moment too. She leant forward and took my hand gently.

'My dear,' she whispered softly, with what looked like tears in her eyes. 'Some people wait whole lives to feel what you feel. And even then, they miss it because they are too *espantado*, too scared. Hold on to this love, sweetheart, because even when you have it, it can be taken away from you too soon.' She wiped a tear from her eyelid and I assumed she was now speaking about her husband, who I knew she had been married to for sixty-seven years, but who had died a few years earlier from sickness. My pity for her was enough to stop me focusing on her comments of love, once in a lifetime and the confusion they stirred within me. I swallowed, patted her hand, exhaled, then realised that I had seemingly passed her test. If it would have been appropriate to laugh then, I think I would have. My lying skills were apparently much better than anyone gave me credit for. I'd managed to bring Grandma Rodriguez to believing tears with fabrications my relationship with Cane. *Yet*...my mind niggled. Somewhere amidst my self-congratulating and tender memories, I couldn't help but doubt myself. Which parts of what I'd said about Cane were the lies? It was becoming blurrier and blurrier inside me.

'Is everything ok?' Cane asked, reappearing at the table to find us holding hands and his Grandmother wiping away a tear. He looked at me intensely, trying to read what had happened. Almost scared that he could actually read my mind, I looked away quickly and took my hand back.

'Yes dear,' Grandma replied, brushing the moment off with wave of her arm. 'Plática de chicos,' she winked, glancing back at me with an affectionate smile. 'Just girl talk.'

I sat quiet through the next hour or so and then finally managed to excuse myself for bed. If I was being honest, I was not only exhausted, but I was confused and worried. The conversation earlier with Grandma had really struck a chord within me. What was happening to me? Who was I anymore? I was beginning to feel like I even I didn't know. I used to be so self-assured and self-righteous, so aware of who I was and what I wanted and what I thought. Now, I barely seemed to know what I felt with any real certainty. It was draining, and it scared me. I pushed my seat out and said my goodnight to Grandma. She patted my hand tenderly, with a sparkle in her eyes. Cane took the opportunity to say goodnight also, and then escorted me to 'our' room. I loitered in the kitchen, waiting for him to kiss his Grandmother goodnight. They exchanged a few quiet and personal words in Spanish, Cane glancing over at me while he listened to what his Grandmother was saying. I was glad I couldn't understand everything sometimes, not knowing what was happening was easier than the alternative. Up the stairs, we closed the bedroom door and I walked over to the dresser in silence. My mind was racing with questions and self-doubt.

'Well, so far so good,' Cane chirped, clapping his hands together. I looked over to him vaguely and half smiled. He watched me pull my pajamas from the drawer and quietly close it. His hands went to his pockets and he leant against the bed post. 'Grandma says that I am 'un hombre de suerte',' he repeated, following me with interested eyes. I glanced at him and translated it out loud with a straight face.

'One lucky man.'

'That was her words,' he teased, receiving no reaction. What did he want me to say? I kicked my flip flops under the dresser and put the watch Edward had given me in the top drawer, as if hiding its face away from seeing. Cane kept watching. 'You're quiet,' he observed from his perch on the bed, folding his arms in front of him. His shirt pulled across his toned biceps and I clocked it, despite everything.

'And?' I asked, turning to face him with raised eyebrows. 'Am I not allowed to be quiet either now? I didn't realise that was part of the deal.' To this Cane smiled gently and lowered his head. I knew it was an unnecessary snap, but I was struggling to stay placid. I could feel my insides spinning and turning yet I had no way to calm it all. I carried on getting ready for bed, hoping to keep it all contained for just a little while longer.

'She already thinks you are in love with me you know?' he spoke. 'One evening in and she is sure of it.' He looked up at me through his long, dark eyelashes. 'In just one night of seeing us together.' I stalled for a split-second, my heart jumping wildly into my throat and my ears beginning to ring. I offered a quick nod, attempting to compose myself.

'Well that was the whole point, right?' I replied with a little more sarcasm than planned, and lifting my hands as if to say, 'obviously'. He didn't react, but continued to watch me with his same assessing eyes as his Grandmother. It was dark out now and the net curtains blew in the night breeze, ruffling his trousers against his crossed legs. He shifted his weight and the big bed creaked slightly in the silence. '*Are* you in love with me?' he uttered quietly, lifting his head to observe my reaction. The question took me by surprise and I dropped my pajamas in shock. The ringing in my ears increased to a sudden deafening roar and my pulse sped up. I could feel my heart thumping inside me and I quickly cleared my throat, stealing time and bending down to retrieve my clothes. I needed to gather myself before I had to stand up and face him. I knew I needed that time because of the petrifying truth that was inside me; I didn't know if I was in love with him. I didn't seem to know anything anymore. The words I uttered to Grandma earlier about Cane, echoed in my head amidst the thundering. Where had those words come from? They were supposed to be lies, but they didn't feel false. What was once hate, was thawing into a pool of uncertainty and I was drowning in a tide of confusion. But there was no chance Cane could know that, no way he could ever see any weakness in me. He would just exploit it and I knew that he would. He was still a businessman, first and foremost, and there was every chance still, that this was all a game. A little flare off defence kicked up inside me, taking my messed-up feeling and channeling them into one I could handle: resistance. How dare he ask me such a question? How dare he presume that love would even be something worth mentioning. We were a deal. A damned, straightforward, black and white deal. Simple. I gathered the nightwear up into my hands, thankful for the new surge of defiance. 'Pardon me?' I said, incredulously, spinning to face him. I was genuinely becoming amazed by his frankness and becoming more insulted by the second. He was sitting there on the bed, calmly and collectively, like he had no cares in the world, as if none of this had any consequence on him. I heard my head growl with irritation. I definitely hated this man. He had this infuriating way of getting under my skin and making my blood boil. And even now, he stood there casually, leaning against the bed post like an easy Sunday morning.

'Grandma said that you may be trying to convince yourself otherwise still, but that she could read it from you.'
'What?' I spluttered, shaking my head and quickly using the excuse of finding my toothbrush to turn away again. Grandma and her bloody Rodriguez eyes. 'That's crazy talk.' I added, flustering around in my belongings. My flare of aggravation was fading quickly as my heart began to interfere. It yearned for the tone of Cane's voice to itch with uncertainty, for it to offer a possibility. My heart wanted him to care, wanted him to be emotionally invested, wanted him to want me. And *that* was crazy talk.
'She said it was clear the moment you started speaking about me.' He wasn't talking in his usual confident and factual manner or even in humour, in fact, he actually seemed quite genuine. Or was I just wishing that? I couldn't even trust my own senses anymore. What was going on with me? Why did Cane have to play these games? I knew they were games, I knew it, yet my stupid heart would not listen. It was on its own mission to see the end of me.

'Oh, she said all that did she?' I replied casually, as I continued pretending to rummage. I didn't want to imagine what Cane would do if he thought for a second that I had feelings for him: blackmail, torture, emotional punishment. It was an endless list of potential. I finally picked up my toothbrush in relief and quickly headed towards the door with desperate focus. 'I need to brush my teeth.' I said offhandedly, praying to be out of the room as quickly as possible, but as I passed by, Cane grabbed my arm with his strong hands and pulled me close to him. I lost my breath instantly, as if being plunged into icy cold water. He pulled me right into his body and I tilted my head up to his, trying to look at him with anger. I prayed he couldn't hear or feel my heart through his chest. 'What are you doing?' I accused madly, trying to pull my arm free and push back. He held tight though, staring into my eyes.

'Me amas, Eva?' he whispered slowly, pronouncing each word carefully. *Are you in love with me?* His pupils widened with curiosity as he tried to get a read. He smelled divine and I could feel his chest rising and falling against mine. I hated this. I was so confused and scared. No matter what I felt it was wrong, every option was wrong.

'Are you insane?' I spat, again trying to pull my arm from his hold. But he wasn't satisfied. 'Am I in love with you?' I repeated bitterly, more so at myself than him. 'And would that love have come from the kidnapping part, the father murdering part, the physical abuse part, the welcome from your brothers part, or the being kept prisoner for the last month part?' I waited with raised eyebrows and hoped that my angry rant would deter him. His eyes danced around my face, then flashed with something new, maybe anger, maybe disappointment. I was too concerned with leaving the room

179

to analyse any deeper. After a few moments more of searching, he let go of me and stood back, placing distance between our bodies. My chest was rising and falling, despite my will, yet his remained still.

'I'll be through in the morning,' he finally said, straightening off his trousers and walking away from me. *'Beunas noches,'* he inclined his head towards me and then silently left the room. As soon as the door closed, my legs gave way and I crumbled to the ground, panting.

CHAPTER TWENTY-FIVE
It was great to be a no one.

Cane had carried on as if nothing unusual had happened the night before. The morning had played out as expected; we had conversed like normal with sarcasm and one-liners, knowing stares and all the delights of our little relationship. We had eaten breakfast with Grandma and then I had thankfully been put into a black car to go shopping for the day- by myself! I was elated! Cane and Grandma were heading inland to visit some old family history sites and I was ecstatic for the isolated freedom. Grandma was concerned that Cane and I were not staying together, but was quickly reassured when I insisted that Cane needed some family time. My comment about desperately needing some retail therapy had received a warning glare from Cane who had slyly slid me his credit card behind Grandma Rodriguez's back. I smiled sweetly when she turned around to commend him on his understanding of the female race. Her birthday party was in two days, which meant I had today and tomorrow until the guests began to arrive and only until tonight the brothers appeared. But that meant today was almost a full day of untainted and undisturbed freedom. Freedom from anyone with the name Rodriguez. Sweet bliss.

At mid-morning, I was escorted by a *short-sleeved* black shirt and found myself in a very up-market shopping plaza. Here I managed to quite happily lavish around the stores for hours. I purchased enough clothes to restock my whole wardrobe and purposely failed to look at any price tags before handing over Canes credit card. I found the perfect dress for Grandma's party and then stopped to have some lunch, packing all my bags down the side of my quaint, outside dining table. The server was Spanish but thankfully spoke enough English to help me order. I knew that I had been followed all day by the black shirt, but he kept his distance and I'd pretended he wasn't there, even when he sat a few tables away and placed his own order for another beer. He held a Spanish newspaper up and I only ever caught the odd glimpse from him as he peered over its top to me. I wasn't too sure why his guard had been required when I had no passport, no ID, no cash, no transport and couldn't exactly run off anywhere. *Anyway,* I thought with smug satisfaction, looking down at my feet, *I have too many bags to run away with.* My lunch arrived, and I thanked the waitress with my broken Spanish. She laughed and smiled, leaving me to people watch and enjoy the warm sunshine. The restaurant looked out onto a courtyard square, which was filled with clothes shops and boutiques. People strolled around, oblivious to my situation and to me. It was amazing to feel anonymous, to be in a random café, eating food I actually ordered myself.

The feeling was immensely liberating after being constantly watched and scrutinised for so long. I sat back and soaked in my undistinguished and unidentified solitude, blissfully content. The sun suddenly blocked out and in the midst of my paradise, a man's voice appeared by my side, attached to a tall, tanned and smart looking Spaniard. He opened conversation, but it took me a few seconds to register that he was talking to me.

'Perdóneme?' he began, in smooth and flowing Spanish, his deep tones breaking my welcomed privacy. 'Discupla la molestia pero nopude evitar verte desde mi mesa,' he rattled off and I struggled to keep up. I picked up a few words here and there, enough to assume a sentence, *excuse me, sorry to interrupt, couldn't help notice you.* I looked up to him, shielding my eyes from the sun and searching for the words.

'Hola,' I began, '¿Cómo se dice?...eh, .how do you say...' I rambled, shaking my hand and trying to remember my Spanish, '¿Hablas inglés?' *Do you speak English?* The man smiled and nodded quickly, switching to a perfectly accented English.

'I do speak English,' he continued, leaning in to me. He smelt like cigarettes and ash and the odour made me recoil slightly. 'Do *you* speak English?' he asked with a lifted head. I wasn't sure why I'd have asked to speak in English, if I couldn't, but I smiled and nodded. 'That surprises me,' he laughed, placing his hand on the back of the opposite chair, as if to hopefully be pulling it out very soon. 'You are very beautiful for an English girl.' He kept his smile but mine faded quickly, as I contemplated his odd backhanded compliment.

'Gracias?' I replied, with hesitation. Maybe it was the language barrier, I excused, trying to assume the best of the new stranger.

'I was sitting at my table and couldn't help but see you. You looked far too beautiful to be sitting alone I thought, so I waited to see if you were to be joined, but it seems not?' He awaited my confirmation with raised brows, his hand still clasped to the back of the free seat. I shook my head.

'No, I'm not being joined.' I confirmed to his look of delight.

'My name is Fernando.' He bowed his head. 'And yours is?' he asked, with his free hand held out to me.

'¿Y a ti que te importa!' answered my escorting black shirt who had appeared at Fernando's side with a stern warning glare. *None of your business* was a great name, I thought to myself with humour, as Canes employee shoved Fernando's extended hand away from mine.

'Oh.' Fernando jumped, releasing the chair and stepping away from the much taller and bulkier black shirt. 'I am sorry, I didn't realise she was spoken for.' I went to correct him and add that I was indeed *not* spoken for, but the opportunity was gone. My guard edged Fernando away from my table, and then out of the café, with severe hostility. I heard him leave a parting comment of 'no quiero ver tu cara de ella o por estos lados nunca mas.' I was pretty sure it translated into something along the lines of 'I don't want to see you near her or here ever again.' Nice and friendly. Poor Fernando scuttled away like a frightened child, not looking back once. I watched him dash across the sunny courtyard, clutching his man bag tightly.

'Adiós.' I called after him, with an apologetic 'oh-well' smile. The black shirt returned to his table without even a second glance at me and took another rather large gulp from his cold beer. I sat for a few seconds wondering if anyone else around us had noticed the rather awkward and confrontational moment. I glanced to the nearby diners, I could see they clearly had not. I picked up my fork and popped a big portion of lunch into my still oddly amused mouth. I was smiling, despite myself, at the black shirt who had glanced my way again. I swore the corners of his mouth twitched up, but the newspaper covered his face and he was out of view again.

I spent the afternoon by the pool. The dress I had brought to wear was a light colour and despite luckily having slightly olive skin, the darker it was the better the dress would be. I knew Cane's extended family and friends would be at the party and as vain as it was, looking good would at least give me that extra bit of confidence. I rubbed the coconut sun cream onto my arms while watching the bright sun dance off the ripples of the cool blue pool water. It looked like heaven. I inhaled, feeling fully relaxed and with no concerns or current thoughts dragging me down. The heat settled into my skin as the rays pushed down from the high sun with a blanket of heat. Every now and then the slight breeze would blow and rustle the dry crisp leaves on the ground, but apart from that, there were no other sounds. I allowed myself to completely unwind, my guard melting down and my defences thawing into a warm summer puddle. It felt like weeks since my heart had beat this slow and steady, since my mind had ceased racing and jolting, since my body felt this rested and recuperated.

'I brought you a drink,' a familiar man's voice began from right above me and I jumped out of my skin. I opened my eyes quickly to see the black shirt from today who had been left in charge of guarding me. He still wore his short-sleeved uniform and was stood towering above me like a tree, casting a shadow over my lower body. In his hands was a large bottle of cold water, condensation dripping down its sides and onto the hot ground. I smiled at him, sure that somewhere beneath the uniform was a man with a personality. I was sure I'd almost seen it crack out of him earlier at the café. I sat up and took the deliciously chilled bottle from his hands.

'Thank you so much...?' I awaited him to finish my sentence with his name. It took him a few seconds of uncertainty, but it eventually came.

'Peter.' I smiled again at him and he shifted awkwardly on his feet.

'Peter.' I confirmed with a nod. He was in his early forties probably, with dark black hair. As he reached down to hand me the drink, I saw the bottom of a tattoo peak out from underneath his short sleeve. I had never seen Peter before until this visit to Spain, but I was sure there were plenty of Cane's employees I had still had not met yet. 'Do you want to join me?' I asked, gesturing to the vacant lounger lying parallel to mine. Again, with hesitation first, he finally agreed and plonked himself, somewhat unsteadily, down into the cushioned sun recliner. It creaked under the bulky man's weight. He must have been roasting, I thought to myself, as I looked down at him over the rim of my water bottle and took a big refreshing mouthful. I was lying in a bikini, he was lying in black trousers, shoes and shirt. 'So, Peter, how long have you worked for Cane?' I asked, taking another sip and placing the bottle on the ground underneath my seat away from the warming reaches of the mid-afternoon sun. Casual conversation seemed like the best thing to aim for, despite the wafts of what I was sure, was alcohol coming off my new sunbathing partner. Was he drunk? Surely not, I thought to myself, casting Peter a quick glance.

'Ten years,' he answered with a hint of pride. My eyebrows raised.

'Wow. That's a long time.' He nodded with a casual shrug and a discrete burp. Charming. A few seconds passed in silence and I took another mouthful of water. 'So, I guess a thank you, for saving me at the café today, is in order?' I joked, looking over to the see the reaction of my new acquaintance. He yawned, stretching his arms above his thick black hair and settling into the lounger, as if he was going to fall asleep. He exhaled loudly and again the smell of warm stale beer drifted my way. He hiccuped, then coughed quickly as if to cover it. He was drunk. I remembered seeing him have a few drinks at lunch earlier, but now he seemed far too relaxed and aloof to be sober. Why else would a black shirt sit down with me and have a conversation as if we were old friends?

'No problem,' he replied with a casual wave of his hand. 'I was just following orders.' This caught my attention.

'Orders?' I asked, with annoying curiosity. He began nodding. 'What orders? Don't-let-Eva-speak-to-any-odd-strangers-orders?' I was saying it light-heartedly, but felt a little cranky at the idea of being so screened. Peter smiled back at me with another small belch.

'Yep. Don't let you talk to anyone,' he repeated, carelessly. 'I *thought* it would be a pretty easy task,' he waved a finger at me and I sat still, watching him. 'Mr Rodriguez was right though, when he said that you attract trouble.' I smiled, delighted that I was causing Cane trouble. 'I think Mr Rodriguez was more concerned with men speaking to you though, rather than odd strangers.' He hiccuped again and wiped his sweating brow. 'I thought he was being a bit over-protective, but he's right, I've seen how men look at you.' I sat up a little straighter, watching him as he rambled in a slightly intoxicated manner. I could feel my head and heart begin to switch back on, the clogs starting to turn again. So long for being carefree and relaxed.

'I'm sure he was joking,' I half laughed, as if it was the most ridiculous statement in the world. Why would Cane care if I talked to men?

'He was quite serious,' Peter defended, glancing at me with a straight mouth and lowered brows. 'He doesn't seem to joke when it comes to you.' My stomach lurched like I was on a rollercoaster and Cane's words from last night ricocheted around me.

'Well, I guess it's all very serious when it comes to *business,* isn't it?' I offered casually, waving his words off. Peter wobbled his head side to side with an upturned mouth, then shrugged clumsily. I was becoming very uncomfortable with the conversation and even more so by how easily Peter was giving up opinions and orders from Cane.

'Mmmh,' he continued, closing his eyes and turning his sweating face up to the sun. 'I think it's more likely that his past experience with women makes him cautious.' He exhaled, taking a swig of his brown bottle and then relaxed into the chair. I bit my lip. I didn't need him to expand anymore.
'Oh really? How so?' *Damn it, Eva!* 'I always just assumed he did well with women. You know, rich, powerful, attractive…' I trailed off, realising that I was sounding very much like *one of* the ladies I was referring to. He sat back up opening his eyes and wiping his head again. He glanced over at me with an assessing twitch. Maybe he was sobering up or just realising that he was being too candid, but after a few seconds of awkward silence, he decided to finish up the conversation and get in away from the heat…but mostly likely, get away from me.

'Yeah, the ladies like him, for all the reasons you said. But after trying with girl after girl and each time discovering its only ever for those things; status, media, money…I think he just decided it was easier to give up. Trust wears away after years of having it grinded at. You know?' He nodded with a note of conclusion. 'This is the first time in years I've seen him care enough to be bothered by who a lady friend of his speaks to.' He gave me a knowing glance and quickly stood up, wobbling to his feet and staggering oddly into the shadows of the surrounding gardens. My heated body became frustrated by the, only moments ago, pleasant sun and I fidgeted, trying to find a comfortable position. My sanctuary, was destroyed by a few minutes of conversation. My heart felt for Cane, despite not wanting to. If Peter was speaking the truth, despite his strangely tipsy disposition, then I could only imagine the disappointment of failed relationship after failed relationship and the anger that would follow. The more I discovered about Canes personal life from his staff and family, the more I found that I was tipping off my pedestal, like a tree blowing in the wind of uncertainty. I stood up and sorted my bikini trying to remind myself that Cane was only a man, a ruthless, manipulating businessman. I dipped my toes into the deliciously, blue pool before quickly diving in head first. The water swallowed me up silently, drowning my doubts and reservations.

It was late afternoon and I was still laying on the sun lounger that I had made home, my eyes closed against the full penetrating sun. The cool evening breeze had begun to stir up and it felt like heaven, drifting over my heated skin. I exhaled with contentment, despite it all. In my relaxed state, I had been drifting in and out of sleep, having strange dreams of Cane and I. The wind would blow, waking me from my doze and then a guilty disappointment would follow. I had just stirred from one such dream of Paris and a moonlit walk, hand in hand, when a shadow blocked out my sun again and forced my eyes open. To my horror, and pleasure, stood the tall, perfect frame of Cane, the sun casting him into a flawless silhouette, as he stood, shirtless, looking down at me. My first instincts, on seeing his chest inches from my face, were not wholesome. I'd been dreaming about that chest for the last couple of hours and now that I was presented with the actual version, I quickly realised my dreams had not done him justice. I'm not sure what exactly I had expected his fine suits and shirts had had hidden beneath, but whatever I thought, it fell short. He was broad and firm, his dark skin tight against his muscles. He had fine dark hairs that tickled the base of his chest and followed that V shape down into his trunks. I flushed, suddenly thankful I was already hot. I dragged, very unwillingly, my eyes from his low sitting swimming shorts, towards his head. Swimming trunks…bikini. Holy crap, I was in a bikini! The instant realisation of my skimpy attire, caused my face to burn even more and me to sit up, abruptly and reach for my towel.

'Eva,' Cane began in greeting and inclining his head, a smile quickly vanishing from his lips. 'Do you mind if I join you?' His voice was as cool as the pool water. He was gesturing at the lounger beside me and I nodded, awkwardly, whilst subtly pulling the towel over myself. 'Please,' he began, as he spread out on the seat beside me, 'don't cover up for me.' The plastic chair creaked slightly as his powerful and strong body lay down, but I barely heard it over the flames that were consuming me. 'You are looking pretty tanned,' he offered, striking up casual conversation as he closed his eyes and relaxed into the sunshine. 'Although, you have great skin anyway.' I swallowed, trying desperately to not look over at his body, let alone hear the fact that he thought I had good skin.

'Oh, thanks,' I muttered, much more timidly than usual. I saw his lips move in reaction. Was my discomfort that obvious?

'Eva,' Cane said in a soft tone, turning his head to look at me. 'Would you like me to leave, if I'm making you uncomfortable?' His mouth was turned up slightly at the sides, but his eyes were genuine. My head screamed the sensible reply, yes, leave now, please, but my heart as always, won out.

'No, no sorry. I didn't mean to…maybe I should just go in and….' My standing up was quickly interrupted by the sweetest voice alive and grandma's head poked over the balcony above us.

'Eva,' she half yelled, pleasure of seeing me evident in her greeting. 'I hope you have good day without us, yes?' She was nodding excitedly. 'Ahhh good, you get some quality time together now, sí?' She waved her hand at Cane and I, lounging beside each other. 'Maybe a pool game, Cane?' she continued. 'Yes, sí, a game is must. I'll get some volunteers.' Before either of us could protest, she was gone from the balcony and back into the house, her shoes leaving a fading echo on the floor. Cane looked back to me and again smiled, seemingly relaxed and entertained.

'So much for running away,' he teased, suppressing a wicked grin. I licked my dry lips, sitting back down and holding back the desire to retort. He was right, I *was* going to run away, but not now. Keeping the pretence up for Grandma Rodriguez was the only thing ensuring me that I'd see my parents at the end of all this. What she wanted, she would get Cane sat up and swung his legs over his lounger so that he was facing me. 'Here,' he said, producing a couple drinks from the floor behind him. The sun danced off the glass as he handed one to me. The ice cubes bobbed around inside and chinked loudly, making my mouth water. I sat up and took the glass from his hand, my fingers brushing his. Fire rushed up my arm and into my chest.

'Thanks.' I said quickly, downing the cold liquid to try and extinguish the burning now inside. His eyebrows raised at me as the empty glass came back down to rest on my bare legs. The liquid began to mellow around inside and instantly made me feel calmer. I exhaled slowly.

'Why do you seem so nervous?' Cane asked, with a perplexed laugh. He held out his own drink for me to take. I saw his eyes dance over me and another wave of self-consciousness flooded my skin. I quickly accepted his glass and swallowed its contents too, hoping it would provide me courage. The second batch of liquid hit my insides with the perfect measure of cold and heavy, and smothered the flames that were continuing to burn. I shook my head, feeling instantly better.

'I'm not nervous.' I replied, enjoying my new, seeping tranquility. 'I'm just really thirsty.' Cane reached out and took his empty glass from my hand, replacing it on the floor beneath his chair.

'Just as well I had a couple before coming out here,' he teased, scratched his chin casually and glancing over at the water. Cane jumped to his feet as two employees arrived, a net and ball in hand. Grandma Rodriguez had rallied up volunteers faster than I had anticipated. Both newcomers had on trunks and were now constructing the volleyball net in the middle of the pool. I recognised Peter from earlier in the day, who now seemed a little bit sturdier on his feet. After a few minutes of organising, the net was up, and the two men were in the pool playing around boisterously. Cane was walking back towards me, his flawless frame getting closer to my body with each step. My mind imagined him sweeping me up into an embrace and gently placing me into the cool water with him where he would lean in slowly and kiss me...

'Eva?' Cane repeated, clapping his hands to get my attention.

'Yes?' I jumped, guiltily, looking up at his smiling face. The sun was glowing off his tight skin and he looked more golden brown now, than he ever had. I felt like I was swooning and very obviously. *Get a hold of yourself, woman!*

'Are you *wanting* to play?' he asked, looking over at the pool. By his tone, he seemed to assume that I wouldn't. 'Have you ever played water volleyball before? You don't have to play if you don't want too.' I shrugged, casually.

'I've played normal volleyball before, does that count?'

'Yes,' he nodded.

'Then of course I'll play.' I stated, sliding to the end of my lounger. Cane extended his hand for me to take and I looked at it quickly, before placing my fingers in his and allowing him to help me up. The electricity from his touch again spread up my arm and into my core, rekindling that heat. Suddenly, the cold water was very appealing.

'Ok, Peter and Paulo, you guys can be on a team and I'll go with Eva. We'll play to ten and the losers have to tidy up,' he shouted over to the guys, jumping into the pool. I watched him emerge, with lustful hunger and an uncontrollable smile. What was wrong with me? I was acting like a teenager. It must have been the sun, or those drinks, or those trunks of his... 'Eva, you want a hand in here?' he was asking, looking up at me easily. It was strange experiencing him be so casual and relaxed, like we had been friends for years and the idea of him helping me into the water, was totally normal. I sat down on the edge to jump in, when Cane's hands found my waist and swiftly lifted me up and in. I was overcome with a desire for Cane to never let me go again and that feeling consumed my every fiber. Once in, he nodded at me to check I was good, oblivious, and then released me to swim to the centre of the pool. I instantly submerged my head under the water, screaming loudly. When I came back up, the boys were already shouting out joking threats, trash talking and splashing water across the net at each other. I waded to the middle of the pool as Cane laughed, running his hand through his dark, wet hair. He turned to me, ball in hand and swam up close. He stopped when he was maybe a few inches from my face and I could see the droplets of water sitting on his long thick eyelashes. He was talking low with his eyes on mine. 'So, Eva, are you actually any good at volleyball?' he checked, very gentlemanly handing the ball over to me to serve. I took it from him, returning his smile.

'I was the school team captain.' I replied, and he began to laugh, shaking water from his face.

'You are just full of surprises,' he winked, walking backwards to stand ready. From the side of the pool came clapping and I looked over to see Grandma, now sitting on my lounger, her hands clasped together with glee. A couple other black shirts had joined her to watch and I suddenly felt a bit of pressure. Not only to not suck in front of everyone, but to remember to keep the role of 'couple' up in front of Grandma…Grandma who missed nothing. I swallowed as I looked back over to Cane, him seemingly reading my mind. If Grandma was here, it was back to the façade. He smiled at me though, with a small head shake as if to say, don't worry about it. I returned his encouragement with a nod and refocused my attention on the net. *Now would be a good time to not suck, Eva,* I thought. I tightened my hold of the ball as I glanced heavenwards, and sent it up. My first serve took Peter and Paulo by surprise, and it sailed past them with great speed and accuracy into an empty space of water. Cursing left their lips, and they playfully blamed each other, throwing lighthearted punches and splashing water. Cane looked at me and smiled, whilst Grandma continued to hoot from her chair, a drink now in her hand. On my second serve the boys managed to return it and a rally got underway. Cane and I worked well as a team, setting up and reading each other perfectly. The laughs were flowing and the scores evenly switching from team to team as the game clocked up the points. It was odd seeing everyone around me interact with such comfort and ease. It was something I hadn't experienced in weeks at Canes manor. I felt nice to be part of something again and I realised that I'd missed it desperately. Based on the conversations from the men, I knew they had all had a few drinks before the game had started and I attributed that to the relaxed atmosphere. Even Cane seemed more mellow and natural, but whatever the reason was, it was infectious and delightful. The crowd at the poolside had somewhat increased in size, now with what I could only assume to be every worker on the estate watching us. There was lots of shouting and joking going on, mostly in Spanish, but I understood them well enough. What looked like a gardener, cupped his hands to his face and shouted at Paulo as he missed one of my returns.

'Paulo, ella es sólo una chica. Why you keep losing to a chica?' Everyone laughed, including me, but Cane pointed a finger at him in jest.

'Watch it, Diego,' he teased, splashing water towards the employee. 'That '*only a girl*', is *my* girl.' Diego put his hands up in surrender with an apologetic smile and Grandma patting his arm in comfort. Everyone laughed some more, but I couldn't help but like how it felt hearing Cane defend me, even if just in play. And why the words, '*my girl*' made me feel like I was on cloud nine, was a thought for another time. Cane waded over and high fived me, passing the ball and offering me an encouraging nod. I sent the ball high over, but Paulo was quick and before either Cane or I could get to it, the ball had been returned and landed with a splash, clean in the centre between us. We both looked at each other, then the ball, and back to our each other's faces. Cane smiled first, laughing at our miss, then I followed. The guys across the net took great delighted with their point and whooped around encouraging the crowd. The roar went up as clapping and hollering spread through the crowd.

'Eva, what is it with men scoring on you today, first at the café, now Paulo?' It was Peter shouting across the net at me, pointing his finger with a grin. My mouth opened and I screwed my eyes up at him, playfully.

'It was only one point, Peter, you're still going to lose.' I shouted, receiving a blow-off shrug and a dismissive wave of his hand. He held up his arms for the ball to be returned, but Cane had stopped, suddenly turning to face Peter with a tense jaw.

'What about a café and men?' Peter's eyes instantly flashed with seriousness, and it was obvious that he not informed Cane about today's events. Cane's eyes darted to me and I saw his look growing with intensity. My smile faded from easy enjoyment to concern, but not quite so much as Peter's.

'It was nothing really, Sir, just a small incident at a café with a random man.' He coughed slightly, hoping to evade the continuing glaze of his boss.

'He did insult me a few times while trying to compliment me, but we pretty much managed to escape unscathed by the whole event and we still have all our arms, legs and appendages intact.' I was smiling again, looking at Cane and narrowing my eyes at him in warning. 'It really was *actually* no big deal at all, Cane.' His head had turned back to me and he was analysing my face, still holding onto the ball.

'Celoso?' Grandma called out to Cane, who quickly switched his attention to her as if just remembering she was present. He forced a smile and shrugged in reply.

'How can I not be Grandma?' He tossed the ball back over the net and waded over to stand beside me, the crowd talking amongst themselves now. His smile was still on his lips, but his eyes were assessing.

'What did she just say?' I asked, glancing back to Grandma's unsuspecting face, who was now, thankfully talking to a maid.

'She said I was jealous.' He was close now, his skin almost touching mine. I became instantly aware that I was standing in only a bikini and that we were sharing the same water and the same space. His voice was quiet, and deep. and it made goosebumps rise up on my arms.

'Celoso?' I repeated in Spanish, copying the pronunciation. 'Jealous, huh? Well that would be crazy, wouldn't it? Considering.' I said light-heartedly, attempting to lighten the darkness that had fallen over Canes eyes. Hell though, if I didn't wish it was true.

'Maybe,' he replied, running his hand through his wet hair. 'Although it concerns me that I can't take my eyes off you for more than a second, without you making a new friend somewhere…and normally a male one.'

To this my eyebrows raised and a smiled tweaked at my lips. I knew it was wrong for me to be happy about the fact that my making male friends bothered him, but I couldn't help myself, it delighted me. My stomach got butterflies as he watched me closely, especially my smile. 'Why are you smiling?' he asked, suspiciously. 'You think this is funny?' I bit my bottom lip.

'I think it's interesting that you would care so much about who I talk to. *Dear.*' I said the last word louder and his eyebrows raised, that small grin of his returning to his face.

'Will you two love birds get back to game?' Grandma called over in her ever-adorable broken English, receiving a yell of support from the crowd. Cane glanced up at her, smiling and nodding.

'OK, OK,' he relinquished loudly, then quietly returned his words to my ears only. 'We can discuss this later, I think.' His eyes were dark and shining as the sun reflected off them. I inhaled deeply and nodded, nerves tickling my stomach.

'If you say so,' I answered. 'But can we win this game first, please?' I pointed towards the net and the two men waiting eagerly on the other side. 'Por favor?' This drew a grin with dimples daring to show and it made my pulse quicken.

'I love it when you talk Spanish,' he said quietly, casting me a playful smile, before returning to his side of the pool. The crowd began to cheer again, and a spectator called out a reminder of the score. My eyes were stuck to Cane's back as he walked away, my heart thumping with pleasure in my chest. I knew that I needed to reign it in, that I shouldn't react so easily to any compliment he gave me, that I should be more guarded and more serious, yet, as I watched his firm shoulders flex and his low waist band dance teasingly in and out of the water, I knew I was fighting a losing battle here. Could I just keep blaming the sun and those drinks? Yes, that was a good plan. A solid plan. The game continued for another few nail biting rounds of laughing and yelling, before finally the crowd fell silent and the last play was about to take place. It was my final serve and we just had to get this one to win. Cane placed his hand on my shoulder and smiled. His cool bare fingers were like electricity on my wet skin. I focused past them.

'I'll set it up for you, ok?' I said quietly, looking at Cane's dripping face. He nodded with a playful wink and went back to his place. I quickly served the ball up high and Cane struck it hard down over the net sure to win, but Peter moved fast and got under it, returning it with lightening-speed. Cane managed to keep it in play and passed it to me, perfectly, ready for a spike. I jumped from the water, as high as I could, and hit the ball back over the net. The boys fumbled to get to it, but it was too fast and too far from them and as it made contact with the water, splashing it up on impact, the crowd erupted into cheers. We had won.

'YEEEES!!!' Cane yelled, bounding over to me with a massive smile on his face. My hands were up with victory as Cane's arms wrapped around my waist and hoisted me into the air, celebrating. I was laughing as the crowd clapped and yelled. Grandma looked delighted with life, as she nudged the maid next to her and said something with a proud face.

'Besarla…kiss her.' Grandma shouted to Cane, who instantly lowered me and placed a long, warm kiss on my cheek, millimeters from my mouth. Thankfully he was still holding onto me, as I was sure my legs would have given way and I would have drowned in front of everyone. The crowd clapped and cheered louder as Peter and Paul swam over to shake hands, fake anger on their faces.

'You tidy up,' Cane said, waving his hand at the now messy pool side. The spectators were quickly vanishing off into the house and gardens. Grandma waved and blew kisses as she toddled off again into the house, always seeming to be busy. 'You can also bring us a couple of celebratory drinks, please,' he laughed, as they shook hands and swung a couple playful punches.

'Sure thing, Boss,' Peter said, turning to me and clapping my shoulder gently in congratulations. 'You've got a good arm on you girl, I'll give you that.' I laughed, shrugging his compliment off.

'Buen juego,' Paulo added too, giving me a high five and then swimming off to take the net down. I turned to Cane with question.

'Good, what?' I asked.

'Game.' Cane translated. 'Good game. He wasn't wrong either, Miss Mack.' He inclined his head at me and began to make his way to the shallow end where there was a ledge to sit on. I followed, feeling delighted with my compliment. 'You must have had a pretty successful school team?' he perched himself on the bank and allowed the water to lap up against his firm chest.

'We did ok,' I replied, modestly, thinking of all the trophies my mum still had up in my old room back home, more evidence of my focused and driven childhood. I sat down by him, sorting my bikini top, long since over my self-consciousness. He had had his arms and hands all over my body this afternoon, it seemed silly now to start worrying about the skin that was on show. Would I have chosen a one-piece if I'd known I was going to see Cane today? Yes, of course! Hell, I would have chosen a wetsuit, but I had dealt with the situation and survived. It fell silent and Peter placed two drinks on the side next to us, then dripped away with Paulo and the net, leaving us alone in the now calm and flat pool. The sun was almost gone behind the trees and we were sitting in the last few existing rays. It was warm and hot still and my top half quickly began to dry. I glanced over at Cane's chest, while taking a sip from my drink. His water droplets were beginning to disappear too, leaving his sheer, flawless skin to soak up the warmth. He exhaled and swallowed a mouthful, then leant his head back with his eyes closed. I licked my lips and pulled my eyes away from him, casting them out over the shimmering water.

'You seem more like you now,' Cane spoke, ending the few minutes of silence. His eyes were still closed but I knew he was listening for my reactions. I bit the inside of my cheek, turning my gaze to him.

'What do you mean?'

'You have a great body, Eva, you look beautiful all the time, I am not too sure why you would feel so self-conscious earlier.' His words were straight and quiet, and my mouth dried instantly, my pupils dilating. Had he just said that he thought I was beautiful?

'Pardon?' I half choked, my eyebrows rising high into my forehead. He opened his eyes slowly and turned his head to face me

'You heard me,' he stated boldly, no shame in his voice. 'Am I not allowed to make compliments?' He turned his whole body to face me now and the sun moved to his strong, carved back, casting his defined chest into shadows. He suddenly felt too close, like his skin was too close to mine and we were both too undressed and too relaxed. I straightened up my spine and swallowed.

'It's a bit inappropriate, don't you think?' I reprimanded.

'There's nothing inappropriate about it, Eva,' he responded with a casual shrug. 'I call things as I see them. Anyway, surely calling my girlfriend beautiful gets me brownie points?' His smile was spreading, making it obvious that he was enjoying himself. Maybe he had had too many drinks…maybe we both had, but I glanced around for company before speaking.

'Yes, well, maybe with an actual *girlfriend,* it would.' I kept a straight face as his eyes danced over mine, then quickly down and back up. I folded my arms over myself in defiance, to which he laughed a little, downing the remainder of his glass.

"Bien, bien, luchadora," he said, shaking his head with defeat. 'Why did you never date anyone but dear old Eddie anyway?' he quizzed, placing his empty drink on the side of the pool. 'It's something I've not been able to get my head around. I'm sure you had plenty of other offers.' Despite myself, I laughed. Mine and Ed's relationship had been complex, especially as of late, but Cane's view of me was obviously very skewed. The person who looked back at me in the mirror each day, with yoga pants and vests on, did not have the sex-appeal he seemed to be talking about. I wasn't sure if this was just another one of his games, but it was a conversation I wasn't willing to take any further.

'Hilarious.' I replied sarcastically, taking another sip of my drink. He laughed, deeply and loudly, his chest rumbling. 'You think I am joking with you?' he challenged, and I raised my eyebrows higher at him with warning.

He lifted his hands in surrender.

'Está bien,' he muttered, shaking his head. 'Fine then, but I was being serious.' It fell into silence again, the voices of the birds filling the void that was now between us. 'But seriously,' Cane's voice perked up again, seemingly unable to leave the topic alone. 'Why did you stay with Edward for so many years? If you hate his business, like you say, and you don't rely on his money, like you say. Why were you with him for so long? I don't get it.' I sat still for a few more seconds, genuinely contemplating his question.

'Did you ever think that maybe it was because I *loved* him?' I turned fully to face him now. The sun shone into my eyes and I squinted slightly to see Canes reaction. He smiled with disbelief and laughed again, as if what I was saying was ridiculous.

'Loved?' he repeated, 'as in past tense? As in, not anymore?' His eyes suddenly burned into mine, like the world hung on my response. We held each other's attention like that for a few moments, everything and nothing being said.

'Well, a lot has changed lately, hasn't it, Mr Rodriguez?' He didn't reply to this, just kept his eyes on me. 'And I guess I was with Ed for so long because of love, yes, but also because after you live a certain way for so long, changing just seems too hard or different or scary.' I swallowed, offering a slight smile. 'You know what I mean?' His shoulders showed the exhale of a laugh, but no sound left his lips. He nodded ever so slightly, and I quietly stood up, getting out of the pool. The breeze rushed in on my bare legs and sent chills over me. 'Thanks for the game.' I added, walking off towards my lounger to collect my towel and flip flops.

'Eva?' Cane called out after me, just as I was away to disappear around the bushes into the house. I paused, looking back at him, still sitting alone in the now shadowy and still pool.

'Yes?'

'For what it's worth, I like that you don't see in yourself what's obvious to everyone else. Edward was a fool.' I exhaled, as a gush of warm-fuzzies overtook my body and I failed to hold in my grin. He always seemed to know the right thing to say to me.

'Thanks, Cane.' I half whispered, smiling slightly and disappearing inside to safety.

By early evening, the maids had made up all the spare rooms for the expected, and unexpected, drunk guests and I moved my stuff from the master suite to the room adjacent. It was smaller with a smaller balcony, but just as beautiful. Maybe even more so for knowing that I didn't have to share it with Cane. I lay on my bed, letting my moisturiser soak in, surprisingly tired from shopping and sunbathing and repeating my conversations with Cane. I was a broken record, going through the same twisted triangle of emotions: attraction, guilt, questioning. It was exhausting. I heard Cane and Grandma downstairs chatting and Cane's voice drifted up to me like a pleasure I could never seem to escape. They were speaking excitedly in Spanish to each other and Grandma was laughing at something Cane was saying. It made me smile, despite myself, to hear them both so happy, the way families should be. I wasn't sure just why, but life was much easier out here and things seemed much simpler. Cane laughed loudly, and it made my arm hairs stand up with delight. *Cane Rodríguez,* I pondered, trying not to think about his comments or about Peter's words from earlier in the day. I kept telling myself that at some time, in the near future, I would hopefully be out of Cane's life and I would never see him again. I would be back with Edward and my family and my life could go on how it was. I could make it all go back to how it was. Couldn't I? I lay pondering on the possibilities and I pictured the glass of grape juice, sitting on my coffee table in my flat. I had been unfair to Ed, I could see that now, but then, he had been no saint either. He would currently still be preparing to take over the business from his dad, becoming the leading man behind the whole driving force. I knew Edward was a fair and kind person, but he was ambitious, and career orientated…and apparently easily led when it came to other women. The thought stirred the echo of what was once hurt. Now, having seen what Canes life was like, I wondered what Edward's future would hold for him as CEO. Would he change to a cold, ruthless and untrusting shell, like Cane had? I was distracted from my thoughts as I heard Cane walk up the stairs. He opened his bedroom door quietly and then stood. He could obviously see that I had moved my stuff out and left his credit card on his bed for him as a parting gift. I'd debated leaving all the receipts too, but decided his bill could do the honours for me. There were footsteps in the hall and then outside my door. They stopped at the threshold and I lay deadly still. Was he coming in? Was he going to knock? He never knocked. I tightened my grip on the moisturizer bottle with waited with baited breath. Seconds passed in silence and then his footsteps echoed, as he walked away again, closing his bedroom door behind him. I exhaled holding my rapidly beating and then feeling something wet on my hands. I looked down to find that I had squeezed lotion everywhere. *Eva!* I thought to myself with deserving reprimand, *he's not even in the room and you are a mess.*

CHAPTER TWENTY-SIX
This will be interesting.

I finally pulled the tag off a summer dress which I'd bought that morning, and having never even lain eyes on the cost once, I discarded the label into the bin. The dress fell over my sun kissed skin and against my body. I put my hands over my rib cage, which was now almost fully healed, and remembered how different things were a few weeks ago. I touched my hand to my neck, recalling. Was somewhere inside of me a micro-chip? Cane's words from my first day on his estate were still vivid, the way he had told me I was now trackable, anywhere and anytime, that I was now his. I doubted his threat more and more every day, feeling that despite what he displayed, Cane really wasn't a monster. So much had changed. I had never imagined any of it would have placed me here, feeling like I did…whatever that was. I stood looking in the mirror at myself, detached, as if I would see a transponder light, flashing, red, through my new dress. Naturally, there was nothing to be seen, but it didn't stop me looking for it every now and then. My life had become a movie; I was transformed from a boring school teacher to a hostage-now-turned-actress. Dinner tonight, as a happy couple, was my next big role. I slipped my feet into my new sandals, still looking at myself in the mirror. I was a stranger. My hair was twisted up into a loose knot at the back, complemented with a pair of simple diamond earrings I'd seen in a boutique window and simply *had* to have. The weight I had lost made me look taller while the time I spent in the gym and walking miles of Cane's garden had toned me. I was sure if Ed was here, he'd tell me that I never looked so good, but to be honest, I didn't feel any better. At least in the days of ponytails and joggers, I knew who I was. Here, now, I didn't really recognise the woman staring back at me. I knew that I was still in there; my stubbornness, my strength, my will to survive, it was all beneath the soft cotton dress, but my convictions, my beliefs, my morals, they all seemed to be more blurred these days. I sighed. Was doing this whole thing with Cane ridiculous? Was pretending to be in love with him, to be his devoted partner, just playing with fire? It was stirring so many feelings and questions, that I was beginning to doubt everything I had once known. In hindsight, I had jumped at the offer of seeing my parents, practically regardless of cost or consequences, which naturally didn't sound like me at all, but now… His flattery and his talk of love last night stayed constantly in the forefront of my mind. Was I in love with him? I mean, who just asks that? Like it would only be natural for a woman to fall in love with him? *Self-centered, egotistical…murderer. Yes, Eva, murderer is the correct word*, I reminded myself, while putting lip balm on and glaring at myself through clear blue eyes. My fingers touched the base of my throat and I remembered, all too clearly, Cane's hand being wrapped around it just days ago. My arm hairs began to rise involuntarily and because I was now this other, new, blurry version of my old self, I didn't know if it was because of the fear I had felt at the time, or because of the passion he had stirred inside me. A knock at the door sent a jolt through me like a gunshot, and I jumped out of my spiraling thoughts. I knew instantly who it was, and I wanted to make him wait. Which he didn't. On the count of one and a half, the door opened, and Cane walked in to me still holding my heart. I went to reprimand him, but the words stifled as I looked over his navy-blue trousers and loose shirt, tailoring him like a Greek God. His skin had darkened in the sun and his Spanish features seemed even more predominant. His dark eyes were alert and his broad, strong shoulders were relaxed. He was flawless in every sense and that not only took my words away, but also my breath. He smiled at me and his eyes did their obvious appraisal, coming back to my head with apparent approval. He leant on the door frame and folded his arms. I swallowed. Why did he seem *even more* attractive in Spain? It made no sense.

'Do I even want to know how much you cost me today?' he asked, referring to the new outfit. I shrugged casually and walked towards him, feeling smug in the knowledge that I had spent A LOT of his money. He cast his eyes over me again, more slowly. 'Well you look beautiful, so I am sure it was worth every penny.' My throat dried up at his praise and my leading high ground plummeted like a dead bird shot out of the sky. And that was the power back to him, then. Cane, ever in control of a conversation. 'Shall we?' he invited, standing aside to the door. I pulled my pathetic self together and continued towards him, now very self-conscious and sure my face was bright red. His hand rested on the base of my back, as he gently guided me out of the room. It felt like home.

Dinner was in the same place as before, served outside in the warm evening air with the sound of crickets and nature gently humming around us. Grandma had taken my hand and pulled me into the seat next to her, her strength still surprisingly frightening for an old woman. Drinks and breadsticks were served as Grandma retold the events from their day. Her and Cane had gone off to do some private things and her eyes watering slightly as she mentioned visiting the gravesides of her husband, son and daughter-in-law. I glanced sideways to Cane, acknowledging that it would have been the graves of his father and mother that they went to. His face remained like stone, no emotions showing, but his eyes, which watched his Grandmother, looked as if they were a million miles away, intense with distance. I gently placed my hand on his arm and he looked towards me, still unreadable. I remembered what Grandma had said about Cane, having to grow up quickly after his parents died and having to step up and run the business. I recalled reading his file and it saying that he had been twenty-one when he took full ownership of Rodriguez Enterprises. Handsome, cold, ruthless...and really young. Maybe when your all-of-a-sudden dead parents leave you a multi-billion-pound worldwide company with no handover advice or guidance, that was how you had to be. I watched him and his eyes as they stayed with me, yet drifted away in his thoughts. It must have been hard on him, I decided with a hint of pity. I couldn't ever remember reading anything about how his parents died, which was odd, but I could clearly see a photo in his file of them both. She was beautiful beyond measure and his dad had been a classically handsome man. Cane's brow creased slightly in thought and I found my hand tightening around his tensed forearm. It was obvious where his flawless features had been inherited from and I wondered what else of him was genetic. The penetrating stare obviously was, as proven by Grandma, but had his gentle, kind side been from his mum? The idea made him seem very human and I felt for him, being now so alone in the world, maybe wondering the same questions. Cane's eyes refocused on mine and I looked into them for answers. Naturally, I found none.

'The way you two look at each other, remind me so much how I used to look at your abuelo.' Grandma said loudly, talking about Cane's grandfather and breaking our gaze. She was smiling, her tanned wrinkled hand placed over her heart. Cane cleared his throat, composing himself, then flashed her a winning smile. No dimples though. I retracted my hand and I lowered my head, taking slightly longer to collect myself. It was still strange thinking of Cane with weaknesses, with human emotions that affected him. He was one of the few people I'd ever met, who could rival my talent for hiding truths beneath the surface; emotionally, mentally, vocally. Cane, like myself, could say one thing, mean another and feel something completely different altogether. Not a talent one liked to boast about and it meant trying to figure Cane out was nigh impossible. Noises in the house distracted the moment and Grandma was suddenly on her feet, gushing excitedly in Spanish. I watched her with confusion until I heard the dreaded voices and my stomach dropped. My jaw tightened as I struggled to practice the talent I so recently reviewed. The Rodriguez brothers were here. I could hear them both exchanging welcomes with their Grandma, voices being muffled as they embraced each other. Cane was watching me, so I swallowed my very understandable anxiety and set my nonchalant expression. This satisfied him, and he nodded gently as if to say, 'that's more like it'.

'They know the drill,' he added emotionlessly, pushing his seat back as footsteps made their way into the back garden. I exhaled deeply. I'd been through worse, I assured myself. And besides, with Grandma here, they could do nothing. The thought was like a piece of heaven and I told it to myself again. While Grandma was around, we were all stuck to the pretences of nicety, *including* the brothers. They could do nothing to me. I smiled at the idea. Here, in the game of make believe, we were all in the same boat. All equal. And we were all a happy family. The knowledge encouraged me, and I sat a little taller and bolder. 'And you know, Eva,' Cane was saying, holding his hand out in my direction. I turned to them, standing up.

'Elias,' I squealed with fake enthusiasm, rushing over and wrapping my arms around him. He froze, rigid, then realising he was being watched by Grandma, awkwardly half tapped my back. 'Andreas,' I continued with equal animation, turning to repeat the same gesture with him. I got much the same reaction, but with a hint of confusion in his pretend smile. Grandma clapped her hands together with delight.

'Sí, Sí! It's so nice to see everyone so happy, feliz. Eva, you make these boys better, hugging and smiling.' She grabbed my hand and led me back to the table, leaving the boys to follow, and Andreas and Elias to give Cane odd questioning stares. I saw him shrug slightly in answer. 'This one's a keeper, Cane,' Grandma advised affectionately, sitting us all back down.

'So how long *exactly* you two been citas...' she searched for the translation. I knew she had said 'dating' already and was preparing my face for the questions end. '...seeing each other?' she ended, dipping her bread into some oil, completely unaware of the stares going on around her.

'A while now,' Cane offered as vaguely as possible.

'Although it feels like much longer,' I sung sweetly, batting my eyelashes at him. He returned my gaze with a firm one, but I could see him holding back a smirk.

'When you two going to find chicas as nice as Eva and settle down? It pain me to see you, coqueteando, *flirt,* around like you are still young. No tan joven!' The two men sat speechless, as if they'd heard this conversation many times before. Andreas rolled his eyes while his Grandmother gave Elias her stare. Their faces, after being told they were 'not that young anymore', were a picture and I couldn't control my smile. Grandma was a smart and switched-on woman and obviously knew her grandsons well. It actually made me a little nervous to think that we were trying to fool her. I took a sip of my drink, trying to hide my smile, but not before Elias clocked it and shot me a dirty look. Naturally, this only added to my amusement.

'It's so hard to find girls who are genuine nowadays though guys, isn't it?' I decided to comment, placing my glass down and grinning as sweetly as I could at Grandma. She nodded zealously in agreement. Andreas's glare intensified at my audacity to weigh in on the conversation. Elias kept his sharp stare locked on me with warning. 'I've told you before, that I'd be more than willing to help you both scrub up and try find someone who's actually worthy of you.' Andreas practically choked on the nail he had chosen to bite, no doubt in attempt to try keep himself silent, and Elias's dirty look turned to murderous. I sat back happy, knowing I was currently untouchable. They deserved everything they got. A few snide and low blow comments didn't make up for hours of being hung over and hugging a toilet bowl. We weren't even slightly close to being even yet.

'Awww,' Grandma sighed, giving me adoring eyes. Normally, I'd have felt guilty for lying, but I was almost telling the truth, they did need to change. I was sure they'd never find the type of girl Grandma was talking about, if they stayed the same brainless, thoughtless idiots they were now. 'Eva, you are too kind.' Grandma said, nudging a now blood-red Andreas. 'You better take her up on offer,' she smiled, pointing at them both.

'In fact,' I continued gleefully, 'I'll personally make sure I find a wonderful young lady for you to spend time with at the party tomorrow night. I am sure Grandma has some great people coming.' Grandma clapped.

'Lo que es una idea maravillosa, Eva.' *Yes Grandma,* I thought smugly to myself, *it is a wonderful idea, thank you.* If looks could actually inflict pain, I would have been writhing around on the floor by now. Still the satisfaction of knowing I was safe from comeback, just fueled my delight and set my brain buzzing with all the cheap, nasty, insults I could say to the pair of bullies. They knew that I could now lump them with the most ridiculous girls I could find at tomorrow night's party and that they would be denied their normal, beautiful models. They would never risk upsetting their grandmother and nor would they oppose Cane's orders. And Cane's orders, were to keep his grandma in blissful happiness. I smiled wider, a delightfully, angelic smile.

'Eva,' Grandma continued, 'if you can find these boys someone who can see them as I do, and as their parents did...'she trailed off thoughtfully, a clouded look coming over her, and her eyes began to suddenly shimmer with tears. Was she thinking about family and all she had lost? No matter, Cane finally stepped in and decided enough was enough. He changed the subject with a final warning stare to us all. He was the boss of everyone after all, and so we all obeyed.

'Abuela, tell the boys where we were today,' he began, changing the subject and patting her hand softly, coaxing her back to settle on happier things. The fog cleared, and her sparkling eyes brightened as she began to recall the old childhood spots her and Cane had visited that day and the love-filled memories they held. They all reminisced and laughed as they expanded on the tales for me. Naturally at every opportunity I could, I would slide in a cheap comment about the brothers, laced with fake love and sickening affection. I'd allow just enough time for the insult to be there, before adding something disgustingly adorable. I was loving every second of this. Grandma missed them all, but the brothers missed nothing and barely managed to stifle their desire to retaliate, less and less obviously, with each passing comment. Eventually, they excused themselves for their plans to catch up with old friends in the town, but not before grandma forced a kiss for me from them both, both of which were not surprisingly rather rough. Cane sat watching with a mixture of unreadable signs, tapping his forefinger off the table and analysing. We small talked for a while longer then Grandma pushed us all off to bed with promise of lateness the next night at the party. We said our good evenings and head off in different direction of the house. We walked in silence until we reached my new bedroom door.

'Interesting evening,' Cane began, putting his hands in his pockets. I shied away from looking at him, not really wanting to be reprimanded. 'I'd maybe sleep with your door locked tonight,' he added, casually. This comment made me look up, eyes wide. He was kidding, right? We were in grandma's house, his brothers would never...would they? He wasn't smiling, and my victorious glee quickly vanished. I hated when he was right. Even without saying a word of rebuke, he'd very effectively chastised me for being foolish enough to provoke his brothers. I turned my eyes to him, feeling full of stubborn frustration.

'They deserved it,' I flared, defiantly. 'I have never felt so sick in my entire life. And I'm finding them an awful girl tomorrow,' I pointed my finger at him. 'They *deserve* it.' His lips cracked a note of humour, but then quickly vanished. There was a quiet pause.

'Can I come in for a drink?' he asked, confidently, as if it wasn't even really a question. My eyes widened. 'At least let me check your door locks,' he laughed, stopping my protests. As much as my head wanted to take the chance to shun him and play the upper hand, the largest part of me wanted him to come in– to check that the door did locked, of course.

'Fine, but only to check the door.' He smiled, with dimples, and walked past me into the room. *Damn it, dimples!* I already knew my resolve was going to melt before the door was even closed behind us. He crossed the room quickly and poured a couple of drinks. He passed one over to me as he headed back towards the door again, flicking the old switch on the handle. He turned the knob, and pulled at the door, but it stayed put.

'Locked,' he confirmed, taking a sip of the strong dark liquid. I eyed mine with suspicion and decided nothing good would come from it. The last time I'd been drunk was when it had been *encouraged* by the brothers and Cane had ended up holding my hair while I threw up, that definitely wasn't happening again tonight. He left the door impenetrable and began walking towards the window. I kicked off my shoes and leant back onto the old desk, watching him. He was relaxed tonight, looking casual, comfortable and seemingly social.

'Do you have any friends?' I asked, seeing him spin on his heels to meet me with an astonished look, then a smile. He choked a laugh.

'Insulting as that sounds, why'd you ask that?'

'I don't mean it like that,' I explained, smiling, 'I just never see you, hangout.' For some reason, the word 'hangout', seemed ridiculous in association with Cane. I tried to explain myself. 'You know what I mean. I never see you relaxed with people over, like buddies and friends and...' I paused slightly, '...girls." The last word caught his attention and he looked at me with his full gaze. He observed me for a full few seconds before speaking.

'You know, I never went to University,' he began, completely changing the subject. He took a full mouthful and finished his drink.

'Really?' I queried, surprised I hadn't known that fact. It made sense that he hadn't been able to attend University once he'd taken over the business, but he had been twenty-one when he had happened. Surely, he had time to fit a course in before that?

'De verdad,' he confirmed, repeating my words. He was back at the desk next to me, filling a second glass. 'That surprises you?' he asked to my nodding.

'I'm a teacher, I assume everyone should go to Uni,' he smiled and raised his glass to me slightly. 'You are known worldwide as one of the brightest and most successful business minds, and yet you didn't even go to uni?' He nodded firmly.

'Corecto. Although, I'm not sure the whole world refers to me as the *brightest and most successful mind.*' I held up my finger at him.

'Actually, yes they do. Classes study you.' He raised his eyebrows at me. 'Not *my* classes, mind you.' His smiled widened, taking another mouthful. 'So, what did you do between school and *this*?' I asked waving my hand up and down at him. He pursed his lips at my term 'this' and then shrugged, as if that was his answer to my question. 'You did do something though, for those two years in between, right?' He finished his glass again, exhaling slowly. I cast my mind back to his file. What had it said? I remembered what school he attended, that he'd done well and graduated top of his class, but there was nothing on him really until he started running the business. 'So, what did you do?' I asked again, getting the very obvious feeling that he was avoiding the answer. That in itself intrigued me more than anything. 'Cane?' I probed, only to be met with a blank face. I narrowed my eyes at him with suspicion and he shook his head as if to say, 'no chance'. 'Can I guess what you did?' I asked with a small playful grin. Refilling his glass, he returned my smile with one of his own and a nod.

'This will be interesting,' he added, signaling with his hand for me to begin. I studied him playfully.

'Were you a porn star?'

'Trust you to lower the tone,' he replied, shaking his head at me with dimples. I laughed, but raised my eyebrows awaiting an answer. 'No, Eva, I was not a porn star,' he stated, incredulously. 'I'd have been far too shy at nineteen for that.' He sat on the bed opposite me, removing his jacket and awaiting the next guess.

'Did you work in the fashion industry, as a model maybe?' To this he laughed, rolling his head backwards.

'A model?' he repeated, as if it was the most ridiculous statement ever made. I smiled at his response, not even entertaining the idea that he didn't know how attractive he was. I was sure that was impossible for even him to deny.

'Fine,' I continued, ignoring him shaking his head and muttering 'a model' to himself.

'Two years?' I queried, to which he nodded in confirmation. He swallowed the remainder of his drink.

'You know, it scares me how well you know my past. How did you know it was only a two-year gap?' He remained perched on the bed.

'Your file,' I began, 'I read it…' I paused, '…once. I just remember it.' He nodded casually.

'You know, if circumstances were different,' I glared at him to tread carefully with his next comment, circumstances were not something he and I could deal with lightly, 'I'd head-hunt you with a memory like that. Reading something only *once* and remembering every little detail. It's very impressive.' I rolled my eyes at him as he rose to get another drink. I was keeping count, this was his fifth. 'Seriously,' he continued, casting a side glance at me as he refilled. I ignored him and continued.

'Did you elope to Paris with some airhead blonde, just for it all to end in a messy divorce and millions of lawyers fees?' He paused before answering, a dry look of 'very funny' written on his face.

'Firstly, you know I've never been married, since you've read my file *una*,' he made air quotations for the word 'once' and gave me a yeah-right look, 'and secondly, I'd like to hope my first marriage will be my only marriage.' I caught his eye and felt the floor move beneath me. That might have been the most romantic thing I'd ever heard a man say, and I'd known some charmers in my time. My skin began to flush with a burning desire and I placed my hands down on the desk to steady my balance. Thankfully he returned to his perch on the bed across the room, putting distance between us.

'Just so you actually do know,' I added, quickly trying to regain some dignity, 'I did only read your file once'. I copied his quotation marks. 'It wasn't exciting enough to read twice'. He laughed again, and I continued before he could say anything else sarcastic. 'Ok fine, then, did you open your own shop of man suits and teach people how to always have their hands in their pockets?' To this Cane choked on his drink, spraying liquid across the floor.

'A what shop?' he asked with a slightly bemused tone, wiping his lusciously inviting lips. I leapt off the desk and picked up his jacket to mimic him, standing all boldly and confidently, my hands in my fake pockets, cocky and casual, like I owned the world. I even gave him a display of his walk and it must have been either pretty good, or pretty ridiculous, because he burst into roaring hysterics, rolling backwards onto the bed. I hadn't seen him laugh so hard before and the sound was like honey and happiness, freezing me to the spot. I don't know why it surprised me, that another quality of his was so addictive, but it was like gravity, pulling me regardless of will. I beamed uncontrollably, then despite myself, I began to laugh. Cane was a force of nature, regardless of the emotion he was displaying, and when he let go, he pulled everything into his vortex. I took off his coat and put it back on the bed next to him as he continued to roar. I watched his lips pull back into a perfect smile and his dimples etch themselves into his cheeks. His eyes were scrunched closed and the lines by his eyes seemed to glow. Even falling around with laughter, he was flawless. Eventually, he wiped his eyes and began clearing his throat, still hardly able to look at me without setting himself off again.

'I'll take that as a no, then?' I finally continued, shaking my head at him.

'That might have been the funniest thing I've ever seen,' Cane chuckled, standing and coming to the table to refill his cup again. Was this glass six? Maybe that was why he was so relaxed and laughable tonight? He sipped a little, then turned to me still with a smile. 'No, I don't own a *man-suit* shop, Eva.' A small snigger snuck out again. 'And for the record, I do not look or walk anything like what you just did, just so we are clear.' He pointed a humorous finger at me. I waved it away.

'Footballer?' I shot out.

'Nope'

'Farmer?'

'No.'

'Army?'

'El ejército?' he repeated, with wide eyes. 'I wouldn't have survived.'

'Ran a dating agency?'

'Like a pimp?' he asked, offended. I shrugged sarcastically, and he eyed me over the rim of his glass, swallowing.

'No.'

'Accountant?'

'Boring.'

'Dentist?'

'Really?'

'Fine! I give up,' I protested, holding my hands up in frustration. 'Just tell me. It can't be that bad, surely?

'I don't think anyone bar my family knows to be honest. I found people judged.'

'I promise I won't judge.' I encouraged, keeping a straight face and batting my eyelashes.

'Bein,' he caved, groaning. 'Fine. Come here.' He nodded to the space on the bed next to him and I walked over, sitting down. I briefly acknowledged, that not so long ago I wouldn't have voluntarily stood in the same football pitch as him, let alone sat by him on a bed. He finished the drink and closed his eyes slightly, as if to recall a deep memory. 'Between the ages of nineteen and twenty-one...' he paused, trailing off, about to change his mind.

'Cane!' I urged. 'It honestly can't be that bad. I won't judge you, I promise, ok?' I nodded my head repeatedly to encourage him and he eyeballed me, sighing and seeming giving up.

'Fine,' he tutted with defeat. 'I worked in Africa teaching kids English.' I laughed instantly, shoving him and telling him to be serious. He sat dead still. Oh, he was serious. What? This man, this still apparent stranger to me, volunteered in a third world country for two years? Working with children? With children! I held his eyes, now showing almost a degree of vulnerability. How did someone change *so* much in the space of so few years? My mouth began to smile with affection, before I could stop it and this strange wave of appreciation swam through me, appreciation for him. For Cane Rodriguez! Something I NEVER thought I'd feel. I had seen another glimpse of the real him and I loved it. He had been a good boy once, innocent and giving, and I knew that was all still inside of him, just buried under the years of his brutal twenties. His voice deep voice broke through my thoughts. 'You said you wouldn't judge,' he half whispered, presuming to already know what I was thinking. But for once, in our bizarre relationship, he was wrong. I shook my head slowly, keeping his eyes and taking in his whole face; his dark skin, his slight worry lines, the tanned creases in the corners of his lids, his long lashes and appealing lips. He was a strange, beautiful creature and I wondered if he'd ever become less surprising.

'I'm not *judging* you, Cane,' I said gently. 'I am just impressed, what an amazing thing to have done. It must have been incredible. And that two years is something to be proud of, not to hide away from.' I nudged his shoulder slightly and saw his chest begin to rise and fall. He exhaled audibly and dropped his eyes, leaving us sitting in silence. I knew that something had just changed, because his disposition clouded like the weather in Scotland, casting the ambience in the room to a very quiet silence. Had I overstepped the mark? The ticking of the grandfather clock was now the only sound around us and I assumed that I'd somehow ruined the night. I was contemplating what to say to break the quiet, trying to pick the right words, when Cane's voice began to speak, his shiny eyes suddenly looking to mine.

'I don't remember the last time someone commended me for doing something truly *good*, Eva.' He rubbed his chin with his strong hands. 'It's been too long. You forget how healthy praise feels.' I dared not move as he poured his genuine, heartfelt thoughts out. Was he admitting remorse just now? Or regret? I watched him like a time bomb, thrown completely by his display of emotions. He cleared his throat, sitting up straight. Maybe he was a little drunk, I considered as he exhaled loudly, standing abruptly to his feet. He poured himself another drink and took a sip, turning to face me. I identified my internal moral struggle. I felt sorry for him, for his obvious lack of love over the years, but more so than my pity, I felt insanely turned on by this honest vulnerable side. It was wrong, really wrong and I knew it. Yet I couldn't control it. Watching him standing there, exposed and trusting, made me want to comfort the man in ways that I knew I shouldn't. I swallowed the pulse-racing thought quickly, trying to shake the images from my very twisted head.

'Cane…' I began slowly.

'You want to know why you never see me at the house hanging out, Eva?' he interrupted, loudly and almost angrily. I silenced and remained still. 'I don't trust anyone enough to have friends.' He laughed bitterly.

'Hell, I don't even fully trust my brothers.' He opened his mouth and downed the rest of the glass in one, banging it firmly down on the desk.

'Two hundred times bitten…forever shy.' He walked towards me, pointing his finger and I stayed frozen. 'I can honestly say, that I trust you more than anyone else in my life right now,' This got a reaction.

'Me?' I repeated in a high pitch, holding my hand against my chest. He laughed, sitting back down next to me and nodded. The resentment left his voice.

'Sí, tu,' he confirmed, nudging me with his arm. The skin on skin contact sent tickles into my spine and I sat straighter, allowing them moving space. 'I always know where I stand with you. You're *honest*,' he added with a strange smile. 'Brutally.' Now I knew he must be drunk. 'I almost forgot what real honesty felt like, until you came along, Eva.' I sat facing him, dead still, afraid that if I moved my heart would burst through my chest and straight into his arms. I could feel my palms begin to turn clammy and my breathing shorten. I recognized the feeling very well from every other close encounter I'd had with him. 'Are you hearing me, Eva?' he asked, laughing at me. 'You look stunned'. I cleared my throat, finding my voice amidst my thudding heart.

'Well, I am.' I answered honestly.

'Do you understand what I am trying to say?' He was looking straight at me, straight *in* me, and to be quite honest, I didn't have a clue what he was talking about anymore. I shook my head blankly.

'Not a clue.' I utter as he laughed loudly, then turned to face me dead on. It normally didn't end well for me when he did this.

'Listen carefully then, I doubt I'll be brave enough or stupid enough…or drunk enough, to say this again.' Why did I feel like I was holding my breath? 'Eva Mack, you are the best thing that's ever happened to me.' He half smiled, 'Hell, I'll say it in Spanish for you too…eres lo mejor que me a pasado.' He nodded firmly. 'Period.' He was pointing at me with a strange look on his face. *Business wise, though right? That's what he means, business wise…I was the best thing that had ever happened to him business wise? Speak Eva, clarify it! Do it now.* Silence. More silence. Even more silence. Cane watched me, then nodded, starting to smile. He pulled off his shirt, suddenly leaving himself in a white vest. I tried to look away, despite my wide eyes, but it was like my focus was glued to him. I literally couldn't have stopped looking if the whole world depended on it. I had never experienced him so honest, so informal, so….sexy. His dark skin and toned arms seemed to be calling out for me, *take me, take me, I can hold you.* I cleared my throat, as he threw his shirt aside and pulled himself up to the pillows on the bed, laying back with his fingers interlocked behind his head. His biceps stretched his skin and I could see his solid chest rising and falling through his thin vest. I yearned for those strong arms to hold me and my head to rest on that chest. He looked like the postcard you sent to people to gloat, *'wish you were here'*, and man, did I wish I was there. He nodded for me to join him, but I was stuck, unable to move. My mind was struggling to process everything, all the words he was saying, their intent and meaning. And if that wasn't hard enough, I had his beautifully toned and muscular body laid out in front of me like a platter of flawless perfection. My head was going to explode. I desperately trying to ignore him and his luring physique, trying to ignore his smooth and enticing words, to assume it was all business and all just a game, but my heart was having none of it. His words echoed in my fully crammed head. *I was the best thing that had ever happened to him? Me?* My hands were held tightly together on my lap, my knuckles turning white as the blood struggled to make its way through my clenched fingers. Did he know what he did to me? Did he do it on purpose? Did he feel even a fraction of what I was continuously struggling to not feel? Questions! I had so many questions inside of me, desperate to be answered. *Ask them Eva, ask them now.*

'Eva?' his voice came as if he'd bellowed beside my ear. I jumped slightly and looked over his way, as casually as I could. He nodded for me to join him again, but I was literally stuck to my spot. His eyes softened. 'I just want to talk,' he reassured, 'I promise.' The problem was, him lying there in his vest, on my bed, late at night, in a romantic foreign country, didn't make me want to just 'talk'. *You deserve some slack*, my heart called out, urging me on. *Even if just for the night.* My heart was right. Damn it, if the last few weeks had proved anything, it was that I had will power. I could handle something as easy as talking, especially because, at the end of the day, I *wanted* to lie there with Cane and talk. I shut my head off and climbed up the bed, lying sideways to face him with my hands under my face.

'What do you want to talk about?' I asked, inhaling his sent as slyly as possible.

'Ask me a question.' He turned onto his side to face me, our bodies now lying parallel to each other. I closed my eyes briefly to block out his proximity and to think of a question. I reopened them to meet his deep, dark gaze watching me so intently I was sure he'd been counting my eyelashes. I cleared my throat.

'Ready?' He tipped his forehead slightly to confirm.

'Shoot.' I inhaled.

'Whatever happened to those three employees from the first day I came to you? The ones in your office?' I didn't say, 'who you were about to shoot', but the meaning was left lingering there. His face quickly flashed with shame, but then was gone. He blew out deeply and very slowly, his drink tinted breathe brushing my face.

'It seems like a long time ago, doesn't it?' he began, gently. I nodded in complete understanding, it felt like forever ago. I could still remember being scared and confused as if it was yesterday, but the fear I'd felt that day, I hadn't felt with Cane in a long time. If anything, those feelings were merging into their very opposites. I now felt safe with him, safe when he was around. He kept his eyes on mine as he began slowly. 'I've apologised to them,' he muttered as a smile began to spread across my lips. The idea of Cane apologising to anyone, let alone three incapable employees, was just amusing. He narrowed his eyes at my obvious enjoyment, but carried on. 'I moved them to a different estate with new jobs and new people.' I nodded, surprised but happy.

'I thought you killed them anyway.' I replied quietly, not actually sure he did want to hear the honesty he'd spoken about earlier. He pursed his lips.

'I almost did,' he confirmed, this time with real shame in his voice. His eyes lowered from mine, being pulled away into inner thoughts and his eyebrows creased in trouble.

'But you didn't,' I added, touching my fingers gently on his hand. Instantly those eyes of his were back on me and I could feel the heat from his body running up me. I took my hand away quickly, changing the focus. 'Ok, your turn,' I offered in a lighter tone. 'Ask me a question.' His easygoing grin returned, and he readjusted his position, propping his head up with one arm, his bicep flexing.

'Who do you *hang-out* with, in your spare time?' I knew he was making reference to my question earlier, but my stomach dropped. I looked down to compose myself and hide my betraying eyes. I hadn't thought about Tammy in a while now, not since I had locked her away in the vault. I wasn't ready to pull her out yet and relive the pain of her betrayal, but that was what he was asking me to do. I gulped discretely, determined not to ruin the moment. I would answer truthfully, in the spirit of tonight's truce, but I would only offer the manageable emotions.

'It was that girl, Tammy. You remember her?' I answered, unable to stop myself from thinking of her and her craziness that I used to love. Cane's face fell with what was unmistakably, regret. He had forgotten. I smiled at him, finding that his concern was somehow helpful in easing my pain. I sighed out loud, feeling considerably calmer than I thought I would have been when I finally had to mention her name. 'She was always there for me, I can't think of any time that she was not there to just listen, even when...' I paused as a hard-to-control flash of rage ran through my veins, '*especially* when it was to do with Edward...' I exhaled and relaxed my jaw, 'and business stuff. We'd been friends for years you know? Since I can remember anyway.' Cane's face had changed, and something crossed his eyes, but as normal, it was gone too quickly for me to see what it was. 'She's also the most snobby, devious, backstabbing, vindictive, malicious, cruel...' I inhaled again, cutting myself off and trying to calm my climbing temper. I sat quiet and still for a moment, breathing, centering. 'She is also the most hilarious and alive person I've ever known.' I laughed slightly, thinking of our last conversation at the cafe where she'd just bought some crazy expensive shoes and explained her current affair with a married man. I wondered ironically if it was *my* married man, but then remembered that he'd had been ancient. Against my better self and despite my resentment towards her, I missed her. I hated her just now and never wanted to see her ever again, but I missed the innocent trust and love I once had bestowed in her. I wondered if she knew what had happened to me? If she knew that her and Edwards secret was out? Had Ed told her? My fists tensed involuntarily, and I looked up to see assessing eyes locked onto me, watching, as if I was a new species. I coughed, suddenly realising that this little episode had snuck up on me unexpectedly. It wouldn't happen again. Back to the vault.

'Ok, próxima preguntan,' Cane announced *next question* rather bluntly, obviously wanting to change the subject. I saw a hint of pity shade his face and that was the last thing I wanted now, pity. I thought of a question quickly, to lighten the mood and return our evening to that of miraculous escape. Who wanted brutal real life when we could stay in denial?

'If you could do anything on a Saturday night, what would it be?' I smiled calmly at him, letting him know that I was fine. He laughed a little, lifting his hand towards me and playfully redirecting.

'What do you think it would be?'. I had a quick think.

'I'd say you'd either choose to work or to be out with some supermodel, at a glamorous restaurant, spending some of your incredible volumes of wealth...' I paused with a smile, 'actually, you'd probably choose to work, wouldn't you?' He smiled back.

'I work, Eva, because a) I need to, and b) I prefer my own company to that of superficial *supermodels*.' He smiled cockily. 'And you're wrong, neither of those are my ideal Saturday night.' I raised my eyebrows in question, waiting to be corrected. 'If I could do anything with my Saturday nights, I'd choose to stay in, to put on lounge clothes, pick a movie, make some popcorn and sit on the couch, relaxed,' he paused, 'probably with you, someone I feel myself around.' His ideal Saturday night sounded exactly like my ideal Saturday night. I let the idea of lazing around in our pj's together float in my mind for a split second, pretending like maybe he meant it for real. I had no idea what had happened to my normal, cool composure or my ability to hide real thoughts and feelings, but for some reason tonight, those talents were gone. I was left bare, open for him to read like a book. And honestly, I actually liked it.

'You just want to hang out with me because I'm the only one who wouldn't sell pictures of you in your pj's to the press.' He barked a laugh, probably understanding that I was dodging yet another personal moment.

'Cierto, true,' he agreed, then continued. 'My turn.' He lowered his head to the pillow. 'If you could know anything for sure in your life, what would it be?' It was a bold question to ask, considering what we'd been through in the last few weeks and the magnitude of events still looming in my future. Surely the obvious answer was, the end to this whole mess? The future of Ed and I? What was going to happen to the business? To my family? What I should have done differently? The possibilities were endless of the things I'd like to know about for sure, but with brutal and selfish honesty, only one real question mattered to me right now. I swallowed hoping to empower myself.

'I'd like to know for sure if you mean what you say or if you are just playing games with me.' I kept his eyes, determined to not look like his answer mattered that much. The volcano inside me knew better though and it was a physical effort to not appear desperately invested in his answer. He didn't reply quickly, in fact, he was silent for what felt like an eternity, just watching me. Finally, though, he exhaled slowly, and his breath gently blew the hairs that had fallen around my face. For that split-second, I imagined that breath preceding a kiss, a gentle, deep, meaningful kiss, which he placed longingly on my parted and wanting lips. My heart began to speed with delight at the thought and my traitorous body lusted for the real thing, for him. Those turned up lips were only inches away, I would just have to lean forward.

'You don't trust me?' he asked quietly, raising his strong hand to my face and tracing a finger down my cheek. My whole body shivered at his touch and despite trying to stop myself, I leant my head into his hand.

'I want to,' I answered honestly, 'but I'm so confused'. I creased my brow in frustration and he gently ran his hand across my head, soothing the lines away.

'I trust you,' he answered quietly, eyes still locked on mine.

'You have nothing to lose though,' I replied defensively, to which he retracted his hand and shook his head.

'*I* have nothing to lose?' he repeated my words with emphasis. 'I have more to lose here than anyone.'

'How?'

'Being with you, Eva, changes me more than I ever thought anything could. I am a different person. I *want* to be a different person, but doing that compromises everything in my life, everything stable that I have.'

'And for me it's all easy-peasy?' I asked, a little louder than I'd planned. 'I don't know if I'm a pawn in a game and if this whole thing we've been dancing around for weeks now is just a twisted little 'extra' that'll sting Edward. I'd lose my whole family, my friends, my life. I want to trust you, I want to fully believe that you're the man my gut tells me you are, but everything I've been raised to know about you screams differently. I don't know if what I feel is real or what I've been told is real. And you're cryptic hot-then-cold attitude doesn't help at all.' He sat silent, breathing as if weighing up everything I'd just said. Then, before I knew it, he reached out and took my hand. I could feel his strength as he locked his fingers around mine into a gentle vice. His heat felt like it was burning into my bones, etching itself in me. I was holding my breath again, eyes transfixed on him and he was looking deeper into me than he had ever done.

'You-can-trust-me-Eva.' He said slowly and firmly. 'I will never do anything to hurt you again.' He squeezed my hand tighter. 'Me crees?' He asked if I believed him, his eyes boring into my soul intently. I hesitated.

'I want to,' I began. 'And I can try, but it takes time to earn trust, Cane.' He watched me as a flash of disappointment crossed his face, only to be quickly recovered. 'This man here, right now, is the man I'll learn to trust.' He nodded slowly, a glimmer of hope settling in his eyes.

'I understand that.' He whispered. I cast my eyes to the clock to check the time, it was late. My hand was still held firmly in his, lying between us like a bridge. His thumb had begun to stroke my fingers in the most reassuringly, comfortable way. I had to stop myself from moaning out loud. It felt so good. It felt like something between us had finally happened; words had been uttered, feelings exposed, and truths addressed. It was all out there now. It was massive and daunting and electrifying all at the same time. But we had taken a step of some kind. This was a moment, a proper movie moment, when the tides changed, and fate was altered. I could feel it inside of me. *He cared. He said he cared about me. About me?* The confirmed hope was settling inside of me with a spreading warmth. I felt like I would burst with pent up delight. His words replayed on loop as we lay still, each run just out doing the last. In my head, I knew I should feel some shame and fear at the steps Cane and I were taking, but while his thumb was stroking my hand and his gorgeous eyes were dancing over my face, I just couldn't bring my heart to care. The clocks tick came back into focus and echoed through the room.

'It's late,' I said reluctantly, to which he nodded his head.

'Can I just stay a while?' he asked, quietly. 'We don't need to talk anymore. Let's just lie here, have a time out.' I smiled at him with a little nod, silently desperate to keep him here longer anyway. His dimples flashed delight and I shuffled my position, letting him keep hold of my hand. We lay there for a while just looking at each other, hearing the ticking of time as it went by us. It felt like a different reality, like a world away from life, away from all the mess. I felt my eyes begin to close as sleep called to me and as much as I fought it, desperately not wanting to fall asleep and leave this magical moment, it was stronger than me and my relaxed body drifted off with Cane's dark, deep, beautiful eyes watching over me.

CHAPTER TWENTY-SEVEN.
This was no fairy tale.

The clock struck one a.m. and Eva had been asleep for a while now. He lay deadly still, not daring to disturb the magical reality he found himself in. It was dark and warm, and for once, he was not alone. He kept his tired eyes fixed on Eva's face, watching her every little move while she slept. He knew he'd thought it before, but now he understood and accepted every part of its truth, that she was perfect. Her long dark eye lashes fluttered as she dreamt, and he desperately wished he could know what she was thinking. Her hair was swept behind her ear and flowed away like a dark silky river. He longed to run his fingers through it, to feel it brush against his skin. Her lips were parted slightly as she breathed, and he had to physically restrain himself from leaning in to kiss her, to tenderly and lovingly place his mouth on hers. Who was this man she roused in him, this stranger? Had this version of himself always been here, dormant, or was it new, created by her and only for her? Either way, he cherished it, and was enjoying the feeling of loving again. When had he last lay awake to just look at someone, to try and force a permanent picture of them into his head so that he would never be able to remove it or forget it? Had he even ever *felt this way? Her breath blew against his cheeks and she mumbled in her dreams, his heart reacting to it with pleasure and surprising satisfaction. He wished life could actually stop, that he could use all this money and power and prevent the hands on the clock from turning and taking away each second spent here with her. The ticking though, came back into focus and filled the whole room again. His influence and wealth meant nothing here, could do nothing to affect her and their time, or affect how she felt and what she did. Maybe that was why it all felt so precious to him? He carefully lifted his hand to her face, knowing their moment was nearing its end and that that he must leave to honour her request; that they didn't share a bed. He touched her lips with such gentle want it made him tremble. How could she ever trust him? How could he ever convince her that he was changed, that he was ready to keep changing? Time was not on their side, nothing was. This was no fairy tale, there was no happy ending waiting for them on the last page. He knew all too well, that the odds were stacking up against them, that some of the most powerful people in the world were determined to see the ending he so desperately wished he could change. He leaned across the bed and as lightly as he could, kissed her cheek. Her warm skin heated his lips instantly and his insides yearned for her with a worrying passion. She stirred at the disruption and turned away from him, letting go of his hand and hiding her head in the cool side of the pillow. He exhaled slowly, his blissful peace and happiness ended, his sanctuary of stillness and harmony over. The cool air rushed in and replaced the space she only seconds ago occupied. Reluctantly, he rose from the bed and quietly made his way to the door. An empty duvet and pillow in a cold room, was all that awaited him, like it had done his whole, isolated life. He flicked open the lock and paused at the handle, looking back to her, hidden in unaware sleep. How he envied her rest from this relentless struggle, from this constant battle inside. He knew, like all nights before, hours of eluded sleep awaited him across the hall, thoughts and feelings of her stirring such powerful emotions, that he could not switch them off or even escape them. But why, he thought to himself, as he closed the door quietly, why would he ever want to sleep and escape her anyway?*

CHAPTER TWENTY-EIGHT.
I'd survived worse situations that this.

I was aware of the door opening, but I was so deep in my sleep that it was too late to register what was really happening. I opened my eyes enough to acknowledge that I was still lying on my bed and that I was still fully dressed. I outstretched my hand for Cane only to find him gone. Disappointment blocked my senses for long enough, that the footsteps were at my bedside before I realised there was someone in my room. That all too familiar panic, flooded with drowning speed, as rough hands grabbed me pulled me from the warm sheets. My attempted scream was stifled by a mouth full of material and a massive hand placed heavily over that. I could smell alcohol, men's sweat and aftershave that I'd only ever smelt on Andreas. I struggled, pointlessly, as his powerful hands tightened around me, constricting my moves and squeezing the air out of my lungs. I desperately tried to calm myself, as Andreas began to drag me from the room. As we entered the hall, I tried to kick my feet out, hoping I'd somehow knock Cane's door. But Elias was waiting, and he locked my legs into a vice that I stood no chance of escaping from. What the hell were they doing? What were they thinking? Wafts of alcohol from Elias, filled my nostrils and I quickly realised that this was not going to end well. These two had zero sense of consequences most of the time, let alone when they were, by the stench of it, highly intoxicated. I swung my elbow back catching Andreas in the ribs, he groaned, and Elias stifled a sniggered, trying to swallow down his laugh like a naughty school boy. Andreas glared at him and then tightened his grip on me, to ensure it didn't happen again. With surprising efficiency, I was carried down the hall like rolled up carpet, away from Cane's room, and with that, the promise of the safety I'd heard of just hours before. We entered into a completely new area of the house and I quickly lost my bearings, suddenly feeling very much now alone. It felt like minutes until my feet were finally dropped onto the old polished wooden floor and as soon as I had my footing, I swung my head back at Andreas catching him on his cheek bone. He grunted, releasing me from his hold and throwing me to the ground like I'd just stung him. The moist gag fell out of my mouth and air rushed into my lungs. I inhaled deeply, trying to regain some steadiness. Whilst I was gasping for oxygen, I heard Andreas curse me from behind. I felt my ribs flutter beneath my skin and I put my hand to them.

'Que sólo la cabeza me tope,' Andreas yelled at Elias, informing him that I had just head-butted him. Elias was attempting to quiet him down, but he himself was laughing too hard to get the words out properly. My hands were shaking, despite knowing in my head the brothers wouldn't really hurt me. Something about being pulled from your safe sleep, by strong strange men, in the pitch black of night, was enough to set you off. I needed to relax and think straight. I imagined I was inhaling strength and balance at the same time as air, like I'd been taught in martial arts classes many times. I forced the calm around my body and quickly, my thoughts and senses began to return to me. I'd survived my last encounter with these men, I'm sure I would again. I reminded myself that this was all just *harmless* fun to them, yet my concern lay with what their interpretation of 'harmless' was. As I began to get my bearings, I realised I was in what looked like a small gym. I couldn't imagine Grandma being able to use it, so it had to be the grandsons. It was a good few halls away from Cane and even if I did manage to break for it and run, I'd never find the right doors. We had come through so many, but could I outrun the brothers while they were drunk? As I began weighing up my options, a new voice quickly caught my attention and I snapped my head towards the back of the room, where a bulky man was standing, arguing. He looked local by his darkened skin colour, and by the comfortable way they were all bickering, he seemed to know the brothers well. He was a solid, muscled giant and stood a good few inches above his, far from small to start with, companions in crime. A tattoo, of what looked like the devil, ran the length of his bare roped arm and he had veins bulging out of his skin, as if he had strained his body too far. He eyed me like a predator seeing its first glimpse of prey and it made my stomach contract and my feet itch ready to run. I inhaled slowly, trying to look away from his chilling stare. They were now all arguing with each other in Spanish, fast and animatedly. I caught only a few words, but they did anything but instill me with confidence; *bad idea...can't get caught...man up....* As I watched, I realised just how drunk they actually were: swaying on their feet, exaggerated hand movements, nodding heads and the loudest quiet voices I'd ever heard. At least that explained the ridiculous, dramatic kidnapping. I knew Cane had warned me to lock my door after my escapades at dinner, but I had thought his strict rules were enough to protect me. Obviously not. I had been beginning to find something appealing about the two brothers, despite everything. There was something alluring in the way they so brashly faced life, with no concerns for the future. It was maybe a hint of jealousy that softened my feelings towards them, but now, as I watched them stumble and slur, that building charm was quickly disappearing. I could, all too well, imagine that this was how they got themselves the name and reputation they had. I swallowed watching them. I knew that at the end of the day I could handle the brothers, I knew they had to answer to Cane. But this strange man, who kept turning his head to stare at me with such intent fascination, well he scared me, a lot. I got up to my knees slowly, then stood, my stomach feeling, embarrassingly, queasy. I hated how panic and nerves played on my body, even when your head willed them not to. I mustered some courage, knowing hell would freeze over before I showed any weakness.

'Guys?' I spoke out, finding my voice. I got no reaction. 'Hello?' I repeated, as they continued to mutter away in a huddle of conspiring Spanish. I raised my voice louder and tried again. 'Hola!' This caught their attention. 'What are you doing?' This silenced their arguing and their attention came back to me, as if the two brothers had forgotten I was even here. Puffing themselves up, they walked towards me, the new one staying behind.

'What does it look like we are doing?' Andreas asked, with a disconcertingly smug look on his face. His eyes were bloodshot and red.

'Kidnapping me in the middle of the night, *in* your grandma's house, *against* Cane's orders?' I spat back at him, as angrily as possible. To be honest, this whole thing was just ridiculous, and despite how drunk they were, they needed to know it. Maybe I could simply talk sense back into them. Andreas laughed, nodding.

'Exactamente,' he agreed, slapping me playfully on the cheek as if I was a pet. I let the small sting settle in, registering that he obviously had no measure of his strength right now. Not great for me. I held his boisterous eyes as boldly as I could, despite mine watering slightly. I heard the new guy snigger in the corner. I definitely didn't like him.

'Andreas, your brother will not be happy with this,' I said as firmly as I could, praying my voice wasn't wavering. He began to laugh again, curtsying to me and turning to face 'his brother', Elias.

'*Brother*, the lady says you will *not be happy with this.*' He attempted to mimic my voice, badly. 'Are you happy with this?' Elias began to chuckle in appreciation, nodding vigorously.

'I am very happy with this,' he laughed, 'please continue.' I let out a noise of frustration and raised my hands to shove Andreas away from me. To my surprise though, Elias stepped in, shockingly quickly for a drunk man, and grabbed my wrists, pushing me backwards. I stumbled as he began to tut at me, wagging his finger from side to side in reprimand.

'Since you are so keen to fight...' he began, with a dangerously excitable smile on his face.

'Keen to fight?' I repeated with confusion. 'Let me go. This is crazy.' I argued, glaring at him with warning. He shrugged and continued as if I hadn't spoken.

'Andreas and I were talking about you at the bar tonight.' He pointed his first finger at me and it wobbled around close to my face. I swatted it away. 'We were saying how all the staff talk about you, from that day in the alley. And from your encounter with Williams and Wyatt in your room when you attacked them…la pelea…' He paused, as if taking a little longer to translate his native tongue for me. 'How good you fight.' He finally spurted out. I rolled my eyes.

'Are you serious? I didn't *attack* anyone to start with,' I defended angrily, shaking my head, 'they attacked me, and barely getting out alive, doesn't sound like the story you are telling.' I tried to play it down, hoping that the boys would realise this was all a waste of time and let me go. No such luck. Elias moved to Andreas in an unsteady turn and flung his heavy arm around his brothers neck, smiling as if everything they were up to was perfectly acceptable.

'Nonsense,' he began, shaking his handsome and drunk head at me. 'Don't be so coy. Credit given where credit is due.' He ruffed his brothers impeccably styled hair, to which Andreas shoved him off and quickly began to remold it. 'Anyway, we decided we'd love to see a girl who could hold her own for a change, you know, not with the nails and the biting and the hair pulling, like normally happens.' My eyebrows raised.

'How many women do you see fighting?' I asked, surprised by how frequent he made it sound. He smiled and shrugged at me, coming over to throw his arm around my neck now. He was heavy and unstable, and he was leaning on me far too much to be masterminding any form of plans tonight. Let alone ones that involved me.

'You know how these things are, Eva,' he answered light heartedly, squeezing my cheeks together. I pulled my face away. 'Girls get protective and feisty and they're high maintenance anyway, throw some *times of the month* in there and wa-boom…' he jolted forward, almost bringing me to my knees, 'it's a girl fight.' He looked at me with half closed eyes, awaiting agreement. I shook my head.

'Elias, you need to seriously look at the girls you are dating. That's not normal.' He looked at me for a while, as if trying to understand my words. Then thinking better of it, or forgetting I'd even spoken at all, he carried on.

'We,' he waved his hand between Andreas and himself, 'don't believe that a girl as educated and as *hot* as you are' he licked his finger and touched it off my skin whist making a sizzling noise, 'is capable of fighting the way everyone says. Es imposible.' I nodded, deciding that maybe just agreeing with him was the way to go.

'Exactly, Elias,' I confirmed. 'It is impossible. In fact, it's ridiculous. The one and only reason I wasn't murdered in that alley, like my dad was supposed to be, was because Cane showed up. Period.' I shrugged with an 'oh-well' face as he regarded me closely, his breathe ripe with a mixture of alcoholic beverages. He waved his hand at me like he was flapping a fly away from his face, his finger not quite lining up with me as he pointed.

'Your dad wasn't supposed to be *murdered* that day, drama queen,' Elias laughed, as if it was funny joke. 'The instruction was just to rough him up, send a message to Bain. Williams just got out of hand and riled everyone on.' He wriggled his finger around in a small suspecting circle, as if he'd be able to tickle the truth out of my now very dry mouth. Was this true? Cane had never mentioned it. I recalled quickly all the times I'd so bitterly brought up that day. If it was true, surely, he would have defended himself? But why would Elias lie about it? I doubted he even had the brain capacity to lie in this state. 'Then you showed up in the alley...' he continued, 'and fought like a *dude*.' He said the word 'dude' like a clichéd surfer, seemingly getting excited at his comments. 'And we want to see it again now,' he yelled, whooping with his arm in the air like he was at a basketball game. I shook my head, trying to prioritise. I could ponder on this new information later, first I needed to get out of this situation. Preferably unscathed.

'Elias, you honestly think I can fight? I mean, look at me, I'm not exactly strong and muscly like you men?' I saw doubt in his expression and preyed on it instantly. 'Seriously boys, you've seen me drinking. Do you think someone who can't even keep a few drinks down would be able to take on any of your brothers *trained* men?' I laughed as if it was the most ridiculous thing ever said, and in my defence, it did actually sound ridiculous. I was far from big and looked anything but deadly. Andreas had begun to nod absent-mindedly in thought. It looked like borderline agreement. Progress. 'Do the staff gossip a lot?' I asked Elias, who was still leaning on me for support.

'Sí,' Andreas answered, slowly lowering his wobbly self to sit on the wooden floor for stability.

'See?' I asked, patting Elias's arm which still hung around my neck. 'It's just gossip. One person tells another, who exaggerates it, then tells someone else. I bet it says that I took down something crazy, like ten men, or something?' Andreas began to laugh loudly, as if deciding that it was the craziest thing he'd ever heard. Elias's eyes were beginning to waver in conviction, seeing his brother's reaction. The doubt was starting to settle in and hopefully it was bringing some common sense with it too.

'They did say that actually,' Elias confirmed, as Andreas began to howl with humour. 'Ten men does seem a bit unbelievable,' he muttered to himself, starting to smile. 'There's nothing of you.' He jabbed me in the belly, which made me yelp and wriggle. My reaction seemed to finally convince him, and he began to laugh with Andreas, throwing his head back into a roar. Personally, I didn't think it was *that* funny, but if it put them off whatever train of thought they were having, it was fine. Elias tickled me again and I screamed, trying to escape. 'As if you could do that,' he wiped at his eyes. 'Decena. Ten! Trained men.' He slapped my bottom and I yelped, loudly, the two of them now doubling up altogether, tears running from Andrea's face. I slapped Elias's hard chest in reprimand, feeling a weight of concern leave me. It was over. They had come to some form of reason, or at least had decided it was all ridiculous. Drunken hilarity had replaced their dangerous curiosity and sighed with relief.

'You two are crazy,' I encouraged, retaliating with my finger into Elias 's ribs. He wriggled like a little girl, laughing and released his hold on me. I pretended to laugh with them for a few seconds, although honestly seeing them fall about with such intoxicated hysterics did have me smiling a little. I exhaled with a conclusive tone. 'Well, you two,' I began, still smiling at them and shaking my head. 'I am up early tomorrow to help your grandmother with organising the party, so I am going to go back to bed.' Elias tried to stop laughing long enough to nod, then wave me off, but apparently it was too tall an order.

'Yeah, yeah, yeah,' he agreed, pointing for the door. 'Vi...go, go to bed. Sorry we woke you,' he was wiping tears from his drunken eyes and I made my way to the exit. My hand had practically made it to the handle when suddenly the deep voice of the giant stranger piped up. The tone of his voice sent my panic off again, it gushed through my body as if I'd just fallen off a cliff. My stomach dropped, and I scrunched my eyes shut.

'Quedarse,' he said loudly, over the subsiding snorts of the brothers. I was sure it meant hold on, or stay, or something, but I quickly rushed faster to the door knob, ignoring his malicious tone. I had just got my fingers on its cold metal, when his rough and aggressive hands slammed down on my shoulder from behind, holding me in place. He spun me firmly to meet his chest, and it seemed that the enormous Spanish Goliath had managed to cross the room much faster than I would have thought. I had to look up to see his face, which was greasy and cold with black eyes. He stank of beer and sweat, and his cheeks were flushed with the signs of too much alcohol. The brothers had got back to their feet, their smiles gone. Maybe even through their inebriated states, they could sense the danger that seemed to have suddenly pierced the room. Elias's face was strangely serious considering just seconds ago he had had tears dripping from his playful eyes. The stranger pulled me back from the door with fingers dug deep into my shoulder. I yelped in protest, trying to wriggle free of them.

'Ouch!' I voiced, yanking myself away and stepping a couple feet back from his massive overbearing frame.

'Que esta haciendo?' Elias began, asking the guy what he was doing. His voice was suddenly quick and fluid. 'Let her go to bed. The joke's over.' His words had no effect on the man though and he continued to stand between me and the exit. I could physically feel, that never far away, alarm beginning to rise within me.

'People don't just make stuff up like that, Elias,' he finally said in mumbled, yet just understandable, English, pointing at me with a condemning finger. 'Ella esta mintiendo! She is lying!' Andreas, obviously trying to quickly smooth out the mounting tension, began to laugh again.

'Seriously, if you had seen her drink, you'd maybe change your mind. Peso ligero...' he clicked his fingers, searching for the translation, '...lightweight, doesn't even cover it.' He waved his hand at me, as if dismissing me. 'Llegado, amigo...*come friend*, let's go get more drunk. The night's still young.' He beckoned his friend away to join him, but the man stayed fixed to his spot, his eyes hard on me with persecution. 'You said I'd get a fight tonight,' he threatened angrily, now turning on Elias with menace. My eyes snapped to the brothers in shock. That had been what this was all about? Yes, I was trained in how to hold my own, but that never meant I *wanted* to fight or that I didn't feel the fear of confrontation. Elias stepped forward with anger on his face.

'No,' he warned, his accent coming through strongly. 'I said you *may see* a fight. You were never going to be involved. Eva is nothing to you.' Elias had walked towards me and stepped between the two of us. I assumed it was supposed to be protectively comforting, but from the way he rocked on his feet, it didn't instill me with much confidence. Yet his defending intent was clear, and my heart melted a little towards him. Regardless of his motivation, he was willing to protect me and that meant something. But it also meant, that he now sensed the danger.

'She's nothing to you either, Elias, so get out of my way. She needs taken down a peg or two.' I backed up a step, quickly realising that this whole thing was going south, fast. Andreas was marching, as much in a straight line as he could, towards their friend.

'Oye!' he shouted, angrily. 'No one talks to my brother like that.' He pulled hard at the man's shoulder, with as much threat in his blurry eyes as he could offer. 'Es hora de irte...*ahora!* It's time for you to leave, now, Andreas had been saying, but before anyone could react, the giant had swung out at him. With a loud thump, Andreas was hit and lying out cold on the wooden floor. I yelped with shock as Elias's temper flared. He roared and swung for his supposed friend. Within seconds, the sociable bond the men had displayed, was gone and the two began to brawl. Elias was actually putting up a good fight, despite the height and weight differences, and especially despite his intoxication. The sound of pounding flesh echoed through the room, loud and aggressive. I stood, frozen. I hated fights, despite everything the last few weeks had brought. I hated the rage and uncontrolled passion they created, the way they instantly caused rationale and reason to fly out the window. There was no control when a temper was lost and when there was no control, there was no safety. The men continued to wrestle loudly, grunting as punches were exchanged. The sounds of impacting flesh made my stomach turn each time. Elias may have stood a good chance, had he been sober, but as it was, he stumbled often and swung wide, unable to focus. He was an easy target and the monster, who was supposed to be their friend, took advantage of his weakness, finally sending a forceful blow to his ribs. Elias crippled to the floor, beaten. Watching his chest take the hit and knowing that it would have been his ribs that would have felt the full impact, it made me cringe. It was only yesterday I had felt that exact same pain, bruised and broken ribs. Elias was stronger and bigger than me though and I was hoping he had more resilience. He groaned from the ground, trying to catch his lost breath, blood seeping from a cut on his lip. I desperately wanted to run, away, to him, anything, but I was frozen, unable to react. I watched as Elias sustained the blow from another three kicks, each one making my eyes scrunch closed. My heartbeat was racing and all the memories of fights and arguments and confrontations from the last few weeks, came rushing back in. The feelings of being boxed and beaten and losing seemed to never truly go away. The temperature in the room was rising and I was stood like a statue with a rapid heartbeat and wide eyes, heat pushed in on me. Despite wanting to help, I just couldn't. Elias was attempting to get his bearings, despite still lying on the floor and he rolled onto his back, coughing. *Eva, run while you can, while they are distracted*. Yet, I was paralysed.

'You promised me a fight, Rodriguez. Still the *mentiroso,* you always were.' The stranger spat the word *liar* with rage, and kicked Elias back down from his attempt to stand. Despite Elias's strength, he lacked enough control and fell back down, looking like he couldn't take much more.

'You're forgetting you're place, *amigo,*' Elias gasped, through gritted teeth. The giant growled with drunken anger and lifted his foot to kick again. It was lined up for Elias's head this time and as I saw it happening the panic in me finally thawed my silence.

'STOP!' I screamed with outstretched hands, desperately looking for the Spanish word. 'PARA!' My voice echoed loudly, and it was enough to disrupt the fight. The man dropped his foot inches from Elias's face and turned to face me, as if remembering all of sudden, that it was me they were originally fighting about.

'Ahhh, chica,' he began, turning to face me with sweat shining on his forehead. 'Why so protective of the man that was talking about having a boxing match with you earlier, eh?' He leered at me, advancing slowly in a slightly off straight line. He was big and strong, and even if not as much so as the brothers, he was still drunk. He laughed coldly, his eyes greedily moving from the top to the bottom of my body. 'I've seen these two speak about women their whole lives, heard them brag about the beauties they've bagged,' he licked his lip with a sick smile, focusing on my chest. 'For once though, they didn't exaggerate you, chica bonita. They said you were a looker.' His eyes jumped back to my face. 'No wonder the big guy is keeping you around, you are a pretty girl. Fácil en los ojos.' He bit his bottom lip. 'How you English say it?...easy on the eyes?' He smacked his hands together and rubbed them as if warming up. 'There's only one good use for a pretty girl like you and I'll happily be the one to remind you of that.' His eyes narrowed with such hate that it reminded me of Wyatt and Williams. How could some have so much unfounded and unexplainable revulsion for someone they didn't even know? 'For once, I'm going to take something from Cane that he can't ever take back or fix with his money. He'll always know that I was the one who ruined you.' Terror cursed through me as I realised his intent. I was in serious trouble here. Suddenly, he lunged for me with outstretched arms, and a snarl echoed through the room. Thankfully, he was sluggish from drink and despite his muscled build, he was slow. I dodged under his tree trunk arms, running to Elia's side, who was now trying to shout at his friend.

'CARLOS!' he yelled through his gasping lungs. He tried to stand again only to fumble and fall. I tried to help Elias, but was too scared to take my eyes away from the predator coming up behind me.

'Don't tell me what to do, Elias, you are not your big brother. This is between him and I now.' He came at me again, a swing for the face. In slow motion it was like watching a boulder sail directly through the air, solid and unstoppable. Adrenaline finally kicked in as self-preservation coursed through me and I ducked, my 'fight or flight' impulse surging through my trained body. With no thought given, other than reflex, I slammed my closed fist expertly into Carlos's kidneys with all my might, watching my prayers to never have to fight again disappear with painful impact. My hand throbbed as the all too familiar sensation of bruised knuckles and clashing bones came flooding back. The giant, whose name was apparently Carols, grunted with shock and pain, stumbling backwards, his hands holding his side. He took a couple of seconds to compose himself, but then he stood up again, taller, a malevolent and smug smirk satisfying his face. 'Sooo…' he began, straightening himself and pacing around me like a wild dog awaiting its pounce. My heart raced as I followed his path, circling, never taking my eyes from him for a second. How was I back in another perilous situation? How could I possibly be in another fight for my life? This world was tough and relentless, and I couldn't seem to avoid confrontation, no matter how hard I tried. At least on my side this time, was the fact that Carlos had already been fighting with Elias and was showing the signs of exertion. He had a foot of height and probably my whole-body's weight of an advantage on me. I knew that one good hit from him was all it would take to wipe me out and that knowledge was both crippling and motivating. 'Usted lucha como un hombre,' he spat to the floor, taking his hand away from his kidneys and smiling at me. I translated his thick accent into English quickly. *You do fight like a man.* Like that was such an amazing thing? Why were men so fascinated by women who could rival them in something? Especially combat?

'Lucky hit,' I shrugged, as confidently as I could. I glanced down quickly to Elias, who was still lying incapacitated. His face was almost as shocked as Carlos's. *Now would be a good time to get up and help,* I thought, as I watched him gasp in and out of focus.

'Un golpe de suerte, eh?' Carlos repeated my words, laughing in disbelief...*a lucky shot?* I felt a cold sweat pass over me. All I knew about this man was that he seemed hell bent on destroying me, in order to punish Cane. The mere mention of Cane's name earlier seemed to anger him more than anything. They obviously had history, bad history, and history I was now being sucked into. 'Lucky hit, indeed,' he said again in English, nodding like he accepted the challenge. 'Veremos...we'll shall see.' Instantly, he lunged at me again and swung for my head with full strength. He obviously had no intentions of holding back even slightly. I ducked and missed the attack, but only through sheer reflex and I heard the whoosh of moving air rush past my ears. *Eva, holy crap, focus.* My legs were shaky, slow in catching up with the rest of my body. I felt totally unprepared for this. Carlos' second shot caught me square on the shoulder, jarring me and forcing me backwards in a falter. I could hear Elias stumbling around in the background, still trying to get to his feet, but it was all happening too fast for his drunken and winded body to process. I shook myself, trying to clear the fog and the throbbing. As I did, I took another jab to the thigh and this one sent me fully to the floor, numbness spreading through my entire dead leg. A self-congratulatory yell of appreciation went up from Carlos. Getting a couple hits in, was apparently, something worth celebrating. I lay flat out, registering the pain, exhaling slowly. Ten seconds in and I was already being beaten. My shoulder felt like someone was holding a fire iron against it and my leg now had no feeling. There was a ringing in my ears that was louder than I'd experienced before, and Dr Miele's warning about fatal head blows circled around my thoughts. He was right, there could be no head shots tonight, not if I wanted to make it to the age of thirty-three. I squeezed my eyes shut. Enough was enough. I was better than this and I knew it. I tensed my fists and set my resolve. If he wanted so desperately to see me fight, then so be it. There was no way this scumbag was going to beat me down like a broken animal. I was stronger than this and I had survived worse situations than this. I *was* a fighter and I'd be damned if I would have it any other way. This pig wanted a fight, he wanted to see how a mere female could measure up to the might of a man? Then so bloody-well be it. I grit my teeth and then inhaled as calmly as I could, forcing down the stirring anger inside. Elias and Carlos were shouting at each other and it started coming back into focus. I watched as Carlos kicked, a half-risen Elias in the stomach again, following it by laughing. Elias began coughing and spluttering, holding himself but the noise wasn't enough to cover the sound of me standing and Carlos quickly returned his attention to me, looking a little disconcerted that I was still conscious, let alone, standing. If getting back to my feet was enough to shock him now, well he was in for some serious surprises. I was done being the victim, I was done being thought of as the prey. He marched towards me, loudly, obviously with the intents of finishing the job and not expecting a fight back. He was wrong. As he reached me, I swung my leg out, swiped and sent him crashing to the floor. He made the sound of a falling tree and the ground vibrated with his weight. While I had a split-second advantage, I ran at him, and kicked hard in his side, as hard as I could, again and again and again until my leg muscles began to feel the strain and my bare foot burned. Carlos recoiled and put his arms up to try protect himself from the attack. It was pointless though and he groaned in agony, vocalising his pain. The sound gave me encouraging satisfaction.

'See how you like it, cerdo,' I spat, sending one last almighty kick into his manhood, before backing away to watch him reel. He gasped looking for air, coughing and spluttering. I prayed that he wouldn't stand again and that he would just concede, but I should have known this type of man's ego wouldn't let it go so easily. He snarled at me calling him a pig and fumbled to find his feet, pushing himself back up. He was winded, but gave me a sleazy smile, insinuating that my attempts hadn't even dented him. I offered his smile back, just as confidently, then indicated with my fingers for him to come when he was ready. The calm motion of the gesture only seemed to anger him more and he lashed out with madness, punching and jabbing at any space he could. I dodged and ducked each one until I forced a wide clumsy swing and took the opportunity I'd been waiting for. I threw my fist and arm up under his chin as fast and hard as I could. I felt the almighty slam in my body as I made impact. It jarred him and I could see saliva spray from his mouth as he stumbled. I took the opening again while he was disorientated, striking him hard to the face and pushing my whole body into the follow through. He lost his balance and stumbled sideways, Elias taking the opportunity to trip him and send him crashing to the ground again. Whilst he smashed into the floor, I used all my remaining strength to kick him again, as many times as I could physically managed, before my muscles screamed from the strain. He grunted and groaned with each impact, blood escaping from his untouchable narcissistic body. I backed away and used the break to try catch my breath, trying to slow my racing heart. My muscles were protesting and despite being in a summer dress and barefoot, I was sweating. I used my shoulder to wipe my forehead and felt it twang from its knock earlier.

'That all you got?' I yelled over to him, forcing a light-footed hop, as if I was still full of all the energy in the world. Which I wasn't. Far from actually. I watched as he literally pulled himself up using the wall, fueled by my provoking taunts. His face was swelling and bloody and he seemed livid now, probably enraged by the fact he was being beaten by a woman. Apparently, this was the ultimate disgrace. He came for me once more with clumsy speed, his feet causing vibrations on the gym floor as he crashed his way towards me. I braced myself for more as it came. I blocked and dodged, maneuvered and swung, each second passing feeling like an eternity. Despite managing to get a couple good hits in that made Carlos bleed more, I was getting tired quickly. His sheer size required me to move and react faster just to get out of the way of his tree trunk arms and concrete fists. His physique alone was allowing him to go longer and take more than I ever would be able. I was like a breeze trying to blow down a house, chipping and chipping away with no real signs of collapse. Then, as if just on cue, my focus lapsed, and he hit me in the stomach. Bile rose in my throat as I crumbled to my knees, unable to breath. My head was screaming like a boiling pot, the pressure looking for an escape. I leaned forward taking my weight on one shaking hand, saliva running from my mouth uncontrollably. My vision and hearing swam as the pain threatened to finish me off. Darkness was trying to encroach from the corners of my eyes, no matter how much I willed myself to stay conscious. I was petrified of what would happen to me if I passed out, and so I pushed, with all my might, back at my fading senses. I knew another blow was coming my way and I awaited its damning hit through my ever-increasing darkness, knowing it would most likely be the end. Suddenly the noise of an opening door burst through the silence like a bomb had gone off, and Cane burst in. I dragged my eyes up to look at him and through the blur, I could see that he had the wrath of God on his face. Relief swept through me with such force, that my arm gave way and I fell to the ground, my body slumping in release. Cane was still wearing his cream trousers and white vest and he stood at the door frame looking more fearsome than ever. He was taller and broader and stronger than he had ever seemed before, with power and authority surging from him. His face was tight and angular, his eyes hard and unflattering. Carlos stood still, just above me, halting his attack at the disruption. I was trying to stay with the scene surrounding me, but I was struggling to focus on that and breathing at the same time.

'Cane...' Carlos began in a welcoming sarcastic tone, as if he had just arrived late to the party.

'BASTA!' *ENOUGH!* Cane demanded in a voice I'd not heard him use in a long time. It was ice and power and weight but even that couldn't quite match the murderous look in his eyes. He was furious, absolutely livid and his entire body emanated that. Disobedience was not a quality Cane accepted well, something I'd seen firsthand. Elias may have been drunk, but he had enough sense still to stay put while Cane took in his surroundings. He stepped inside the door and slammed it behind him, the walls shaking from its bang. He looked at Carlos and then his brothers, then me, his eyes flashing with anger. When he spoke again, his words were precise, firm and unmoving. 'WHAT. IS. GOING. ON?'

'Cane,' Elias began, coughing, and struggling to get to his feet. 'We were just...'

'Sólo estábamos un buen rato,' Carlos interrupted cockily, informing Cane that they were *just having some fun*. He lifted his clenched fists and jabbed a few air punches casually. 'Still the same old Rodriguez, eh? You should learn to chill out brother, join in maybe? I hear this one's being making a fool of you anyway. Maybe it's time to finally restore some of that manhood.' Cane's full attention had now switched to Carlos, his head turned to face him, his jaw set the same way it had been on the few times I had seen him lose his temper. He looked flawless and powerful as he advanced across the room towards Carlos, each step sending a shiver through me. Carlos stood firm and arrogant, obviously having no idea what was about to be unleashed on him. Cane reached him in what felt like two steps and then suddenly, he stopped abruptly, as if trying to reign himself in.

'I will give you one chance to apologise and get your pathetic, pitiful body off my land, Carlos, before I extend you the same courtesy that you have shown here.' He nodded towards me, still lying on the floor. Cane was standing statue still, staring directly at Carlos, who now didn't seem that big or strong anymore. He also didn't seem to quite understand the magnitude of the danger he was in. He laughed, looking to Elias.

'Always so demanding and serious, Cane,' he began. 'Hay cosas que nunca cambia, *some things never change*. You think you scare me?' he taunted, angrily. 'Have you seen me lately?' He pounded his hard chest like he was Tarzan. 'I can take anyone on now, Rodriguez, even you.'

'Yet you still feel the need to beat up women who are half your size,' Cane spat callously. He danced his eyes over Carlo's swelling and bleeding face, then smiled. 'Although it doesn't look like *this* woman is going down easily.' Carlos face flushed red with torment, his eyes turning to me with frightening hostility. 'Is a female finally getting her own back on the great and mighty Carlos? Maybe its penance for the damage you have done to her kind over the years?' Cane talked slowly and clearing but with utter disgust in his tone.

'Like you are so high and mighty,' Carlos roared, squaring up to Cane who still hadn't moved. 'I haven't seen my sister in years thanks to you,' he hissed, his face now inches from Cane's. I was sure Cane would have smelled the alcohol on him long ago and I wondered if that was why he was restraining his reactions.

'You used to beat her, Carlos, she *rogó* me to help her leave.' He emphasized the word *beg* with his eyes narrowed to slits and his arm muscles tensed. 'I can see you haven't changed, even slightly. You're *pathetic* still.'

'And you the ever-reigning judge and jury, Rodriguez. You think your money and your fancy clothes make you better than me? What about her?' Carlos pointed to me on the floor, like I was faeces. 'She's here of her own free will, is she?' he argued, a smug smirk on his horrid face. 'Yes, your brothers spilled it all while I got them purposely drunk earlier. Kidnapping, ransoms, beatings…it all sounds so *proper* Cane. You are a *true* gentleman.' Cane's temper flared with violent rage as he bellowed back at Carlos.

'YA TI QUE TE IMPOTRA, CARLOS'. *She is none of your business.*

'You're being played again, just like my sister did. This one's a hot piece of…' Cane's fists tightened, and Carlos saw it, stopping his sentence. He registered the nerve he had so obviously hit, and he smirked at the identification of it. 'She's a looker, I'll give you that one, Cane, and I can't blame you for having your way with her while she's at your disposal, but at the end of the day, she's just a *woman*. Yet you always choose the girl over your family, don't you, you piece of…'

'You stopped being my family the day I realised that you enjoyed beating up women, Carlos. You are nothing to me anymore, no matter how big you make yourself.' He cast a filthy assessing look at Carlos's bulky body and the no doubt thousands of euros of steroids pumping through his veins. Cane's eyes were dark and filled with ferocity. His perfect face was tensed into tight, sharp angles and I inhaled with anticipation, feeling their argument reach its peak. 'You make me sick,' he condemned, his chest rising and falling with anger. Seconds of dead-lock passed in silence and then, as if it took everything in him, Cane suddenly let his fists relax. 'Now get off my land and never come near me or my family again, so help me, or I'll show you the same courtesy you bestow on women.' He stared at Carlos with fierce warning. 'Comprendes?' Seconds passed while Carlos kept his defiant stare locked on Cane's, then finally, he relented, stepping back and lowering his head in submission. This seemed to satisfy Cane and he nodded, moving past him to finish helping Elias with his attempt to stand. As soon as Cane's back was turned, instead of leaving like commanded, Carlos made for me. He had obviously clocked that I was Cane's Achilles heel and he came straight for me, quicker than I had time to process. I heard the movement beside me before I realised what was actually happening. I was just in time to focus on Carlos's foot making its way to my face, sailing sure and steady on a collision course. He was relentless if nothing else and seemed hell bent on destroying me tonight, even if it killed him, and I knew, as I raised my arms to try protect myself, that it probably would. Cane being Cane, had read Carlos's move and had reacted at the same time as him. Unfortunately, he had a little more ground to cover and by the time he impacted with Carlos, knocking him over, Carlos had made impact with me. Cane's attack spared my head but instead my raised arms took the brunt of the kick. They provided minimum protection as I felt my shoulders shudder with the force and I was propelled back with nothing to break my fall. I crashed to the ground and lay there, trying to stay conscious through the pain. I felt my mouth water and I swallowed, trying to calm myself and the uncontrollable tears rolling from my eyes. I lay in a daze, lost and confused, feeling throbbing and the slam of my heartbeat. I wiggled my fingers and found them thankfully cooperative. It was just pain, I knew that, and I knew that pain passed. I exhaled slowly, beginning to finally focus again on my surroundings. It took a lot of effort to block out the buzzing in my head, but quite quickly, I managed to focus on the strange sounds close by me. I knew the noise well; the scuffle and heavy breathing of a fight. CANE! I shot bolt upright, too upright, and black crept into the corners of my eyes. I screwed them shut, breathing air in deeply. As it passed, I saw Elias, standing to the side, looking unsure on what to do. Just across from me was Cane. He was straddling the limp body of Carlos, whose face was beaten and bloody. I jolted as I saw Cane hit him again, and again. Cane! I'd seen such protective rage in his eyes earlier, but now they looked empty and vacant as he slammed his fist into Carlo's face, repeatedly, heavily. Before I could register what I should do, I was already stumbling to my feet, running forwards and ignoring my pain.

'CANE!' I screamed, my arms stretching out to reach him. 'STOP.' I shouted as I landed at his side. 'PARA, STOP!' His one hand had hold of Carlos's collar, lifting him from the floor, the other was raised in the air for the next hit. I grabbed his raised hand in mine, feeling the warm smear of blood, and I threw myself directly in front of Cane's face. 'Cane!' I begged urgently, eye to eye. 'No, no, stop!' His pupils were cold, and I could feel his fist shake in mine. Yet his lost gaze found me, and his hand slowly relaxed its clench. 'He's not worth it.' I pleaded, pulling his fist down towards my other hand and holding it tight. I kept my eyes locked on his with worry. I shook my head, rubbing my thumb across his swollen knuckles. 'Enough. You're better than this.' I whispered to him, leaning so close that I could feel his rapid breath on my lips. The tension left him instantly as my forehead met his. His eyes locked back onto mine, seeing me and he nodded, almost unnoticeably, exhaling. He released his hold on Carlos' shirt and his body dropped back to the ground with a grunt. Cane climbed off of him as I assessed his beaten body. He was beaten up pretty bad, but would survive. I glared at him and his swollen eyes as he managed to focus on me through them. 'You deserve everything you get, you pathetic pig,' I spat. 'But I won't let Cane carry the consequence of killing you. You're not worth that.' I turned away from him and back to Cane whose lips, despite the situation, were turned up at the corners slightly, his eyes searched my face and body.

'Está herido?' he asked with such concerned sincerity that it made my eyes water. He was so focused on me that he even forgot to translate his question. Thankfully, the look in his eyes transcended language barriers and I knew that he was asking if I was hurt. I smiled as casually as I could and shrugged lightly, taking his hands into mine and looking over his bruised knuckles.

'Me? Hurt?...nunca!' I answered with a tough smile. *Never*. To this he reciprocated, gently shaking his head.

'Luchadora,' he whispered, smiling affectionately. A shuffle of feet reminded me that Elias and Andreas were still in the room and I looked up to find them. Elias over at his brother's unconscious body, shaking him. Cane's eyes moved to them like daggers and I felt his muscles tense again with anger.

'Let's go, Cane?' I asked quietly, casting a glance to the door. He relaxed at my request and instantly turned back to me with a nod, standing up and helping me to my feet. I felt the tug of pain on my body, but they would only be bruises, and bruising I could manage. My brain replayed the way Cane instantly reacted to my request just now, how he had softened at my words. I thought quickly of how he had submitted and yielded to my voice as if I was the only thing that mattered. Heat surged through me. That was a power I knew I'd never learn to manage. I brushed the acknowledgment aside as we made it to the door. I turned the handle and opened it. Fresh, bloodless smelling air rushed in passed us. I inhaled it slowly as Cane turned back to his brothers. Andreas now awake and sitting up with a very confused expression on his face. Unsurprisingly, they both looked pretty sober now.

'You disobeyed me for *him?*' Cane asked loudly and firmly, his voice echoing in the silence. It was a tone that was not to be argued with. 'Clean up this mess and get him off my land.' He pointed to the body of Carlos who was stirring on the floor. They nodded, and Cane added with a cold and threatening voice, 'I'll deal with you both later.' I saw fear flash through their eyes as Cane led me out the door and shut it behind him. He held his hand gently on my lower back, guiding me without words. It was warm and protective. He opened my bedroom door and led me across the threshold, locking it behind himself. He rested against the wood as I crossed the room and I could feel him watching me like I was fragile doll. Suddenly, he began banging his head off the doors old panels.

'I should have stayed longer,' he cursed, nodding towards the messed up bed covers that I'd been pulled from. 'I left you. I thought it was the right thing to do. You fell asleep, I unlocked the door and left you alone.' A strange, warm feeling was starting to spread through me. I briefly acknowledged that it was wrong, after the last hour, but seeing Cane so upset and frustrated because he thought he let me down, was...well, it just melted my heart. Him blaming himself for tonight only showed that he actually cared about me, that my pain caused him pain. I quickly thought back to minutes ago where I had urged Cane back off the cliffside that was Carlo's beaten body. I would have done anything to spare him the weight of killing that pathetic man. It had been a reflex to try save him from pain, to try affect his wellbeing. Now, as I watched him stand against my door, deflated and discouraged, I understood exactly why he wanted to take the fault as his own. Not too long ago, this would all have very much been his fault, and only his. But now… He sighed heavily, distracting me back to the room. I smiled at him, despite the heaviness in his eyes, and shook my head. I didn't want him to have to carry more guilt and remorse than he already did. In the life of the new me, I wanted to protect him.

'No, Cane,' I began gently, pulling my hair up into a pony tail. 'This was no ones doing. I provoked your brothers at dinner which led them to get crazy drunk and rant about me. Then this all happened because apparently you made some nutter angry years ago doing the right thing. Your brothers didn't know it was going to all go wrong, they weren't actually to blame,' I paused with a sarcastic smile, 'for a change.' I waved my hands back towards the direction of the gym. 'Once they realised that Carlos was out of control, they tried to stop it. It was just your brothers' typical antics gone wrong.'

'Eva, you shouldn't even have to be concerned with them at all, I promised you safety and I failed you.' He shook his head at himself, in disgust.

'Cane,' I sighed, 'we could pick and blame away at each other for absolutely everything that has happened to us, for this whole thing in the last few weeks, but no good will come from it. We'd still be *here*.' I pointed to the spot I was standing on. 'We'd still be in the same place, no matter who's to blame. And I'm tired of it all.' I turned around, so my back was facing him. 'I'm tired of the thoughts and the heaviness and the second guessing. So, let's just not go through it again, ok?' I finalized, attempting a light tone. I was too drained, too hungry and too dirty to deal with it all tonight. And anyway, considering everything, I had made it out unscathed. Maybe I was becoming both physically and mentally stronger, but sweeping this whole ordeal under the rug seemed like an easy enough thing to do. I genuinely wanted to just forget it and get to bed. Was that weird and wrong? I vaguely thought how different I was from before this odd and eventful deal happened, sitting marking papers in my living room, my life smooth and easy. I had changed so much. I sighed looking at Cane, his inner torment still plastered all over his beautiful and lowered face. I turned myself back around again and took a step towards him. 'Now can you come and unzip my dress please, cause I'm pretty sure I won't ever be able to wear it again if I don't get it off soon.' He exhaled, sensing my determined tone and understood that arguing was pointless. Maybe he was getting to know me pretty well. His reluctant footsteps crossed the room to my back and his fingers touched my neck. My stomach leapt with pleasure and instantly erased all my bad memories. 'Don't get any more blood on it,' I warned him, playfully. 'You paid a lot of money for this dress.' I could feel him shake his head at me with silent laughter and he pulled the zipper down, his fingers leaving a trail of tickles down my spine. I held the front and turned to him, offering a grin.

'How about we just forget tonight?' I suggested, suddenly desperate for a bath. The temptation to invite Cane to join me was strong, but I managed to keep my mouth shut.

'How about we don't *forget* about it, but I'll not talk of it to *you* again?' I knew that meant he wasn't finished with his brothers and I also recognized the stubborn set of his brow. Cane was obviously still determined to make himself and his disobedient siblings suffer. I sighed in defeat.

'Fine. Deal,' I said, shrugging my shoulders, relenting. To this his face broke into a playful smile, dimples penetrating his cheeks and he shook his head at me.

'You should know by now, not to make deals with me, Eva.' I let out a bark of a laugh, almost letting go of my dress. I grinned at him, unable to stop myself.

'Well, aren't those words of truth?' I teased, shaking my head playfully. Cane sunk into the armchair by the door and fell quiet, watching me while I collected my bath stuff.

'Eva,' he began, reclaiming me attention. 'you know I'd do anything to protect you, right? I'll *always* protect you now, no matter what. Even if it's from me.' He practically whispered his words and I could hear his sincerity, let out in a moment of weakness. I stopped what I was doing and turned to face him, so that he could see my eyes. I sighed slowly, looking at his worried and honest expression. 'That's the truth, Eva,' he offered.

'Yes, Cane.' I said with a small smile, nodding. 'I believe you.' He swallowed, and his frame relaxed a little, as if my belief removed an actual weight from his body. His words reminded me of my conversation with his brothers earlier and I cleared my throat. 'Cane?' I asked quietly, and surprisingly timidly. He didn't answer, but kept his eyes on me, waiting. I exhaled loudly, suddenly feeling the magnitude of my question. 'That day in the alley when we first met?' I watched him as he nodded his head slightly, his eyes softening with uncertainty.

'Sí?'

'Were your orders to *kill* my father?' Cane's eyes flashed with a fleeting emotion. He moved uncomfortably in his seat and quickly took his gaze from me, casting it down to the floor. I saw his throat move and he rubbed his strong hands over his jaw. 'Cane?' I prompted, waiting for him to look up at me and reply. My heart was beating much louder than I had anticipated and I struggled to maintain a casual façade. 'Cane?'

'Does it matter?' he finally said, still looking downward towards his lap. I exhaled loudly with exasperation. *Did it matter?*

'Elias said something tonight, that it was never supposed to go that far in the alley, that you never meant for my dad to be killed.' Cane cleared his throat, putting his hands into his trouser pockets, yet still looking down. I could see his discomfort, and that alone was massive when coming from the man of stone. 'Cane? Is that right?' I pushed at him, with a little more authority in my voice. There was no reaction still. I crossed the room until I was directly in front of him, one arm still holding my dress against my body.

'It matters Cane,' I said, answering his question and kneeling down to see into his eyes. They were heavy with memory, sadness and remorse. 'It matters to me that I know the truth.' I encouraged with longing eyes. He shook his head with a loud inhale and exhale.

'No, your dad was never supposed to be killed. That was never the intention. I know you think I am an animal, and I maybe was, but a roughed-up advisor to Bain, was better than a dead one, purely for the message it sent and the tale he left to tell.' He paused as if I would recoil from him in disgust. 'Knowing that I only meant to have him beaten, doesn't make any of it better.' He lifted his head and quickly took my hand in his. 'The second I laid eyes on you in that alley, Eva...' his grip tightened as if it would soon be gone. I could feel the warmth from his soft skin radiate into my fingers and travel up my arms. I looked down at our hands. Our skins were still shades apart from each other, despite my time in the sunshine, and their colours seemed to mark the differences that would always be between us. Yet, as Cane's hand tightened around mine and our skin sat side by side, I couldn't help but notice how much I liked the look of them together. They were complimentary colours, not contending ones, I saw that now. Cane spoke again, a little pleading hinting his words. 'The very instant I saw you, Eva, everything changed. I felt something I hadn't felt in a long time. I had to try so hard to look composed...and then I realised what had been done to *your* father...I felt like I'd just lost something before even getting to have it.' He bit that bottom lip of his, staring at me hard. 'You changed everything.'

'Why didn't you tell me before?' I asked, exasperated. He shrugged.

'What would it have mattered? It still shows that I was a monster and you'd have still thought of me what you wanted.' He had a point, I was blinded by hate and rage for so long, just like I had been raised to.

'It matters to me now, Cane,' I insisted, squeezing his hand in return. 'I know the man you are...now.' He let out a massive exhale, clenching my hand even surer and dropping his forehead to rest on mine. I could literally see the relief lift off of him, like one more battle between us had been faced and, against all odds, conquered.

CHAPTER TWENTY-NINE.
There it was. Like fireworks.

The next day was just as the rest, hot and sunny. I pulled back the curtains to the same postcard picture. It was easy to forget the night before when you consciously decided to and when you were surrounded by so many thankful distractions. The sun was up, and it was a new day. Could I spend hours of agony going over and over everything from last night, from the new developments with Cane, to his brothers, to that man Carlos and to the new sore parts on my body? Yes, I could. And could I get angrier and more bitter and blame everyone around me? Yes, I could. And would it help? Not even close. I was learning this lesson quiet quickly. I yawned as the sun shone into my room, making me squint and my eyes water. What I had said to Cane last night was true, blame changed nothing; not our past, not our present and not even our future. I stretched carefully, very aware of the morning stiffness that accompanied a sore body and as I extended my arms above my head, I quite simply decided not to dwell. I was sick of analysing, of being morally torn and mentally victimized. This was life, with its curve balls and erupting volcanos, but it was also all *mine;* my life to live and to control. And I could do that much if nothing else; control myself and my reactions. I didn't know when I would next see Elias and Andreas, or Cane for that matter, but when I did, I would deal with it. Until then, I wouldn't worry about it. Instead, I headed for a shower, a normal, everyday, run-of-the-mill shower. After all, it was party day. I inhaled as I opened the bathroom window, loving the smells and the sights and the sounds here. Maybe it was the being away from home and all its complications, but I was officially in love with Spain. The heat washed away worry and minimised fears, spreading warmth and assurance in its path. I was beginning to think that I never wanted to go home. Would staying with Grandma for the rest of my life be an option?

I made my way down the stairs in a new pair of shorts and a sleeveless vest, sporting my somewhat darkened tan. I felt renewed and remarkably fine considering the bruises my knuckles and forearms held. Maybe it was the darkened tone or that my skin was toughening up, but surprisingly and thankfully, unless you looked, you couldn't really see any evidence of battle. Downstairs, the house was in military mode with caterers and designers, tables and musicians, all swarming the normally tranquil villa. I found Grandma bossing a chef around in stern Spanish and interrupted politely, asking her what she wanted me to do. She had of course insisted that I was a guest and should relax by the pool, but after I assured her I would much rather help. With hardly any argument, she happily gave me a list a mile long of things needing completed, *rápidamente*…quickly. I smiled at her instructions and went promptly on my way. I was happy for the distraction to be honest and keenly went to work amidst the organising chaos. I saw Cane once, briefly, as he crossed the driveway and slipped into a car. My heart had stopped as his smiling eyes met mine with a nod. A nod that said everything and nothing.

'Do not worry, dear,' Grandma had assured me, sneaking up out of nowhere. 'He go to pick up family friends from *aeropuerto*. He be back in plenty time for tonight.' I smiled at her gratefully and watched the car drive away, Cane sitting effortlessly at the wheel. I was given the afternoon off to sit by the pool and relax and in what felt like no time, it was early evening and the house had transformed into a magical Spanish fairytale. Garden lights hung everywhere, illuminating the mix match of dining tables and chairs. There was a buffet table and a chef with an open cooker, his white hat bobbing as he sizzled and prepared the food for the evening. At the far end of the garden was a band with a large wooden dance floor and candles that hanged from the trees, dancing in the breeze. Fairy lights sat in the trees like little stars, creating the most perfect backdrop I had ever seen. I had admired the final product with Grandma for a few moments before she had pushed me up the stairs to get ready and then run off in the direction of her bedroom. There was a young Spanish girl at the door, ready for arriving guests, and she watched me curiously as I made my way up the stairs to my room. I hoped I didn't stand out as much as her look made me feel. There were seats enough for eighty people in the garden, but Grandma didn't seem too sure on just how many were coming, cracking some joke about people her age making plans one week and then being dead by the next. I had laughed, but more from shock, to which she had chuckled wickedly and vanished off to her room. The woman had spirit for her age, that was for sure, and a lot of people still in her life. I thankfully hadn't seen anything of the brothers all day and despite inner pep-talks, I wasn't quite sure how to react when I did. They had dragged me from my bed and scared the crap out of me, but they had also tried to protect me when it had all gone south. That was something I was sure I would never have witnessed in my life time and it had created this new side to them, a new strum in my heart that beat with less apprehension. Maybe they weren't too bad, maybe somewhere deep inside, beneath the rough and playful facades, were just two broken men?

I showered and dried my hair, then sat in my dress applying my make-up, something I hadn't done in a long time. The dress I'd gone with, in the end, was an elegant flowing one to my knees. It was delicately decorated on the scooping neck line, flattering and timeless. The whole thing was ivory, graceful and gorgeous. Spending a small fortune on it really had made a difference in the quality and I bit my lip at the thought of how much rent this little baby could have paid for back home. It drew a small smile, despite myself and I shook my head slightly ashamed. I had never been luxurious or frivolous at home, but I kind of liked how it felt. I exhaled and stood, looking into the mirror. I was nervous for some reason and really wanted to look good, to draw confidence from at least that fact. Why I was so anxious was a whole other minefield of unanswerable questions that I quickly brushed away, smoothing my dress down. I looked over myself with only the critiquing eye a female could bestow on herself. I had been unsure about the light colour, but thankfully the sun had been kind over the last few days. I gazed at myself in the mirror lost in thoughts. Earlier while I'd been helping Grandma organize, I'd fallen upon a room with photo frames all over the wall. In the centre of all the old frames had been a massive family portrait from when Cane was young. In it stood the three generations from which now, sadly only really one still existed. I'd smiled at the young Cane. Even then you could tell he was going to be a looker. What had really caught my eye though had been his mother. She was beautiful, classic and striking. I watched her for a while, identifying Cane's characteristic in her; her eyes and her distinctive dimples. I wondered if he remembered she'd had them, the exact same ones he did? She had been flawless, which was something else her and her eldest son shared. I had hoped maybe if I had stared at her for long enough, that she would have given me some answers to everything, but after what felt like an eternity, nothing had come, just a sense of appreciation for her, her beauty and her son. I slipped my feet in to my heels and put on all my jewellery. I stood back in front of the mirror again and assessed myself. I would never be in the league of his mother, there was no questioning that, but my dress made my eyes seem a deeper blue and my genes seem not so plain. I could honestly say that I hadn't looked this good in years or arguably not since the Charity Ball magazine picture. This time though, it wasn't Ed's selected professionals that pulled it off, it was all me. That gave me confidence, confidence I'd never really had before and confidence I so desperately needed tonight. I could already hear the party starting downstairs, yet I lingered at the door with nerves. *Get out there, Eva,* I told myself firmly, knowing that this might be the last time I had to socailise with other people that weren't me or black shirts. Still, it was hard acting happy all the time, pretending life was fine every second of the day, when inside I was wrenched with torment and confusion. I scrunched my hair and summoned strength at the thought of getting to see my parents after all this. I descended the stairs and was met with a hallway full of people, all speaking in loud and animated Spanish. The girl still stood at the base of the stairwell, collecting personal items and directing people through the house to the gardens. Her eyes caught mine and this time she smiled, her head nodding to acknowledge me. The atmosphere was hot and happy as everyone embraced and laughed. I had never seen so many colours at a party, every lady seemed to be wearing a beautiful frock and all the men paraded in floral shirts and linens. It was dazzling to watch but somehow made the whole event more fascinating. I made my way out to the drinks table and was poured a beverage by a man I recognised from the set up earlier in the day. He handed it to me with a smile of recognition.

'Te ves Hermosa,' he offered with a little smile, as he handed me my drink. *You look beautiful* he had said kindly and I accepted the compliment with much needed encouragement. I smiled brightly back at him with warm eyes, grateful for the small confidence booster. I wondered if I looked like I had needed it.

'Gracias,' I replied, blushing slightly. Compliments were nice to hear, but I never found them easy to take. A flaw all women held, I was sure. A loud familiar laugh from across the garden made my smile drop, and Andreas's dangerous, yet oddly charming chuckle, alerted me to his presence. My eyes quickly found him in a small crowd of plastic girls, displaying and showing off his biceps through his patterned shirt. I watched him, rolling my eyes and sipping my drink, my heart steadying. I wondered a few steps closer, curious as to if I would ever be able to trust or like these men? It was peculiar to be so unsure of them when I was so completely opposite in regard to Cane. Elias appeared in the group with a large beer in one hand and a tiny woman in the other. I remembered the panic I'd felt the first time I'd met them, especially in comparison to Cane. It had been very different. Cane had had an unnerving effect on me that day, to be honest he still did, but he had been intimidating, commanding and dominant, with complete control. Elias and Andreas were utter loose cannons. I sipped my drink again with my pulse returning to normal. I guessed it wasn't really their fault. They'd been raised in a strange and parentless environment, where trust and compassion didn't exist. They'd had no discipline and no course of guided direction. Maybe they couldn't be blamed too much for their blatant disregard of decency and normality. Exactly as I thought this though, Elias slapped a lady's bottom as she walked by with, what I could only assume, was her husband. She yelped from shock and the man went to defend her honour. All too quickly though, he saw the assailant and bowed out of the confrontation, ushering his abused wife away without any further words. I swallowed my mouthful of drink and shook my head with a deflating exhale. Nope, who was I kidding, they were definitely just idiots. *Idiots and bullies, no excuses.* I sighed and cast my eyes around the crowds in the garden, recalling my promise to grandma at the dinner table a couple of nights ago. I was going to find those boys a suitable woman and I now knew, the exact type of lady I wanted. I was spurred by what I had just seen and with the knowledge that all bullies can be humbled with the right action…or the right woman, I got to searching. I was sure there was at least one of these types of women here, it was a rife opportunity, too good to be missed by a true professional, I just had to locate her. I'd been to enough fancy events, full of rich people and gold diggers, to know how it all worked. I wandered around the crowds for a few minutes, watching everyone. Of course, I could find the most unattractive and awkward lady at the party with poor dress sense, bad body odour and no personality, and pass her off to the brothers with Grandma's approval, but that was too easy and too fair for them. They deserved to be messed with, the way they messed with everyone else. Yes, I had a new appreciation for them which I never expected and surprisingly I didn't hate them like I was sure I would, but I also didn't agree with their callous actions and blatant disregard for thought. Humility came when you passed through challenges. They just needed the right challenge. I took my drink as I continued to wander around the party. My heart leapt every time I thought I saw Cane, only to be disappointed when it was not him. I pushed his absence to the back of my mind and continued on my mission, sure that at some point, he would show. I should be enjoying my free time away from the Rodriguez boys, not constantly looking over my shoulder, hoping to see a particular one. I shook my head at myself in reprimand and carried on with my task. I analysed everything I saw as I passed groups of people, checking body language, facial expressions, positioning, until after an hour or so, I finally witnessed exactly what I was looking for; complete and utter professional female manipulation. I'd noticed her earlier actually, made up to perfection, elegant and stunning, yet flitting from man to man, anyone who seemed to take her on. Women that beautiful didn't flit, they always normally belonged to another perfect being, like themselves, secure and looked after. It was a giveaway if you knew what you were looking for and thankfully I did. Gold diggers were some of the cleverest beings alive on the earth and the best ones were always women. I watched her as she very politely excused herself from the company of two middle aged men as their wives appeared. She glided through the crowd gracefully heading towards the bathrooms, turning the heads of men and a few women, as she passed by. *Perfect.* I quickly followed her with a fleeting buzz of excitement. Once inside the Ladies, I casually stopped at the mirror beside her, then suddenly realised that I'd never actually done this before, whatever this actually was. I fluffed my hair inconspicuously, trying to make a plan. I was pretty much baiting a con-artist, something I was sure wasn't done often by everyday run-of-the-mill people, like me. She retouched her lipstick and pulled her boobs up into her low-cut scoop dress. I cleared my throat and watched her with jealousy, and not just at the boobs, the whole of her was stunning.

'I just adore your dress,' I began, quite genuinely. It was a daring dark red that I knew I could never pull off, mostly due to the fact it was tiny and feminine, and I was not. She turned to me and smiled with a warm, welcoming face, quite happy with the compliment.

'Gracias, thank you,' she replied with perfect, white, straight teeth. 'You are not Spanish, no?' she continued. I shook my head with a slight shrug of disappointment.

'No, I wish I was though,' she laughed. 'I'm a close friend of Grandma Rodriguez and the family.' She was suddenly was very interested in my story and stopped fiddling with her chest to listen. 'I'm just here for the birthday party.' I turned my attention back to my hair in the mirror. 'Do you know the family well?' I asked casually, to which she shrugged one shoulder elegantly, very non-committal. I already knew that she wouldn't personally know the family or necessarily anyone really for that matter. She most likely gate crashed, after all, this was a job to her, not a social event. Her career was this: to attend occasions and find a rich, powerful man to seduce and eventually marry, thus securing a lifetime of wealth, luxury and influence. Simple.

'Sadly, I do not know them at all very well. But I hear they are a...maravillosa familia...' She paused, 'especialmente los tres hermanos.' I smiled. *Yes, especially the three brothers,* I repeated to myself happily. She applied more lipstick while eyeing me attentively from the side.

'They are wonderful,' I gushed, flattening my dress against my stomach. 'I should introduce you!' I announced suddenly, as if the idea had just come to me. A quick flash of excitement passed through her eyes before she professionally composed herself again.

'I hear Cane, the oldest son is a very nice man, sí?' Something stirred inside me at the thought of her elegantly and professionally seducing Cane. I forced the thought from my mind, quickly swallowing the feeling that was definitely jealousy, irrational as it was. 'He is, but always so busy. You know, the younger brothers Elias and Andreas, they could really use a nice woman like you in their lives though. They always have such awful girls around them.' I thought she might burst with delight.

'Tú eres muy amable.' *You are too kind,* she purred back at me, placing her perfectly manicured hand on my arm. I smiled. I liked this one.

'You know what, let's go introduce you now *and* I'm going to tell Grandma Rodriguez about you. She'll be sure to keep those boys straight and let them know when they've got a good thing.' At this she literally jumped for joy, skipping into the air with glee. 'The tip I give you,' I continued, as I took her arm and led her from the toilets, 'is not to let any of those other *chicas* get around them.' She nodded in understanding. 'They are only after one thing and can be very vicious trying to get it.' I at least felt like the last part was true, any girl I ever saw with the brothers surely wasn't after them for their personalities. She straightened her red dress to her tight body with confidence, then squeezed my arm gently.

'I understand exactly,' she whispered with startling force. The more I talked to this woman, the more I was genuinely amused by her. I hoped she ate the brothers up and spat them out again. 'I can be very…dedicado…' she searched for the right translation, despite me knowing fine well what the suitably used word meant, '…dedicated,' she finally offered, 'I can be very dedicated, when I need to be.' She puckered her lips together to smear her lipstick and my mouth twitched at the sides with a smile. I bet she could be. Butterflies tickled my stomach as I approached the brother's group. This was the first time I'd spoken to the men after last night's fiasco. But, just like the little actress on my arm, I reminded myself, it was all about confidence. Fake or not.

'Elias, Andreas,' I called out loudly, pushing past Barbie, Malibu Barbie and Tropical Barbie, until my new friend and I stood in the centre of the circle, directly in front of the brothers. They eyed me with an odd mixture of what looked like apprehension and then suspicion. I was sure if they had not caught sight of the beauty on my arm they'd have instantly marched me away to Cane's side, demanding I was locked in my room. I seemed to cause them nothing but trouble, but the feeling was very mutual. I planted smug, sweet kisses on their cheeks and continued to talk before they could make a scene. 'I'd like to introduce you to my very good friend here…' I paused quickly realising that I hadn't asked her name. Thankfully she was true a professional and stepped forward, boobs upright and alert. She extended her elegant hand and long slender arm to each brother with such seductive force that I had to stop my mouth from dropping open. I couldn't imagine ever being able to command such feminine supremacy.

'Rose,' she purred, musically, flirting mercilessly with her eyes. I gathered my wits and continued while they were distracted.

'I was telling Rose how wonderful your family is, especially your adorable Grandma…' I let the implication of Grandma linger just long enough for the boys to think that she was somehow involved. 'And I decided she just had to meet you two.' They looked somewhat confused. The night we had shared previously, had been heated and disastrous and left many questions between us, but now, in a polite crowd, I was presenting them with the most beautiful woman in the room and telling them Grandma had approved of her. I smiled sweetly and continued. 'I am sure you will look after Rose here, like gentlemen,' I pat her hand gently, 'while I go find Grandma and tell her of your manners.' I winked at Rose as I turned to leave. I'm pretty sure she knew I was up to something, it took one to know one after all, but the opportunity was too good for her to question. She acknowledged my wink with a slight head incline and then dawned an immaculate smile. I hoped she played the bullies for all they had and made them look like fools. I wanted them to be humbled, to realise people had feelings and actions had consequences. If Cane was too busy to teach them that lesson, then I would. As I walked off, I could hear Rose instructing the brothers that they were to dance with her, immediately. I glanced behind to see them following her off to the dance floor, leaving behind a very angry group of plastic dolls. I smiled with victory, returning to the same beverage table from before, feeling very much like I deserved another drink. It was a different man serving this time and he quickly poured my order and handed me my newly filled glass.

'Para una bella dama, mirando.' *For a beautiful looking lady.* He passed me the glass with a gracious nod and I smiled at him, thanking him kindly. I liked this drinks table.

'You look more than beautiful my dear, you *are* beautiful. I see what Cane mean when he tell me, that you have something special, something he never see before in anyone.' Grandma appeared at my side with a somewhat confusing opening statement, but it was quickly forgotten when I turned to face her. She was sparkling in a deep purple dress and heeled sandals. Her hair was styled and her jewellery glistening in the lights. She was radiant, and I hugged her with delight, thinking how easy it was to forget that she was an old lady, and not in the prime of her youth.

'You look absolutely amazing.' I beamed with, for once, full genuine honesty. She nodded in agreement.

'Not bad for ninety, hey?' she laughed, collecting a drink. 'And you my dear, look glowing. You give some of this Spanish chicas a run for money.' I shook my head, positive she was being far too generous with her compliments. 'Now, come, I want to introduce you to family and friend.' I smiled and took her hand, following her across the party with unexplainable butterflies returning to my stomach. I glanced as casually around as I could whilst walking through the crowds, but I could not see the person my heart was searching for. Maybe it was a good thing. I didn't need to see him anyway, did I? Once upon a time I'd have avoided him at all costs, but times had changed. Grandma extended my hand into the palm of a young and somewhat, attractive man, telling me his name was Rafael and that he was Cane's second cousin. She said the word English in Spanish and then wondered off with a mischievous wink. What was she up to? Why did this feel like a test?

'English?' the young man confirmed, looking me up and down. I wasn't too sure how I felt about being so openly eyeballed by someone who wasn't Cane, but I smiled and nodded with a yes. 'If you do not mind me saying so, you are a very pretty woman.' I choked on my drink, laughing awkwardly. He was bold.

'Umm, gracias, thank you,' I replied shyly, 'but its dark out and I'm pretty sure these lights are doing wonders for everyone.' He nodded, licking his lips.

'What is your name?' he continued, still holding my hand. I pulled it out of his firm grip and placed my drink in it to make sure he couldn't take it again.

'Eva,' I answered, wondering if all Spanish men were this forward? Hadn't Grandma maybe mentioned to him that I was with her grandsons, that I was her beloved Cane's other half? Not that I was actually *with* Cane, but you know, pretending to be with Cane…not that she was supposed to know that part…ahhhh…I shook my head, almost losing myself to a very complicated train of thought. It was a messy tangle of lies and was always in the back of my mind, especially now, as we were joined by another man.

'Excuse me, may I join you? I couldn't help but overhear your conversation. You speak English, sí?' Rafael glared at the newcomer with a smile, but nodded in agreeance.

'Please,' he mumbled, extending his arm and stepping back to allow him to entry to our circle. We introduced ourselves again and began to talk about our lives, what each of us did, where we did it and general chit-chat. My answers were all slightly fabricated, in light of the fact that the last few weeks had seen me a captive and used for ransom, but I answered all the same, keeping it vague and general. The conversation trickled on and some forty long minutes later and I was stood in a larger circle with six men, each speaking English mixed with Spanish to me, and asking me question after question. It was pleasant enough, if not a little hard to correctly translate their words, but maybe this was how people socialised in Spain? Or maybe it was just the few drinks they had all had now, making the whole thing seem a bit overwhelming. The party was well under way and people were eating and laughing, and the noise created a joyous blanket of happiness. Servers moved amongst the guests clearing plates and filling drinks and the dancefloor was full of couples. People passed by our group frequently, as they walked down to the pond. The night was magical, a little strange at present, but magical none the less and was a perfect celebration for a wonderful woman.

'So how do you know dear old, Mrs Rodriguez?' Rafael finally asked, leaning in past the man standing next to him. They all listened intently as I opened my mouth to speak, but as I did, the crowd parted slightly and at the other end of the garden, I saw a man in cream trousers and a loose white shirt, standing and looking our way. My voice disappeared from me as my eyes settled on him. His skin seemed to darken each time I saw him and where he stood, the fairy lights illuminated him into a spectacle. His thin shirt danced in the evening breeze, floating against his tight body, and his strong arms were placed at rest in his pockets. His eyes were alive and alert, ever watchful. Of all the times I had found Cane Rodriguez attractive, this moment maybe topped them all. In his natural surroundings, he looked even more like deity: strong, confident, gentle and reserved. He roused in me uncertainty and lust and every emotion mixed up into the other. He both settled and excited me, and my body yearned for him beyond control, coming alive whenever he was near. His eyes quickly found mine across the garden and locked on, my insides beginning to simmer. In an instant everything around me changed. My breath slowed, and my chest rose and fell in silence, failing to claim any air. The scene became a movie, a still shot, where everything around had paused and where everyone else had blurred, disappearing into nothingness. I watched him through the crowds, every inch of him, intently, as his eyes travelled up and down my body in return. He inclined his head towards me with acknowledgement and I licked my lips in subconscious delight. I nodded back at him with a lingering smile, feeling the blush on my cheeks deepen. If I had ever had had an issue with Cane's longing and reading stares, it had passed. His eyes on me now surfaced emotions I was quickly failing to suppress. I had his undivided attention and it was welcomed. He saw me…and I liked it.

'That would be, Cane Rodriguez,' a voice said close to my ear, snapping me back to reality. I felt the men's faces on me, each watching where I had been very obviously focused. Rafael's voice shattered the moment like glass and my surroundings came crashing back in around me, breaking my connection to Cane. I moved my head with irritation, trying to catch another glimpse of him, but he gone, lost to the moving crowds.

'Cane Rodriguez is, erm, how do you English say it…*bad news.*' One of the men warned, joined by a chorus of muttered bitter and snide agreements. 'Any lady who is with him is loco, un idiota. If you ask me.' Again, agreeing mumbles at the words *fool* and *idiot* echoed around in our circle, ripe with resentment and dislike. The adjectives made my fists tense slightly. 'Oh great, he's coming our way.' The small, thin man added, with what sounded more like anxiety. My stomach muscles contracted, and my heart began to beat faster. I could smell him before he arrived, my every sense acutely aware of where he was and where he was heading. His aftershave caught at my nose and sent butterflies through my skin, a prickling delight that spread rapidly to every part of me. There was a heat beginning to build inside, pooling and yearning, and I could feel it beginning to consume me.

'So how did you say you knew, Mrs Rodriguez?' Rafael was asking again, trying to bring the conversation back to him and close the circle, of what was apparently very insecure men. I finished my last sip of drink and turned my head to look him straight in his eyes, making sure my words were clearly understood.

'I'm here with her grandson, Cane.' I stated boldly, smiling sweetly and turning just in time to have Cane reach my side. He stood taller than all the other men and I could feel them shrink from behind me, cowering away with sheepish nods of acknowledgement. I surged with unmistakable pride. I was proud to have Cane's attention, proud to have him stand at my side, proud for him to be searching for me through a crowd. I knew what the men in our group had said about him, may be true, he had been a dangerous and dreadful man, once, but that person was no longer. Our private moments of intimacy and honesty were forcing themselves up, all the promises and whispered hopes inside me were now dancing by the fire and desperately wanting to be set alight. Yes, he had been a monster, he had done awful things, but even with that past, I knew I could no longer deny what I felt. He was rapidly becoming *my* monster, *my* claim, *my* attachment and *my* cross to bear. Fate had twisted its sarcastic dagger and I had become defensive over Cane Rodriguez. The understanding was insane, but blatantly there nonetheless. He was mine now, and I would stake that claim.

'Eva,' he offered simply, reaching his powerful hand out for mine. I couldn't stem my smile, it conquered me quickly, and I placed my hand, unquestioningly, in his. Tingles of pleasure fired throughout my body. 'Podemos bailar esta pieza? Luchadora?' he requested with alight eyes, as if no one else was around. I nodded without hesitation, disposing of my glass to a shocked Rafael. *May I have this dance?* I repeated his words to myself with quickly spreading delight. I'd dance with him till the end of time if he asked me to.

'I'd *love* to dance.' I swooned, following him off to the dancefloor without even casting a second look backwards. His hand felt like fire, foreign and new, but it burned into my skin, searing away doubts and reservations. I forced myself to look up from it and focus on something else, on any another feeling, but just like it had been the other night in my room when he had taken my hand, nothing else seemed to matter. Once we reached the very centre of the dancefloor, he stopped and brought me into his arms, taking me by my waist. His hand sat on my hip, steady and firm, pulling me tight into his chest I could feel his strength through my thin dress, and just like moments ago, the world vanished again; the crowds surrounding us and the colours and noise of the party evaporated into mist. We were alone, and Cane's body held me firmly against his. He was so close to me that I could feel his heat radiating through his shirt and my pulse quickened as we began to dance slowly. His eyes stayed locked on mine, not missing a beat and I could hear my heart and my breathing. We moved to the music that I knew was playing somewhere, with no words being said, just the exchange of glances and provoked smiles. It was our language, wordless and loud. He spun me gently under his arm and when he pulled me back into his body, he finally spoke.

'Te ves estupenda,' he whispered intimately, leaning his head to my side and his lips brushing my ear. 'You look stunning.' I blushed uncontrollably, thankful that it was dark. I could feel myself falling under his unexplainable spell. I tried to keep myself together, to remain controlled, but as his eyes continued to read into me more deeply, it was proving useless. I was lost to him, and I was sure we both knew it. I swallowed for composure as his hand moved on my lower back.

'Well, some kind gentlemen bought me this really, super, expensive dress,' I glanced down at myself with a playful smile and Cane's eyes sparkled with humour, 'so I thought I should probably wear it.' His mother's dimples appeared on his day-old stubble and my heart filled to capacity, ready to explode. Just like fireworks. His smile was like fireworks, erupting inside me. Maybe it was the sincerity or the genuineness that I knew his dimples signified, but Cane's real smile was as striking as it was deadly.

'He has good taste then,' he laughed gently, spinning me again.

'Some would say so.' I inclined my head slightly towards him, every movement laced with intention. His eyes left me, scanning around briefly, then returning to my face. They were gone for only a second, but it allowed me to breathe, deeply.

'How have you been today?' he asked, relaxed and casual, moving us slowly across the dancefloor. I felt like we were alight and leaving a glowing trail of embers behind. We traced a pattern of our movements, in a world where the presence of others ceased to exist. And it was perfect.

'Bien, gracias,' his hand on my waist squeezed slightly in reaction, and it sent tingles up my back.

'I love it when you speak Spanish,' he whispered in a low playful voice, tightening his hand around mine. I wouldn't have thought it possible to be so aware of every touch on my body, but I was, and immensely so.

'How was *your* day?' I asked, trying to control the explosions of sensations coursing through me.

'Bien,' he answered with an odd tone. 'It's been good to spend time with mi abuela this week.' He said his grandma's name with a tone of sentimental fondness. 'I was unsure what to do tonight,' he suddenly admitted, looking down at me, 'I wondered if it was best for me to stay away from you for a while, give you, give *us,* some space' I dipped my brows, concern and disagreement crossing my face. Cane read it easily and smiled in response, pulling me slightly closer to him. 'Abulea had a chat to me, don't worry,' he continued, 'she has this uncanny knack of giving everything...clarity.' I laughed, knowing exactly what he meant. I recalled the moment she had told me to hold onto love, despite anything. Her advice was half the reason I was stood here in Cane's arms, it plagued me with knowing.

'I wonder if that clarity just comes with age?' I said, glancing at her socialising and laughing across the garden. Her eye caught mine for a second and she smiled with delight and knowing.

'I don't know,' Cane answered, following my eyes to her, 'she's always been a bit crafty.' I watched her a moment longer and could tell that Cane was most likely right, she did seem to have something mystical about her.

'I think she's buying this whole crazy act though,' I added offhandedly, instantly realising my words and regretting them. We were living in a fairytale and voicing the truth was like breaking a spell, a spell I very much wanted to stay under, for as long as I could. Cane swallowed and nodded to my comment, but did not continue with the topic. I inhaled with baited breath, awaiting his next move and praying he didn't walk away. The music around us stopped and quickly changed into a fast paced salsa song. The band announced something in Spanish and people around us cheered, filling the dancefloor with enthusiastic bodies. Cane's eyes twinkled with challenge and his hold of me tightened. I gasped in surprise and looked questioningly at his suddenly mischievous face.

'Can you dance?' he asked, nodding in gesture to the music now in the air. There was a playful smile on his full lips and I returned his grin, quickly pulling away from his hold. He stood motionless, his eyes travelling up my body with appreciation. Looking through my eyelashes, I stepped in to him again, placing one alluring finger on his hard chest. His eyes shot down to it, his teeth biting his bottom lip with intrigue. I began to move slowly and provocatively around his body, trailing my single finger across every inch of his large and enticing frame. I could feel his shoulders rise and fall quickly with his breathe and his eyes danced over me with rousing delight. I reached his face again, moving in close to his ear, my breath heating his neck. I felt him lean towards me, a low rumble in his chest.

'If you'd actually read *anything* about me, *Mr Rodriguez,*' I began, whispering seductively into his ear, 'then you'd know, that I took dance classes since the age of three.' It suddenly felt like play time, like we were due some light-hearted fun, some unbridled enjoyment. Now was time to let a little of that pent-up tension and steam out, to touch and flirt in a place where it was unseen. He smiled wickedly, as his hands quickly grabbed my waist and pulled me in against him. I inhaled sharply with pleasure and his eyes lit up at the sound. 'Yes, I can dance, Senor.' I mouthed, thrill and anticipation bubbling up inside me like a volcano.

'Bueno…*good,*' he muttered looking me in my eyes, 'cause I'm not willing to share you with the group of idiots over there who are waiting for their turn.' I glanced to the side of the dancefloor where the men I had previously been talking to, waited and watched. I smiled at Cane, playfully.

'Well, as long as you can keep up,' I teased, 'I guess you can stay.' He laughed loudly, grabbing my hand and spinning me into the middle of the floor. Even being modest, I had to admit that everyone was watching us with jealousy. We had the moves: spinning, dipping, lifting, reading and knowing each other perfectly. I wasn't sure when it had changed exactly, but the chemistry felt like never before, like fire heating up and reaching a near boiling point, intense and consuming. Every time we returned to each other our bodies would collide, sending sparks through me like I had never felt before. I was aware of every part of him touching me, aware of his hands on my waist, his chest against my chest, his body pressed up against mine and his eyes never leaving my smile. Who knew that dancing could be so seductive, so powerful and consuming? It had certainly never felt like it before. And who knew that Cane could dance so well, that had definitely not been in *his* file. As the song ended we finished, holding tight to each other, breathing heavily and our chests rising and falling quickly from the exertion. Upon the last chord, the crowd erupted into cheers and the sound flooded back in like an explosion. It pulled us both back to reality as we looked around, instantly realising that the noise was applaud, and applaud for us. I wasn't sure when it had happened, but apparently, everybody else had stopped dancing at some point and had stood, watching us instead. Embarrassment surfaced quickly, and Cane laughed again with that gravitational laugh, pulling me down into a bow with him. His eyes were alive with enjoyment and I blushed at the attention, hiding my face in my hands and quickly following him off to the pond for some air. He grabbed two drinks from a server as he passed and led the way to the bottom of the garden where the water lay, covered with floating candles. We were still laughing by the time we reached the pond side, joking about the public display. It was hypnotic to see Cane so relaxed, so at ease, so normal. He was confident and infectious and sexy and everything a man should be. It was impossible to not want him.

'Eva, I'm impressed,' he began, taking his pretend hat off to me. I laughed, curtsying.

'As am I, Mr Rodriguez. Where did you learn to dance like that?' He shrugged with humour like it was nothing.

'I'm from Spain. We all learn to dance like that.' I shook my head at his modesty.

'I'm pretty sure that if I'd have danced with one of those other guys, it wouldn't have been like *that.*' I took a sip from my glass, letting the cool liquid quench my worked-up thirst.

'Cierto, that's probably true,' Cane agreed, 'but then cousin Rafael and the Mendez brothers have about as much *chemistry* in them as a tea-spoon.' I smiled slightly, and my stomach turned at his use of words.

'Is that what we have, is it? Chemistry?' I asked quite suddenly, hesitantly lowering the glass from my uncertain lips. Cane looked at me, his smile quickly vanishing. 'Chemistry?' I repeated. 'Because chemistry has the potential for disaster, you know?' He had put his glass down and was stepping towards me, his eyes deep and searching. They locked on mine and didn't move, as he reached inches from my body. His finger came to my face and swept over my check, across my lips and left a blazing trail. My whole body was pulsing, vibrant with excitement and confusion.

'Sometimes though, chemistry makes new discoveries,' he whispered slowly, his hand sliding around my back and pulling me closer to him. Our bodies melted into each other as if it was the most natural thing in the world. I was breathing deeply, desperately searching for a sign or a reason to have faith in him, to take the biggest chance of my life. Everything in my body and heart told me to trust him, but everything in my head still spoke caution. Still counselled to be safe. I was stuck, constantly stuck. Caught in the middle of an all-consuming passion and an intense fear, both of which wanted to devour me. Cane leant as close as he could be without actually kissing me. His breath warming my wet lips and he looked me dead in the eyes, piercing straight to my soul. He inhaled deeply. 'Are you in love with me, Eva?' he asked again, whispering slowly the question from the other night. My glass slipped from my hand to the grass and I lost my air. My heart pounded against my chest with such intensity I thought it would break out of me.

'I...,' I hesitated, 'I, I don't know,' I whispered. 'I just don't know.' I watched his eyes flash with something had never seen in him before. 'What do you *want* me to say?' I begged with exasperation, pleading for help.

'I want you to tell me that you love me...' his voice deepened, 'the way that I'm in love with you, Eva.' His eyes searched mine for what felt like an eternity, as if he had finally said IT and everything now hung on the next few seconds. *He was in love with me?* I said the words to myself again. My heart felt like it was going to explode through my skin, like it didn't have enough room inside of me anymore. I struggled to breathe and stay grounded. *He was in love with me? Those eyes and that smile are in love with me? That body and these hands holding me, are in love with me?* How did I feel? I knew that I wanted him to kiss me, I knew that I had never felt this strongly about anyone in my life before. I knew I couldn't remember where I was or what I was wearing. HE WAS IN LOVE WITH ME! My heart screamed it out to my head. HE. LOVED. ME. He hadn't breathed yet and his eyes searched mine like the entire universe depended on me. He needed a response, he needed me to react, and I could physically see that desperation in him. The closest I'd come to seeing him this vulnerable was the night of the camera, when he had held me whilst I cried. But this was different, now he was bare and laid out, waiting, desperately exposed. He was alone and out on a limb, and I was sure that wasn't a place he frequented often. He whispered it again, firmly, as if needing to make sure I'd understood. 'Eva, did you hear me? Te amo.' His eyes pleaded for a reply and it was that look that drew me in, that weakened and defenseless side of him that could still love and trust someone. I only managed to nod slightly before his lips crashed into mine and he kissed me. It was a full, yearning kiss, strong and deep and passionate. His tongue demanded entry and I parted for him, as if it was what I had been created to do. It was fire, spreading through my body, consuming any fear or doubt I'd ever had, burning them out with an intense and immediate heat. The world dissipated, dissolving into nothingness, with no sound, vision or gravity. My whole being merged into him and his hold on me, as his arms wrapped around my body and pulled me closer. Everything that ever existed melted away and I couldn't care if I ever saw it again. His strong arms encompassed me, and I could feel his bones pressing into mine. He let out a small noise of pleasure as he kissed me harder and deeper, his hands running to my lower back. It was hot and intense, and I kissed him back like I was lost from reason, hardly able to breathe through my desire. I wanted this. *I wanted this*. The knowledge was freeing and liberating, and I wrapped my arms around his neck trying to still get closer, as if to merge into him, willing him to kiss me harder and longer and to never stop.

`Are you two ever coming up for air?' Grandma's voice interrupted, shattering us with a startling jolt. I jumped away quickly, holding my hand to my mouth, a million emotions coursing through me. My heart was beating faster than my body could keep up with and it made me sway with dizziness. I was panting, unable to catch my stolen breath. Cane didn't break his stare, he watched me like I was an atom bomb, either away to explode or become forever dormant.

'We'll be back up in a minute, Abuela,' Cane called to his Grandmother, still keeping his eyes locked on mine. She accepted the brush off and wandered away muttering that it was her party. Neither of us moved as the seconds of silence passed. We were both either too scared or too confused to do so, and so instead, we remained silent, only looking at each other. The sound of crickets humming all around and the noises of the party had all come back in, the sounds of music and people laughing now drifted down to the empty pond side with us. Finally, Cane spoke, but not with his normal, confident and commanding manner. It was a whisper, a begging plea from a reaching man.

'Eva,' he began quietly, making as if to step towards me, but thinking better of it. 'I meant what I said.' He was shaking his head, as if already expecting me to retreat and run. 'I love you. I love you completely. We can work this out.' I stood frozen, unable to process anything but breathing. 'I just need you to stay with me. Please?' He had spoken those words to me before, the night we had had dinner and he had had that same pleading look in his beautiful eyes. I had expected myself to panic, freak out and run, as Cane obviously did too, but those reactions weren't coming. I had never felt more alive in my entire life, than I did when Cane was with me. I looked into his eyes. He held such a power over me it was unnerving. How was it possible to feel so connected and attached to him when I hated him so venomously my whole life? I *wanted* him to be mine now, *so* much that it physically hurt. I wanted to always have those eyes looking at me, trying to read me. I wanted to make him happy and ease his lonely life. I wanted to stay with him so much that I could barely form words to reply. He kept his longing eyes on mine, awaiting my response. *Stay with me...*his words would plague me until the day I died, I already knew this. How could I stay with him? We both already knew the answer to his question, the impossibility of it, but apparently only one of us was willing to admit that. So, with strength I didn't know I even had, I finally spoke.

'I can't be with you, Cane.' At my words, his head fell, severing our eye contact. It was heartbreaking to watch him look so defeated and hurt, this giant of a man. Remorse began to fill my veins like cold ice water. I felt like I was losing something more important than I'd ever had before, like I was making the biggest mistake of my life. My fingers touched my lips, trying to hold onto the rapidly fading feeling of him there. He was a man who had caused me so much pain, my family so much pain, the world I lived in so much pain. He was a man who despised my side of life, my people. He was a man who had done unspeakable things to those I loved. And yet, despite everything, hurting him outweighed it all. Watching the strongest man I'd come to know, look utterly destroyed, mattered more than the things I knew he'd done. *Stay.* The word echoed in my head like it was etching itself into my soul, stuck there to haunt me for forever. *Stay with me.* My eyes stung and when I shut them, I felt tears flow from my lids. I was a grown woman crying over a decision I never had the luxury of even making in the first place. Life had ensured that even though I was filled with these powerful new emotions, I was never allowed to use them. I could never make it work, I could never make a right choice. I couldn't stay and be with him anymore than he could leave his life and be with me. It required change, so much change, that it was just too much. How could we ask our families, our friends, our associates, anyone in our polar opposite lives to understand and forgive? To trust us to be in love and happy? And if us being together caused so much pain to the people we cared for, how would we survive that? Even if *we* were ready, the world we belonged too, was not. I stepped towards him in desperation and placed my hand on his strong chin, lifting it to my eyes. 'You know we can never be.' I whispered, wishing I could break down and sob where I stood. His arms reached out and pulled me in to him, embracing me desperately, clinging to me like his life depended on it. *How has this happened,* I asked myself as my fingers grasped his back with all the strength I could muster. I was sure I had hated him all my life. *Hadn't I?*

CHAPTER THIRTY.
Stolen time.

The crowds parted, and his heart almost stopped beating...there she was. He felt like he was in a movie and someone had pressed the slow-motion button, Eva's face coming into focus across the dance floor. The lights were glowing around her and she had never looked more beautiful than she did now. His breath stalled in his chest and he felt like he should hold onto something to stop himself from crumbling. She was perfection, standing feet away and looking straight at him, an arrow to his chest. He just about managed to swallow before the crowds mingled again and she was lost. He used the cover as a chance to move from her view quickly, and to gather himself. He stood in the shadows for a second, composing himself, catching his stolen breath back. His mouth had turned up at the sides and his hands turned warm in his pockets. He exhaled loudly and wiped his palms on his trousers whilst trying to stop his goofy smile from spreading. On command, his heart began to slow, and he regained control. He bit his bottom lip with anticipation, if he was about to walk over to her, he needed to at least look a bit cooler, even if he felt on fire inside. After a couple more calculating moments, he stepped out into the party again, placing his hands back into his pockets. As he made his way through the oblivious and noisy people, his eyes quickly found Eva and locked on. She was standing in a group of men and he quickly noted that he couldn't leave her more than a few minutes before the sharks circled. But Eva was looking outward and around, and he allowed himself the hope that she was maybe looking for him again. She disappeared behind a group of men for another few seconds as he crossed the drinks area. He glanced fleetingly at the company she was with and as one man placed his hand on her shoulder, a jealous rumble sounded inside him. He tightened his lips as she again vanished from view behind a rather large and loud woman. A few steps more and he found himself almost at her feet. Her shoulders straightened, and he could have sworn her lips twitched before she bit down with her teeth at them. Did she sense him coming, the way he had become so acutely aware of her? Then, never losing sight of her rising and falling chest, he was beside her, her body's heat radiating in his direction. He knew he should acknowledge the other men in the circle, but something in the way her eyes locked onto his, made him simply forget they even existed. He asked her to dance as bravely as he could, and his heart soared as her countenance lit up at the request. As her hand slipped confidently into his, every doubt and morsel of hesitation vanished from him and he knew nothing but the feel of her soft skin touching him. He was left fresh, clean and weightless.

After what had felt like only moment of perfect joy and hope, of utter happiness and bliss, he had somehow had to watch her walk away from him, again. Her dress blew in the breeze behind her and as she put distance between her skin and his; between her life and the one he wanted. They had danced, he had held her, they had laughed...they had kissed. They had kissed! The memory of it still lingered on his lips and he touched them. A kiss. And it was unlike anything he had ever felt before, unlike any feeling or sensation that had ever entered his body. It was a moment of purity, of harmony and peace. He had had everything he could have ever wanted right there in his hands and he had allowed himself to believe. Now though, she was gone, and it was harder to watch than he had ever thought to be possible. It was suddenly colder and loneliness than he had ever experienced before. He collapsed to the wall, his legs barely holding his weight. The air rushed in on him and threatened to suffocate him where he sat. He had uttered the most sacred, yet scary, words in the world to her...te amo, 'I love you'. He had said it, out loud, to her ever-guarded flawless face, and then...and then she had left. It was a bitter, hard slap to the face. As he closed his eyes, he could still see the tears making their way down her cheeks, he could feel the heat from her hands in his and he could hear his heart crack with pain. Was this love? Was this what happened to people who cared and who opened up? Well, it was tragic and sad. He cleared his throat and lifted his head, looking up around at the happiness and enjoyment surrounding him. He deserved this pain and disappointment, he reminded himself quickly, trying to collect some composure. He had known from the start that getting involved, getting attached to Eva, was crazy, was suicide. Hell, even his brothers had warned him. Yet, he hadn't been able to stop himself and even now, sitting alone in agony, he still couldn't control what he felt. It seemed to be the one thing in his whole life that his mind could not manipulate, that his will could not bend. No matter how desperate his attempts. Well, he thought to himself, tilting his head back up to the star filled sky and exhaling long and slow. If this pain is what I am left with from my time of having Eva in my life, then I'll burden it gladly.

CHAPTER THIRTY-ONE.
Patience, you'll see it soon enough.

We avoided each other as much as possible over the next couple of days and not because it was awkward or because we were angry and mad, but because it hurt too much. Cane spent well needed time with his grandmother and I made excuses to swim or to walk. There was a strange atmosphere amongst us now, and as the next couple of days passed, a numbing sadness settled over everything. It felt like the end of something that could never start and despite talking when we had to, we found ourselves silent when we were alone, always exchanging looks, understanding, yet disappointing.

At night, when we left, I had said my genuine sad goodbye to Grandma. She was an amazing soul, full of life and clarity. I had bent down to hug her, and she had whispered into my ear something that had stayed with me the whole journey home and the whole way back into my lonely cold room. '*Sometimes, even when the whole world is against you, things can work out, if you take a chance.*' Maybe she knew not all things were perfect in fairytale land, maybe she knew something had changed, but her words echoed in me every time I was alone. I sat on my bed, the familiar surroundings of Cane's room twenty-seven offering me no comfort. Where did Cane and I go from here? Where did I go from here? Back to being a prisoner? Back to being a life wrecker? Back to being a simple business deal?

A few days passed and the two of us managed to avoid each other almost completely successfully. And not because we didn't want to see each other, but because it was too hard. Spain was fading into a dream and our realities were quickly consuming us both up again. I had seen Cane watching me walking the dogs and I had seen him come home from work late at night, but our communication was limited to an acknowledging nod and a smile. Thankfully, with each passing day, the bounce in my step grew and my positivity returned. The memories and feelings from Spain were slowly diminishing and had begun fading away into a blurry fairytale, a what-could-have-been and a once-upon-a-time. Surely, soon enough I would be free from this place and once Cane was out of my life I could get over him. I would never have to worry about seeing him again and feeling all of *this*. Out of sight, out of mind. I could go back to my old life and start to try re-build it again. I had made it thirty-two years never bumping into Cane Rodriguez, I was pretty sure that I could easily go another thirty-two without trying. And surely now, that was the best option? Even if the idea of it made me want to cry. I kept telling myself that I would be able to get over him once I was gone, once we were apart, and that was helping me pass each day. But the sinking truth was ever loud and undeniable behind my rehearsed speech. It knew my hopes were false and that my wishes were useless. I would *never* get over Cane, not ever.

On a morning like any other, I awoke to a letter that had been slid under my door. It was a piece of ripped and muddy notebook paper, tattered at the ends and scribbled on messily. I opened it with curiosity and was delighted to see a friendly name at the bottom. I quickly dashed back to the top to read it, happy that it was not bad news.

Eva

I postponed my trip to the east side forest knowing that you would be back at some point.

I am needing to go out there today though and was hoping you would join me? If you're able, meet me at the fountain at 9am.

Gideon.

I exhaled with glee looking out the window to the yet again blue sky and singing birds. It was no Spain, but I couldn't think of anything better to brush the cobwebs away than an adventure with Gideon. I checked the clock and quickly bounced into the shower, my steps encouraged by awaiting fresh air and a friendly face. At eight-fifty-five I was stood by the large stone fountain in the front drive. The granite sparkled in the morning sun, as if millions of diamonds were embedded within. It was mesmerising to look at and listen to, and the sound of splashing water covered Gideon's approaching footsteps. I jumped as he stabbed me in the side with a strong finger, yelping like a puppy who just had its tail stood on. I spun to see his crazy blonde hair dancing in the breeze and his blue eyes sparkling in the bright rays. He laughed.

'You're a jumpy thing, aren't you?' he joked, nodding for me to follow him around the side of house. I smiled and swung a small smack of reprimand to his shoulder.

'Only when people creep up on me.' Our feet crunched loudly on the gravel as we made our way to a gardening buggy parked to the east side of the manor. In the back of it was some wood and wire and other gardening machinery. To be honest, I was never really a keen caretaker, I just enjoyed the finished products beauty, and so I paid little attention to the accompanying equipment, as I climbed into the passenger side of the cart.

'So, how was Spain?' Gideon asked, turning the little key and starting the engine. I glanced at him with a small shrug, quickly looking away again.

'It was fine,' I answered as nonchalantly as possible. He laughed slightly, shaking his head.

'That good, huh?' He put us in gear and we moved off with a start, heading towards the east side of the estate. The breeze blew against our faces and the buggy's wheels followed the made path with bumpy ease. The sun warmed my skin against the cool of the wind and we sat in silence, enjoying the scenery. Gideon pointed left to a gated area which I hadn't seen before.

'That's a private area for Elias and Andreas.' He raised an eyebrow. I looked at it closer, wondering what disturbing and mischievous secrets it held.

'What's in there?' I asked. He shrugged not fazed by his lack of knowledge.

'Don't know, I don't take care of any of that area.' The gate disappeared from site as we drove further off into the gardens and I put it from my mind, hoping I would never need to know what was in their little play yard. As we continued for a few more miles, the terrain became more rocky and unsettled and our surroundings became thicker and thicker with forest. The sun was blocked by the towering trees and the chill from the breeze lifted goosebumps on my arms. I folded them into myself to offer some protection from the draft.

'Are you cold?' Gideon asked, looking at me quickly as he maneuvered around a large puddle. I smiled at his concern.

'I'm fine, don't worry.' He slowed slightly and shrugged off his bobbled and faded black fleece, handing it to me with an encouraging nod. I took it from him with a thankful grin.

'I should have told you to take a warm top. It's cold in the forest, but when we clear it again, the sun will warm you back up. You OK?' his concern was touching, and I slid the warm and heated material over my prickly arms.

'Thanks,' I nodded, zipping it up over me and smiling back at him. Gideon felt a little like the big brother I never had. Maybe that was why I was so fond of him? He was thoughtful and easy to be with, like life rolled off his back untouched.

'So around us now are some of the oldest trees on the estate.' He pointed to our right where a sea of bark filled the view. They climbed tall and strong up into the atmosphere above, reaching for the sunlight and its warming rays. My head was tilted back fully trying to find their tops. 'They are one hundred and eighty-year old sycamore trees.' Gideon beamed with pride as we drove by them, climbing higher along the path. 'A lot of the trees here are old English Oak,' he continued, patting a trunk as we passed by it, the bark scuffing under his weathered hands. 'Did you know, that oak trees grown from British stock are heavier branched and have a better growth rate?' I glanced over at him with interest as he kept one hand on the wheel and the other dancing around us, pointing to plant life. 'Spain have their own oaks too, as do Italy, but they are more susceptible to root death here and can spread their diseases all too quickly to our indigenous plants.' I thought of Spain and of susceptibility as he mentioned them. I found the words oddly ironic considering my recent experiences there. He continued with the plant lesson, unaware of my thoughts. 'Mr Rodriquez wanted a bit of Spain in his land and we dabbled with a few imports, but I'll show you them as we get to them.' We drove further into the estate and time began to disappear from me. I glanced at my watch to find it was already half past ten. I loved when a morning flew by. We hit a flatter ground and a much more sparse field appeared with more deeply rooted and stronger trees surrounding us. There was a small two wheeled path maneuvered through the grove and we followed it at slower speed. To our right I could see the grassy ground dropped away to a steep slope, indicating just how high we had traveled on our tour. The sun broke through the leaves here and danced on the cushioned ground while birds sung with approval. I smiled.

'It's pretty here,' I said, looking over to Gideon. He nodded with a lift of his closest shoulder.

'Yeah, Mr Rodriguez has some spectacular lands that's for sure.' He touched a low branch as we drove by, the twigs bending easily under his fingers. 'These are, when in season, apple trees. The kitchen gets us to collect up the apples when ripe and they use them for the menus.' He smiled with thought of pudding and that made me smile too, my stomach rumbling at the memory of missed breakfast and sweet desserts. I turned to face Gideon more with a lifted finger, delighted to finally be able to contribute to his wealth of environmental knowledge.

'Did you know that many common apple trees lay claim to being *the* inspiration for Issac Newtons '*notion of gravity*'?' Gideon laughed, with a shake of the head.

'I did not know that.' I copied his actions and let a branch brush off my hand as we passed by.

'The original tree though, if you ask me, is found in Woolsthorpe Manor, where Newton's family home was. I studied his notion in one of my uni classes, one semester. I loved the picture of that tree. It's was called the 'tumbling tree' because it stood at a forty-five-degree angle and looked like it was going to fall over. But that thing was solid as ever because of its roots'. Gideon was watching me with a happy grin.

'That's pretty cool,' he added with a nod, steering us out of the apple grove. I thought quickly of deep roots, versus how things looked on the outside. It was an inspiring lesson and one I could take note of just now in my life. I unzipped his fleece, as we opened back up into undisturbed sunshine and its warmth began to radiate into me.

'The tree fell down finally in 1820,' I added with a passing pang of reality, quickly looking behind us again, 'but anyone of those trees back there could be a descent and have a famous relative...' I began to grin, '...in their *family tree*.' I burst out laughing at my joke. Gideon hit the brakes and sat still, shaking his head with a smirk. 'You get it?' I asked with a shove of his shoulder, 'family tree?' I laughed louder at myself, and Gideon kept his disapproving smile.

'That was awful,' he said, looking away from me with an indulgent grin still on his lips. He put us in gear again and drove on. 'And you are supposed to be super smart?' He added in jest. I giggled to myself a little longer, ignoring Gideon's lack of appreciation. Finally we pulled up to a clearing at the top of the drive and I could see the fence that was down ahead of us. Gideon stopped the engine and hopped out as I sat and let the sun and view soak in. There were hills and trees covering the rear of the estate with the bright sunbeams highlighting it all. It was quite breathtaking.

'It's impressive,' I said to Gideon, who was now removing things from the back of the buggy and making his way to the broken fence. He glanced over to see where I was looking and smiled in agreement.

'It's not a bad job really, is it?' He grinned, dumping the heavy equipment to the soft grass with a thud. I nodded enthusiastically.

'Well, all except from your boss, maybe.' I added with a small shrug. Gideon came back to the cart and lifted a heavy mallet from the back, swinging it over his shoulder with ease.

'Actually, if you mean the big boss,' he began nodding me over to follow him to the fence. 'Mr Rodriquez, he's pretty decent. I've only really met him a handful of times while working here, but he's super fair to his staff, has great benefits, treats everyone well, knows our names.' He leant the hammer against a rock and proceeded to put on thick working gloves. 'My supervisor won't have a bad word said about him. Something about how Mr Rodriguez saved him from becoming a homeless loser and we could all learn something from him about kindness.' He shrugged casually, as he repeated what was obviously a very commonly said praise. He scratched his cheek through the dirty glove and it left a line of dried mud on his skin.

'Oh really?' I asked, against my better judgment. Gideon began to pull the broken fencing out of the way.

'Yeah,' he continued, with strained breath, dragging an old post to the side. 'I think he made some bad investments, lost all his money, lost his gardening business, house etc. He says he was living in a cardboard box on the streets when he decided to write to Mr Rodriguez with a plea letter, a charity letter, or something,' he paused as he began to dig a bigger hole, 'apparently, next thing he knew, he says Mr Rodriguez turned up at his cardboard box one rainy night, saying he needed a caretaker for his land

and was he interested? My boss says that Mr Rodriguez packed him into the back of his car there and then, took him back here, gave him a roof over his head, a wage and a job and never once mentioned that night again.' Gideon stopped speaking as he focused his strength on lifting a new pillar into the hole he had just created. His forehead was beginning to glisten in the now almost afternoon heat. I stood stunned for a few seconds, letting Gideon's casual words unknowingly start back up feelings I was still trying so desperately to extinguish. There was becoming a list of character witnesses for Cane, all from unsuspecting and undistinguished people, the ones nobody cared about. I snapped out of myself and rushed to Gideon's aid to hold the beam upright as he packed soil around its base. 'Thanks,' he said with relief and surprise. I laughed, feeling the muscles in my arms and thighs already begin to strain with the weight.

'That's a pretty impressive story,' I said, watching Gideon stamp the mud tightly down with his working boots. He had soil marks all over his face and trousers now, which only worsened, as he stood exhaling, loudly, and rubbing his hands off on himself.

'That should do it.' He indicated that I could let go of the beam and I did so, carefully. To my delight, it stayed upright and firm. He went for the mallet, which he had leant against the nearby rock. 'Yeah, I thought it was a bit farfetched to be honest, such a powerful man like Mr Rodriquez, just turning up himself one night in the streets. But then my boss runs a homeless outreach program that Mr Rodriguez funds and he says that they started it together not long after he began working here. So maybe it is true?' He motioned for me to step back as he swung the hammer wide and hard down onto the top of the pillar. It hit directly with a massive thud, pushing it further into the fresh soil below. My eyes twitched uncontrollably with each impact, like watching a balloon pop, and while my face showed no other emotions, my insides were all over the place. Cane did all that? Yet again, I was back in my dilemma, I was back in Spain, having to choose between him and my family. I shook off the predicament that was my life and let it go with the breeze that blew through my hair. I wondered if I would *ever* really know the whole truth of who Cane Rodriguez was.

'Anyway!' I announced, with a bit too much finalisation. Gideon looked at me oddly. 'It is a beautiful place.' I looked out again to the view, hiding my flushed cheeks and clouded eyes. He stood up to get the next beam from the cart and came to my side, looking at what I was seeing.

'Yes, it is,' he agreed, 'but don't give away all your excitement yet,' he teased, a small smile on his wet lips. 'I have a surprise for you once I've finished here.' My eyes widened, and I turned to him with questioning plea. He laughed and shook his head firmly. 'Patience. You'll see it soon enough. I only have three more posts to do then we can head off again.' He lifted the beam from the back and carried it over to the fence. I followed quickly, dragging the mallet over to him to hurry the process.

The last three fence beams went in faster with me helping and after an hour or so, we were packed up and in the buggy again, moving higher up the hillside. Gideon was somewhat dirty and sweaty from the work and I even sported the signs of a fruitful labour. The warm sun and cool breeze were welcomed companions as we traveled through more of Cane's property. I had never realised just how vast the land he owned was, and as it kept spanning out in front of us, the magnitude of his wealth started to become a bit more apparent. I smiled to myself as I thought how attractive Cane must be to women, he was not only handsome, but also filthy rich. I briefly recalled Peter telling me in Spain about Cane's failed relationships and all the women who only wanted him for his money. I inhaled the fresh country air with another quick smile. *Who could blame them?* Gideon interrupted my wicked thoughts, with a pointing of the finger to the new set of trees growing parallel to our path.

'These,' he began, as if we had been waiting to see them this whole time, 'these are the imports I was mentioning earlier when I said Mr Rodriguez wanted a bit if his homeland here.' I looked past him over to the forest of solid barky trees, all standing tall and straight. 'They are called the Spanish chestnut tree. These ones are roughly thirty-meters high and their foliage is a striking yellow colour. You'd love it,' he stated, smiling at my tilted heavenwards head. 'We got these ones from a castle estate further down south where they boast a thousand-year family history.' We reached the end of their pasture and continued to drive upward on marshy grass now. 'Here's a question for you, university girl,' he joked, nudging my side. 'Legend has it when it comes to those Spanish Chestnut trees, that they were grown from nuts that came from the wrecked Spanish Armada.' My eyebrows lifted with excitement and intrigue.

'Really? That's exciting,' I held the buggy frame as it bumped to the near top of a clearing and looked back at the now, much more interesting trees. Gideon nodded energetically.

'So, storytelling has it. But,' he waved a finger at me. 'can you tell me, smarty pants, what year that would mean they were seeds?' He put his hand back on the wheel as the last part of the hill steepened. I squinted with thought.

'Spanish Armada wreckage?' I checked, quickly recalling my history knowledge. He nodded with a quick glance my way.

'Fifteen-eighty-eight?' I half answered, half questioned. He yelled out loud with a laugh, smacking his hand off the steering wheel with defeat.

'Damn it! Correct.' He joked with false annoyance. I fist pumped myself with congratulations. Gideon shook his head at me. 'You really are a smarty pants, huh?' I laughed with a shrug, as we cleared the top of the hill. The breeze swept my hair from my face leaving my eyes unobstructed to the view that now lay before us. My breath caught in my throat and my mouth dropped open, as the buggy came to a stop and the whole of Cane's estate lay ahead of us, in a stunning and perfect aspect. I stood up in the cart, my eyes widening with appreciation. Gideon smiled at me. 'Thought you'd like this. Here's your surprise.' Gideon put on the breaks and turned off the engine, climbing out of the cart and walking to the front of the buggy. I followed with my hand shading my eyes from the sun. The estate was massive. It covered as far as could be seen and ranged from forest to flat fields to lakes and houses. Sat in the centre though, was the masterpiece of it all, the main house. It shone like a beacon in the distance, the windows twinkling in the sunshine. My heart beat increased with affection for it. Despite everything, my fondness for the place was very apparent to me and probably anyone who watched me close enough. The manor was old and strong and had defied the wear of time, still immovable and erect, proud as the day it was built. I couldn't help but have deep routed feelings for something that managed to stay standing against all odds, and do it with grace and poise. Gideon was watching me from the side and I turned to see his smile.

'What?' I asked, blushing slightly.

'Nothing,' he muttered, shaking his head and going to the back of the buggy. 'It's just nice when you meet people who appreciate the same things as you do.' He pulled a box forward and began to take out some juice and wrapped up food. It was a picnic.

'Gideon!' I exclaimed, with a massive grin and small laugh. 'You brought a picnic for us?' He was spreading out a rolled-up blanket onto the spongy grass and placing the food down on it. 'That is so thoughtful and sweet.' He laughed, as he signaled me to sit down.

'Well, I'm afraid I can't take credit for it all. The spot was my idea, but Mr Rodriguez came to see me a day or so after you guys got back from Spain and asked me if I had planned to take you on a tour of the estate. I told him I'd mentioned taking you to the east side. I won't lie,' he said quietly, leaning forward towards me, 'I thought I was going to get into trouble for being with you.' I sat quite still, the breeze blowing at my quickly and intensely heating cheeks. 'But all he said was, that I should take a picnic and that you deserved a break from everything for a while.' He shrugged, opening the food packets and placing them out for eating. My heart was pounding. I inhaled and exhaled the fresh and cool air, hoping that it would somehow steady my butterflies. Cane organised this picnic? He thought to seek out Gideon, the Gideon he had already voiced concern about, and to ensure I had a nice time away from the house for the day? Even after everything that happened in Spain? In that second, my head imagined Cane sitting opposite me, the wind blowing his dark, thick hair, while he organised his thoughtful and caring and sweet and attentive and considerate

and romantic picnic. The sun would be beaming down on his golden skin, while he offered me a small time out from a hectic world, knowing that I needed it desperately. 'How he even knew I'd asked you to come out here is beyond me,' Gideon continued, shaking his head with wonder and blowing my imaginary Cane away from the blanket like a summers day cloud. 'I'm telling you,' he said with conviction, 'that man *knows everything.*' He popped the lid off the juice and poured it into the two glasses. I swallowed trying to look composed and not like my inside were turning to liquid. *Yes Gideon, that man does seem to know everything.*
We ate our delicious lunch and talked about the estate and the things that went on in the gardening world. Gideon was delighted to chat about his passion for the outdoors and quite happily sped along with himself, leaving me to sit, relax and listen. Every now and then I would glance over towards the main house and see it glisten in the afternoon sun. I wondered what Cane was up to at this moment. I wondered if *he* ever got the chance to just sit and soak in his epic estate? If *he* ever got time to unwind and slow down. Gideon's watch beeped, and he glanced down at it, announcing that we needed to be heading back. Mr Rodriguez had arranged with his boss for him to have time to take me out here, but Gideon's boss still expected him back to do some tasks before the end of day. Again, another thoughtful gesture from the all-knowing Cane. It made the corners of my mouth turn up with delight, despite myself, and I quickly bit my lip to hide it from Gideon.
As we got closer to the house again, I started to recognise landmarks and felt the bitter arms of inevitability reach out for me. I sighed heavily, wondering what I would do for the rest of the day now that I had had such a pleasant morning. We glided quietly past a bed of beautiful blue flowers and their smell tingled my nostrils with memory.
'Gideon,' I asked pointing over to their patch, 'what are they?' He tapped the break slowly and we came to a stop, him leaning by me to see the flower. He nodded with a smile.
'Another part of Spain Mr Rodriguez had us import here. They are called Hyacinthoides Hispanica,' He said it in a Spanish accent, then quickly back to his own. 'Spanish Bluebells,' he translated. 'They are really similar to our own native bluebells and are in fact now more commonly grown here than our own ones. They come in white and pink actually, but Mr Rodriguez was adamant that we had to stick with blue ones.' Then as he said it, my mind recalled the last time it had seen the flower. It had been in Spain, in Grandma's garden. That was why they had had to be blue and had to be here on his land. They reminded Cane of home and family. I looked at them differently, as their stunning blue petals danced in the afternoon breeze. Yet another layer of Cane that revealed a gentle and sentimental side. Gideon started the engine back up and drove us off, I quickly glanced

back to captured one last look of the little flower and all it stood for.

CHAPTER THIRTY-TWO.
It couldn't be. It just couldn't be.

I made my way back to my room, the late afternoon sun starting to make its way down the sky. It had been a wonderful day and I felt lifted. I had been here weeks now and the once '*black shirts*' were becoming friends; names, people I recognised and had passing comments with. I was acknowledged by most at the very least and after today's escape, I felt rejuvenated and vibrant. Life wasn't actually that bad, was it? If I didn't say it out loud and didn't let my head into the secret, I could easily admit that I liked it here sometimes, even loved certain aspects of it, such as this house and that garden we spent time in this morning, and...and well, other things. As I walked passed a couple of the female maids returning from the staff quarters, I smiled and wished them good afternoon. They returned my greeting with head nods and quiet sayings of my name. I had passed them by a few steps when a hand on my arm and a gentle voice from behind stopped me.

'Miss Mack?' It was saying timidly and as I turned, I found a maid with her hand stretched out to me. She smiled kindly, as I grinned back at her with question.

'Hi...' I paused for thought, I was pretty sure her name was Maria. I'd spoken to her a few times briefly around the pool area, but nothing extensive or overly friendly. 'Maria?' I finished with apologetic raised eyes.

'Sí. Maria,' she answered, nodding with confirmation. She was a Spanish lady, short and round, with dark wavy hair and olive skin. She had bright brown eyes that shone when she smiled and hands that seemed to always be moving.

'Call me, Eva, please,' I prompted, reaching out and softly touching her arm. It seemed to put her at ease and her nerves disappeared with another smile.

'Eva,' she nodded, 'I was wondering if you could help me, por favor?' Her eyes glanced away from mine with uncertainty.

'Yes of course, I would love to help you if I can. What with?' I clapped my hands together enthusiastically. My reaction seemed to settle her hesitation and she smiled at me, carrying on with her request.

'My daughter, Antonella, has school dance and needs a...' she trailed off while she looked for the translation, 'vestido de fiesta de graduation...prom dress. She is difficult size though,' she added, with another flap around of her busy hands. 'There is talk that you make dresses?' I smiled and nodded.

'Yes, I can make a dress,' I agreed with delight. 'Would you like me to make one for your daughter?' She began to nod vigorously, clapping her hands together.

'Sí. Please. Por favor. If you are able?'

'It would be my pleasure to do that,' I sang with genuine truthfulness. A project. I couldn't think of anything better. 'When does she need it by and does she have anything in mind- styles, material, colours?' Maria began to fumble in her apron pocket and produced a mobile phone. Once upon a time my head would instantly have begun to think of ways I could use it call home, but now... She unlocked it and scrolled through a few screens until she found what she was looking for. Turning the phone to me with pride, I was presented with a picture of what I could only assume was her daughter. I took the phone and looked at the teenage girl. She was a little tubby with frizzy hair but had a pretty face and her mother's shining eyes. I could see under the rough and awkward exterior she was a budding beauty, something I felt I could still relate to.

'She's really pretty.' I smiled. 'How old is she?'

'Antonella is sixteen.' Maria returned with a modest smile and took the phone back from me to flip through for another photograph. When she handed it back this time the picture was of a dress. I presumed the prom dress she wanted. I looked at it with a seamstress's eye trying to decide if I would be able to recreate it. It was pink satin with a square framed neck, fitted bodice and flared bottom. It had no sleeves but lots of frills. It wasn't the prettiest dress I'd ever seen but it wasn't the worst either. I could probably make one pretty close to this, I could maybe even insist on some changes to stop the bullying I knew would come from replicating it to its exactness. I had seen all too well what teenagers were like nowadays if they saw something they thought wasn't *cool* enough, or didn't fit in. And despite *my* preferences for a simpler taste and style of life, I still knew what was *in* these days...and frills were not.

'Yes, I can do this,' I said, handing the phone back with a happy and excited smile. 'Can your daughter come here for a fitting?' Suddenly realising it was doubtful. Cane would not allow a random employee's daughter to come and play dress up with me- the hidden and top secret kidnappee-slash-asset. Maria began to shake her head.

'Mr Rodriguez says when he tells me about your skills, that she not be allowed here to see you, but since we are same sizes almost, that you be able to model me?' I hesitated with surprise. *When Cane told her about me?*

'I'm sorry,' I began, before I could stop myself, 'Cane...I mean, Mr Rodriguez, *told* you I could make a dress for your daughter?' She tucked her phone back into her uniform safely.

'Sí,' she confirmed, completely unaware of my astonishment. 'He come to see me and say he heard I worried about Antonella not getting dress and

he say you are…talentoso…talented, at making dress and would most be happy to make one.'
'Cane suggested this?' I repeated, still a little astounded. She nodded absently, delighted to have found a solution to her daughter's problem. Would Cane Rodriguez ever stop surprising me?
'You think you use me for dress size?' Maria was asking, brushing her overalls down. I focused back on her and pushed away the tormented and never-ending argument of Cane's split personality.
'You are the same size?' I asked. 'Same height and shape?' She nodded with a smile and a shy shrug. 'Then yes, there's no reason that you wouldn't be fine. When do you need the dress by? We'll need to get material and things ready.' She began to nod more vigorously, taking a pen and paper from her pocket and handing it to me.
'You write what needed and I get it all. Gracias, Miss Mack.' I smiled at her widely beginning to jot down everything I could think of that I could possibly need. I wrote a couple of shop names down too that I knew she would be able to get the required items from quickly. I handed back the paper and pen and her busy hands collected it, stowing it away with her phone. 'Antonella's dance in two weeks, is that time enough?'
'If you can get those items speedily enough, yeah, its plenty time.' I shrugged thinking the end of my sentence, *it's not like I'm going anywhere.*
'Gracias, gracias,' she sung, nodding her head towards me.
'No problem,' I replied, as she began to back away in the direction of her fellow workers.
'I need go work now,' she announced, pointing over her shoulder. 'Thank you, Miss Mack.'
'Call me Eva, please,' I repeated with a warm grin. She returned it with a wave goodbye and trotted off down the corridor. 'Hasta luego.' *See you later,* I called after her as she disappeared around the corner with the clicking of busy heels. I turned to continue my walk to my room. It had been an interesting and eventful day for me. I thought briefly on Cane and how different a man he was, to who I had thought him to be. Everything I had ever learned about him had come from a brown file, filled with pages of notes made by someone behind a desk, with a chip on their shoulder for the Rodriguez family. A tainted, biased, hate-laced opinion, based on years of bitter rivalry. Now it seemed the more I learned of Cane for myself, and the more I found out from the people around him, the more the once irrefutable facts were becoming disputable fictions. I continued walking towards my room lost in my thoughts. As I rounded the corner to my door I saw Scott walking towards me. He stopped briefly, which was unusual, but welcome.
'Afternoon, Miss Mack,' he opened, nodding politely. 'One of the staff, Maria, was looking for you earlier, did she find you?' He was a little

awkward and I was taken back slightly by him chatting, but I smiled warmly. He was always polite, but never chatty.

'She did, thank you. It was about making a dress for her daughter's prom.' He nodded, and I assumed that was our conversation over. I went to open my door, but he loitered still, like he needed to say something, but was uneasy doing so.

'If you don't have any plans this afternoon, Eva, could I suggest having a look around the stables? We have some new horses coming in and Mr Rodriguez has some fine breeds. They are beautiful, especially when they are *first* settling into their new surroundings… so you would need to be there as soon as possible to see it.' I looked at him quizzically, but he simply nodded and then carried on down the hall. *Well that was a little bit odd,* I thought to myself, brushing it off. My hand rested on the door handle still, with plans of watching television, but with the idea of the stables planted in my head, and Scott's weird behaviour, I began off towards the back of the house instead. It had been such a pleasant day so far, admiring the magnificent creatures could only add to its perfection, surely. The stables were impressive and Cane, naturally, only had the most expensive and handsome breeds. They were strong and amazing and had I not been warned by Dr Miele not to ride them, I would have. One fall, the Doctor had told me, would be plenty to snap those ribs of mine. I had remembered the pain of healing bones far too well still, to tempt that fate. Instead, I spent a while with the animals and chatted to the livery workers, enjoying more human company. They were mostly, and unsurprisingly, Spanish so the conversation was disjointed and hilarious.

'How many horses does Cane have?' I asked as they looked at each other blankly with smiles. I squinted, trying to think of the Spanish words. 'Cuántos caballos?' They nodded, beginning to understand me.

'Cinco,' one of them answered back, in his deep voice. *Five.* I smiled with a confirming nod. They showed me the new breeds that had just been delivered and talked over how to groom them. On request, they had allowed me to have a go brushing one down. For some reason, they had found my flip flops hysterical and had all fallen around in laugher every time I nearly stepped in something. Each time a call would go up, echoing through the stables, '*por los pelos'* or '*casi*', which I was pretty sure translated to 'close call' and 'almost'. Their obvious delight was infectious, and I found myself laughing each time with them. I was left to my own devices for a while, as the men continued their work and after a few minutes I took a rest, glancing out the doors towards the manor. The sun was shining brightly, and the house stood erect as always, proud and superb. I breathed deeply, patting the horse's neck and letting the sun warm my face. His ears twitched as voices from the kitchen door, across the yard, caught his attention. I squinted my sun stricken eyes to see a lady leave the house and walk towards one of the black cars. It was odd to be leaving via the back, staff door, I thought, watching her long slender silhouette. The sun bounced off her pair of hideous red shoes and my mind tugged back to when I had last seen a pair like them. My eyes struggled to focus, as something familiar about the lady's walk nagged at me. The horse shifted and blocked me against the gate, obstructing my view. I awkwardly tried to move him to get a better view, my curiosity urging me on. Alarms were going off in my head, like it knew something my eyes and heart hadn't quite caught onto yet. My first theory was, that she was a lover of Cane's, sneaking out the backdoor, but I quickly brushed that off along with the unsettling feeling of jealousy that it stirred. The driver got out of the car and was walking around to open the passenger door for her. I pushed the horse out of the way, knowing I only had seconds until she was closed in and away from view. I jogged out into the yard, letting the hot sun blind me temporarily. I threw my hand up to shade my eyes, my heart unexplainably beating wildly against my rising chest. My focus settled in time to see the face of the lady, as she placed a large packet of money into her expensive bag and climbed into the back seat. My heart stopped, and vomit rose in my throat uncontrollably. It couldn't be. It just couldn't be. I drifted aimlessly, further out into the courtyard, towards the car as the engine purred into life. My ears were ringing and my mouth watering, as information, emotions, and pain all came flooding out of my vault, unable to contain the sudden resurfacing. Tammy. The tinted window could not hide her as the sun illuminated the perfectly painted features of my once best friend. *Tammy.* What was she doing here? My head continued to repeat her name to itself in shock, as if it was mistaken and my mind was deceiving me. Her eyes widened in recognition as she leant forward, her hand against the window. Time seemed to have stopped, both of us stunned frozen. I wondered briefly who was more astounded; me to find her here, or apparently, her to find me? Once upon a time, my first instinct upon seeing her would have been that she had to come to rescue me, my dear, loyal persistent friend. Now though, that notion was the furthest thought from my mind. She blatantly was not here for my interests and by the look on her face, was completely oblivious to the fact I was even indeed around. The money pack she had slid into her bag nipped at my subconscious, and my mind quickly and bitterly connected the dots. Tammy's face remained horrified. She was collecting a pay. I lost my air and felt myself become light headed. It all started making sense, and just like a jigsaw puzzle, the past few years of my life flew before my watering eyes and the pieces started to fall into place. Why had Tammy always been so dedicated and interested in my rants about Edward and the Brice's business, why had she always been so determined to listen to every last detail I had to entrust in her? Why had Tammy always had more money than she could explain? How had Cane known about the

Shanks Building Campaign and that Edward and I had been arguing a lot lately? How was Cane always one little step ahead of everything? I was a fool. Could I trust *anyone* in this world anymore? *I* had been hand feeding Cane with information. It was me. I would confide in Tammy and she would get paid for my ignorant loyalty, by passing it onto Cane. She was an informant. I remembered the horrid thought from the camera room, where I realised that Bain must have had a mole amidst his company. I whimpered in disgust of myself. It was me, I was the mole. The bile rose in my throat again and I put my hands to my head to try and stop its nauseating spin. The car door opened slowly, and those disgusting red shoes touched the courtyard ground. I looked at her with such horrified detachment it made my eyes sting. How could she? I burned inside with such a mix of painfully overpowering emotions; betrayal, hate, anger, stupidity, guilt, and it was impossible to tell which was strongest, let alone process them all at once. She began to step timidly towards me, but I shook my head at her firmly, holding my hand out to signal she was to come no closer. I couldn't trust myself right now to be any nearer to her. The things my head wanted to do, I knew would not be what my heart would want to live with afterwards.

'Eva?' she questioned hesitantly, her shoulders lowered and subdued. I had never seen her look so apprehensive in all her bold, lying life. I watched her, still trying to calm my erratic breathing and hear past my thumping heart. I could not find my voice to reply though, it was lost amidst inner confusion. 'Eva?' she said again, taking a tiny step forward. 'How long have you been here? Does anyone know you are here? Are you, all right? Poor Edward's been going crazy trying to find you.' Hearing her say Edward's name sparked a reaction inside me finally, and motivated my voice…unfiltered and unreserved. The feelings of the camera room came blasting back to my already overwhelmed heart as if it happened yesterday. The lies. The cheating.

'That almost sounds like concern, Tammy.' I spat, venomously. No, I wasn't going to play the damsel in distress, I knew all about her now and the look in my eye must have confirmed so. She straightened up, the defiant Tammy I knew all too well resurfacing. If she thought she was going to get to be self-righteous, she had another thing coming. There was nothing she could say to me right now that could ever diffuse the fire I felt cursing through my body. I knew who she was now and what she had done.

'It was concern, *actually*,' she snapped with raised eyebrows and a sassy voice, all pretenses apparently gone. Playing the defence was not going to make it all right for her conscience, no matter how much she may have hoped it would.

'How could you Tammy?' I accused harshly, my hand still held out to stop her advancing towards me. '*How could you*?' I spat. 'How long have you been working for Rodriguez?' I was shaking my head at her now, begging to understand. '*I trusted you*, my whole life Tammy. I told you *everything*. You were a *sister* to me.' Tears welled uncontrollably and fell from my eyes. They ran heavy and fast down my cheeks onto my heaving chest. And then unable to stop it, I sobbed, my shoulders crumbling with the weight of loss they were feeling *again* on Tammy's behalf. I bent over, feeling so much weight I could hardly stand, and the tears poured from my heart. Tammy stood still, motionless. Moments in silence passed where I struggled to not fall apart with sadness, all the while, Tammy stood cold and still like a statue, bold and unmovable. If she felt any remorse, it was not being shown. It made the whole thing worse, seeing her so remote and blank. What had I expected though? A breakdown and begging for forgiveness? If this Tammy was the Tammy I thought I had known, that would never happen…and that thought proceeded anger. How dare she? How dare she stand there so casually and indifferent, whilst I felt the weight of it all. I stopped crying and inhaled deeply, standing back up, taller, bolder. Even in ridiculous ugly stilettos, I was taller than she would ever be, and I wanted her to feel that now. I had seen Cane grow in height as his wrath was felt and I wanted that for her, to feel how vicious and pitiless I could be. I was strong now and two could play this game. I was not the weak girl she thought she once knew, I had changed. I was tougher, smarter and more resilient than she would ever have thought possible. 'How-long?' I demanded loudly and coldly, my demeanour changing quickly. She stood still, her eyes widening as I wiped mine dry. I repeated myself slower and with much more annoyance. 'I said, *how-long-Tammy*?' Still nothing. It enraged me, and I advanced towards her, her high heels clicking as they backed up towards the car. 'How-long-have-you-been-using-me-to-sell-secrets-to-Rodriguez?' I demanded, and she shook her head slightly. 'ANSWER ME!' I screamed with resentment, slamming my hand down on the car beside her. It was too late for secrets and quietness now, the cat was out of the bag, the time of innocence was long gone. Now was the moment to come clean and let it all out, if for nothing else, but for closures sake. 'HOW LONG?' I bellowed, feeling like I could smack her in the face any second.

'YEARS!' she screamed back, breathing heavily. It was a stinging slap in the face, but one I knew was coming. 'Years, Eva.' she returned to a harsh, yet normal tone. 'I needed the money. Mr Rodriquez's men approached me in a club one night and it seemed harmless.' She folded her arms. 'You were already telling me everything, I thought I might as well get paid for it. It's over now anyway, Rodriquez just cut me off.' She waved her hand angrily towards the house. 'Does *that* make you happy? The money is finished.' I bit my lower lip, trying to gain some composure and stop myself from wrapping my hands around her pathetic, scrawny, lying neck and squeezing every last false and artificial breath from her.

'MONEY?' I shouted. 'You did it for money?' I inhaled, feeling my hands shaking with resentment. 'How did it work? Tell me how it worked?' Tammy shook her head. 'TELL ME!' I threatened.

'Why? What does it matter now? It's all over, Eva' she laughed, bitterly.

'Because I want to know how you snuck around and betrayed me so *easily*.' She exhaled, shaking her head with boredom and putting her hands on her hips. But her eyes were shimmering with tears, being held back. 'HOW?' I pushed with disgust.

'Oh, for goodness sake,' she retorted, throwing her hands in the air as if I was a pestering child. 'I'd email when I had something, and he'd send a car and I'd meet him. I'd get paid depending on how useful the information was. I don't see why it's such a big deal anyway.' She nodded towards me. 'I only told him business stuff, the stuff *you* don't even care about. Is that not what you kept telling me, that you hated Bain Enterprises, that you wished you never had to deal with it all?' She was right, I had said those things on multiple occasions...in private. But it didn't make me wrong and her now right. 'You would go on and on about you and Edward fighting because of his work. Like *Edward* would really ever be separate from Bain Enterprises? Why was it so hard to deal with having lots of money, Eva? Most people would do anything to be rich.' Her words hit a chord, a very tender and sore chord, in my heart. Edward. I lowered my hands and looked away from her treacherous painted face. When I finally looked back, I had managed to get my temper under control. For this moment, I wanted an honest response, not one laced in thoughtless retaliated anger.

'And Edward?' I asked quietly, finally feeling brave enough to meet her adulterous eyes. This time hers did widen, with shock. She was not prepared for this particular secret to have been discovered. Her cheeks flamed red with what I prayed was shame, and her eyes shot away from me like lightening. Finally, a sincere reaction. At least her not being able to look at me, showed that, somewhere in her twisted and manipulated head, she had feelings. 'Was that for money too?' I pushed. She cleared her throat and folded her arms again, avoiding my face. She shifted awkwardly from one foot to the other. 'Well?' I prompted, frostily. There was a pause, until finally she lifted her head, her eyebrows creased.

'You had everything I wanted, Eva.' she said in a wavering voice. A single tear dripped from her lower lid. She quickly wiped it away with her bright red painted fingernail. 'Money, happiness, an engagement, a future...Edward.' She swallowed. I inhaled slowly letting her words sink in. She was jealous of me? She had always been so independent and self-sufficient. I thought of how many times I'd been jealous of her. How ironic.

'You are *in love* with Edward?' I asked, incredulously. She shook her head.

'No, just in love with his life. I thought maybe he would come around one day and then I could have all the things you could have had, if you'd have welcomed his lifestyle. A hot man, a life in the media and magazines, designer clothes and shoes, parties and cameras...money to burn.'

'You could have had that,' I retorted, defensively. 'You could have met someone rich and had all of that. But you had to take it from me?' Disappointment surged through me. 'Take it from the one person in the world who loved you and would have done anything for you?'

'What do you want to hear, Eva?' she asked candidly, her face almost betraying her more than she wanted. 'You want to hear me begging for forgiveness and see me crawling on the ground clinging to your cheap clothes hems?' She shook her head. 'It won't change what happened.' A tear slid from my eye and as she saw it, she quickly looked away again. I wiped it with a trembling finger.

'I knew you were ambitious and motivated, Tammy, so in a twisted and completely unacceptable way, I can see why you felt abusing my trust to sell information was a morally justified thing to do. Apparently, your only drive in life is money. But Edward,' I paused to compose myself once more, determined not to cry or let my anger take over again, 'Edward was too far.' I looked her dead in the eyes, like Cane had done to me so many times, making sure his words and intent were very clearly understood. My words came out slowly and unsympathetically. I needed her to fully comprehend the seriousness of my final interactions with her, now a stranger to me. I wanted her to remember the last things I would ever say to her, for those words to burn into her memory and haunt her for forever. 'We are done. Finished. I can't stand to even look at you.' I exhaled loudly, composing myself still. 'I sincerely hope one day, someone breaks your heart like you've done to mine.' I faltered slightly, and a sob escaped with my breaking voice. She swallowed and blinked back watering eyes, obviously desperate to look away but too proud to do so. I bit my lip until I could speak clearly again. I wasn't done. 'Now get in that car, Tammy and go. Leave the country and run, because I swear to you, my hate and anger will be nothing in comparison to Brice's, when he finds out what you have done. Even Rodriguez's money will not shelter you from his retribution. And trust me when I say, Ed will choose me over you any day. There will be nowhere safe for you now.' Panic spread across her eyes and she held onto the car for support. Fear lingered on her face, questioning if I would really turn her in. My eyes blazed strong and fierce. Yes, I had every intention of making sure Bain knew she was the reason he had lost billions over the years, that she had double crossed us all and sold us out. She must have seen my resolution and she swallowed quickly, shaking her head. I walked boldly towards her, seeing her shrink inwards. She turned her face up to meet mine. I placed my hand on the door, holding it open so I could look directly into her false, deceitful face, one more time. With both anger and remorse, I watched her eyes begin to falter and I spoke very quietly and firmly. 'I-NEVER-want-to-lay-eyes-on-you-again. You are dead to me.' She stared blankly and fearfully at me, and I pushed her into the back seat of the car, slamming the door closed on her ugly face. The car immediately took off and I watched it drive away, the lowering sun reflecting like a mirror off its shimmering roof. I hoped that beacon followed her wherever she went and brought her the justice I so desperately wished she receive one day. I looked down to my hands to find them shaking. The livery workers had obviously been watching the whole event and as they quickly began to scuttle away from my view, I found myself collapsing to the ground with my head smothered in my hands. I was breathless, so breathless. I noted vaguely, as I tried to steady my breathing, that my hands still smelt like straw. It was only moments ago I'd been blissfully stroking and admiring the horses. Now, I was crumpled and broken on the ground again, like a beaten shell. How quickly the rug could be pulled out from underneath me. I remained squatted while everything continued to circle in my head; Tammy's pathetic reason for betrayal, her single tear running down her face, the way she spoke of Edward like a winning prize, the money she stashed so smugly into her expensive and flashy bag, the confession of working for Cane for years now…for *years*…my brain suddenly switched gear. *Years*…years meant that they knew each other long before all of this…which meant that this whole time Tammy was not just a name to Cane, he knew exactly who she was and what she had been doing, not just with Edward. My mind flew back to the camera room and to Spain where I'd talked so broken-heartedly about her, where I'd confided my intimate and shattered feelings about her to him. My pulse began to heighten again with each new thought, and my ears returned to their ringing with each recalled fact. My head raced through them. Cane knew she was a lying, backstabbing fraud, yet he said nothing. *I'll keep you safe, I'd never let anything harm you*…promises from him stung at me, as if they were stuck on an internal repeat. They were all lies. He was a liar too. I'd been used and used and used again my whole life, and only now was I realising what a pathetic fool I was. I trusted too easily, it was that simple. I put faith and hope out there like an innocent idiot, unaware of the sucker that made me. I was sick of being made a fool of though, sick of being used for other people's interests. It was dinner time and I knew exactly where Cane would be. I was mad. Mad at *him*. I wanted to shout and flare, directly, at his perfect face. He deserved my wrath as much as anyone. I tensed my fists and stood up abruptly. I *needed* to scream, and scream loudly. Without any more thought, I marched for the house. I was done, done waiting, done playing this game, done pretending I was fine and that everything would be eventually ok. My life was falling apart, every last piece of it, and I was sitting by, casually letting it happen. Every time I thought something was ok, it was taken from me, tainted and ruined. I stormed through the house and up the staircases with a face of thunder, doors slamming and feet banging beneath my weight. My mind was reeling with memories of Tammy and Edward. And now Cane was with them, laughing at me, taking notes and passing over money. I could see them all sniggering at me, together. It was unbearable. I reached the door, past the wooden carved squirrels, and threw it open with an almighty crash. The waiter jumped out of his skin, almost spilling his tray load, but Cane seemed to be expecting me, sitting there as cool as ever.

'HOW COULD YOU?' I screamed, madder than I think I had ever been in my whole, entire life. Everything had just built up and was finally erupting in an explosion. Cane signaled for the server to leave, which he did, quickly and gratefully. 'You lying piece of-'

'Eva,' he interrupted, quickly. 'who do you think made sure you were out there when she left?' He kept a controlled manner, placing his napkin down on his lap and leaning back. 'I wanted you to know who she really was.' I angrily grabbed the silver candle holder from the table in front of me, and before I could stop myself, I launched it at him, with as much force as possible. It went hurtling across the room and smashed off the opposite wall loudly, breaking in half and denting the woodwork. He didn't even flinch as the silverware hurtled towards his head and missed him by mere centimeters. He sat, constant and steady and watching, all the while, I panted and paced like a caged animal, unable to escape bondage.

'How long, Cane? How long has she been your spy?' I screamed at him, advancing menacingly, my voice echoing around the massive room. He sat still, listening. His lack of fight was infuriating. I grabbed a glass next, throwing that at him too. It sailed across the table, smashing past Cane into a million pieces. He remained motionless still. The noise of chaos, mixed with my bellowing, had obviously set off alarms and for the second time since being here, black shirts burst into the room, eyes alert and guns raised directly for me. Unlike before though, this time I couldn't have cared less if they shot me. I had nothing left to be scared of losing anymore. All I knew, was that before I left this room today, I wanted Caner to admit it, to admit he had lied to me, that he had cheated me again. I wanted to hear the words from his mouth, the mouth I so easily trusted and felt for these days. He waved the men away dismissively and they immediately left the room, closing the door behind them. I could hear their muttering as they retreated. But I didn't care.

'Years, Eva, but you already know that.' He remained calm whilst watching me explode, and the fact that my meltdown seemed to completely unaffected him, was making it worse. Was it all ok, now that he had allowed me to see what Tammy had been up to? No, not even close. Dropping Edward's infidelity on me apparently wasn't enough. That had healed now, and so he obviously felt like he had to break me even further, with more treachery.

'How could you do this?' I raged, pointing at him accusingly. He nodded slowly.

'It was business, Eva, sólo negocios.' *Just business.* He finally stood, placing his napkin politely on the table and beginning to walk towards me.

'Don't you dare come near me. I don't *trust* you or *anyone* anymore. You can't change, I was an idiot.' I screamed at him, slamming my hands down on the table with such force it made the cutlery and plates rattle. 'You'll always be a lying coward.' I must have hit a nerve, because the Cane I used to know, reared his provoked head.

'Have I not changed enough for you, Eva?' he shouted back, now advancing on me. 'I've spent the last two months learning to be someone new for you, learning to try and be a better man, in ways you'll never even know. But you are unforgiving.' My blood boiled. How was he turning this on me? How was he now the one shouting at me? I was the one who had been screwed over, yet again. I was the damn victim, yet again. The fact that he *dared* to be mad with me just now, only enraged me more.

'WHAT?' I roared, pushing away his solid frame as he approached me. He slammed against the table and the glasses fell, sending liquid across the white cloth. I ignored the mess, unable to see past how livid I felt. 'How can you turn this on me? *I trusted you.* I thought you were a good man with a hard life, but I was wrong. You lie about everything. You only do what serves you best.'

'I never claimed I was a good man, Eva. You're the one who seems hell bent on proving that. I made a deal, years ago, with a social-climbing woman who meant nothing to me or anyone I knew. It was sometimes useful and sometimes sparse,' he yelled at me with animated hands. 'I didn't even know you then, *let alone* care about you. It was a simple business deal; information for money. No personal agenda towards you, whatsoever.' He straightened himself up to his full height, as if it would affect my arguing. But he had forgotten that I was no longer afraid of him or intimidated by him. I was certainly no longer the girl who would be pushed around by anyone, that was for sure. That girl was dead, stabbed in the back. 'And the last thing I need is your pity, by the way,' he added, raising his hands at me. 'Yes, my life has been complex, and I have done some awful things due to that, but at least I don't use it as an excuse for everything.' My eyes widened in response.

'Excuse me?' I yelled, in disbelief. 'Don't *dare* pretend that you know me. You think having me held hostage here for the past few weeks, and kissing me once, that, *that* qualifies you to talk about my life? About my feelings? At least I have damn feelings, Cane.' He laughed, bitterly.

'Yes, yes, Eva. El Diablo. I am *the Devil.* I am the reason for *everything* bad in the universe. No one else in your perfect, little world, could ever do a thing wrong. It's all me. It's *my* fault our families hate each other, Tammy and Edward are *my* fault, your parent's divorce is *my* fault, your crappy life is all *MY* fault! RIGHT?'

'Well if the shoe fits, Cane!' I spat, my heartbeat pulsing through my body making my blood boil.

'Yes, because Princess Eva could never do anything wrong, she could never make a mistake or wish she could take something back. Have you ever thought that maybe, in all this mess, that *you* are the common denominator?' I saw red and before I could stop myself, I slapped him clean across the face. I did it with such force that it knocked his head to the side and his cheek instantly reddened. The noise of it echoed in the instantly silent room and Canes eyes froze. My chest rose and fell with angry, laboured breath, and I stood motionless, staring at him. Then like lightening striking from nowhere, he closed the distance between us and was in front of me in seconds, his lips crashing into mine, hard and fast, his body seizing mine. He kissed me with no question and no permission and as my hand wrapped around his neck to pull him closer, I quickly realised he would need no forgiveness either. His lips were hard on mine, claiming me as if I was his, and always had been. My breathing deepened and instantly, I was aware of every part of him that was touching me. It was intense and consuming and hot. Then just as quickly as it had started, it stopped, and he pulled away from me. I was left breathless, my lips pulsing from the pressure they had just felt. I panted audibly, watching him. He spoke quietly, his hand reaching up and ever so gently, tracing over my bottom lip. I almost moaned out loud, unable to control myself. 'I am so madly and overwhelmingly in love with you, Eva,' he whispered. The words felt so undeniably right, and a passionate heat coursed through me, disbanding any cold and emptiness. 'Te amo,' he breathed again, in beautiful, gentle Spanish. I had fought this, I'd fought *him* for so long and I was so tired of fighting, so sick of being at battle with myself. He loved me, he was saying it out loud for heaven's sake, *he loved me!* Why the hell was I holding back anymore? What did I think was left in my life to justify holding back for? I repeated it again in my mind with exhilaration and the words forced thoughts of Tammy and betrayal and lost friendships, and everything, far away. They erased the last few minutes of fighting, all the heated and untrue words we had voiced, and they left no more questions in their wake. My hands moved to his face and I held him in place, keeping my eyes locked on his. I wanted him to see it all, to see everything as I gave it over to him, to see all of me. I inhaled.

'I'm in love with you, too, Cane,' I said firmly, watching his eyes widen and then begin to glisten. His hands tightened on me and his dimples appeared, lighting his striking face into a beam. He truly was the most beautiful man I'd ever known, and my stomach flipped at the sight of his reaction. His eyes danced down to my mouth again and before I could speak, he had crashed his mouth back to me, claiming me once more. I could feel lust on my skin, feel it in the air we both breathed, feel it in every fiber of my being; want and desire. We had been through so much, battled so many feelings, and now, at the pinnacle of it all, I knew the truth. I loved him. I loved every inch of him, every morsel of his being. I loved him like I had never loved another being in this world and was sure never to again. I was so attached to this man in a way I never knew possible, and it was vulnerable and liberating all at the same time. His kiss intensified and deepened as he lifted me up and crossed the room to the wall, my back colliding with its old oak surface. I wrapped my legs around his waist, feeling his hands everywhere, knowing that he was everywhere, and he was kissing me hard, with such a craving that I never thought I'd be able to stop. He pulled me firmly into him and I could feel our bones meet. He groaned with desire as I began to frantically unbutton his shirt. His mouth was so soft and so hard as it kissed my neck and my chest and my face. My skin was electrified at his command and I couldn't breathe. His shirt fell to the floor as his hot bronze skin carried me to the dining table, placing me down on the end where he proceeded to remove my top with swift precision. The candles still burned around us in the dim evening light, and the smell of dinner lingered in the background. I tightened my legs around his strong body, determined that nothing would separate us now. I needed this, I wanted this. Guilt and concern could arrive later, but now this was the only thing that felt right, the only thing that made sense. With moist skin and a blur of breathing, Cane's belt was undone, and we found ourselves at the line, waiting to fall, fire burning around us. Suddenly, out of nowhere, he pulled back a little, pausing, panting, searching to check I was all right, that *this* was all right. It instantly switched to a gentle moment and he took my head in his strong hands, kissing me softly, tenderly, gently. His eyes looked into mine for confirmation, for agreement, for me to say he was not alone here.

'Are you sure?' he whispered carefully, into my ear as his hand ran down my naked back, pulling our bare skin closer to each other, closer to his lips. His head was lowered, eyes looking at me through thick lashes. I kissed his forehead softly, then lifted his mouth to mine, offering a simple, easy nod. His dimples appeared with such definition, that I almost laughed. Cane's true smile was a sight to be reckoned with and it melted me to the core. I touched a dimple tenderly as he kissed the inside of my hand.

'You are so beautiful,' he breathed, looking at me, like I was his universe. My heart almost stopped at the sincerity of his words and at the look of adoration in his eyes. Damn, I was so in love with this man, I barely knew how to control it. 'We don't need to, if you're not ready or not sure,' he assured gently, kissing my hand again. I let my smile spread across my face, looking up to his dark, melting gaze.

'I'm sure,' I replied clearly, dragging his perfect lips and body back to mine to finish what had started weeks ago in a back alley.

CHAPTER THIRTY-THREE.
Just a business deal.

I woke the next morning, comfortable and dazed, and inhaled the warm air from around me. My eyes were closed still as I became aware of a pressure leaning on my chest. I opened them quickly to find myself, in what I had come to accept, as my bed and my room. The windows shone with morning light and blue sky hung like a painting. I slowly glanced to the side to find Cane lying next to me, asleep. My heart stopped, and my body tensed instantly. I had forgotten for a split second, in the morning fuzz, about last night. Cane was lying under the covers with me, his muscled arm relaxed over my chest. His head was facing me on the pillow, his skin glowing in the fresh sunlight. *I slept with Cane!* The realisation swept through me in an exhilarating frenzy. A blush came over my cheeks and a warmth swept through my belly, as I began to recall last night's actions...every-single-one-of-them! The heat spread through me once more and I couldn't stop the smile that crept onto my lips. I turned my head to look at him. He seemed so at peace as he slowly inhaled and exhaled, blowing warm air onto my skin. I watched him quietly, not daring to move. I wanted a camera to take a picture, to capture this innocent moment of his, where the pressures and concerns of life eluded his shoulders and he could dream. His long dark eyelashes fluttered to themselves, holding secrets beneath. His morning stubble sat across his lower face and I straightened my lips, feeling them pull with dryness, and quickly remembering what that stubble had done last night. My stomach flipped again as certain moments from the previous evening flashed through my mind. My smile betrayed me again and I couldn't keep it in. Had I ever felt this before? Felt this overwhelming blissful excitement and joy? I couldn't *remember* ever experiencing it and surely this much intensity would be something that would stick with you? If felt so...amazing, so fulfilling and entire. Was this what being *in* love was? I ever so gently took my free hand and touched his cheek, stroking it. He was warm and inviting and so soft. I was transfixed on him, watching him just be, seeing him so quiet and calm. Another smile surprised my lips and my heart thumped with excitement. Crap, I was in trouble; I was so in love with this man, it was ridiculous. I loved him, and I had absolutely no idea when and where it had happened. The urge to wake him and kiss him filled me, but I held still, not wanting to move just yet. I knew once he awoke, it would all be over. The magic would be gone, as it always was with us. I contemplated how I felt as I stared at his dark, relaxed skin. I ever so gently brushed my fingers through his thick, hair, recognizing my thoughts. Yes, there was guilt when I thought about Edward and Bain and my family, who thought I was being punished, tortured, held in a dungeon and who knew what else. The worry they felt for me while I lay in Cane's arms, dreaming of happiness and joy, was enough to make me run screaming from the bed. But it felt so right here, it was so hard to comprehend why it was wrong. Why couldn't we stay like this? Why couldn't we be in love and live happily ever after? Didn't we deserve that? Didn't *I* deserve that, after everything I'd been through? I exhaled as a painful sadness crept into my stomach and began making its way to my heart. Questions danced through my mind, endless questions, which I could find no answer for. Each one was like a pin, bursting holes in my protective bubble, and leaving me feeling confused and worried. How, where, when…what would they say, what would they do, what would they think? Questions began to taunt me, wiping my childish smile away and chasing it to the shadows of doubt. *Reality*, I thought to myself as I took my hand away from Cane's perfect face, *I hate you.* Cane maybe sensed the sadness that had crept into our bed, but he began to stir like a waking lion, muscles and limbs flexing and stretching in the morning light. His deep eyes opened with a few blinks and settled their first day's gaze on me. His dimples appeared instantly, and he pulled me closer quickly before I could speak. Maybe he already knew what was coming, but he left no space to voice it, as he lay his warm and dry lips onto mine. Resolve and rationale melted into butterflies and twinges, as his hot skin pressed into me, wrapping his hands around my back. I moaned slightly with ecstasy, unable to stop myself. He chuckled in response and my heart sped up. Cane's lips left mine before I lost myself to him and he pulled back to look at me.

'Buenos Dias, bonita,' he began, his voice gruff with first use. It was attractive beyond belief and drew an unavoidable grin from me. I could get used to hearing that sound every morning, and get used to him calling me beautiful too.

'Morning,' I replied through my smile.

'You been watching me sleep?' he asked, yawning slightly and stretching his arms around me. I laughed innocently and awkwardly, shaking my head.

'No,' his chest rumbled with silent amusement, which made my stomach tighten. Was there anything this man did that did not affect my insides?

'Sí usted fuera,' he teased in Spanish, pulling me fully into him and kissing me ever so tenderly on the forehead. I practically swooned out loud as he did it, butterflies traveling to every appendage in my body. 'Yes, you were,' he repeated. 'You were lying here wrestling with yourself trying to stop the inevitable panic.' I opened my mouth to start a retort, but realised there was no point. He was right. He was always right when it came to my thoughts. His smile stayed, but the dimples left, and my heart dropped slightly. He kept me pressed against him, my face turned up to his. Underneath these covers with Cane, was where I wished I could stay, forever, never to deal with the real world. 'Well before that panic does set in and we do what we do ever so well…el drama,' he winked at me with a heart melting grin. I smiled, shaking my head at him and squeezing him tighter. 'Let's just agree to lie here for a few more minutes, ok?' He kissed the end of my nose so adorably that I couldn't have said no even if I wanted to.

'Fine,' I agreed softly, running my hand down his bare skin of his tight and sculptured chest. We lay in comfortable silence, listening to heartbeats and touching skin to skin. It was homely and secure. Like Christmas morning or a holiday, or something you would quite happily experience daily. The sun was climbing slowly into view through my window, bringing the day with it. We could hear the odd noise of moving life from outside the door as employees began their day, rushing to begin work. Cane's phone began to ring on the cabinet next to his head and it made me jump. We laughed a little until Cane hit the silence button and put it back down. I sighed, and he nodded slowly, both understanding it was time; time to talk, to move apart, to go back to life, to try figure this out.

'Well,' he began with a heavy voice, pulling me in abruptly and kissing me on the lips, 'I don't want to go, but I *need* to go, I have work.' He stayed put though, his fingers still tracing invisible patterns on my back. Physically, I wasn't stopping him, but mentally I was tying him down to the bed posts with navy seal knots.

'Ok,' I agreed quietly. He nodded as if trying to convince himself, then quickly sat up, as if he'd change his mind if he didn't move instantly. The covers fell from his body and cold air came rushing in where he had been laying pressed against me. I shivered and pulled the covers back, watching his toned back and flawless skin begin to dress.

'So, I will see you later?' he half asked, half stated, now pulling on his suit trousers and buckling the belt. I shrugged, trying to focus on his words and not how he looked shirtless.

'As you command,' I muttered casually, but as the words came out and settled in the air, I realised how they sounded. They summed up our relationship perfectly. I had to do whatever he commanded, I was after all, his captive, here at his will and for his use. His eyes flashed with something that was too quick to read and he pulled his shirt on, buttoning up in a, suddenly, very loud silence. The atmosphere changed between us instantly and that harsh, ridiculous situation we had just been talking about avoiding, came crashing back in. 'What do you want me to do now?' I asked, folding my arms across myself defensively, feeling all of a sudden very exposed. He turned to look at me, no expression on his face.

'What do you mean?' his jaw was locked tight and I swallowed, knowing the stubborn look all too well.

'You said you wanted to see me later, I assume it's because you need something?' His eyes narrowed, and his hands went into his trouser pockets.

'I get your point, Eva,' he answered a little louder than I had expected. It took me by surprise.

'Hey!' I reprimanded, feeling somewhat defensive. 'What's the attitude for? It's a fair question. You normally call for me when you want me for a business need. Yes? And you just said, that you would see me later on.' I raised my now, angry, eyebrows at him. 'What am I supposed to think?' He grunted with what sounded like frustration.

'And that's all this still is, is it, Eva? Un acuerdo de negocios?' He was mad at me and I was unsure why to be honest. What he was saying, was exactly what we were.

'Yes.' I snapped. 'This IS a business deal, remember. You've told me it a million times. I surrendered to you for your use, you've kept me here under lock and key, you've dangled me to bate Brice, you threatened my family if I try to leave, you put a tracker inside me and my dad…' I stopped abruptly, seeing the water in his eyes. It stunned me into complete quiet and Cane just stood there, looking at me.

'*Just* a business deal?' he asked simply, no trace of emotion. 'Nothing else to you? Last night was nothing to either of us?' I'd hurt his feelings and I sighed, relaxing my shoulders and pulling my knees into me. I shook my head slowly.

'You know that's not what I meant. You and I Cane, it's so complicated. Look at us. Is this what we can be?' I lifted my hands around me. 'This is *your* house, *your* rules, *your* family, *your* life. What about, me, everything I left behind?' He stood motionless. 'Do you want me to just give that all up and come live here with you, as your prisoner?'

'You know I had a speech all planned for this morning,' he exhaled, shrugging at me, 'begging you to stay here with me, make a life here with me.' He gave a beaten smile and a defeated shrug. 'I guess that won't work now though, will it, knowing you want your life back *more* than this.' He lowered his head from me.

'That's not fair, Cane. You make me feel this way, you make me fall for you and trust you, but yet you think you can keep everything the same…*your* way. With this same *stupid* deal?' I was exasperated. 'Have I crossed your mind at all in it? What's to become of me once you've *taken* everything dear to my family and loved ones…'I swallowed, 'once you've taken *my* heart?' He didn't answer. He stood a safe distance away with a guarded expression. 'What's the plan for me now?' I asked, suddenly feeling

I was due an explanation. The only way I could currently see any form of a happy ending for us, meant Cane backing out of this deal, calling it all off and letting me go. But would he do that? Would he? 'I've been here for weeks and weeks. You've told me nothing and I've been a good sport, Cane, I've not pestered or questioned or made things hard for you, I stuck to my end of the deal. But it's wearing thin and my heart can't handle all of this for much longer.' I stopped and waited for a response, but he kept silent. I stood up, wrapping the duvet around me and walked to his side. He watched me approach him with a worn-out look on his face, his eyes heavy. 'Your grandmother told me that even if the whole world is against you, that sometimes things can still work out, if we take a chance.' I looked up at him as my eyes began to fill with tears I couldn't keep back. 'Well I've taken every chance I can possibly take, I've given you everything, and I mean *everything*, Cane, and things are still not working out, are they?' More tears fell from my eyes, laying me bare. 'I can't keep doing this. It's *killing* me. You need to do *something* with me. Please. This right now, this life, it isn't real, and it isn't fair. I love you, Cane, I do, but you hold all the cards here. You are the only one who can fix all this.' He closed his eyes and lifted his head up away from my view. Seconds passed away in silence, until finally he answered in a heavy sigh.

'Eva, I don't know what to do with you, I don't want you to leave, I don't want you to go away, I don't want to send you back to your life to be with Edward,' he tensed his hands, 'DANM IT! The thought alone of you being with Edward makes me sick with jealousy.' He swallowed, and I watched his Adams apple move. 'I don't want to not see you from my windows or hear the staff speaking about you. I don't want you to leave my life…' He stopped, his chest heaving with frustration. He looked back down to me and locked his dark and heartbroken eyes onto mine. I held them despite desperately wanting to cry and yell and tell him to stop it all and cancel the deal, to pick me, choose me over the Bain's and revenge. Yet I stayed silent, hoping this was one of the times he would read me. He inhaled gravely. 'Yo no quiero harcete dano,' he finally whispered.

'Then don't,' I pushed firmly, don't hurt me anymore. It's simple.' Shaking his head, he stepped back.

'It's not that easy,' he stated, now moving towards the door as if the conversation was over. My insides turned with failure as he crossed the room to leave.

'Then just do *something* with me, Cane,' I yelled after him with frustration. It made him pause, his hand on the doorknob. 'Sell me, jail me, shoot me…' He turned to look at me with disturbed eyes. '*Anything* is better than to keep on doing *this*. I can't take it much longer.' Tears poured from my eyes and he stood, for what felt like a painful eternity, looking at me. Then, with no reaction at all, he opened the door and walked out, leaving me standing cold and alone, wrapped in the covers we had so intimately shared just moments ago.

CHAPTER THIRTY-FOUR.
What a mess.

As he walked away from her bedroom, the early morning sun was beginning to rise in the sky and cast its rays through the windows. He was bubbling over inside, like a pot that had been on the stove for too long, he was going to blow, and he knew it. He marched back to his room, ignoring all the greetings from his staff. It was too much to bear, too much to take. Did he honestly think that by sleeping with Eva, that it would have solved all his problems, that they would wake up this morning and it would all be fixed? If anything, it had only made things worse, only complicated matters. He was an idiot and he was angry, at himself, at the world and at allowing himself to believe. He slammed his bedroom door shut with such force that he heard the furniture rattle. His blood was coursing through his body so quickly he could literally feel the pressure building, racing to explode. He breathed heavily as snap images from last night with Eva flashed through him, each one creating a greater rage of frustration. He wanted her, he wanted that life, the one with her waking up beside him. He wanted what he knew he couldn't have, and the fact that he allowed himself to get this close was now killing him. Without thought, he grabbed his desk chair and with all the strength in his body, he threw it across the room. It smashed like it was made of matches, sending splinters and shards everywhere. The release felt good and before sense could take its hold, he let his wrath free on his room, smashing and destroying everything he could get his powerful hands on. Sweat ran down his back and his limbs trembled with tension as he ripped apart the place he knew so well. Each piece of destroyed furniture restored a part of control in his head, draining away the irrational, emotional boy that was taking the lead in his life. Eventually, when his muscles could handle no more and his room was utterly ruined, he stopped, slumping his back against the cold wall and sinking to the ground. He sat there for a while, inhaling and exhaling. What a mess, he thought bitterly, not referring to his once orderly and tidy room. The maids would not be happy, but then, neither was he. Eva's words plagued him with painful replay as he sat panting on his floor like a broken boy, 'sell me, jail me, shoot me...*Anything* is better than to keep on doing *this*.' *His head dropped into his hands with defeat. He was backed into a corner and no matter what way he tried to escape, Eva could never be his. He had been warned by his brothers countless times, cautioned and counseled to steer clear of her, but his heart had not listened,* he *had not listened. Now, he was madly in love, and had no way to ever be with her. The knowledge of it was excruciating. He had dealt with loss in his life, felt bereavement and failure, but this was a new ruin, even for him. A knock at the door drew his head up quickly and snapped him from his suffocation. It opened before he could stand, and Scott entered, his face quickly turning to dumbfounded shock.*

'Erm, Sir?' he called out amongst the rubble, looking for his boss.

'Here, Scott,' Cane replied, lifting his heavy arm into the air to be located. Scott closed the door behind him firmly and made his way to his boss' side. It was a maze of broken wood, shattered glass and smashed breakables, and each step Scott took, made a crunch that echoed through the unsettled atmosphere. He reached Cane's side and with no questions, knowingly turned and sat, his back resting next to Cane's.

'You're first appointment is in an hour, Sir,' he began, ignoring the strange circumstances around them. Cane laughed, banging his head purposely off the wall as he dropped it backwards to exhale.

'Oh, Scott,' he assessed with a smile on his lips. 'You are constant and loyal, my friend.' He patted his number two on his shoulder and Scott shrugged with a grin.

'Do you want to talk about it?' he asked, picking up a piece of what was once a mirror and throwing it to the side. Cane shook his head in exasperation.

'No, talking about it will fix nothing. But thanks.' He brushed his hands down on his trousers readying himself to stand.

'Sir?' Scott said, before Cane moved away. Cane looked over at him. 'You may not want my opinion and I'm sure you've thought this all over a million times...' He paused as if waiting for permission to continue and Cane gave it, nodding, ready to hear the advice that was surely to follow. 'She is one in a million, that girl,' Cane smiled despite himself, nodding in complete agreement. He shrugged and laughed quietly at the hopeless knowledge of it.

'And what do I do with that, Scott?' he asked, looking into his old trusted friend's eyes. Scott lowered his head and popped his knuckles, awkwardly.

*'You once gave me advice that saved my life, Cane,' he half whispered, using his boss's name with respectful esteem. Cane looked up at him in surprise, both knowing what Scott was referring to. 'You said to me something that I can now say to you...*when you find what makes you that happy, hold onto it for dear life.'* He let the words settle in the air for a few seconds, silently. Then nodding his head with finalisation, he stood up and made his way back to the door through the fall out. Cane sat still watching him leave. He hated when advice came back to bite him in the ass, especially good advice.*

CHAPTER THIRTY-FIVE
Let's play a game.

I had a new clarity that was overpowering enough to dull out the pain in my heart. It was simple: self-preservation, through denial. No more self-pitying and moping. This is what had happened to me, through either my fault or the fault of others, but what was done was done. I was moving on. I packed my room up, ready to leave at any time. The homelier it felt, the easier it was to stay. Cane obviously had no intentions of stopping this deal, so I needed to accept my fate. I needed to stop making roots, and stop imagining a happy ending. I now spent all my time locked in my room, where I couldn't be distracted by the beauty of the house and grounds around me. Admitting to myself that I actually liked it here, only made it all worse. I was on emotional and physical rations; I ate only when I had to and only in solitude, I talked only when it was completely needed, and I felt, only when I could do so with detachment.

Three days had passed since I had slept with Cane. And I was coping fine with my new resolve. I was committed to not worrying about complications and instead I just wasted moments until I was told my fate. Material and items for dressmaking had arrived in my room, but they gave me no joy, unlike before. They were just a distraction. I would still make the dress for Maria's daughter, but only because I'd agreed to do so. I didn't want to keep these ties, these friendships I was developing. I didn't know where they would end up, or when I'd have to say goodbye. This was not my home and I needed to keep reminding myself of that.

A knock on the door finally came and I knew it was here, the end was coming. I opened it to Scott. It had been a while since I had talked to him and I briefly wondered what he thought. He was Canes second, he must have known something was going on.

'Mr Rodriguez would like to see you, Eva,' he said quietly, casting his eyes at mine.

'Yeah, I figured he would, sooner or later.' I stated, keeping the emotion from my words.

'You all right?' he asked, in what was an uncharacteristically caring tone, as he pushed the door open for me. I looked back to him for a few seconds, feeling the sudden massive urge to just tell him everything, unleash my whole heartache upon him, to confide in someone...but the seconds passed quickly, and I remembered my new resolve. I shrugged casually instead, hiding all the pain away.

'I'm stronger now than I have ever been in my whole life...so, I will be just fine, thanks.' I gave him a half smile for his unexpected concern to which he swallowed and returned back to his normal, nonchalant manner. He nodded in the direction of the hallway and I inhaled deeply for strength, stepping out of the door. As the office lock went green, I tensed my muscles and stood tall. The balcony was closed for the first time I had ever seen, and the curtains were shut. Cane was at his desk, sitting with a single chair directly in front of him. He barely looked up, but motioned for me to take a seat. I did as was asked, silently. Once sat, I glanced at him through my eyelashes of my lowered head. He looked tired and was unshaven. His usual air of confidence was lacking, and his normally bright eyes were cold and grey. He looked like I felt; exhausted and spread thin. I swallowed. This was going to be interesting.

'Miss Eva,' he began, back to our formal addresses. 'You have been so *desperado* for me to do something with you, that I thought you should be one of the first to know of the actions taken on your behalf. The final deal has been made.' His eyes looked at me, but only superficially, and I could see nothing of the Cane I loved. I knew that man was now locked inside, shadowed by the man that now sat in front of me. I nodded trying to look brave, despite the nerves inside. 'You are getting married to Edward Bain, as has always been your life plan. The date is set for next week.' *WHAT?* He left me no time to question as he looked back down to his papers and continued. 'You will be wed legally and in the limelight, like I am sure Edward always had planned. You will stay married for the legal requirement of time and until he has become CEO and owner of Bain Enterprises, which I know through our dear friend, Tammy, will be soon. You will sign the paper work given to you that will put the highest holding of shares into your name and then with no pre-nup, you will get divorced. You can blame his infidelity if you wish, I really don't care for the reasons, but you *will* take everything from him; his money, his status and most importantly, his business.' He paused for a breath. *WHAT?* What was he saying? His words were sharp and cold and confusing and no matter how I tried to process the bitter things coming out of his mouth, I couldn't. 'After the divorce is settled, you will be required to sign any and every document that is placed in front of you, by me. I will be making all decisions and running Bain Enterprises, even if it's legally in your name. Then when the time allows, you will gift your ownership to me. That tracker in your dad will stay active for the rest of his life and I will use it if you try to screw me over in any way. All you have to do is sign things and you can be free of me and return to *your* normal life, since I know how important that is to you.' He dropped his pen to the papers, conclusively. 'That is the deal. Easy and simple.' No eye contact or physical display of remorse, he just sat rigid and still, his hands clasped together with a bit too much force. I though, was beyond stunned and didn't know how to keep myself sat still on the seat. I wanted to jump up and smack him in the face, to shake his stubborn body and knock some sense back into him. Instead, I was speechless, silenced by shock. This was the deal? The final end? Why not just force Brice Bain to sell his shares over? Why this ridiculous drama of marriage and divorce and prenuptials? As if reading my mind, he answered my question. 'I am not allowed to own such a dominating market share as set by law, buying dear Edward's company would not be passed, even with my influences. If the ownership were technically in your name, ' he lowered his voice, 'and I control you, then that's good enough for me to start. I'll still be able to do whatever I want with the company, with Bain's legacy. It'll be mine.' He raised his eyebrows, waiting for a response, a stone façade on his face. *This* was the plan? *This* was months of my life? *This* was plotting and scheming and revenge? *This* was how we were going to end? It was ridiculous. It felt ridiculous. Had he lost his mind?

'Edward will never go for it, he will never sign his company over to me,' I protested, shaking my head. 'And what's to stop me just running once I'm with Edward, hiding and never coming back. I can't sign anything if I'm gone, Cane. Your deal is ruined then.' He shrugged, casually.

'Apparently when your life is on the line, Edward darling will sign anything.' He paused. 'The reminder of that tracker in *you*, was enough to convince him that if he turned me down, or tried to cheat me or tried to run and hide, that I would always be able to find you. That I would always take what was rightfully mine.' I saw an echo of the old Cane behind his straight face, as if it was fighting to fully take control again. 'And make no mistake, Miss Mack, I've said it before and I'll say it again, I own you.'

'You don't own me, Cane!' I began, defiantly. 'I may have given you myself, but that was willingly, not because you demanded or commanded it. Do you remember that?' I watched for a reaction as he sat erect and still. 'And you're lying,' I continued, with a little less conviction, my mind becoming cloudy and my heart sinking. 'There's no stupid micro-chip inside of my dad, or me, and you know it.' He watched me with his ever perfectly practiced mask.

'Is there not? Are you one hundred percent sure about that?' I wavered, his cold eyes throwing me. I shook my head at myself. Yes of course I knew that, of course I was sure. It was a bluff, there was no tracker in me. I *knew* him, I *knew* him now. And this wasn't him. It was a lie and he was acting cold to push me away, acting mean and detached to make it easier for me to leave, easier for him to let go. This whole thing was ridiculous. 'The papers are being prepped as we speak. Your church is booked. Your marriage needs to be real to the world. Once you have the majority of shares at the end of it all, I'll just need you for authorising signatures. Apart from that we will be strangers again…as you wished. But mark my words, Miss Mack, you will sign whatever is placed in front of you in the future, no questions, no scheming, no trickery. If you do try anything, I will take you back and lock you up in that windowless cell you originally thought me capable of. Do you understand me?' I sat motionless. I hadn't seen this coming. I hadn't known what to expect to be honest, but this? 'Me hago entender?' he repeated blankly, his emotion creeping in slightly through his Spanish. I was astonished and astounded and disturbed and a million other things all at once.

'Yes, I understand you, but I don't believe you.' I begged, searching for his eyes. He glanced up one more time, then nodded towards the door.

'You can go.'

'Cane?' I whimpered, begging. He barely registered me. 'What are you doing? This is crazy. This is not you.' To this he finally looked up.

'Miss Eva, it's quite the opposite, this *is* me. And you were the one who said *anything* was better than being here and with me. So, you have your wish. A life without me is better for us both anyway.' He signaled towards the door again.

'I didn't say that, Cane, and I definitely didn't mean it like that and you *know* it.' I argued. 'What am I supposed to do? Do you honestly want me to marry Ed? Go back to life with him...sleep in his bed?' To this I got a slight reaction and his eyebrows straightened in concentration. I knew that he didn't want me to go back to Edward, I knew it. I just needed to break through his stubbornness, through the stupid idea in his head that *this, this* was the best option. 'I don't love him, Cane, and you know that. *I love you.* This is crazy. This will change everything. Don't do it, I'm begging you, please. I can't just marry him.' I pointed between him and I, pleading and searching for his eyes. 'You said it to me Cane, te amo, do you not remember that anymore? Or was it all just a lie?' His eyes flashed with something that looked like pain, and then were back to the cold business mode. I knew what he was doing, pushing me away and making it impossible for him to ever be happy, for him to ever get what he wanted. But he was also making sure I would have the life he thought I so desperately wanted now. The life I so desperately *didn't* want now. What I wanted was him, a new life with *him*. I knew he thought making me mad and acting like the animal he may have once been, would be enough to make me run, to make me leave, but it wasn't. It made me frustrated and angry, but not any less devoted. What part had he not understood? I loved him. I knew he was better than all of this. Making me hate him was not the selfless and kind act he thought it was, he was not sparing me in the end. I was willing to stick by him, to see it through, to weather the tough times, I was willing to do that. But I knew that despite me being ready, he was not willing to watch me suffer, just to be with him.

'Cane, I love you. Not Edward, not the businesses, not the money or the power, but you.' I tried one more time, my voice quiet and firm. 'Are you listening to me? I choose you. Why are you doing this?' The office doors opened, and a black shirt came in, obviously to escort me out. 'Cane?' I tried again, knowing I was about to be removed.

'It's Mr Rodriguez, to you,' he added conclusively, with a nod to the black shirt, who literally removed me from the seat. I went willingly, casting a last glance back at the man I was sure I knew, the man who didn't even flinch as the door closed.

I was left to find my own way back to the room, wondering aimlessly through the halls and paying no attention to my surroundings. I didn't know how to process any of it. I was too confused and lost to be mad or scared or sad or relieved...or anything. I knew I should be partly happy at going home, but the fact was, I wasn't happy at all, not even slightly. I was going to be married to Ed, even after all this? Then get divorced? How could I do that? Yes, I'd found my heart softening towards Edward over the last few weeks that I had never thought would come so quickly, but I would never date him again, be in love with him again...share a bed with him again. The thought flashed me back to waking up in Cane's arms and the warmth that had brought. I could *never* have that with Edward, I didn't *want* that with Edward. And how would I be able to just blindly sign anything Cane lay at my hand? How could I not look at the paper work, look for a way to save my father's job and Brice's company? How could I not plan to run and try free everyone from the mistakes I had made? Cane must know I would never roll over and play dead, when the people I loved were being hurt...and that included him. Too distracted by my turning questions, I failed to notice that I had company, and by the time they had caught up to me, it was too late. I hadn't been alone with the brothers since Spain, even though I had seen them about. Their stares were always a strange mixture of unreadable emotions and their passing comments were just as confusing. I exhaled. Of course, they would show up now. It was perfect timing really, wasn't it? I hear my damning fate and then the devil's pets show up to add salt to the open wound.

'Look who we have here, Elias,' Andreas announced, throwing his heavy arm around me. I sagged under its weight, too weak to even try force some resilience out. Elias grabbed my hand and began pulling me along with them.

'We had such an interesting experience last time we hung out, Eva, we were thinking you would like to join us again?' He flashed his devious smile at me and my stomach dropped with dread. It must have shown on my face and Andreas laughed loudly, pulling me off towards the grounds.

'We're not that bad, surely?' he teased, nudging me with his shoulder. It knocked me forward and Elias kept my hand to keep me in place. 'We actually owe you, in a way, to be honest,' Andreas continued in a loud and boisterous manner, despite the strangely thankful words that were leaving his mouth. Against my better judgment, I took the bait and spoke.

'You do?' I asked with raised eyebrows. *Owe me in a bad way?* Elias slipped my hand through his strong arm and left it there, while they continued to escort me outside to the gardens.

'Sí, I guess so,' he continued, agreeing with Andreas. 'Maybe even two-fold.' He held up a first finger. 'One, for smoothing things over with Cane about that night in Spain. Whatever you said, the punishment we expected wasn't half as bad as what we got. Cane said he was being lenient due to your defence of us.' I looked over to Andreas, awkwardly.

'Very cool of you,' he added, with a thumbs-up. This was all very alternate-universe. Elias continued before I could dwell on the strangeness too much.

'Secondly, for setting us up with Rose.' Elias smiled a sloppy smile and I quickly remembered about Rose, the beautiful gold digger. I had forgotten about her amidst my troubles and dramas. But by the look of Elias's face, she was very much on his mind still.

'It's going well with Rose, then?' I asked timidly, feeling slightly guilty that all too soon she would eat him up for breakfast and leave him broken hearted and penniless. I was sure I remembered him deserving it, but now, as we walked along with my heart so destroyed and heavy, it seemed wrong to do this to any other person on purpose, regardless of who that person was.

'Ella es perfecta.' *She is perfect,* he continued, smiling. Andreas began talking about her super-hot friend she had set him up with. Maybe it was the pain I felt for me and my losses, or maybe I was just turning soft, but I spoke before I could stop myself.

'Maybe just be careful with Rose, Elias, she's a, emmm...' I searched for a more delicate word than *gold-digger.* Elias just laughed.

'I know exactly what she is, Eva,' he said with a goofy smile. 'But we are surprisingly well matched.' He winked, and I dreaded to think what his comment meant. I quickly brushed it off, they were big boys after all and I had my own troubles to deal with. 'Which is why we are going to cut you some slack today and insist on doing something fun with you.' This made me lift my head and glance at them both with concern.

'*Drinking,* was your idea of fun,' I began with loud skepticism. '*Boxing,* was your idea of fun.' I raised my eyebrows and a knot of worry formed in my stomach. They both burst into grunting laughter, scaring away a flock of birds from a nearby tree.

'She has a point there,' Andreas agreed eagerly, staring very obviously and directly at Elias's face with delight, '...caterpillar eyebrows.' Elias erupted into laughter with his brother and the two literally fell to the ground with childish hysterics. I stood upright, waiting for them to regain their composure. I didn't get the joke, but something felt familiar about it.

They rolled about like children in a frenzy of loud and manly laughter for what felt like minutes, each time I thought it was over, one would mutter something about eyebrows and they would be off again. It was somewhat bizarre to see them so happy when I was not. I was jealous of their carefree lives and their happy-go-lucky outlook. Oh, to be so care free and easily amused again. I yearned for those days.

'She has no idea what we are laughing at,' Elias finally spoke, gasping for air and holding his side. I shrugged at him blankly, with no expression.

'De verdad?' Andreas asked, standing to his feet and wiping tears away from his cleanshaven face. He looked at me with disappointment. 'Really?' he repeated. 'Black caterpillars?' He watched me as if it would draw the desired reaction. It didn't 'Owww, that's a shame,' he added, with another small burst of laughter. 'Cause it was freakin' hysterical.'

'Do you remember anything from the first night we met, when we had a couple drinks?' *Couple?* Elias had a smirk still stuck to his handsome face and I looked at them both as if they had gone mad.

'No.' I answered, shaking my head. 'I do remember being violently sick for hours after it though,' The laughing stopped and they both kind of shrugged at each other as if to say, fair enough.

'Oh well,' Elias concluded, 'maybe one day we will remind you of what you said, when you're in a better mood.' He put his arm behind my back and continued to pull me along with them.

'This is so much more *fun,* than our previous encounters, we promise,' Andreas said, leading the way to an area of the gardens I had once thought to never enter. It was their own private section which Gideon had pointed out to me before and I remembered wondering what horrific and crazy horrors took place behind those gates. I was now away to find out and I had no energy to argue. After a few feet of silence, Andreas spoke again, but this time in a lowered tone. 'You got the business deal plans today, sí?' He kept his eyes away from mine like they would betray him somehow. I swallowed the sickening feeling that the scene from Canes office had left with me, and nodded simply. Andreas sighed, and Elias patted my arm in what almost felt like pity. Was this a joke? When did the brothers have feelings or care about *my* feelings? Was this all just a cruel prank about to be exposed at my further expense? As I thought it we rounded a corner onto what looked like an outdoor shooting range. My fear was confirmed as I was put into a seat and guns were pulled out of a locked cage.

'Look how scared she looks,' Andreas laughed, waving a gun in my face. 'We're not going to shoot you, Eva, for goodness sake.' He laughed, shaking his head at me.

'We're not actually allowed to anyway.' Elias added, with a playful wink at me as he took a pack of bullets and began to load two guns. *That* gave me great confidence. He then sighed loudly, coming to perch by my side.

'Look,' he began, with a quiet and weirdly sincere voice. 'I know we've had a rough start, but surprisingly, to both of us, we don't think you're all that bad.' He scratched his chin awkwardly, as if saying these words made him uncomfortable. I knew the feeling. 'We just figured that after hearing the business deal news, what with you and Cane as you are, that you would want to vent a little and *this*,' he waved his hand at the range laying in front of us, 'is a great way to do that. Dispara…shoot things.' I turned to look at him. This was the closest we had ever been, his face near enough to mine for me to see laugh lines in the corners of his dark eyes and his long eyelashes. The intimate moment obviously made him uncomfortable and he cleared his throat loudly, standing back up quickly. 'This or we could give you some pads and let you spar, since we all know how good you are at that now.' He smiled at me with a wink. I said nothing, and he let it go with a small nod of his head. I watched him as he stood, continuing to load the gun. Andreas gave me a small geeky smile, as if to echo his brother's, oddly, thoughtful words. I never thought this would have happened. The day I saw humanity and compassion in the two younger Rodriguez brothers. It felt like everything I had ever known about this family was wrong, completely and utterly wrong. How did I go back to a life with people who still hated them? Who would curse them and judge them and despise them with every breath? Did I stay silent when I heard people unfounded, false nonsense about the Rodriguez men? The brothers weren't so wild and careless and irresponsible as they were made out to be, they also had a soft and caring- as if on cue, the blast of a fired rifle went off next to me without warning, taking the branch of a nearby tree off and sending it crashing to the ground in an almighty ear-piercing racket. Andreas began to whoop with excitement. I shrugged to myself in reflection. Then again, maybe they didn't have any soft sides at all. I watched Andreas high-five Elias, who was now beckoning me to the line next to him. I walked over and stood by Elias's side, my feet touching the spray-painted perimeter.

'Can you see the target board at the end of the field?' I followed his finger to the small round stand at the far end of the long clearing. I nodded, squinting through the sun. 'We will move it closer for when you take your first shot, don't worry,' he added in full confidence, that I would never hit it that far away. 'Now these are just rubber bullets, but will hit that target just fine. This is how you ready your rifle.' He showed me the safety rules and how to hold the barrel against my shoulder. 'Rifles give a fair amount of kick back so be prepared for it in your hombro, shoulder, sí?' He clasped my right shoulder and looked for understanding. I nodded as expected. They obviously had no idea that my father had forced me to a shooting range from the age of being old enough to hold a gun straight. He had pretty much prepared me, my whole life, for the last few weeks of events: martial arts classes, dancing classes, shooting practice, masking my emotions, strength and independence under pressure. The thought gave me a swell of appreciation for him, my very much alive and well father. I pictured the first-place trophy that sat in the cabinet at his house from the last competition I had won. It was a gold statue of a gun with a number one being shot from its barrel. I glanced back to Elias, who was still reciting rules on firing a weapon safely. I didn't have the heart to tell him, not when they were going out of their way to be so nice. Andrea's phone rang in his pocket and he stopped reloading his rifle to answer it. I couldn't hear the conversation, but it ended with Andreas raising his voice slightly in frustration. Elias had stopped his instructing to watch his brother with curiosity.

'Elias, we need to go back to the house for a few minutes. Rodeado de idiotas.' Andreas yelled with irritation, putting his gun down. Elias turned to me.

'Surrounded by idiots,' I translated, nodding with a small smile. 'I got it.' I'll just wait here, if that's ok? I don't want to go back to the house yet.' Elias shrugged and walked off towards his brother.

'We won't be long,' he added, jogging to catch up with Andreas, who was now ranting in Spanish about incompetency and marching off around the clearing. I watched them go, then sat back down on the chair, finally alone with my torturous thoughts and breaking heart. Words and sentences from Cane's office ran through my head like they were stuck on a broken record, the painful parts just replaying and replaying. I closed my eyes and could see Cane's cold face as he brushed me away from him. I leant forward and put my head between my knees to stop the nausea that was circling my stomach. I was to marry Ed? And never see Cane again? I was lost in my thoughts, trying to imagine how my marriage would be to Ed each day, each night, when I knew that my heart now belonged with Cane. I was so consumed with confusion, that I never heard the footsteps of approaching bodies.

'Look who we have here,' a voice spat coldly, making me startle and my heart turn to ice. I spun to see two men, two men I hadn't seen in weeks, and two men who I hoped to never see again. Their faces were fresh in my mind still, vivid from our last encounter. It was the day of the camera room, they had burst into my bedroom and ripped me from my bed. Wyatt and Williams. A cold shiver ran over my body, as the summer breeze blew warning. I stood up with the ice spreading to my stomach. I hadn't seen or heard of either of these men in weeks, and I had purposefully put them from my wandering mind after Cane had so sternly instructed Scott to 'deal with them.' That implication had plagued me afterwards with uncertainty. Now, as I watched the sadistic faces of those two men walk towards me with hostility, I almost wished that my worst assumptions had been true. Their determined and threatening pace left no questions, they were not here for a happy reunion. I glanced with unmoving dread at the black shirt, Williams, the pervert from the day I had first arrived at Cane's home. I could remember all too well how much he enjoyed lingering over certain areas of my body as he searched me with a cruel and belittling smile on his face. Then later on in my bedroom, he had licked my face with disgusting enjoyment. The memory made me shudder with revulsion. He was no longer wearing a black shirt and was dressed in sports bottoms and a scrappy old t-shirt. His round face was covered with a messy growth of unkept beard, but he looked nonetheless just as angry and intimidating as he did when he had had me pinned against the wardrobe by my neck. I swallowed with memory of the pressure squeezing in on my esophagus.

'Just who we were looking for,' Wyatt sneered, as if Christmas had come early. They approached me at great speed, with purpose in their strides. Wyatt was taller than Williams and was built better, but he too, now looked worse for wear, in his ripped and faded jeans. He had a baseball cap on, but it couldn't hide the contempt his eyes held as they moved aggressively for me. I quickly remembered he was the one who I had given a black eye to in the alley, the one who I had seen kick my dad. My palms clammed up and I closed them to try and keep control of my emotions, the recall of him slapping me across the face flashed through my mind with realistic stinging.

'It's comeuppance time, missy,' Wyatt hissed, extending his finger and pointing it at me with force. They reached me quickly, despite my backing up and Williams grabbed my arms, shaking me violently. I tried to keep a composed face, but I was desperately looking around for help. Where were Andreas and Elias? I never thought there would be a day where I would search for their aid.

'You ruined our lives, princess, and it's payback time,' Williams shouted in my ear, shaking me hard again. My panic was starting to spread as their tempers flared. I could feel his fingers digging into my skin with painful strength and I tried to pull myself free. Williams shook his head, irritably. 'You are going nowhere until we are done with you, life wrecker.' He yanked my arm and pulled me to the painted line of the field that I had stood at previously with Elias.

'I have no idea what you are talking about,' I protested, as confidently as I could, struggling against his strength to free myself. Williams shoved me forward, so that I was now a couple paces in front of them.

'I'm sure you don't,' Wyatt spat menacingly, folding his arms. 'After your little prank that day, we got the beating of our lives and then the sack.'

'Not just fired, little girl,' Williams barked, 'but black listed from any other work.' He literally spat on the floor at me and I jumped out of the way with disgust. 'Because of you, we have no work, no money, no way to pay certain people we owe.' I shook my head.

'It's hardly my fault, I didn't fire you,' I replied as boldly as I could. I was a little angry if I was being honest. After the news I had had earlier and with my heart in unexplainable pieces still, I just had no patience for this. I was reaching the stage where I wished people would just get over things or just kill me. I was sick of being bullied, used and pushed around. I exhaled loudly, with my annoyance blatantly obvious. 'No,' I continued, defiantly. 'No. You had your orders and you disobeyed them. Don't take your failure and pitifulness out on me.' Their tempers raged and instantly I realised, as per normal, I had not helped the situation with my loose tongue. Wyatt stepped in, and all too quickly slapped me across the face with such force it made me stumble. My eyes ran with tears and I held my throbbing cheek with surprise. They laughed, and I quickly remembered just how much I had hated them both. I steadied my breathing and stood back up again, straight, my cheek pulsing with heat and my anger pounding with desire to defend myself.

'Thankfully, we still had a couple favours to call in, to get us back in here. And now that we're here, let's play a game.' Wyatt began, walking towards me and picking up one of the rifles from the grass. My eyes widened uncontrollably, and my heart quickened with fear. How did I always manage to end up in these situations? Moments where my life was on the line? I suddenly realised that they had no reason to not kill me. They were no longer Cane's employees. The thought was scarily sobering. 'Have you ever seen a gun before, princess?' Wyatt asked degradingly, waving it close to my face. I wanted to rip it from his hands and slam it into the bridge of his nose, but Williams now had the second rifle aimed at me. I knew they were both loaded too, so instead of fighting back, I looked down with pretend submission and fear. 'Sheltered life like yours, I bet you've never even held a gun before.' He jabbing the barrel into my shoulder and I closed my eyes, taking the prodding. I reminded myself that I was a medal holding marksman and given half the chance I would show them it gladly. But for now, I could act like the scared girl they wanted to see…it wasn't entirely untrue anyway. Wyatt laughed bitterly. 'Don't worry too much, poppet,' he pushed me forward with his free arm, further onto the field. 'It's only the first couple strikes that hurt.' He glared at me with hate. 'And then you'll be dead.' To this I looked up at them. There was no hint of pity or remorse in his eyes, he was utterly and completely serious. They were going to try and kill me. I desperately looked around again for help, for anyone, but we were in the private part of the grounds and no one was here. They were hooting each other on now, edging each other forward with manly satisfaction. My only relief in all of this was, that they didn't seem to know the bullets were rubber. The idea of having even one of them fired at me though, when I'd seen what Andreas had done to the tree earlier, was not something I wanted to experience.

'Are you scared?' Wyatt asked, lifting his rifle towards me. This time I *was* actually scared, and sadly, my face must have shown it. I was getting sloppy.

'Good,' Williams spat. 'Now you know how we feel every day. How it feels when you have lost everything.' I swallowed down my laugh at the comment. They had no idea just how much I could relate to that feeling. I held my hands up to them in defeat, hoping to stall. Elias and Andreas had said they'd be back, surely it was soon?

'You haven't thought this through,' I began in a quiet voice, shaking my head. 'When Cane finds out what you have done to his business deal, he'll find you both.'

'And kill us?' Wyatt interrupted, with sarcasm. 'Lady, we are dead men walking anyway. The people we owe money to don't let you off free when you miss payments.'

'I'm sure you could work something out with Cane, he's a businessman after all?' I begged, slowly stepping back away further from them onto the range, my feet struggling to stay steady on the grass.

'The last time we saw Mr Rodriguez, he said he'd kill us both if he ever laid eyes on us again.' Wyatt said the words with resentment. 'The fact that he didn't kill us then and there was strange enough, I doubt he'll extend the courtesy twice.'

'Enough talking and stalling,' Williams piped up loudly, he was itching to get his gun in place. 'I've been dreaming about this moments for weeks now.' He nodded his head towards the field to inform me to go, but I stood still, motionless. I could picture all too clearly the distance between here and the end of the range behind me. I had focused my eyes on the target down there just earlier with Elias. I would never make it that far unless they both happened to be awful shots. I knew for fact that I would be torn to shreds if I was shooting at me. With these two though, I didn't know their skills, and it was the only sliver of hope I had. I stood firm, hoping that my defiance would be enough to change their minds. It was a pointless game though. The sweat ran down my back and I could feel my fingers prickle with fearful warning, itching to defend myself. Even if the bullets were rubber, being shot with them, would definitely break the skin, if not embed in it. With enough of the right shots, hell, they *could* kill me. 'I'll count to three, shall I?' Williams had begun, evil flashing in his eyes. I stood firm, trying to not show my panic. I would not run like a fox with the hounds chasing after me. I had just thought that my life had been through as much crap as I could take, and I'd hit rock bottom, and then this happened. Playing cat and mouse with two psychos. I kept my feet planted on the ground, Williams staring me down. Next to his shoulder, I could see Wyatt already standing with his rifle aimed. My heart began to beat faster with acknowledgement. I was going to be shot, and multiple times. And there was nothing I could do about it. 'One...' Williams started counting. My breathing stopped. Was it better to be shot in the back, while running away, or to be shot at close range with the defiance of no run at all? 'Two...' A cruel and satisfied smile crept across his face. I stepped back uncontrollably, and Williams leapt forward, shoving me hard, forcing me further out into the field. 'Three...' he yelled, jumping back to line with Wyatt, his gun at the ready. I paced back a few steps, watching the two men with fear, surely this was just a game, surely, they wouldn't- but before I could finish my sentence, Wyatt let off a round and a bullet flew passed my shoulder, almost too quick for me to react. I jumped and instantly all my fear and panic turned to adrenaline, pumping through my body. My eyes widened with dread and like a puppet, I began to run. The field seemed to stretch and grow as I sprinted as quickly as I could towards the far end. Three bullets had missed me now and I was slightly encouraged by their poor aim. But just as I was getting hopeful, an almighty sting pierced my calf. It made me stumble, my hands instinctively going to hold the wound. Tears filled my eyes, as I lifted my palms to find blood. I winced in pain, at least thankful that I was far enough away for them not to hear me cry out. I pulled myself to my feet, practically halfway down the field. The first few steps shot pains up my calf and leg, but I pushed through it, my adrenaline working quickly as an inhibitor. I was three quarters of the way down by the time the second shot finally hit me, piercing into my shoulder. It stung more than the first one and hit me with such force that it knocked me forward off my feet. The tumble down winded me and tears poured from my eyes. I stood as quickly as my shaking legs would let me, and ran the last few feet, knowing my life depended on it. I could hear over my heaving their sickening laughter in the distance, and I finally threw myself behind the wooden target frame at the end of the field, grasping for breath. My whole body gulped for oxygen and the two shot wounds stung like I had hot irons rammed in them. I glanced at the black bullet still half showing from my calf and wiped away the tears from my wet face. I pulled it out with a painful wince and threw it to the side, hearing it bounce off of something noisily. My eye quickly found the small gun lying on the ground next to the target refill sheets. My heart skipped with hope as I dropped to the floor, praying for bullets. As I pulled the papers away I found a small cardboard box and my pulse sped with relief, as I opened it to find a half full carton of rubber pellets. I quickly took the gun and loaded it, pocketing a handful of remaining bullets. With a weapon in hand now, and already knowing that my aim was better than theirs, I began to think clearer. I looked up at the fence which was now in front of me, giving way to the wilderness of the gardens. I could hear the men laughing and making their way towards me.

'Don't hide now princess, you've got to make it back down the field again still.' They howled with enjoyment and it made my blood boil. I looked at the gun in my hand and for a split second, I imagined firing a round straight into one of their eyes. It would blind them instantly, if not travel through the soft tissue and straight into the brain, killing them in moments. I knew I could fire the shot off before either of them had to time lift their rifles. The possibility made me shake with desire. I hated them so much and their poorly timed revenge, the idea of letting all my pain out on them, was scarily tempting. I shook my head at myself, knowing it was just my fear and anger talking. I held the gun firmly in my hand, trying to steady my thoughts and get control of myself. They couldn't have been more than ten feet away when I dashed to the fence and hopped it as quickly as I could, sending them into yells of warning. A shot went off and flew past my ear in a whizz. I ran for cover behind the bushes, knowing I didn't have long until they were on my tail. I could hear them climbing the fence and calling my name with every disgusting word they could think of. I crouched as still as I could behind a large green shrubbery and took the gun, locking it in my left hand and holding the barrel tightly. It steadied instantly, and I let my finger find the trigger. The back of the knee would do nicely, I thought, remembering the best places for incapacitation. If I broke an artery, so be it. Wyatt was the first to show me his leg and as he cursed me loudly, I pulled the trigger with a smile. The gun fired with a piercing bang and before either of them could figure out what was happening, Wyatt was on the floor, screaming in pain. I took the opportunity to run, but Williams had spotted me already and leaving his partner in crime reeling in agony on the ground, he took off after me. I knew I couldn't outrun him, he was stronger and faster than I could ever be, especially with two bullet wounds, so I double backed quickly, sliding under a brightly coloured plant that was humming with bees. I tried to ignore them as they swarmed around me, upset with their disturbance. I felt a sting in my arm and a couple others break my skin, but I was instantly distracted from its pain as Williams came into the clearing.

'Princess, you have nowhere to run,' he taunted, his gun raised still. 'You might as well come out and face your fate. I might even make it quick for you, if you beg.' He continued, circling the opening. 'You know you're from a family of cowards, right? Your dad was just as pathetic as we kicked him to the ground.' I tried desperately to ignore him as he rounded towards my hiding place, the bees still hard at work, oblivious to the protection they were offering me. The head of the rifle passed directly by my face and I held my breath. One shot now and I'd be dead. Sweat ran down my back into my already soaked top and my legs shook. It felt like the gun was aimed at my face for a lifetime, then, all of a sudden, it moved on, continuing round the perimeter. I released my breath, vibrating with fear. If I could sneak away from him now, I was sure I could make it back to the house before being caught, I could get some help. Just as I went to move though, Williams spoke again, his voice deep and bitter. 'You know,' he began, maybe only two paces away from me now. I could see his back rising and falling with enjoyment. 'I was looking forward to finishing your dad off before you stopped us that day,' he sneered with a vile laugh. 'And I would have happily taught you some manners too in your bedroom given half the chance. You women are only good for one thing,' he spat on the ground and something in me snapped. Maybe the casual reference towards my dad's life, maybe the insinuation of deserving to be raped, but the same anger I had felt days ago, watching Tammy drive away from the house, rose back up inside of me. This time though, it was mixed in with all my pain and disappointment from earlier today. My skin began to flush, and my hands shaked with fury and I struggled to keep myself in check. I was sick of being treated like something people had stepped in, sick and tired of everything. Despite knowing somewhere inside that I should run and ignore everything I was hearing, I couldn't, I couldn't let it go and I couldn't bring myself to back down anymore. I was done being trampled on. Before I could stop myself, with one fluid movement, I was out of the bush and had my gun pressed against the side of William's temple, forcing its barrel hard into the soft exposed skin. He froze, stunned.

'Throw the gun away now or I swear I'll pull the trigger and end your pathetic life with a small piece of cheap rubber.' At least he was not stupid and whether he could hear the point of no return in my voice, or could feel the dedication of the gun placed to his head, he dropped his rifle quickly, raising his hands into the air and holding very still.

'I want an apology,' I began, something inside me taking over. Scarily, I knew that given enough time with him, I could in fact shoot the pathetic weasel. My legs shook with that knowledge, frightened of the person I had the potential to become. Maybe it was true, you could only push someone so far before they finally began to push back, regardless of the consequences. Is this what had happened with Cane? His life had pushed and pushed at him until he finally snapped? Williams stammered, his hands still lifted into the air. 'I want an APOLOGY!' I screamed, pushing the gun further into his temple.

'You're just like the rest of them,' he argued back, yelling at me. 'Go on, pull the trigger, your father-in-law will be so proud. Given, an employee will never match his murder of the Rodriguez's, but its close enough.' His words stalled me slightly and a flash of Cane making demands of truth to Bain, echoed in my head once again. My mind seemed to know something I hadn't caught onto yet.

'What are you talking about?' I snarled, shoving his head with the gun. He laughed, his hands still high in the air.

'Like you don't know,' he barked, his shoulders tight with hate. I searched my mind, desperately thinking about what he could be meaning. 'What are you talking about?' I pushed again, releasing the safety. He stammered at the sound of the gun in his ear.

'Bain killing the Rodriguez's parents. You're all murderers!' he yelled with despise, 'like you didn't know,' he spat on the ground by my feet again in disgust. 'You deserve everything you get; your family is scum.' He was talking still, but I wasn't listening. What was he saying? Obviously, it was a lie, a pathetic and desperate lie.

'That's a lie.' I screamed defensively, shoving the gun harder against his head so that his upper body was tilting. 'THAT'S A LIE!' I bellowed. But somewhere, deep inside me, I knew there was every chance that it might be true. And that was petrifying.

'EVA!' A voice came from behind me, snapping me back into reality. It was strong and gentle and familiar and pulled me back to the ground, away from my spiraling descent. What was I doing? Cane was walking up slowly towards me, his face heavy with concern and worry. I could see Elias and Andreas in the background, watching me with wide eyes and still bodies. 'What are you doing?' Cane whispered again, looking at my bloody wounds and my pale, white face. He shook his head at me, slowly. 'You don't want to become this person,' he begged, his hands raised slightly towards me, like he was trying not to spook a frightened horse. I shook my head, struggling to concentrate on anything.

'Is it true?' I asked desperately, tears forming in my eyes. My physical pain had vanished, consumed with dread that the man I had known as family all my life had taken away the parents of the man I had fallen in love with. It was too much to process. It couldn't be true. Yet I could still see the face of Bain as Cane had told him, the day of the conference feed, that he had to finally announce to the world the truth. His eyes had flashed with fear and knowing. A tear fell from my eye and ran down my numb face. In my heart I already knew the answer.

'Es cierto,' Cane replied, quietly. 'It's true, but Eva, put the gun down, please.' I was not even aware I was still holding the gun. My mind reeled, and my throat constricted as I released the cold metal weapon, it dropping to the grass with a thud. Williams turned as if ready to continue his attack, but was met with my tears. He hadn't expected them, and he stopped, his mouth closing into silence.

'I didn't know,' I whispered to no one, my heart breaking further than I thought possible. Williams must have seen the truth in my eyes and he began to back away in silence, knowing he had lost. I could see the brothers take hold of him aggressively, but everything was muffled and quiet. I slowly looked up with blurred and stinging eyes to find Cane's longing and deep stare. 'Why didn't you tell me? I didn't know.' A sob escaped my lips as shame and guilt threatened to devour me. I could remember all the times

I had accused Cane of not being able to let go of a *petty* family feud. *Petty*! He stayed still and silent, shaking his head slowly, but watching me like I was on a cliff edge. I pulled my eyes away from his quickly, unable to bare being watched as my mind battled to make sense of everything. I felt like I was falling, literally falling, my nails scraping at crumbling rock as I slid down into a dark, black chasm. I dared not look back up at Cane or his brothers, knowing now what I did. All this time I had accused Cane of being this murdering, heartless and cold person, devoid of emotion, having come to the conclusion that he had *had* to become that way. It turned out now, that I was part of the family that *made* him become so detached and alone from such an early age. It was my family that orphaned them all and left them to become cold, hard orphans. I turned silently and began to walk to the house, no one trying to stop me. The gardens merged into nothingness and the house melted into grays and browns. Did I have anything left in my life that was not built upon a spoiled and disgusting lie? The foundations of me were ruined and I had no idea where that left me, no idea how to live anymore. The Eva now, the Eva that knew too much, could never go back. I was aware of my bed beneath me and tears falling from my eyes, but then they were all gone, and it was dark and quiet.

CHAPTER THIRTY-SIX.
There is talk.

A couple of days passed again, and I stayed to myself. Cane had let me cope in my own way, sending Dr Miele to me daily as a way of checking in. The old man could deal with my physical pains, but not the ones inside. He had sat on my bed with me the next day and told me the story of the night Cane's parents had died. He patted my hands with the comfort that only someone who had seen it all could offer. He sighed in recollection, bringing himself back to a time when sad things were all that existed in the Rodriguez family.

'It was an accident, I am sure,' he began with his thick, Spanish accent, 'and I am sure Bain has suffered his own devils for it over the years.' I cast my eyes upward from my bowed head, almost afraid to look at him. I was ashamed. Ashamed of my family, ashamed of their actions, ashamed of all the self-righteous things I'd said, which now turned out to be nothing but hypocritical. Dr Mieles thumb gently stroked my hand in comfort, as if he knew exactly what I was thinking and feeling. 'Mr and Mrs Rodriguez were kind people, family people, rest their souls, but business was big part of their lives. They were in process of a hostile bidding war with Bain, over a pharmaceutical company, that Mr Bain already owned. They were going to buy it, I think whether Mr Bain was selling or not. There had been lot of controversy over it in media. The day Mr and Mrs Rodriguez were visiting one of pharmaceutical factories, there was massive explosion at the wing they were in. Them, plus two other workers, died.' I sniffed quietly, as Dr Miele paused to collect his thoughts and emotions. A *factory explosion* had killed Cane's parents? Why had I never heard anything of this? I know the fact that I had never been told anything about it all, that it was nowhere in any of Cane's files, was almost confirmation enough. Had Mr Bain caused the explosion on purpose? As if reading my thoughts, Dr Miele continued with an answer. 'There were never murder charges raised, but evidence proved on-site negligence. Cost cutting measures, directed by Bain, had led poor safety standards for factory of that type,' he sighed. 'You could argue coincidence, bad timing, or that explosion was set to conveniently kill Bain's biggest rivals, but sadly, you know this world, Miss Mack, evidence be changed, lost or altered at good price.' He rubbed his old chin, thoughtfully. 'God will deal with real truth in end.' He let the words linger. Could the Mr Bain I know, purposely have murdered four people? The fact that I honestly couldn't answer the question with any degree of surety, scared me. 'I remember the weeks that followed their deaths,' he continued, lost in his memories, 'the reading of will, Cane being told he was in charge, watching him all too quickly turn to stone on outside, yet hearing him cry himself to sleep in nights. The media dragged their deaths through headlines for months, pictures of them everywhere. It was awful period, with no escaping. After a time though and some very hard learning curves, I watch Cane build a wall round the once young, caring, boy he was. His guard became that of what is now, hard and polished.' I wiped a tear from my cheek. I couldn't imagine losing my parents in such a way, let alone being left alone with the crushing weight and legacy of a multi- billion-pound, world-wide, business to manage and run.

'Why did Cane never out Mr Bain then, prove he was guilty and send him to prison, get justice?' I asked, trying to understand it all. 'Why have I never heard about any of this? Why is it not still spoken about in the press?' Dr Miele stood up off the bed, straightening his crumpled trousers and sighing deeply.

'I remember day vividly, when it all seemed to peak. Elias and Andreas were yelling for action, threatening revenge, planning Bain's downfall. There were guns and anger flying round room, tempers at breaking point. It felt like there was nothing else in world that mattered anymore, except Bain's sins upon Rodriguez family.' He stopped speaking and a long pause settled over him. I looked at him, questioningly. 'Cane sat quiet through it all. He was in the office where his dad had done so many times before him, and at peak of anger, he had simply and firmly said, "They are gone, and they will rest. That is final." The room had gone silent and even if brothers disagreed, they never mentioned it. From that day on, Cane demanded that level of obedience and respect. If he carried mantle, including making the hard decisions, then when those decision were finally made by him, they would be honoured, media and all. And they have been since.'

'Why do you think he's never taken revenge on Mr Bain, if he was so sure it was not an accident, even after all these years?' I asked, with bloodshot eyes. 'Why not just expose him or kill him?' Dr Miele paused.

'Love and respect for parents' memories,' he said, quietly. 'Emotions I have not seen him use so openly again until he met you.' My eyes flashed to his, widening. They were met with a small, all-knowing smile. He nodded slowly. 'On your first night here, I watch him lift you into your bed from where you had fallen sleep crying at window. He had such look of intrigue on his face, but a glimpse of something else too, something I not seen in him for years. On second night, when you fallen asleep by the lake, I saw him lay the blanket his mother had given to him, over you.' My eyes dashed to that same blanket, still sitting by the window on a chair. 'He watched you sleep for while, his face different. His guard came down for split-second and I saw boy once again, curious and unsure, but possibly willing to take chance, with no guarantees. The way he watch you, those first couple nights, is still the way he look at you now, when you not see. But I see it when others do not.' He paused with a small nod. 'I remember the look from when he was carefree, happy child.' He smiled slightly and then with no more words, crossed the room and quietly left. My brain turned with thoughts of murders, schemes, and lost innocence. I stood up and walked to the window seat, picking the blanket up into my arms. I held it closely to me for comfort, knowing now where it had come from. How did I deal with any of this knowledge? Every time I learned something new, my life solidified in complexities and the web of tangled thoughts and feelings, just continued to thicken and blur. I sighed deeply, inhaling the smell of the blanket. I sat recalling Dr Miele's words. The only silver lining in the whole account was, that there was no certainty that Bain had deliberately murdered Cane's parents. They still could have just been in the wrong place at the wrong time. How easy it was to let anger, hurt and pride rule you. I remembered holding the gun to Williams' head, thinking to myself, that I could pull the trigger. Only a few weeks of hell had led me to there. Years of torment and pain existed between these two families, what actions had that led to? They had been turned into bitter and twisted people, living with consequences they may have wished had never even happened. That was a feeling I knew well. It saddened me to my soul. What a mess it had all become, and what more of a mess I had made it into.

With a heavy heart, I stuck to my arrangement with Maria, to complete her daughter's prom dress. I'd done a lot of work on it in my room, while avoiding human contact over the last week or so, and it was now ready for being fitted to a body. Maria had arrived, chatty and forthcoming, naturally oblivious to my inner turmoil. She stood on a stool as directed, with her arms stretched outwards as I measured her.

'There is talk,' she began quietly and timidly, her arms wobbling in the air around her. Her sudden change of tone made me look up from my tape measure, to see her lowered brows and creased eyes. She glanced at me quickly, then lifted her head again, away from my sight. I ran the tape along her limbs, making notes as I did. After a few seconds of silence, she continued. 'People say that you be leaving soon?' She kept her eyes heavenward and I was thankful to not have to answer to them. Instead, with a pencil between my teeth, I nodded casually. Memories of Cane's office and his ridiculous plan stabbing back into my heart. I bit down on the wood between my teeth for support. 'It is true, then?' she asked, lifting her arms away from her waist, as I ran my tape around it.

'Yes, I think that is true,' I replied, jotting down another measurement. 'I will have Antonella's dress ready in time though, don't worry. As soon as I am done, I'll have it delivered to you, maybe in a couple of days.' I smiled at her reassuringly.

'Estes feliz de irte?' she asked hesitantly, as if knowing she was stepping on tender and fragile ground. *Was I happy to be leaving?* It was a good question. I dropped the tape measure with a sigh, signaling that she could stand down now. She did, with a loud thud, and the furniture around us rattled slightly. I asked myself her question again. Was I happy to be leaving?

'I guess so.' I replied, turning my attention to the pieces of fabric lying on the floor, all pinned together in random shapes. I picked up some chalk and began to mark out the new measurements. 'I will get to see my family and friends again.' I added, as optimistically as possible. Or at least I'll see the friends I have left, I thought sadly to myself, Tammy's face crossing my mind.

'It is good to see family,' she agreed, with a big smile and fidgety hands. I nodded back at her trying not to think of the whole drama that was ahead of me with Cane's business plan and a stupid wedding to someone I was no longer in love with. 'Yet, you are...triste?' Maria added, looking across at me and my focused face. Her comment caught me by surprise and I dropped my chalk. *Sad?* She walked over to me and ran her hands over the satin material lying cut on the bed. 'My friend works Mr Rodriguez room,' she said quietly in her broken English, keeping her eyes on what her hands were doing and not me. 'She say that Mr Rodriguez seem sad too. That he was sad before you, then very happy and now sad again.' I swallowed the dry lump in my throat, determined to not cry at her words. If Cane was so sad then why was he making me marry someone else, why was he still carrying on with this crazy plan? A swell of frustration coursed through me.

'Well, Maria,' I said, a little more standoffish then I meant, 'Mr Rodriguez is a complex man, who seems determined to keep everything complex. If he wants to stay, triste, then by all means, he can stay triste. Without me here.' I grabbed the chalk off the floor with a loud exhale and began to mark up the material again. Maria had gone silent and I felt a little bad for taking my aggravation out on her. She approached my side and I felt her warm hand lay gently on my hunched over shoulder. I stopped drawing and turn to look at her. Her eyes were sympathetic.

'The girls talk say, Mr Rodriguez keep a expediente...' she struggled to find her words, scrunching her eyes in concentration, 'expediente, erm, a *file*, a file on you in his room, on he escritorio...his desk.' Her voice was quiet and kind as she continued. 'They say he look at your picture every night.' She smiled at me now, but all too late. Her hand tapped my shoulder with a final, quick squeeze. 'They say it...romántico.' She glanced at her watch and began to gather her things together. I sat still with my breath, just trying to function. Romantic? Cane and I? The staff thought this was a romance story? I wanted to laugh out loud. My impending marriage plans were obviously not public knowledge yet, or they would be using different words, I was sure. Romances had happy endings. Cane and I would definitely not be having one of those. I zoned back in to hear Maria explain she had to get to work and that if she was needed again, to just let her know. She was thanking me and opening the door to go. She paused suddenly though, with one foot in and the other out of the room, seemingly undecided about whether to say anything else or to just leave. Her sentimental side must have won though, and she turned back to me, clearing her throat.

'Nobody *want* to be sad,' she said, in a timid voice, 'but sometime people think they not deserve happiness. But everyone deserve happiness.' She smiled quickly and with one last small nod, she disappeared out the door. I exhaled so loudly it felt like a scream. I threw the chalk across the room with irritation, watching it hit off the smooth cream wall and crumble into small chunks on the carpet. I felt exactly the same as it, broken and falling to pieces.

CHAPTER THIRTY-SEVEN
Unscathed?

It was evening and he sat alone in his freshly decorated bedroom. The smell of new furniture lingered in the silent air and reminded him of his moment of weakness. His finger was tapping repeatedly on the cover of the file that he had delivered to him the night Eva had arrived into his house. It was a report on her; everything about her life, about her family, her hobbies, her education, her habits, her loved ones... As his finger rose and fell on the collection of pages, so did his breathing, each inhale and exhale bringing new thoughts and painful memories. It had been so long since he had let himself think about the circumstances of his parents death that he had forgotten the amount of anger and pain it boiled up within him. Now though, after recent events, that frustration and resentment was simmering dangerously near the surface and it seemed like only the thought of Eva was keeping it all at bay. He had told Dr Miele to attend to Eva and that when he did so, that he should account the painful and dreaded past to her. He knew that she would be wanting to know what had happened, that she would be seeking the truth, and quite frankly, she deserved the truth, deserved to know what happened the day his parents were killed. He knew that maybe he should have been the one to tell her, but he also knew the restraints of his own heart. Dr Miele had silently nodded his head in agreement, but with heavy and reluctant eyes. He couldn't blame the old man for being displeased with the task. He had known his parents for years and served diligently by their sides. His loss on that awful day had been great also. A knock at the door drew him from himself and back into the room.

'Sí?' he answered, stopping his tapping and straightening in his seat. The door opened, and Scott's head appeared through the frame.

'Just checking in with you, Mr Rodriguez,' Scott said casually, both of them knowing that it was far from just casual. Cane nodded coolly, shrugging.

'I'll survive, Scott,' he answered with a small smile. 'Do you know how Eva is doing?' Scott stepped into his room and closed the door.

'Doc says the bullet wounds will heal fine in a few days...he said that her body's seen worse.' Scott swallowed as he finished his sentence, knowing fine well how Cane felt about the abuse Eva had endured since arriving here. If nothing, Cane was a gentleman at heart, especially with women, and seeing Eva go through more than any innocent person should, tortured him. Scott had never known Cane's parents, but the old doctor had once told him that Cane's mother had

always taught her sons the importance of respect and value of women. That message may have got lost on Andreas and Elias over the years, but Cane had never been anything but chivalrous and courtly with the opposite sex. Scott knew that seeing the woman he had grown affection for, whether Cane would admit to that or not, be hurt on his watch, was an unforgiveable sin...and one he would hold himself accountable, forever.

'Bueno,' Cane replied, flatly.

'She's pretty resilient, Sir, I'm sure if anyone can recover unscathed, she will.' To this Cane let out a small, sad laugh, rubbing his forehead slowly.

'Unscathed?' he repeated, 'Scott, you didn't see her earlier...' he trailed off as the memory that was now embedded in his mind came back into focus; Eva holding a hand gun pressed into a man's temple. He would bet that even in her wildest dreams, she would have never imagined herself capable of doing such things. Now, after only weeks in his life, she had come face to face with killing someone. She'd had to make a decision on whether to take a life or not. The change was too dramatic, too extreme and he felt nothing but guilt for it all. He had put her here. He swallowed again, lifting his eyes to Scott's. 'It's pretty safe to say I've ruined her, Scott.' His trusted second, stood motionless at the door for a few seconds longer, before deciding to talk. He was never a big talker, something Cane liked about him, so the times he chose to speak of his own accord, Cane generally listened, knowing something worthwhile was about to come out.

'That's funny, Sir,' he began, clearing his throat, 'because according to Eva, she's never felt so strong before.' To this Cane looked back at his friend with quizzical eyes.

'What?' he asked, his fists tensing slightly in anticipation.

'She said that to me, a while ago, Sir,' Scott continued, shifting his weight. 'And I don't think she meant just physically.' Cane sat still, digesting the words. 'Yes, this whole thing has been a complete nightmare for her, given, but if anyone will take a positive from a situation, Cane, I think we both know it would be Eva. She's experienced more in these past few weeks then she probably has in her whole life so far. She's felt more ups and downs and had to deal with more trials than she ever knew could exist, yet she's come out standing and still fighting.' He put his hand back on the door handle ready to leave. 'I think she knows she's a stronger person now, despite it all. So, I wouldn't say you ruined her, Cane...' he cleared his throat, 'changed her definitely, but not ruined. And change is not always a bad thing.' Without leaving any space for further discussion, Scott nodded to his boss and backed out of the room, closing the door into silence again. Cane sat bone still, Scott's words numbing his self-loathing and guilt, softening their pain. There was no excuse for what Eva had been through, he reminded

himself sternly, but maybe he should give her more credit. Scott was right, she was not a fragile glass doll that was broken, she was a strong and resilient woman, some of the qualities Cane admired and adored in her most. His mind cast back to how cold he had been to her in his office, telling her the deal. She had looked so hurt and that alone had almost broken him. It had taken every fiber of his strength to keep his harsh and detached façade up. He had told himself that it was for the best, the best for her. The less she liked him, let alone loved him, the better. He was a walking disaster and she needed to be with people who could give her happiness. Yet, now alone and hearing Scott's words, maybe he had been wrong? Maybe he should have trusted her, given her the credit she was due, let her choose her own fate. She was woman enough to decide if she could weather a life with him in it. How had he not seen that? He stood up, and cleared his dry, scratchy throat. Well it was too late now, the deal had been struck and he couldn't change anything about that, even if he regretted it. No, he reminded himself, it had been the best thing to do in the long run. He opened her file and looked down at her unassuming face, feeling all the want and frustration in the world come down upon his shoulders. Well, he thought to himself with a fleeting moment of joy, there was actually one thing he could change, one thing he could do for Eva to try and compensate. He could keep a promise.

CHAPTER THIRTY-EIGHT.
Why do I feel nervous about that smile?

The wedding dress fitters had arrived sooner than I thought possible and happily fussed over me, whilst I smiled in the right places and nodding when expected. I guessed for them, a wedding dress was a cause for celebration. For me, not so much. At the end of the painfully forced session I had chosen a simple gown, white and elegant. Fancy and showy didn't seem quite right. With the dress now chosen, the whole thing was beginning to feel a bit more real, almost like an actual genuine wedding was going to happen, and it was coming at me in a speedy blur. Last minute invites had been extended and replies received. Scott had delivered papers to sign that were bound in official looking covers and I had done as commanded, with no questions asked, placing my forced and reluctant signature on the dotted line next to that of Edward's. The sight of his handwriting made me smile with memory, then cry with guilt.

It was an afternoon and I lay on the grassy bank next to the water outside the house. I found the pains of thought could easily be controlled by quite simply, just not thinking. Zeus lay by me, panting in the warm afternoon sun and I ran my hands over his shiny coat. He was still good company, no questions, no challenges, no constantly having to second guess myself. I stretched my legs out, feeling the healing skin pull on my calf. The rubber bullets had fairly left their marks on my body, but not as bad of a mark that a bullet close range to the temple would have left in Williams. I shuddered in shame as the emotions I had felt that day resurfaced. I swallowed and forced the thoughts away again, back to the vault with everything else. I was sure one day the storage unit would fill up and it would all come pouring out into a massive breakdown and subsequent years of therapy, but for now, they were better lurking there, than disturbing the present.

'Hi, Eva,' a familiar voice called out, from across the water. I looked up to see Gideon, hands full of gardening equipment and dirt smeared over his clothes and face. I smiled, thankful to be pulled from my thoughts to a pleasant distraction. I waved at him with enthusiasm.

'Hi, Gideon,' I replied loudly as he propped his stuff against a tree and jogged around the shimmering water to meet me. He brushed off his hands on his bottoms and sat down next to me on the grass, a warm and kind beaming grin on his face.

'It feels like forever since I last saw you,' he began, with a thoughtful shoulder nudge. I nodded, still smiling at him. I had been locked in my room for the last who-knew-how-long, avoiding people and life. So, yes, it had been a while.

'It does, doesn't it?' I agreed, tucking my knees up under my hands. 'How are you? How have you been?'

'Busy,' he laughed, dusting his face off on his dirty T-Shirt. 'But in a good way. I love this time of year, there's so much to do on the land, you know?' I loved how excited and passionate Gideon got over his work, it was infectious.

'No, I have no idea I'm afraid, but I'll take your word for it.' He laughed at my words, then glanced out to the water.

'So, the talk is that you are leaving soon?' he began, still looking away from me. 'Is it true?' He picked up a twig and snapped it into small pieces, awaiting my reply. I sighed, casting my eyes after his.

'Yeah, I think it might be pretty soon.' I confirmed. He threw the pieces of stick into the pond.

'That's a shame for us, but I guess its good news for you, right?' He glanced at me sideways, keeping his blonde hair covering most of his eyes.

'I guess so,' I agreed, with guarded emotions. 'I'll miss our little adventures though.' I said with a smile, bumping into him gently. He laughed.

'Well, at least Mr Rodriguez won't have to worry about our time together anymore. Last time I saw him, he made a comment about how much of it we seem to spend together.' Gideon had my attention now.

'Oh, really?' I asked. 'Why, what did he say?' Gideon stood up and began to brush the grass from his trousers.

'Just that normally he'd have been suspicious of us by now, but that he trusted you.' He looked over towards the sun. 'Or something like that. It was a bit weird to be honest. In fact, it seems like all my encounters with him, when they are about you, are a bit weird.' He gave me a quick, knowing, smile. 'It's getting late, Eva, I need to get going.' I nodded in understanding, starting to stand. 'No, you stay there, I'll see you around though still, yeah?' I lifted my shoulders.

'I don't think I'm going anywhere in the next day or so, so yeah, I'll see you Gideon.' He nodded, satisfied with the answer. He threw me a wink as he jogged off back to where he'd stowed his work tools. I waved him off as he stomped away to the back of the house, leaving me and the dog alone again. His words echoed, as did everything Cane said or did. He *trusted* me? I let out a small bark of sarcastic humour. It didn't feel like that. Zeus's ears pricked, and he lifted his head quickly, in the direction of the house. I followed his attention to a black shirt, walking my way. It was Scott. He was a strange man, I concluded, as he made his way towards me. He was almost mechanically obedient to Cane, more so than any other worker. But he had a human, compassionate side, which seeped through the metal armour every now and then. He had never been friendly or warm, but he had never been cold and vicious, and over the last couple months, that was a big difference.

'Eva,' he began, greeting me and bending down to clap Zeus and his wagging tail.

'Hi, Scott,' I replied, already knowing that only approached me if he had something to say or do involving Cane. His eyes clocked the bullet wound on my calf and his lips tightened slightly. Anger, pity, who knew, and what difference did it make anyway?

'I heard about what happened,' he said, nodding to my leg. 'Did the doctor see to those?' I nodded with a slight shrug, playing it cool.

'Yeah. I've had worse, though.' Which was true of course. His eyes lingered on it for a few more seconds, then returned to business.

'Mr Rodriguez wants to see you.' He nodded towards Cane's open balcony window behind him. I could see the curtains gently blowing in the breeze. It had been a few days since I'd seen him now, since I'd learnt how his parents died. And those days had felt like an eternity. If I was being honest, I missed him. I missed him so much that I could physically feel his loss. I pulled my eyes away from his balcony.

'Do you know what it's about?' I asked, squinting my gaze back at Scott through the afternoon sun. He shook his head, rubbing Zeus's belly.

'I don't ask questions.' I considered him for a moment.

'Why is that?' I challenged, with an inquisitive gaze. 'Why don't you question him?' I expected a quick stern, 'mind your own business', but instead he cast his eyes towards Cane's balcony and let out a low sigh.

'He saved my marriage.' He nodded, patting Zeus's belly in conclusion. 'I owe him more than just following orders.' With a very fleeting glance at me, he stood up, brushing his knees off. 'You ok to head up there now?' I nodded quickly, not sure who was more taken back by the moment of honesty. 'Ok,' he finalized, quickly exiting as his big frame cast a shadow on the grass where I sat. I watched him go, repeating what he had said in my head. "*He saved my marriage*". I shook my brain and ran my hand through my hair. Would there ever be a more intricate man than Cane Rodriguez? I doubted it very much. I stood up, clapping my hands for Zeus to follow. I walked up the oh-so-familiar wooden staircase to the hall with Cane's office. I'd given up expectations, or trying to guess what new fate awaited me. I had no anger or frustrations left anymore and as I walked towards the guarded office door, the reality settled on me, that more than anything now, I was just sad. Sad that things were ending this way. Sad that things had gotten so bad in our lives. Sad that I'd caused so much pain I could never take back. And sad mostly, that if I had met Cane in another time and place, he probably would have been the love of my life.

'Afternoon,' the black shirt greeted me, pressing the buzzer on the panel. It flashed green and he opened it for me. Cane, for once, sat to the right of the office, on the sofa. I quickly recognised that the last time I'd seen anyone sat in the same place, had been the first day I'd arrived here. His head dashed up to me with a deep look of concern. How much he had changed, I thought to myself, as I crossed the room to sit by him. No nerves, no fears, none of the emotions I had had that first day, they were all gone. He watched me quietly until I rested next to him, eventually meeting his eyes. Almost instantly, as his pupils set on me, every emotion I'd been restraining from the day on the shooting range resurfaced. I could feel my eyes begin to fill and I quickly blinked to try and stop it. Did I apologise? Did I ask the questions I desperately wanted answers for? Did I pretend none of it happened?

'It is what it is, Eva,' he began quietly, keeping his gaze on me. 'No se puede cambiar el pasado…the past can't be changed.' He nodded gently, as if asking for my understanding.

'But the future can, right?' I whispered back, referring to our situation. He exhaled, looking away from me. I didn't move my eyes from his dazzling face, which for once, was showing some form of emotion. It was silent for a bit, not awkwardly, but not contently. I knew that I still needed to say it, at least once to him, and I knew that I'd probably never have another chance. I swallowed, leaning forward to him slightly. 'It was wrong of me,' I began quietly, but surely. 'To judge you and your past when I didn't know anything about it.' He looked up at me quickly, surprised and intent. 'I took everything I read in a file to be gospel and I held you against that, my entire life.' I swallowed. 'It was wrong, *I* was wrong.' *I was wrong*, I knew it now and I needed him to know that I knew it. It needed to be said out loud, put into the atmosphere, ever to remain uttered. 'I'm so sorry, Cane.' I exhaled, still locked in his inquisitive gaze and still fighting tears. Slowly his hand took my face, gently placing his thumb on my lips. It felt warm and safe and sent peace through my whole body. I could feel his pulse in his hand as it stroked my skin slowly, my head leaning into his hold. His eyes softened as he looked at me, then in an almost whisper, he replied.

'We were both wrong, Eva. I can see that now too.'

'A right pair, huh?' I whispered with a small smile. He exhaled loudly and with a final nod, took his hand back. My cheek instantly felt cold, craving the heat it had had seconds before.

'Let's not talk of it again, ok? It is in the past, Eva.' He sat back casually and crossed his legs. His light suit trousers strained against his muscles and I remembered all too well what it felt like to have those legs around me. I dragged my eyes from his thighs and my mind from the gutter, to find he had a smile on his face, an almost mischievous looking smile. I eyeballed him suspiciously. 'Why do I feel nervous about that smile?' He laughed at my words and drew a grin from me. To this, his own smile increased again, and I glimpsed slight dimples beginning to dent his golden face. He put his hands up innocently.

'I have no idea what you are talking about,' he said, almost cheerily. I narrowed my eyes at him, waiting for the next part. He surrendered quickly, laughing. 'OK, OK, fine,' he relented. 'You're leaving in an hour to go see your parents.' He said the words quickly, almost too quickly for me to process.

'What?' I snapped loudly.

'Tus padres. Your parents,' Cane repeated, without the smile or laughter. 'You're meeting your parents this afternoon.' I must have looked confused, as Cane felt the need to further explain. 'We made a deal in Spain. You kept your end, it's my turn. Your parents are on their way to a secret location, where you'll meet them.' I think I'd understood what he'd meant the second he'd said it, but the excitement of the idea was stopping me process the information logically.

'REALLY?' I yelled.

'Verdad,' he repeated. I jumped up. There were a million emotions buzzing around my body all at once: excitement, anticipation, relief, panic, joy, worry... I stood trying to process it all quickly. A flash of my parents' faces came to me and the happiness it brought won the battle inside, sending me running to the door. My sheer excitement blocked out the sound of Cane's voice calling after me and it wasn't until he whistled loudly, as I was paces from the door, that I heard it and stopped. I realised instantly I'd got carried away and very openly displayed everything. Once upon a time, I'd have instantly regretted letting Cane see my reactions, but I'd learnt that keeping anything about my thoughts or feelings from him was pointless.

'Eva,' he was saying, with a serious tone. I turned and slowly walked back to him, more professionally and more composed. I sat perched on the sofa like I was at an interview, poised and proper. I caught a flash of a smile from his face, but it was quickly replaced with a more business tone.

'Yes,' I said calmly, letting him know I was focused and ready for him to speak. The rules. In my flurry of surprise and joy, I'd forgotten about the rules. There always had to be rules.

'Reglas,' he repeated, echoing my thoughts. 'I said you were leaving in an hour, but you won't see your parents until later tonight. I've had a look-alike stationed at a building I own for a few days now, guarded and watched as if she was you. You'll be taking her place in a few hours, when we arrive through a secret tunnel. That way, if we are followed, they will take that building to be your holding place. No one knows of the tunnel and, so they will assume you have been kept there. After you leave to go play happy families, I'll stay for a while and then will be going to deal with business matters out of the city. Eva,' he inclined his head at me to stress the importance of his next line. 'I've told your parents a rescue mission of any kind this close to the final deadline dates would be deemed needlessly risky, keeping in mind your tracker and the danger *you* are still in.' To this I scanned his face. Everyone else thought I was in danger still, the Bains, my family, all of them. It was a horrible lie, considering that with Cane I now couldn't have felt any safer. He cleared his throat and continued. 'I needed assurance that you wouldn't be taken and to get that, I had to warn some pretty serious threats.' I eyed him with suspicion. What a weird position we were in. 'I need your word that you will not run. I don't want to be made to take drastic measures with you, Eva, but the stakes are high right now. Do you understand?' I swallowed, revisiting my thoughts from a second ago about how safe I felt with Cane. Could he still, for business, hurt someone I loved? Did that Cane still exist? He held his dark eyes strongly, as I looked into them for answers. As deep as they were, they gave nothing away. My heart told me no, he would never hurt me now, he was bluffing.

'I understand,' I said plainly. There was no point being mad, hurt or insulted, we were where we were. 'I won't run.' He nodded as if my word satisfied him.

'Confió en ti,' he continued, 'but I trust no one else.' Just as he said it, the door opened, and Scott entered, holding what looked like a waistcoat. My eyes caught the small cylinders attached to its front. I'd seen enough movies to know what a biological weapon looked like, strapped to a suicide vest. My eyes must have been popping from my head as Scott walked towards us with it, holding it out to Cane.

'WHAT THE HELL?' I yelled, catching a quick smile in Scott's eyes as he turned and left the office. I was on my feet now, backing away from the waistcoat. 'I just told you I wouldn't run!' Similarly, to Scott, Cane was smiling too.

'Bien,' he said, turning the item around. 'Good, it's convincing then'. He laughed to himself as I relaxed and stopped backing away.

'That's not funny,' I said, slightly angrily. Cane stopped laughing at hearing my tone. I wasn't sure what he had expected I'd do when faced with being strapped to a bomb. He nodded.

'I'm sorry, you're right, that wasn't funny.' But even as he said it, another small smile danced across his face and a dimple appeared for a quick second. He caught my folded arms and somewhat unimpressed look and quickly resumed his business mode. 'As I said, I trust your word Eva, I don't trust anyone else. Your parents have been told that I have the trigger to activate a chemical bomb on your clothing, if at any point a rescue mission is attempted.' I sat back down, taking hold of the cylinders gently.

'That is sick and wrong,' I muttered, looking at him sternly. A dimple appeared again, but was gone just as fast. 'And it makes no sense.' I continued, choosing to ignore his attempt of hiding his enjoyment. 'If you blow me up, the whole deal falls apart.'

'You won't be blown up,' he replied, tapping the glass tube. 'These are chemicals which if mixed, will burn and eat away at your skin like acid. It would cause such agony and disfiguration that you'd never look the same again, nor be able to live a normal life again.' I quickly pulled my hand away from the purple and clear liquids, aghast.

'Who makes this kind of weapon?' I asked, in disbelief and disgust. Cane sighed standing up.

'Too many people I am afraid.' He motioned for me to come and try it on. I froze. He actually wanted me to wear it?

'What if it goes faulty or leaks?' I was talking pretty loudly, shaking my head at the waistcoat now being held open for me.

'Eva,' he said, trying to talk to me.

'I'm pretty clumsy, Cane, what if I fall and smash them?'

'EVA!' came Cane's voice, louder than mine. I flashed my eyes up to his. 'Do you honestly think I'd put you in a real chemical bomb?' My eyes danced to the cylinders again with wary suspicion.

'No?' I replied with question. To this, he dropped his arms and stood looking at me like I'd just slapped him in the face.

'No!' he repeated, very firmly. 'I wouldn't!' He shook his head and then the coat. 'It's a fake, por el amor de Dios!' He rolled his eyes at me, muttering under his breath, 'for goodness sake'.' I continued to eye it and then him, which just seemed to add injury to the insult.

'Well what do you expect?' I asked, quite genuinely, finally standing and holding my arms out for the coat to go on. But only after I'd seen Cane shake it around so close to his own body. 'When it comes to business, you are single minded to the point of scary sometimes.' He slid the waistcoat onto my shoulders, smoothed it, then turned me to face him.

'Well that was the old me,' he uttered, zipping me up. 'This,' he continued, tapping the two cylinders, 'is water and food dye, so the worst that will happen if you fall over is, you'll ruin your clothes.'

'I'll ruin *your* clothes,' I added, smugly. 'You bought them, remember?' He raised his eyebrows at me and shook his head, a small smile dancing around the corner of his lips.

'Smart ass.' he muttered, stepping back to look at me. I dragged my gaze down to myself. I looked like a suicide bomber. I rolled my eyes. If I'd have made a list of things I thought I would NEVER do in my life time, this would still have not made the cut. I shook my head and exhaled loudly.

'You are crazy, and this is ridiculous.' I stated, far from impressed.

'Maybe so, Eva,' he replied, 'but your parents won't risk you being harmed and you won't risk them being harmed. It's a good system.' I didn't reply. Business wise, it was sound. Normal wise, it was insane and sick. 'Right, you can take it off now,' he instructed, pulling on its side. 'You have half an hour until we leave, go get ready.' I gave the waistcoat back happily and made my way to the door. 'Eva,' he called out after me, and I turned around to find Cane standing with his head now lowered towards the ground. His smile had vanished, and his face turned serious. He spoke quietly, completely differently from the conversational tones we'd just exchanged. 'You know I'd never hurt you, right?' I nodded slowly. I guess I did know that. 'Letting you see your parents today is a massive risk for me, yes?' I thought about it quickly and nodded in agreement. 'Please,' he continued, 'don't make me regret it.' I watched him keep his eyes to the ground, probably to hide what they were showing. I nodded one last time and then left the room.

CHAPTER THIRTY-NINE.
What a cliché.

The car journey was long. It was either my excitement or my panic or my nerves or my mind pacing ahead at a hundred miles an hour, but it seemed like we were on an endless road. Countryside after countryside passed, until finally the world went black and we entered a tunnel. I'd played the scene ahead of me out a thousand times in the last few weeks. Would they be mad at me? Angry? Disappointed? Distraught with worry that wasn't even merited? Was I ready to hear the full extent of the mess I'd made? The car stopped, and Cane got out of the front passenger's seat. He had left me alone to the back, knowing I needed time with my thoughts. Instead, Scott had kept me silent company, sitting opposite me with his eyes ever watching eyes trained on the windows.

'Time,' Scott announced quite calmly, tapping my leg as he got out and opened the door. We were inside what looked like a rundown warehouse. What a cliché, I thought, as I looked around at the cracked windowpanes and the dust dancing through the beams of sunlight. Cane was hanging up on a call as he walked towards us. Black shirts were everywhere. He hadn't lied when he had said that anyone who was looking for me, would assume I was being kept here, under lock and key. I remembered, originally, that this was how I had expected to be kept. I glanced at the small room at the far end of the building, which had a camp bed set up and some books on the floor. Who was this girl who had been posing as me? I hoped she was getting paid a lot because, as I looked around, I clocked the toilet bucket sitting on the floor in the corner the room. I shuddered slightly at the thought. Scott moved towards another car, opened the door and gave instructions to the driver. My focus came back to Cane, who was now putting the waistcoat on me.

'You're on your own from here,' he was saying. 'Scott will take good care of you.' I looked back over to his loyal steed, who stood by the second car, back door opened and ready.

'Scott's coming with *me*?' I asked with surprise. Cane never went anywhere without Scott and Scott never took his eyes off his boss. He nodded, doing up the zip.

'I want someone keeping an eye over you,' he smiled, encouragingly. 'You have a tendency to get into trouble, especially when I leave you alone.' I offered him a small grin back, trying to calm my weird nerves.

'Where are *you* going?' I asked, as he nodded to Scott, indicating I was ready to be taken.

'I'll be here for a while, then I'll be out of the city for a bit. I'll be back by morning though.' I bit my lip, puzzled why I suddenly felt off centered. Was it because Cane was leaving me? Was it him going far away that was creating this unsettling inside me? I shook my head, trying to get a grip, but my eyes continued to flit, sensing my anxiety.

'Eva,' Cane's voice spoke calmly over the humming of the AC fans. I found his eyes. 'It's all fine. You're going to see your parents, you did all this for your dad and he knows that, so enjoy seeing him. I know how much you can miss family.' I nodded, exhaling. He was right. He seemed to always be right. 'You know, he's a good man, your dad.' Cane added, quietly, as he checked over the cylinders one last time. His words took me by complete surprise and I tilted my head at him in question, my eyebrows raised. Cane held onto my collar for a second longer than needed, pulling me closer to him. 'He raised an amazing woman...luchadora, pero increíble.' *Feisty but amazing.* My heartbeat stopped as his eyes flashed with a blaze of warmth. Then, all too quickly, with a slight nod of his head, I was led away by my arm, waistcoat and all, to the car and an awaiting Scott. I watched Cane's face for as long as I could, until eventually it was out of sight and the car door closed behind me. The engine purred to life and we drove off. It took me a few minutes to get my wits back, sitting in the leather seats, thankful for the dimming shadows. If Cane had spoken those words to me, even a few weeks ago, I would have called it a manipulation, a maneuver to help ensure my compliance. Now though, well now it was all a bit different. Now, I *believed* him, every word he said, even from his office earlier today, where he claimed he had changed. I believed that too. Maybe that made me a fool, maybe that made me gullible, but it was what it was, and there was no point pretending otherwise now. I trusted every single thing Cane Rodriguez said to me, my doubts were gone and left in their stead was conviction. I glanced up to find Scott watching me with a strange look in his eye.

'What?' I asked, feeling a little defensive. He didn't reply, but kept his peculiar eye on me. I changed the subject. 'How long until we arrive at where ever we are going?' Scott glanced at his watch.

'A little while,' he replied, vaguely, turning his attention to the window. I nodded and returned to my thoughts, instead thinking of my family. I realised I was rubbing my rubber bullet wound scab and instantly became very aware of it.

'Scott,' I asked quickly, 'do you have a jacket I can wear? I'll leave it open. I just don't want my parents to see my arm.' He glanced at the bruised wound and nodded, taking his coat off and handing it to me. I put it on, pulling its warmth over my arms. 'Thank you,' I whispered to his simple nod. We rode in silence for the rest of the journey, him watching everything like a hawk, me trying to harness the tidal wave of emotions washing through me. It was fully dark by the time we arrived and as the car pulled off the road and the engine stopped, my heart did too. My palms were sweaty, and I still hadn't decided if I was more excited or scared about seeing my parents. The two feelings very much in competition with each other and neither had currently prevailed. Doors all opened and then slammed closed and the perimeter check was carried out. Finally, my door was opened with the all clear and I followed Scott out into the night air, to find a port-a-cabin standing in front of us. It reminded me of the old town hall from when I was a child; musty, cold and with lots of exit doors. A familiar single car was already parked to our left and a light on inside. I ran my palms on my jeans as the first set of black shirts entered the cabin. I glanced around to fields and trees. In the distance was a small town. In the sky was bright stars. But I had no idea where we were. Scott nudged me ahead and my focus left the escape of the clear night air and went to managing the three cheap rickety steps. As I entered the room, the same smell of my old town hall came back to me, where I'd taken my first ballet classes as a tiny tot, my parents watching so proudly from the sidelines. Then just like remembered, I saw them, sat at a round table at the far end of the room. I stalled my run awaiting Scott's nod, and when it came, I took off towards them, without any of the pre-concerned hesitations I'd be plaguing myself with as we drove here. I ran at them with full pace, suddenly desperate to be in their arms. They were both on their feet, with arms outstretched, before I was even halfway across the old moldy room. Tears of relief flooded from their eyes as their arms embraced me with forceful strength and encompassed me into their safe embrace. It was home and it was love, and I had missed it more than I had known. It hadn't been so long ago, that I had thought I would never see them again, but now, we stood reunited as a family unit and that harrowing and sickening thought was gone. They said my name a million times, running their hands over my cheeks and down my hair, holding my face into the light so they could see me. The waistcoat bomb had been whimpered at with fearful tears and then avoided like it would smash any second. It felt wrong not telling them that it was fake, that Cane wasn't really a monster, but I knew it would not only break the rules, but it would waste the little precious time that I had with them now. *How would they ever understand anyway*, I thought to myself, *even I don't understand why I feel what I do.* When I married Edward in this whole twisted business plan, I'd see my family all the time and then, I kidded myself, there would be time to tell them the truth about the real Cane. So, I kept quiet and enjoyed their relief, pushing my guilt back to where I'd learnt to keep it. Are you OK? Are you all right? Are you hurt? Are you fine? Are you in pain? Are you managing to hold on?... Their questions bombarded me, a million ways to check that I was fine with words, but never waiting for a response before embracing me again. I waited it out and let them vent their anxiety and relief, knowing I'd not be able to speak properly until their initial fears were settled, until they could see I was OK. When the opening questions had run their course, I gestured for us to sit down, and they did, mum wiping tears from her face.

'I'm fine,' I confirmed again, nodding confidently. 'I'm fine, honestly.' I looked at dad, no real evidence left of the thing that started all of this. The human body could heal almost anything, given enough time, something I knew all too well now.

'How are you, dad?' I examined, watching him exhale and shake his head.

'I should be dead. And you should be free.' My eyes filled up and I blinked it away. I grabbed his hand tightly and looked him very firmly in the eyes.

'No!' I stated loudly, hearing it echo around the whole room. 'No. I would do it again with no hesitation. I made a choice and it was the *right* choice.' A tear slid from his eye, despite him trying to be tough. 'My children will have a grandfather and I still have a dad. I will *never* regret that.' I squeezed his hand tighter, boring my sincerity into him. He obviously recognised my stubborn tone and gave up his argument. I smiled to lighten the tone, which seemed pointless when I followed it with, 'How's Edward?' My mum blew out a long, dramatic breath.

'Surprisingly strong,' she proclaimed. 'He had a lot of guilt at the start, to do with how you found out about...' she paused, uncomfortably, '...found out about those other girls,' I waited for the sting, it didn't come, 'but since then, he's been very sensible, and level headed.' I smiled. *That's my Edward. Sensible and level headed.*

'Have I ruined everyone's lives?' I asked bluntly, deciding it was better to just know the honest truth. Dad cleared his throat, looking at my fearful and hesitant eyes.

'Does everyone agree that your life is worth more than a business? Yes, they do. Does that make it easier to hand it all over to that disgusting retch of a man, no.' He swallowed the venom that laced his mouth as he spoke of Cane, and I swallowed my urge to defend him. I heard Scott shuffle on his feet nearby, probably stifling the urge to do the same thing. I had to stop myself from looking around at him for strength. 'No one blames you for anything though, Eva. Mr Bain and I blame ourselves for not properly ridding us of this problem, when we could have done so many times before.' My eyes widened.

'Dad!' I scolded firmly. 'We are better than that and murder was never the answer, no matter whose side you are on. *You* taught me that. Wasn't that what this whole thing started with, you looking for a peaceful future?' I shook my head at him and he relaxed his tightened jaw, nodding slowly.

'I know, Eva, but it's hard to not wish that man was dead, when we know what you've been through.' Mum began to cry again, and that wave of guilt surged through me. I smiled, a big smile.

'Do I look rough?' I began, positively. 'Do I look like I've been dragged through the wars? Do I look like a defeated person, like I'm mentally scarred or sociologically damaged?' I shook my head. 'You taught me to be tough.' My dad cracked a small smile. 'I sleep at nights,' I threw in, 'and people who have been through too much, don't sleep at nights.' My mum dried her eyes, seeming to find the words reassuring. 'Now, tell me what's going on with the family and in the normal world, I'm sick of talking about business.'

We chatted for a while about cousins, jobs, sporting scores, all normal things I had been missing out on. It was almost easy to forget that I was wearing a fake bomb and that we were surrounded by black shirts, or that my time here was going to end soon. Saying goodbye, was not something I was looking forward to. Amid a story of mum's neighbors, I noticed Scott's hand quickly go to his ear piece. His face told me instantly that something was wrong and like a ripple effect, the news spread quickly to all the other black shirts, who all, very suddenly and loudly, began to mobilise. My mum jumped, screaming slightly, as Scott's massive frame crossed the room in loud precise steps and grabbed me from my seat.

'What?' I demanded loudly, looking around from door to door. 'What's going on?'

'The holding house was just hit. They're under attack. This was a set up.' Panic flooded my body with a sickening knowledge. Cane was still at the holding house. He said he would be staying there for a while before leaving. I could hear screaming and yelling and gun fire coming through Scott's ear piece and I suddenly felt vomit rise in my throat at the sound. *CANE!*

'Did you tell anyone?' I yelled at my parents, who looked as shocked as I did. They both shook their heads, fear spreading across their faces as their eyes shot to my waistcoat bomb.

'No, no one. We would never have risked harming you. Rodriguez was very precise in his instructions. We told no one.' The way they both kept frantically looking to the bomb as if it would irrupt any second, assured me that they were being truthful. They hadn't told.

'It wasn't them.' I yelled to Scott, who was grabbing me and pulling me away. My mum was screaming after me, running across the room with my dad to the door, where I was being pulled out into the night.

'EVA!' I could hear my mum scream, her hand outstretched to me. But my concentration was on Scott. What was happening at the warehouse? Was Cane ok?

'I'm fine, mum, I'm fine. Go, go home.' Scott threw me into the car and it was screeching off before the door had even closed. I could see my parents left terrorised outside the cabin, eyes wide with fear, but despite them, my heart was with Cane. Was he alive? 'Scott, what's happening?' I shouted at him.

'The warehouse was hit. I can hear gun fire still. There was a massive explosion, a bomb I think.' He pushed his earpiece closer into his ear to keep listening. 'There's talk about a drone tracing the safe house.'

'Is he Ok?' I asked loudly, on the edge of my seat. Scott seemed as concerned as I was and when he didn't answer, my worry began to increase. 'Scott, where's Cane?' I yelled at him. 'Look at me,' I tried to pull at his shoulder. 'Where is he, Scott? Did he get out?' He turned square onto me, doubt filling his normally so cool face.

'I don't know,' he stated, 'I don't think so.' His words hit me harder than I would have ever thought possible. My air vanished, and my heart screamed. Scott climbed over into the front seats, leaving me in the back. I couldn't handle this. I wasn't strong enough. My mouth began to water, and I put my head between my knees, feeling the car swerve at high speed. I could feel my pulse in my head as my heart struggled to keep pumping. He was dead? Cane was dead? A loud sob, painfully and consuming, escaped my mouth. It couldn't end like this, it couldn't. But Scott's face showed such concern and loss, that it was hard to hope otherwise. Cane was gone! He was gone, and this was all over. *We* were over! 'Straight to safety point C.' Scott was telling the driver. *What? Where are we going?*

'Where are we going?' I began, frantically. Scott, we need to go back and help.' I shouted over to Scott, but he was ignoring me. 'Scott, we need to go to the warehouse and help them.' I was properly screaming now, off my seat and leaning over to the front to get Scott's attention. Why wasn't he listening? Why were we heading the wrong way? He quickly climbed back into the passenger seats, obviously seeing what I couldn't; that I was quickly losing control.

'It's a blood bath, Eva. My orders from Cane were to keep you safe, regardless of anything.'

'WHAT?' I screamed, struggling against him and trying to reach the driver. 'NO! NO! We need to go back and help them!' I pushed past Scott. 'Go back to the warehouse, go back, we need to find Cane, we need to go back for him.' The car swerved as I yanked wildly at the driver's arm, bellowing for him to turn around. He tried to push me off as he straightened the car and kept his course. I felt Scott's arm around my neck, pulling me away from the driver and back into the passenger area. I caught the eye of the driver as Scott manhandled me down before I caused an accident. *What was I doing?* I could see in Scotts face that I was acting like a maniac, and I knew I was out of control, but I couldn't seem to find anything to calm me. I felt like I was spiraling down a rabbit hole, clawing at snapping weeds and plummeting into blackness. I was acting like a crazy woman but all I could think and see and feel was, *Cane is dead!* Everything we had been through, everything we had experienced, and he was now dead? No, it couldn't be. I wouldn't survive it. If we could just get to the warehouse and see that he was alive, everything would be ok. I could feel my heart literally pounding against my chest and my face burning with heat, my parents' faces raced through my mind as Scott rushed me away from them in a flurry of fear. Cane's last few words to me roared through my mind as if someone was bellowing them into my ear, *'he raised an amazing woman'*. I could feel sweat start to drip down my back as I struggled against Scott, and I was vaguely aware that I was still shouting about going back, kicking to get free and desperate to get to the driver, desperate to persuade him to change his direction. Then I became aware that my vision was blurring and that Scott's hold around my neck was tight and getting tighter. I could just hear him issuing orders to maintain course, before my struggle ended and I sunk into unconsciousness. He'd knocked me out.

CHAPTER FORTY
Earth please swallow me now!

It was peaceful around me when I began to wake. I was cloudy and confused, but I could feel that everything around me was fine. My eyes began to focus on the small room I was in and my new surrounds began to form. I was in an apartment, sleek, stylish and modern. I blinked a few more times, attempting to get my bearings. Where was I? How did I get here? I lay still, trying to remember what had happened, and all too quickly, the memories came flooding back. I bolted upright instantly, desperately looking around for Scott. My noise attracted his attention and he appeared from the adjoining kitchen, where I could see other black shirts were sat. He had an odd look on his face and my heart raced with dread. Cane, the attack, the warehouse, the sound of commotion through the earpieces…it was sickeningly vivid still, and my ears rang with the shouting of men. Scott's eyes were heavy and unreadable, as he left the kitchen and quietly headed my way. Was that the look of someone preparing to give bad news? Tears pushed at my eyes, unable to bear what I was about to hear.

'You're awake I see,' he opened, coming to stand over me. I looked up at him with petrified anticipation, my hands literally trembling uncontrollably. Was Cane dead? The question practically screamed from me as I watched him swallow and exhale with weighty knowledge. I knew that for once in my whole life, my emotions were written clearly all over my face. I was petrified, and I couldn't hide it.

'He got out,' he said quietly, nodding. My whole body instantly gushed with utter relief and tears leaked from my eyes. The relief spread through me like a tidal wave and I exhaled loudly, collapsing back onto the sofa cushions. I wiped at my eyes, trying to stop their silly reaction, but it was fruitless. I had never been so thankful in my life, never been so scared and then so happy. My body was struggling to contain, let alone process, those emotions, and so the tears fell with zero control. Moments passed in silence as I settled myself, Scott stood awkwardly above me. I tried to process exactly what had happened to me, to figure out why I had handled everything so badly. Embarrassing as it was to admit, I had freaked out, plain and simple. I glanced down to find I was still wearing the bomb waistcoat.

'Can I take this off now?' I requested, tapping the cylinders. He nodded, and I began to unzip it. 'What time is it, Scott?' I asked, looking around? How long had I been sleeping?

'It's morning,' he replied. 'You were out the whole night.' I glanced over to the window to see clear blue skies and exhaled again, long and loud. I dumped the waistcoat on the table away from me with a clunky bang. I looked back to Scott with a slightly more self-conscious expression, now that the fear had left me.

'Sorry about last night,' I muttered quietly, still picturing my crazy reactions in the car. I was desperately thinking for a justifiable reason to explain myself and why I had lashed out like I had, but I was coming up short. The truth was obvious; I had thought Cane was dead and I broke down, simple as that. I had felt like my world had crumbled and I hadn't been able to handle it. I sat for a minute longer, going over my actions and recalling how I had dealt with the thought of my dad being dead just weeks earlier. I exhaled, running my hands through my tangled hair. I wish I'd kept it together like then. Scott was still watching me, and I fumbled for something to say. 'Last night...I eh, I think with being pulled away from my parents and ummmm...' I paused, unconvincingly, not knowing what to add to make an excuse for my behaviour. Scott continued to stand over me in silence, looming with quiet understanding. Then finally, after what felt like an eternity of awkwardness, he decided to end my obvious torment.

'Sorry I had to knock you out.' The corners of his mouth twitched, and I could see he was struggling to hold in a smile or a laugh. I let out a small bark, dropping my head into my hands.

'I'm really embarrassed,' I admitted, feeling my face begin to warm. 'I'm not normally so...*unmanageable*'. I said, lifting my head to see him. At my words, his eyebrows raised, and a small smirk grew on his tired face.

'That *must* be sarcasm,' he declared. 'You're *obviously* feeling better.' I feigned an insult, but smiled when he did.

'Scott?' I mumbled, turning to look at him with serious eyes and a fading smile. '*What happened?*' To this, Scott sat down, releasing a heavy sigh and creasing his brow. He was sad and concerned and his obvious display of emotions disturbed me. I breathed in slowly.

'As far as our intel shows, your parents were tracked to the meeting point. We were recorded arriving then our journey traced backwards to the safe house using a drone. From there, we assume they monitored footage to confirm that you, or at least look-a-like you, was situated in the warehouse and had been so from days earlier. They didn't know about the tunnel and so assumed that Cane was still stationed there too. And they were almost correct this time. It wasn't about you, Eva. It was a hit for Cane.

'But he got out ok?' I asked again, biting my lower lip, just needing it confirmed one more time. Scott nodded, and I let that feeling of relief wash through my body once again.

'Only just, though,' he replied. 'Through the tunnel. Not all were so lucky.' As he said the words my veins ran cold again. I could understand the desire to kill Cane, Bain would be freed from this whole mess, but killing anyone who happened to be standing nearby? Even black shirts had families, lives, children, something I now knew. How many of those men would I no longer see around the house and grounds? Guilt rushed through me with a nauseating reality. Their deaths were on my shoulders, they had died because of a decision I made weeks ago in a back alley. How could Bain go this far? How could I have not fully known the capabilities of my future father-in-law? I knew he was underhanded and devious, but so much bloodshed? I felt shell shocked.

'I just don't understand how Bain could go this far.' I whispered, swallowing the bitter taste in my mouth.

'Intel says it wasn't Bain.' Scott announced.

'What?' I exclaimed, a little louder than I had intended, and feeling a little more relief release inside me. Scott scratched his stubbly chin.

'It's a bit unclear still, but looks like the work of the Russians.' Seeing my confused expression, he expanded slightly. 'Its business, Eva, ongoing politics that were around before you arrived. You just provided an opportunity while Cane was...' he paused, 'while he was distracted'. He said his words carefully and watched for my reaction. I shook my head and exhaled with confusion. How would Cane deal with this attack, how would he retaliate? The thought scared me. This life, *his* life, was so extreme and drastic that it was hard to fathom.

'This is crazy,' I said to myself, as I played it all over in my mind. 'People just kill and hurt each other so *easily* in this world.' Scott was silent whilst watching me and he finally gave a small nod of agreement.

'If it helps at all, Eva,' he muttered very quietly, turning his back to the other black shirts in the kitchen, 'there's been none of that authorised or sanctioned on our side in a while now.' He paused. 'I'd say, since about two weeks after you showed up.' He inclined his head gently towards me, then stood up and made his way back to the kitchen. I watched him. Was that true? Cane had said that he had been trying to change, but I hadn't known how. Was he not only changing himself, but also his business too? And if that was the case, then *any* change was possible... Cane, Bain, the companies, the war, it all had potential to change, right? My mind was whirling. If that *was* the case, did that mean my fate still had a shot at being altered? A phone rang, breaking the silence and it was our move authorisation. I was packed into a car and driven back to the place I'd come to know as home. The time alone in the backseat let me think, organise and justify everything that had happened in the last twenty-four hours. It all needed to be sorted and rationalised if I was ever to make sense of it and live with it. The massive gates closed behind us and I recalled the first day I'd driven up to them, determined and scared. Now as they closed me in, they felt almost safe and protective. As we rounded the corner, the house appeared in all its sunlit grandeur, the stairs, the water feature, the sparkling old brickwork, the stained glass, all of it, just as it had been on that first day. Except now, I thought to myself, I was happy to see it. I leant forward to look through the window, my eyes wide with appreciation. Scott smiled across from me, ducking his head to see it also.

'Never gets old, does it?' he muttered, as the car came to a stop. I glanced at him in agreement. I was escorted inside along the usual route to the office. The panel on the wall went green and Scott opened the door for me, but lingered back outside. I stopped as I passed him, placing my hand on his arm gently and giving him a small smile of thanks. He inclined his head discretely and with that, closed the doors behind me. I found Cane instantly. He was standing by the balcony, the curtains dancing around him in the afternoon breeze. He had a drink in one hand and his other resting, as normal, in his trouser pocket. For some reason, he looked more magnificent than ever, like he had intensified in perfection, like knowing he could have been gone had added to his value. His head turned to me immediately and his eyes fixed with intent. They stayed locked, as he put down his drink and in what felt like two paces, was across the room and in front of me, pulling me into him. His solid frame crushed me into his chest, his strong arms wrapping tightly around. His chest rose and fell with such pace, that it felt like he had just run a marathon. He smelt like every memory I had of him and I inhaled, desperate to keep those memories alive. His hand stroked my hair as his breath came loud and relieved and I held on, feeling all the pain disappear into nothing. I pulled away gently at the same time as him and he moved a strand of my hair from my face.

'Close call last night,' I began, quietly, to which he smiled, still looking at me and nodded.

'Very close,' he echoed. 'Were you worried?' A teasing dimple showed on his face and I rolled my eyes playfully at him.

'Not really. You're a big boy, aren't you?' He laughed a little, letting the moment linger, before countering my sarcasm.

'Hmmm,' he muttered, his eyes dancing with indulgence. 'Because I heard that Scott had to incapacitate you.' My eyes instantly flew to his with mortified horror. Earth please swallow me now! Not only did I act like an irrational, crazy idiot last night, but Cane knew it too. *Thanks a million, Scott.* I dropped my head into my hands, trying to hide my face.

'Urgh,' I moaned, 'I erm...I eh...' I fumbled pathetically to find words, despite my head reeling off hundreds of rationale explanations which could save face. Cane began to laugh loudly, his dimples appearing on both cheeks.

'Escuchar,' he pronounced, through his smile, but with a very serious tone. It meant 'listen' and I closed my lips quickly, as he pulled my head up with his finger beneath my chin. 'No one has cared so much about me, since my mother and father were alive.' My brow creased in sympathy.

Surely that wasn't true? He nodded at me intensely. 'You of all people, Eva, would stand to gain from me dying, yet you wanted to save me'. My face burned even more as the temperature in my body began to rise to critical. 'I will *never* forget that.' His voice was a barely audible whisper and he looked at me like I was his world.

'Then cancel this deal,' I begged, before I could stop myself. His expression changed instantly, and he immediately began pulling away. *No, I thought to myself, not after what you just put me through, not after I was forced to admit just how much you apparently mean to me.* 'You say all these things to me Cane, but you are sticking to this ludicrous deal when you could so easily just end it. I don't understand.' I begged passionately, watching him step back and sever his eye contact.

'No es asi de fácil,' he replied firmly, shaking his head. I moved towards him again, my hands open for him, begging.

'How is it not that easy?' I pleaded with frustration. *'I don't understand.'*

'You're right Eva, you don't understand,' he exclaimed powerfully, walking away back to his desk, his retreat. 'I can't undo what's been done, what's been set in motion.' I laughed as he said it, was he joking, right? There was nothing this man could not do if he wanted it enough. I knew that, even if he didn't.

'You are the only one who can fix it all, Cane,' I pushed. 'But you are standing by and doing nothing. It's like its fine when we are alone, and you can say what you want to me, and no one hears it, but then you act like none of its true.' My fists were suddenly tensed with frustration and my temper flared. 'Like none of this really matters to you.'

'Like none of it matters?' I struck a chord, and his anger matched mine. In the old days, I would have shrunk away from his wrath, but not now, not when so much depended on him. If I could just convince him. He marched towards me and stopped inches from my face, repeating himself. *'Like none of this matters?* Where the hell have you been, Eva?' His hands were in the air. 'How many times have I told you? How many ways can I show you how much *you* matter? You're the one who is running away,' he was pointing at me now, 'you're the one who is running back to perfect, little Edward.' To this I ignited, furiously. Like this whole deal was *my* idea?

'WHAT?' I screamed. 'YOU are pushing me back to Edward. YOU set this whole ridiculous scheme up. YOU have given me no choice.' Despite the blood pumping in my ears, I recognized that this was becoming a practiced talent for us; switching from peace to insane anger in seconds.

'You would have chosen him anyway!' he argued back, his eyes sparkling. I pushed him away from me.

'Is that what *you* decided?' I ranted. 'What YOU decided? You say you love me, Cane, but *you* are sending me away. It's not my choice.' I shoved him again in frustrated anger, with stinging eyes. 'I WOULD HAVE

CHOSEN YOU IF YOU'D LET ME!' I screamed as loud as I was able, my voice breaking. He stopped. We both stopped. This was our pattern, I thought to myself as I watched his chest, that had held me so tenderly just minutes ago, rise and fall with exhaustion. We would reach a passionate pinnacle and then it would tip off the end, leaving nothing but sadness. And as I thought it, I watched his strong shoulders drop and his eyes fill with dejection. Sad ending it is again, then. He exhaled deeply.

'I care too much, Eva,' he whispered, looking at me longingly. 'You should never be made to choose me. I am not a good enough man to have you. After all I've done, I don't deserve the happiness you make me feel. My hate and need for justice backed me into this corner and there is no way out. Estoy Atrapado.' *I'm trapped.* He closed his eyes heavily. I watched him, and it made me so sad I could barely keep it together.

'Why can't you make a way out?' I sobbed, with a single tear escaping and tracing its way down my tired face. 'I love you, Cane. I don't want to lose you.' His whole frame crumpled at this, collapsing to the chair, his head held in his hands.

'I don't know how to undo what I've done. How do I undo *so* much? It's not just *my* deal, Eva, it's a network of businesses and wealthy influential people throughout the world who I have promised *a lot* to.' I sat down next to him, starting to understand a bit more. He lifted his head to look at me. 'I've promised more than I wish I had, more than I can take back.' I nodded, slowly swallowing. It was complicated, I got that now, but it didn't change anything to me. I placed my hand over his, looking desperately into his distressed eyes.

'Then disappoint them, Cane, and we'll figure the rest out, but please, I'm begging you, don't give up on us.' I gently kissed his cheek, my cold tears smudging onto his burning skin. His eyes closed. I quickly stood and with painful silence, left the office, walking past the assessing looks of black shirts, praying to make it back to my room before everyone saw me break down.

CHAPTER FORTY-ONE.
Rather a broken heart.

Once again, he watched her leave his office and the sickening thought occurred to him, that it may be for the last time. The wedding was happening in two days. He felt suffocated and heavy, weighed down by things too substantial and real to bear. He had fallen so deeply in love with this woman that it jeopardized everything in his life. He'd finalised a deal which, weeks ago, would have been his finest feat. Now, he would give all he owned to take it back and undo it. His heart had changed, his mind had changed, his life had changed...his future needed to change, too. He knew it, he knew it had to, but he did not know how to make it so. Every avenue he explored led to a dead-end of broken contracts, failed promises and angry influential men throughout the world. He didn't mind losing his wealth or his stature or his name, if that was what it took to be with Eva, but he knew that the kind of people he would be making enemies of, were the kind of people who held grudges. They would take from him as retribution, anything that was dear, and that anything was now Eva. He swallowed feeling his dry throat constrict at the thought of permanently losing her, his hands clamming up at the idea of never being able to see her or hear her voice or know that at least somewhere she was alive, even if with Edward. It was too much. He knew what he had to do to keep her safe, and that was to go through with the deal. Rather a broken heart and a ceasing love, than her life taken and a heart that could never mend. She would hate him for it and they would never be together, but she would live and have a chance at life again, even if it was a life with someone else. He stood up and walked to his desk, firing up his laptop. His dreams of movie nights on the sofa, of walking in the park and doing the dishes with her, all those normal life things, they were fading into painful failed hopes. He pulled a large brown report folder from his desk drawer and opened it slowly. Eva's face stared up at him from the picture attached to her file. She really was beautiful, he thought to himself, as he brushed his finger over her face. He exhaled as if it could blow the pressures and strains of his life away. But he could not, his breath merely sent the file pages scattering across the desktop in a messy gust. He inhaled again, watching them flutter and spread, Eva's picture landing out of his reach. That's about right, he thought angrily, stretching out to collect it and then the rest of the papers. His eyes caught a file, hidden under the other papers and his eyes zoned in on it like a hawk; it was the proposal from Eva's father, from the day they had first met in that alley. He lifted it, having forgotten about its existence. It brought back memories of absolutely everything, playing out like a crystal clear film inside of his head, he could see it all, their whole story so far…the alleyway fight, the deal, Eva sleeping by the pond and him placing his blanket over her, the camera room and the moment they shared afterwards in the dark, the library, dinner and an almost kiss, sitting with her hungover, having her pinned by her neck to the wall, the heat of her body and the look in her eyes, the jealousy over a gardener boy and their friendship, Spain, lying together in bed, that dance and that passionate kiss by the pond, the argument about Tammy and then the amazing night spent with her in his arms, waking to her and her warmth, the frustration of being trapped in a deal released on his room and then finally now…right at the end, the disappointment in her eyes as she just left his office…it was all there, inside his head, ready to replay over and over again for the rest of his lonely life. He could see it all, hear it all and feel it all, just like it was minutes ago, so bitter sweet that it physically hurt. His eyes watered as he struggled to control himself amidst the overwhelming heartbreak, the pages of Eva's fathers original file crumpled in his clenched and angry fists.

CHAPTER FORTY-TWO.
Full circle.

The day arrived. Just like that. Scott had come to my room to pass on all the information I was allowed to know. No Cane, no more dramatic encounters. We hadn't talked since the heated and sad conversation in his office, and to some degree I was glad. My heart couldn't take much more and if this was how it was all going to end anyway, then at least I didn't have to do it while looking at the man I was now so in love with. Weeks of pain and tears, confusion and love, it had all come and gone, in what now seemed, so fast that I could barely remember the first day in that dreaded alley. I looked out the window to the morning sun, the clear blue skies beaming. I showered, numb, and dried my hair, twisting ringlets around the hot tongs. I applied my makeup, casting a small thankful smile that my healing bullet wounds were all below my dress. It was the second time I had applied make-up since my time with Cane, the last occasion being in Spain. I sat motionless, remembering how much easier and simpler things had seemed in Spain, as if everything was on pause and the possibility of hope still existed. I breathed deeply, looking at the clock. It was almost mid-day and my wedding was an hour away. I was happy to be seeing family and to be seeing Edward, who I now knew that I loved more like a brother than anything. It was strange to think that after all this, he was the man I was going to end up with still. It had all come full circle back to when Edward and I had been in love and planning our wedding, except this time, my heart belonged very much to someone else. I slid my white dress on, the beautiful material sitting coolly against my heated skin, and then I stood. I was alone. No fussing, no gasps of appreciation from loved ones, no flashes from bridesmaids cameras wanting to capture the moment...I was totally alone, and there I waited. The clock ticked, and the clouds moved past my window. On the twelve-thirty chime, there was a knock at my door and Cane entered.

'Can I come in?' he asked, politely. Cane was wearing a dark suit and a white shirt, his tie high and knotted ready for business. He closed the door behind him and stood, looking at me.

'Well?' I asked as light heartedly as I could, looking down myself at the finished product. He smiled deeply, looking into my eyes.

'Te ves hermosa.' he replied too quietly. It wasn't the first time he'd called me beautiful, but today, I knew it was most likely to be the last. He stepped towards me and produced a delicate silver chain from his pocket. Hung on the end was a breathtaking single, elegant diamond. I smiled at it, touching it with my fingers. It was obviously expensive.

'I got it in Spain. To remind you of our time there.' he said. 'May I?' he requested, holding it up to my neck. I nodded slowly and turned around, lifting my hair and watching him in the mirror. He dropped it over my face and I felt it touch gently against my skin. He did the clasp up and I felt his safe hands brush my neck. The diamond sparkled against my skin and I touched it with my fingers, holding it as if it contained all my hopes and dreams. Cane placed his hands down on my shoulders, soft and gentle skin spreading warmth through me. I leaned my cheek against him, closing my eyes. When I opened them, I found him watching me intently in the mirror, his eyes deep and sad. Then like lightening, the clock behind us rung out, breaking through our silence. He nodded in what I only assumed was goodbye, and with one last, longing look in my eyes, his hands were gone, and he left the room all too abruptly. I stood holding the necklace, the cold stone boring into my hand, remembering Spain, the dance we shared at his Grandmother's party, the moment by the water, the emotions, the passion...*oh my goodness, breathe Eva.* I leaned over placing my hands on my knees for support, as my air vanished painfully. It was all I could do to not break down. Had I ever felt so sad and so disappointed in my whole life? Would I ever be alone with Cane again, see him, talk to him? A knock sounded at the door again and Scott opened it. He paused slightly to look at me, before informing me it was time. Maybe I looked how I felt, but he obviously decided I need some slack, and he hung back in the hallway.

'I'll just see you at the car?' he muttered, graciously allowing me the courtesy of pulling myself together, alone. I nodded with thanks, swallowing my encroaching sobs. *Here we go. This is the end.* I took one last look around the room that had been my haven for the last three months or so, and touched my hand to the wall. We had seen some rough times together, but it had done me well. I walked out and closed the heavy door into its frame, turning to walk down the beautiful old staircase again for one last time and running my hand over its smooth and flawless wood. It really was beautiful. As I touched the last step, I found myself face to face with Andreas, who was watching me with an odd look. I gasped, slightly startled. I had to stop missing him when he was so close by. I held his stare as surely as I could, despite how I felt inside. I was too sad to experience anything else just now. Elias had steered clear of me after the shooting range incident, but Andreas was not quite so easily put off by emotional displays. He walked towards me and I backed up away from him, until I found myself against the china cabinet, which rattled as I bumped into it. He stopped when his face was centimetres from mine and his body just as close. I stood quite still with his alcohol laced breath heating my face.

'You've changed things around here, you know?' he began, looking over my dress and my made-up face. I cast my head down, not wanting to hear tales of how I had ruined the family and disgraced his brother. Not today. He swallowed loudly and then lowered his voice. 'It's been better since you've been here, Eva,' he whispered, like it was a dirty secret. My head shot up, meeting his small secretive smile, and he gently traced his finger down my cheek, as if he would miss me and was taking stock. He leaned in closer to my lips brushing them briefly as he made his way to my ear. 'Don't marry Edward Bain today.' he mouthed, my heart fluttering with confusion. 'Cane loves you. I've never seen him so happy, Eva,' he pulled away and stood inches from my face, waiting for an answer, a reaction. But what could I say to him?

'Andreas!' Cane's strong and firm voice bellowed from behind him, as his body was pulled away from mine by powerful hands. Cane was on him in seconds, his dominancy forcing Andreas to cower. 'You will not forget that I am still the boss here.' His authority echoed off the walls and Andreas nodded, sheepishly, backing away. 'Go to the car, now,' he instructed, pointing to the door. Andreas shuffled away without a backward glance. I stood watching Cane collect himself.

'He wasn't doing anything wrong,' I defended, shaking my head slowly. Cane turned, breathing heavily.

'Maybe,' he muttered, walking to the door and holding it open for me. I passed by him and out into the piercing sunshine. I shielded my eyes, glancing behind, but I was met with nothing. Cane had gone, and I was alone. My heart sunk further as I walked, with my head held as high as I could, towards the car. I could see from the windows, staff watching and pointing at my departure. The wedding dress must have been a fair sight, and I glanced sideways to see more staff pointing my way. I caught sight of blowing, blonde hair and quickly found Gideon's eyes. He waved at me slowly, but with no smile on his weathered and dry lips. I lifted my hand to him and waved gently, knowing I would never see his blue eyes again or hear his passionate words on nature. He had been a good friend to me and I would miss him. Scott was holding the car door for me and he inclined his head politely as I got in. More car doors slammed and then the convoy was off. I turned to watch the house disappear and as it vanished from view, I held back my tears. The gates appeared ahead and slowly creaked open, the stealthy black shirt watching me as I drove past. As they closed and crashed shut, I jumped, their echo piercing into me with finality. I would never cross that threshold again and I knew it. I turned to the front of the car, desperate to hold it together. I tore my eyes from the what-could-have-been now behind me, and set my face ahead to the future. I was to be wed to my childhood sweetheart, in twenty minutes time, and then everything else would be history.

CHAPTER FORTY-THREE.
Then finally, there was Edward.

The church was a beautiful, old, stone building that sat remotely, in a small, insignificant village of Scotland. It stood picturesque on the edge of a cliff, overlooking the North Sea. The sky was clear and blue and endless, as if a blessing from above, and the slight breeze gently ruffled the daffodils that lined the path leading to the old church doors. The whole thing was beautiful. More than a bride could ever really wish for. I knew it, but I still couldn't find any joy from it. Inside the church, cute little wooden aisles ran down either side of the room. The stained-glass windows cast an array of multi-coloured patterns on the old, stone floor and onto the wedding guests, who sat separated on each side. The left of the chapel sat the family of the bride, all dressed and ready for a ceremony, despite the multitude of tissues and tears. My mother was wearing a canary yellow dress with matching hat and looked practically near hyperventilation, as she desperately clung to my father. My father. Mended and well. He locked eyes with me searchingly, tears welling up in them. Seeing him here, alive, it was what it had all been about, right? I had seen what broken families and lost loved ones did to people now. Especially when those loved ones were taken away from you through vengeance and anger. I at least, through all of this, still had parents to call my own. At the opposite side of the room, the benches were laden with the support of the Bain family and my father-in-law to be, Brice. His expression was somewhat more difficult to read, although fear stopped me settling on him for too long. What he must think of me was beyond my comprehension. Did he hate me for this, would he welcome me back to the family? His face gave away nothing, a practiced talent, especially when there were so many Rodriguez's watching. I guessed that his stance on the whole event would be determined soon enough, considering how close I was getting to the altar. I knew there were other family members, from both sides, scattered around, but truthfully, they had all just blended into the background. If I was being selfishly honest, there was only one person in that chapel I really wanted to see, I really *needed* to see, but I couldn't find him anywhere. It didn't surprise me that he hadn't come, but it did hurt more than I could fathom. The guests had all come out of the woodwork for today and church was full, but that one missing body was more obvious than anything to me. Despite it really looking like a proper wedding, well except the black shirts lining the perimeter of the room. I felt like I was falling. I looked again through the Rodriguez men, searching. I recognised most of them now, each with fixed stares and ear pieces mounted to their well-trained faces. Their presence was far from supportive or welcoming, despite their final goal being the same as the rest of the congregation, to see a marriage, but their presence was also no longer threatening. They stood like sentinels; arms folded, scowls, muscles flexed, not a smile to be seen, not even from Scott, who glanced at my panicking eyes with pity. Sat in the centre of the pews, I caught vision of Elias and Andreas, squared shoulders and grim faces. By their side was the perfect body of little miss gold digger. Any other time, that would have drawn a smile from me, but not today, not now. I looked around again in the corners of the chapel, in the alcoves and the doorways, searching for the eyes I yearned to see, but all spaces were empty, and my despairing heart knew I was here alone. I finally looked forward. Standing with unwavering loyalty, at the altar, was my devoted groom, Edward. The things he was giving up for me, was enough to literally leave me indebted to him for the rest of my life. I would never be able to repay him for his love, his kindness, his selflessness; even though I knew that I would spend the rest of my living days trying to do so, all the while, shamefully wishing he was someone else. He stood ahead of me, tall and fully suited in a tuxedo. His hair was parted smartly to one side and he had a flower in his button hole, just like any proper fiancé would. Even with a shine of sweat glistening off his forehead, he looked gallant and proud. He had given up *everything* for me, maybe from love, maybe from history, maybe guilt, but what did it matter now? I stepped down the aisle closer to him, drowning in dread. Edward was giving up everything he held important for me, everything he was passionate about, and he didn't even know that I didn't love him anymore, that I hadn't been in love with him for a long time. His saving act of selfless charity, was in fact, the worst day of my life and my heart was breaking with each pace closer to him. I searched around again, still desperately looking for Cane, but the aisle was getting shorter. I could see Edward watching me, itching to lay his hands on me and feel that I was safe, and so with one last backward glance to the door, I committed.

Step, step. *Breathe in and breathe out.*

Step, step. *Where is he?*

Step, step. It was too late, I was there. The pulpit was at my feet and there were no more steps to be taken. It was game over. Edward's face beamed at me from inches away and I tried to retaliate his emotions. He reached out for my hands and grasped onto them like a vice, clinging to me with all his worth. I heard my mum sigh with relief and Mr Bain cough uncomfortably. His hands felt so familiar, but so tight. Had they always felt like this?

'Dearly beloved,' the priest began, my heart racing with anxiety. 'We are gathered here today on this blessed occasion, to witness the marriage of Eva Mack to Edward Bain.' I held Edward's elated eyes, trying not to get lost in my head, trying to stay present. This was my path now, this was the consequence of the decision I made three months ago in an alley, my life for my dad's. Would I do it all again, if it meant saving him? I knew I would, in a heartbeat. I knew now, more than ever, that sometimes all you had in this world was love and that was worth sacrificing everything for. I held Ed's gaze with a partial smile, but he was already figuring out that something was wrong. His eyebrows were lowered at me and I felt myself nodding at him, encouragingly. 'If any of you here have reason why this man and this woman should not be wed, speak now or forever hold your peace.' The chapel plunged into deathly silence. I was sure that more than half the people in here were desperate to say something, but the seconds ticked by and it stayed quiet. I had kept focused on Ed, praying for a miracle with all my might, but that hope dissolved as the Priest's voice continued. My knees went to buckle, and I held my sob in, clinging to Ed's hands for support. Was this the true weight of a broken heart, an actual physical heaviness which pulled down on every muscle I had. It was too much, far too much to bear, yet, the Priest continued, oblivious to my falling apart.

'Marriage is a sacred bond between man and wom-' Then it came!

'WAIT!' Elation, utter elation, swept through my whole being. 'Hold on,' Cane's voice echoed, confidently through the chapel. I spun to find him, standing at the top of the aisle by the doors, his hands in his trouser pockets. He looked strong and certain, and more magnificent than ever. His eyes found mine and he suggested a smile, whilst joy consumed me.

'What's going on Rodriquez?' Bain yelled accusingly, getting to his feet. His face was red with anger and distrust and he was waving his fist at Cane menacingly, his men rising to their feet. The black shirts stood to attention also, ready for action. The two brothers were on their feet in seconds, proclaiming threats and hostile warnings. I was aware that Ed was watching me, but I couldn't take my eyes from Cane's face, as he began to walk the length of the aisle, stopping at Mr Bain. The whole room was balanced on a knife tip, ready to fall, and I could feel the heightened and desperate need to explode.

'Mr Bain, if you would give me a few moments of your time, I would like to speak to you outside. Alone' Cane raised his hand towards the doors and awaited the reply from a speechless and skeptical Bain.

'What's going on?' Edward yelled out, his father casting him a concurring look. He leaned into me, watching my eyes glued to the situation. I ignored Ed, pinning all my attention on the two businessmen, making or breaking generations of hate, in the middle of my wedding. THIS was the moment. THE moment that could change it all. Cane was taking the step, but would Bain follow? Did he have it in him? Bain stood abruptly, maybe seeing the look in Cane's eye that could persuade anyone to do anything, or maybe going on his gut, but he walked to the end of his aisle and with a warning glance at Cane, walked out the doors. Cane's eyes flashed by me, showing a hint of surprise, but he turned and followed his old business nemesis to the blue skies and sunshine outside. As soon as the doors closed the chapel erupted into chaos.

CHAPTER FORTY-FOUR.
If we are laying it all out on the line.

He held the door for Bain as the old man approached him with sour caution on his wrinkled and worn out face. His eyes jerked with suspicion and hate, as the wooden frames banged back into place, leaving the two old enemies alone for the first time in years. The sun was shining still, and fresh air blew the tension in the atmosphere surrounding them. He couldn't help but wonder what Bain would think was up to. Years of backstabbing and underhanded, despicable things could only ever lead to mistrust and wariness. Cane's heart raced with fear and uncertainty, as Bain turned to face him, squinting against the bright stark sun, his eyes screwed up with caution and defence. Looking at the weathered man, Cane could understand why he was ready to hand things over to his son, Edward. Time was catching up with Brice Bain and he wasn't quite the vicious, hard-faced villain Cane remembered him to be. It had been so long since they had stood face to face, that his bitter memories and stubborn recollections no longer matched up to the man standing opposite him. In all honesty, Bain looked tired and frail and old.

'Well, Rodriguez, what the hell is the meaning of this?' Bain began angrily, pointing his finger, his defences instantly up and his accusations immediately taking lead.

'Mr Bain,' Cane began, summoning the courage he knew he so desperately needed right now. 'I want a truce.' Bain's eyebrows shot into his forehead with such vigorous speed they looked like they would disappear into his hair line.

'A what!?' he exclaimed with question, practically shouting with surprise. 'Is this some kind of trick, some kind of joke? I won't have it Rodriguez, I won't let you manipulate anything more. Have you not had enough fun, have you not ruined enough people's lives?' He was yelling at him, stabbing his finger into the space between them with anger. 'Not to mention what you have done to that poor girl's life.' He thrust his hand towards the church doors, where Eva stood inside, waiting at the altar. To this Cane stopped him with a lifting of his hand.

'Enough, please, Brice.' Bain stammered at the interruption and the casual use of his first name. Whilst he did so, Cane continued quickly before he lost his chance, and his resolve. 'I am in love with, Eva,' he declared loudly and confidently, lifting his hands openly in front of himself. The cagey mumbling from Bain ceased instantly and his mouth literally dropped open into stunned silence.

Cane stifled a smile at the reaction. 'But with hate in my heart and head, I made a deal involving her. I promised a lot of powerful people a lot of great things when this whole affair was through. But things have changed.' He looked down, away from Bain's astonished face. 'I have changed.' he uttered the words quietly, almost so that the wind covered its sincerity. It felt weak and open to be so honest with the man he trusted least in this world, but Cane knew it had to end and to do so, he knew he needed Bain's help. Eva trumped his own pride any day of his long and lonely weeks. Bain's mouth was still locked open in bewildered shock and he began to shake his head, starting to laugh.

'This is a joke, right?' he declared, with a sinister snigger. 'Am I supposed to believe you?' Bain looked around, as if expecting something to jump out on him and reveal the actual truth. Cane kept his head lowered, humbly.

'En serio, Brice. It's no joke.' he exhaled steadily. 'I love her.' He looked back up into the distrusting man's eyes, hoping that he would see the sincerity now living in his own. 'I love her enough to end all this.' He put his hands into his trouser pockets and inhaled, lifting his shoulders back into their strong and sturdy frame. He had said it, admitted it, he had done the first part, and now, he needed to pitch the rest before the doubtful and guarded old fool stormed off. 'I'm tired. I am sick and tired of this constant battle,' he continued, pointing between himself and Bain. 'I want out of it, I want a normal life, I want normal chances and opportunities that aren't ruined by paranoia and suspicions. I want to start living, Bain,' he paused, holding the shrewd opponent's eyes, 'I want to start a life with Eva.' Bain began to cough, choking on surprise and disbelief.

'You are serious, aren't you?' he strangled out, clearing his throat. 'You are actually serious?' He shook his head. 'What did you do to her while you had her? She loves my son, not you. What makes you think that she'd want anything to do with a monster like you?'

'I'm not a monster...not anymore,' Cane stated firmly, with a set jaw. 'And I am sorry, but she no longer loves your son.'

'This is ridiculous, completely insane.' Bain was shaking his head from side to side with incredulity. 'You set this whole radical and vindictive deal up, then drag me out here in front of a church full of people, to tell me you have a crush on the girl you kidnapped and tortured for the last few months?' He was yelling now. 'What do you want from me now?' he bellowed, with flushed cheeks. 'You want me to hand Eva over to you, so you can fulfill your newest whim? Well, I won't,' he roared, folding his arms defensively. 'I won't do it'. Cane stood listening until the end and waited for Bain's breathing to begin to settle before he finally spoke.

'Mr Bain, I don't need you to give me Eva, that will be her choice. What I do want from you is your time, talents and trust.' To this Bain's whole expression

changed. 'I want to launch a new business with you, a new company, a new leaf.' Bain stood still, his ears obviously not believing what they were hearing. 'I want to build up things, create ideas, start new possibilities. I'm sick of manipulation and endings, ruining things that were perfectly fine before either one of us came along.' Bain's face was stone still, plastered with sheer astonishment. Cane could see his chest rising and falling, but no other reactions left his body. It was like he was stunned and frozen by shock. Cane held in his urge to smile again, knowing it was definitely not the time nor the place to see humour in the cynical old man's reactions. He exhaled with conclusion. 'Brice, I am asking you to take a leap of faith. Mr Mack, Eva's father, presented me with a proposal a few months ago, one that I have only recently read. It was about us joining our industries and creating a new brand, a new company. It was a very detailed and convincing pitch, showing growth and development, which could be off the charts. A new business like the world has never seen before, a new force to be reckoned with.' Bain continued to watch him, ever so closely, as if daring him to show even the smallest hint of a scam, to give him any glimpse of trickery and deception.

'I don't trust you, Rodriguez.' Bain finally spoke, boldly and coldly. 'Why would you want to work with me now, after all these years?' He puffed up his chest, his suit jacket buttons pulling at the strain. 'If you love, Eva, like you say, what does that have to do with business?' Cane nodded as Bain questioned him.

'I understand your reserve, Brice, if I was you, I would be dubious too, but my coming to you today is twofold. As I just said, I want a new life, I want a new start, a new honest challenge…with you, not against you for a change,' he paused watching the old man's face start to slowly thaw with possibility, 'but I also need you to help me protect Eva. If I break this deal, I'm losing a lot of money and burning a lot of weighty men throughout the world.' He looked into Bain's eyes for some understanding and generosity, anything that showed the old man's heart to be melting with even the slightest form of compassion. 'No one does influence and counter-control like you, Brice, between us, we can keep her...seguro, keep her safe.' Bain's eyes looked into his for a long length of time, searching for confirmation of truth. After what felt like forever and what must have been a mighty internal battle for him, Bain spoke.

'You care that much about Eva, that you are willing to lose it all?' he questioned in disbelief. To this Cane laughed in a 'if-only-you-really-knew' kind of way, shrugging in confirmation.

'Brice, if I could give up my name, my money and everything I had, to keep her with me and keep her safe, I'd do it in heartbeat.' Bain's eyes narrowed slightly with a new look in them, a look of a changing mind and an altering opinion. He inhaled deeply, as if trying to push his pride aside.

'If we are laying it all out on the line, Rodriguez,' he began, in a lowered and quiet voice, 'and you are willing to start trusting me...' he stalled, as if his words wanted to come but were caught in his throat. He cleared his voice, as if hoping to mask any emotion that was surfacing. 'Your parents,' he began, more timidly than Cane had ever seen him. 'I swear to you, on my mother, it was an accident. I've carried the regret of it my whole life son, always too full of arrogance and hate to say what I've needed to say for so long.' he paused and swallowed, 'I am sorry for any part I played in your parents' death. Yes, we were rivals and we had a complex history, but there was respect on some level.' Cane's heart began to beat so rapidly he thought he was having a heart attack. He had not expected such an open and honest conversation. Not expected to deal with such deep routed and sensitive issues. It knocked him off his game, off his centre. His hands clammed up and his breathing shortened. The sincerity in Bain's eyes was hard to look at, hard to accept. All these years he had blamed Bain, held him solely responsible for everything...and now, seeing him face to face, apologise, well it was hard to stomach, hard to let go of, hard to believe. He swallowed, trying to stay composed as his inside spiraled into turmoil. Then as he began to feel the anger swell in his breast and the urge to retaliate with hurt, Eva came to his mind. She had dealt with the same thing, been so sure of someone's character, someone's evils, only to discover that she was wrong. She had had to inhale that new air and learn how to live with it for every breathe; Edward, Tammy, Bain, his brothers...him, they all flipped one-eighty on her, shredding her once so strong and sure convictions. He was now faced with the same challenge and it seemed oddly fitting. He exhaled, long, gaining control of himself. If she could navigate her way through new territory, new emotions and new opinions, change what was once utter hate, then he knew he could too. He focused his eyes back on Bain who had been standing very still, watching him with intense interest, his breath held.

'I have hated you for so many years, Brice,' Cane announced with a soft and honest voice. 'I blamed you for everything and let that pain turn into my father's bitter vengeance and into his father's angry revenge and so on and so on. I used it to carry on the family feud, as expected,' he sighed, loudly. 'It's taken Eva to show me that I've wasted so much of my life.' Bain's eyes began to sparkle with what could only be astounded tears, and his cheeks flushed as he looked at Cane. It was a moment. It was THE moment. Here was where it would all turn around. Cane could feel it in him, as the weight he had been carrying his whole life started to finally lift, finally lessen. This was it. This was when he could finally start to heal, start to move on. He could let go of the devastation and the resentment that had held him captive for so long. He looked into Bain's eyes and although he saw hesitation and reserve in them still, he could see honesty and remorse. *He cleared his throat, gaining control of his himself, and then doing something he never thought to ever do, he held out his hand to the old man, feeling it shake with the sheer magnitude of the moment. 'Gracias. Thank you,' he said, watching Bain's face mirror the almost exact range of feelings that was in him. 'That means more than you will know, to hear you say that to me.' Bain's hand reached out and grasped hold of his, in one strong and quick movement. His grip was firm and steady, and they shook in truce.*

'All right then,' Bain began, resuming his poker business face. 'It's a deal,' he confirmed. 'We can go over the plans with Mr Mack on Monday, we'll set up a meeting.' Cane nodded, taking his hand back and putting it in his trouser pockets. He felt different, like his whole life had literally changed in the last ten minutes. Like everything he had ever known was gone and replaced by lighter, easier versions. His shoulders felt weightless and his heart more manageable then he could ever remember. Was this freedom? Was this closure? They turned to the chapel doors and Bain flashed him a sideways hard stare. 'If you screw me Rodriguez, there'll be hell to pay,' Cane smiled, shaking his head.

'You remind me of him, you know?' he offered, referring to his deceased father. He placed his hand on the door handle to pull it open. 'You are both stubborn as anything.' To this Bain let slip a small smile, which he quickly changed back into a straight-laced stare and then nodded, indicating for Cane to open the doors. There was a lot to speak about, to deal with and to face awaiting them inside and it was not going to be a smooth transition. Cane knew that. Despite their few minutes of ceasefire, the two old enemies still had a vast amount of differences to sort through. But for once in his life, as the warm chapel air poured out over them, he actually felt hope.

CHAPTER FORTY-FIVE.
Interesting wedding.

Edward pounced on me as soon as his father and Cane walked out of the chapel doors. He wrapped his arms around my body and squeezed so tight that I could feel my ribs complaining.

'Are you ok? Are you hurt? Did he hurt you? I'm so sorry, I'm so sorry I let this happen to you. Are you ok?' His questions bombarded me all at once and all in one breath and I smiled at him, taking his familiar face into my hands. I looked deep into his eyes that I knew so well. He felt like home, like family, like my safety net. His eyes deepened with concern, he knew me well, well enough to know that something big was about to be said.

'I can't marry you, Ed,' I whispered gently, with a smile. His eyebrows raised with shock and he shook his head.
'What are you talking about?' He searched my face for reason, holding my hands tightly. 'It's my decision, Eva. It's my business, my money. You owe me nothing.' He shook his head at me, desperately.

'I'm not in love with you anymore and you haven't been in love with me for a long time now too.' He was shaking his head in confusion, about to start arguing. 'Edward,' I voiced firmly, taking his cheek in my hand. 'Do you trust me?' I looked into those familiar eyes of his and he nodded, instantly.

'Of course, I do, Eva. But I really don't think your feelings are even a slight concern for Rodriguez and this deal, he's a piece of-'
'Without all the pressure and craziness of the last few months,' I interrupted gently, 'I want you to answer me honestly, with what's in your heart.' He stopped his quizzical searching and stood still, seeing the seriousness in my face. He nodded, glancing towards the door his dad and Cane had gone through, then back to me.

'Are you still *in love* with me?' I waited and watched as he thought, his eyes studying mine in confusion. Seconds passed and eventually his shoulders dropped. I smiled at him brightly. 'Edward Bain, you are a kind and generous man with a good heart. Don't let *anything* ever change that, ok?' I demanded firmly, wrapping my arms around him. He held me tightly, for what felt like a long time, then slowly let me go, keeping my hand in his.

'I'm not going to pretend to have a single clue about what's going on here, but *you* seem to know what's happening, don't you?' He eyes me suspiciously, motioning towards the doors again where Cane and his father were still alone together. I shrugged.

'No,' I replied, with a full smile from my very soul. 'But I think I have a good idea.' I could feel this weight start to lift off me and this feeling of warmth spreading through me. It was happening? This whole mess was turning around.

'How long have you been in love with him?' Edward asked quite openly, keeping my hand in his still. My eyes darted back to him as if my dirty secret had been discovered. Lovers or not, we still knew each other inside out, and he knew when I felt something. Did I lie? Did I make an excuse, for what to him, would seem to be a heinous thing? I stalled, but Ed didn't look mad or upset or betrayed. 'You've always had a good judgment of character, Eva. Maybe not with me,' he frowned at himself, 'but with everyone else in your life. I just hope you are right with this one, because I can't understand how you could love him after everything he has done to you.' I exhaled the breath I hadn't even realised I'd been holding. All the fear I had of what people would think of me and how they would judge if they knew what was truly in my heart, it disappeared. What a man he was to trust me enough to see past the last few months, especially when he thought the worst of what had been happening to me. I smiled at him in awe, squeezing his hand with mine as he spoke again. 'You've always trusted me, Eva, even when that trust was abused.' He swallowed hard. 'I didn't know if I was ever going to see you again and I so desperately wanted to explain and apologise for mistreating your trust...' I put my hand to his mouth to silence him.

'You don't need to apologise for anything, let alone mistakes in the past. Everything before this, before now, it has to be forgiven Edward, by both of us.' He swallowed again and exhaled, giving a few small nods. 'And I know it will be hard for everyone to understand...Cane, especially you Ed, but things aren't what they seem. He's not what everyone thinks.' Edward inhaled, obviously struggling to understand, but knowing he trusted me.

'You seem...different, Eva,' he offered gently, with a quick scan of my face. I nodded, smiling slightly at the observation. He was right, I had changed, I was different. I was stronger and more confident than I had ever been in my life. I was also very much, with every fiber of my being, in love.

'I am different, Ed,' I confirmed proudly, glancing back to the doors. They had been out there for a while now. Edward followed my eyes.
'If you tell me that this will all be fine, that *you* will be fine, and this isn't some twisted confused mess, I'll trust you.' Tears welled in my eyes towards this giant of a man. I turned back to look at him.

'He's a good man, Ed. You'll see it in time, I promise. The last few months haven't been what everyone assumed, you'll see.' He nodded with obvious skepticism, but still always the gracious gentleman. 'You know someone told me something when I was away,' I continued, clearing my throat and blinking my tears away. I was looking out to the congregation, who sat bickering amongst themselves or looking wildly around for an explanation. 'They said, that sometimes even when the whole world seems like it's against you, that things can still work out, if you take a chance.' Edward followed my eyes out to the crowd and watched the chaos, hopefully seeing the same wasted emotions that I did. He nodded. All those years of anger and hate, of wasted lives and regret.

'Sounds like a wise person,' he observed, exhaling loudly. I smiled at him brightly.

'She is. And you'd love her.' Before we could continue anymore, the doors at the back of the chapel opened like thunder and Cane walked back in with Brice. The whole chapel dropped into utter silence, anticipation and curiosity rife in the air. The two men walked down the aisle to the centre and couldn't help but noticed that they both looked, different, somehow.

'The wedding is off,' Brice announced immediately, to which the whole room erupted into bellows and chaos. Edward glanced at me quickly and then straight to his dad's face. Cane's brothers stood noisily, to which Cane pointed at them firmly and commanded them to sit back down. Brice looked over to his son with forgiving eyes, expecting to have to deal with the aftermath of whatever he had just done. But Edward held his head high with trust. 'Mr Rodriguez and I have been discussing an idea that was developed and pitched to him a few months ago by an esteemed college of mine, Mr Mack,' I quickly looked over to my dad, who straightened his back and sat taller, as all eyes moved to him. I saw my mum take his hand affectionately and squeeze it for strength. My mind flashed back to the day this had all started and the folio my dad had put down on Cane's cafe table. It had come full circle, then. I beamed at my father as his eyes, maybe recalling the same event, found mine. He breathed deeply, and a small smile came to his pinkening face. I nodded at him discretely. *Yes dad, in the end, it still might have all been worth it.* Brice had continued, and the limelight was back onto him. 'We are going to start a new company,' he announced boldly and loudly, over the roar of discussion and confusion that had erupted from the congregation. Cane's brothers were now on their feet again, advancing towards him, questions on their faces. Cane, who had stood silent so far amidst the ear-piercing disorder, finally spoke, loud and firm.

'*Sit down!*' he commanded to his brothers, with a pointed finger. Scott had appeared closer to Cane's side as the atmosphere in the room had turned from noisy disorder to confused anger, but now to Cane's unassailable voice, the whole room dropped into silence. I heard the Priest behind us swallow with nerves and I held in a proud smile. 'The details will be decided by Mr Bain and myself at another date, but the business will be favourable to both our companies and address a new opportunity that neither of us have truly explored with much passion.' He had a rapt and gripped audience, many of the people there never having heard the famous Cane Rodriguez speak, let alone with so much authority. But Cane shunned the attention, and being the respectful gentleman, I knew he was, he quickly passed the conversation back to Brice to deliver the punch line. Glory never was Cane's thing, Mr Bain on the other hand...

'We are going to develop and build,' Brice declared. 'Mr Mack has already put an immaculate model and pitch together for the new venture, so Mr Rodriguez tells me, and so we will move into a new chapter of the business world with that at the centre'. Cane cut in from the side.

'And Mr Edward Bain will be at the forefront.' This obviously hadn't been discussed as Brice looked as shocked as Edward did, whose grip on my hand tightened suddenly. Mr Bain turned to Cane with questioning eyes, fully understanding the implications of putting Edward in charge of *their* shared new company. It required *a lot* of trust. But it was a gesture, a grand gesture, a final peace offering. Cane didn't want more work, more publicity and even less of a life, I knew this. He wanted change, change for the better. Edward on the other hand still wanted it all and as Cane had been told by me a million times, Edward was a good-hearted man. I smiled at him, his face showing how massive a deal this was. He swallowed though and tried to compose himself, coolly.

'I guess I should go and see what new adventure I am up to now,' Ed stated, beginning to leave. He paused and turned back to me, lifting my hand and kissing it ever so softly. 'You will always be loved by me, Eva Mack, no matter where time and business take us. And you will always have a home here.' He tapped his heart once, then winked and turned to walk back down the aisle. As he passed Cane, he stopped, hesitating and fighting with himself, then abruptly and almost as if his inner self had forced him to do it, he out stretched his hand. Cane stood stunned for a second, the obvious shock showing on his face. Then, as if quickly collecting himself,' Cane took his hand, nodding graciously at whatever Ed was saying. Edward let go and continued to make his way to his dad's embrace and to no doubt hear explanations. *He truly was a good man, wasn't he?* I thought to myself as I watched him. What other man would shake the hand of someone he hated his whole life, just because seconds ago, I had told him that he was ok? Part of me was sad that Edward and our old life together was over, I knew we would never be the same again, that we would never go back to how it was, but as I watched him return to his father's side, I knew it was there and not at my side, that he truly belonged just now. The business and commercial world was where Edward's heart and passion still lay. How he and Cane could ever work together though, that was beyond wonder. I followed my thoughts to Cane, just as he turned and locked his eyes on me. He began to walk to me, slowly, amidst the commotion, with his hands in his pockets. It reminded me of when I had first laid eyes on him in the alley way and his men had parted like the red sea to let him through. He had been beautiful to me even then. Now, now though, he was so much more than just a handsome face.

'Interesting wedding,' he opened, reaching my side and cracking a proper smile. His dimples lit up his face. I nodded with a full-hearted grin in return. Could it be true? Could he finally be mine? Could that smile, and those dimples, finally be just for me? I reached for his hand and quickly glancing around at the manic and distracted congregation, led him discretely away behind the Priest's alter into the small back room. I closed the door behind us, flicking the small catch to the locked position. The noisy crowd disappeared into a hushed muffle as I turned to face him. He was watching me with a suspicious smile.

'You knew this was all going to happen, didn't you?' he quizzed, taking my hand and stroking it gently with his thumb. I shook my head with genuine honesty.

'No. I only *hoped* it would.' He laughed, his eyes sparkling with happiness. 'So…' he whispered, inhaling deeply and kissing my palm ever so gently. I pulled him in close to me, so his body was pressed hard into mine. His playful smile changed instantly, and his breathing deepened. The grin left his lips and was replaced by a mischievous satisfaction. His strong arms wrapped around me tightly as he spoke into the quiet. 'Where do we go from here?'.

'You could start by kissing me,' I replied, as his warm breath danced teasingly on my lips.

'As long as you promise not to run off again, luchadora,' he teased, his hand running up to my neck where it touched the beautiful diamond necklace. I smiled, looking into his deep, penetrating eyes.

'I'll make a deal with you,' I laughed, running my hand down his back. He barked out a gentle appreciation.

'Because deals work out so well for us,' he smiled, and I bit my bottom lip, imprinting his image into my mind.

'I promise you, that I am not going anywhere from now on, unless you are there too.' He grinned, a proper true Cane smile, as happiness and contentment burst from him. He pulled me even closer and then paused, just barely touching my lips with his. I moaned as his eyes danced over my face and back to my parted and waiting mouth. Then, with one more dimpled smile, he kissed me, sending fireworks into the sky and ecstasy into my heart. Every fiber of me was alight with love, every muscle, every hair, every single thing, melting into him with sheer and utter happiness. I was in love more than I could ever have dreamed possible, ever have known to exist. The Priest's room disappeared, as joy swept through me and Cane lifted me into his arms. Everything was finally right, finally perfect, the way it should be…his hand in mine, his kiss on my lips and, us, eventually and deservedly together. I smiled to myself through his tender and passionate embrace…HE was mine and it had all been worth it in *the end*.

EPILOGUE.

It was evening time and the sun was setting. The smell of sweet popcorn drifted through the room and I stood by the microwave watching it turn and pop, lost in my thoughts. So much had changed over the last few weeks, but looking back, it didn't seem like life had ever been any different. I watched the kernels begin to heat and crackle, ready to change form. How fitting, I thought as I reviewed how much the people in my life had changed since this had all started. I thought of each person who had been affected by my decision, that day in the alley, and how, just like this popcorn, they had become something new under the heat.

Cane and Brice had launched their new business, with Edward as the leading man. He was the face of a new, worldwide industry that was successfully sweeping the nations. Obviously, it helped that it was backed and financed by Bain Ltd and Rodriquez Enterprises; two of the most successful businesses of all time, but Edward Bain was the hottest new bachelor in town, and he was enjoying everything that meant. There had been moments of tension between him and Cane, that was expected, but I wondered as the popping continued, if they would ever understand each other, or come to peace with each other. They had already proved they could co-exist in business, but on a personal level, that was a tall order. I sighed quietly with sadness for that. They were two of the best men I knew, and I hoped the future would bring peace. I had grown a strange affection inside of me for Elias and Andreas surprisingly quickly. They'd come around to certain events, but they hadn't been let near to the new company yet. Cane had the charisma and the patience for proper manners and society, but the brothers were still somewhat lacking in that department and we feared they would never learn how to tame and control their crazy and unruly hearts. Yet, those very same hearts had found a spot in mine, against all odds. I had learned from firsthand experience that people could change, and I believed that was still true of them. They had developed a fierce loyalty to me since the day of the wedding, and despite still speaking ill of Bain and Edward, especially Edward., they were quickly on route to becoming the brothers I never had. They escorted me places when Cane was away or busy, called me for advice, welcomed me into the family and even invited me out drinking with them- which I almost always declined. There was still an ongoing in-joke about caterpillars, which had never been explained to this day, but the promise of doing so was there always, and that reference to my still being around in the future, was enough for me. I had never imagined the relationship I found myself developing with these two men and it still pleasantly surprised me when one, or both of them, would show up on my door with take out. Cane had increased Elias's and Andreas's responsibilities within the family business and to the brothers' credits, they had flourished. It seemed that the less time they had, the less trouble they could get into. I grabbed a bowl to empty the popcorn into, as the erupting kernels started to become less frequent. I wondered briefly about the Rodriquez's parents, I hoped they would approve of me and everything that had changed because of me. I smiled to myself with hope, thinking of Cane's mum's dimples smiling with assurance.

On a happy note, I had my job back, after my 'leave-of-absence'. I had missed my kids and their bright insights. My classes became more involved and demanding, encouraging the kids to learn for themselves and not rely on what a teacher told them. I had learned lessons I never thought I could, and it was time to impart some true knowledge and skills onto the future generations. To match Cane's productivity, I had taken a part time lecturing spot at the top university in the country. It was only a few classes a week, but I got to teach with more passion and conviction and with no limitations on topics. I was loving the demand it placed on my views and my convictions, which I had learned the hard way, can always be changed. Then thinking of changing views, my parents came to my mind and the popcorn began to grow more silent. They had taken a little longer to come around to things. They couldn't help but still think the worst of everything and more importantly, they feared for me. They still both assumed the most inconceivable things that happened whilst I had been with Cane and I was sure they thought I had Stockholm syndrome. It wasn't until a couple weeks ago, when they had first kissed again, that they could look at the last few months of their lives with new thankfulness. A returned love is something to be grateful for after all, and I had never thought it would be possible for them to rekindle the love that they lost so long ago, or for them to rebuild the relationship and the companionship they had once held so dear. My heart soared with joy anytime I saw them together, dating and flirting as if it was all new to them again. They were currently in Spain with Grandma on a second honeymoon and I knew that if anyone could iron out those last few kinks of concern, it was that magical old woman. I smiled at the thought of her and her beautiful old home, my eyes still clearly seeing the bluebells in her garden, dancing in the warm breeze. The striking little flower also reminded me of the day I had first recognised them in Cane's gardens whilst touring with Gideon, my newest best friend. The smile vanished from my lips as I thought of my old best friend, Tammy. She had left the city, or so Cane told me, and to be honest, I was quite happy being lied to, if that was the case. I missed her daily, even to my surprise, but I was still so sad and angry at her. I hoped that day when our paths both crossed again, that I would be over it. That we would be able to address each other as once-friends and not enemies. I turned the bowl angrily between my hands, lost in thought as the last few seconds of the microwave ticked away. I shook my head and flushed her from my thoughts. What-ifs had hung around more than I would have liked, but less than I had expected. There was still a lot unsaid between all the families, a lot of questions not asked, and a lot of harsh assumptions made, despite the time which had passed so far. I wondered if the truth of it all would ever surface, or if it would always just be the unspoken period of time that changed all our lives. The deal that altered everything we once knew.

'You're going to miss the beginning of the film, Eva,' Cane's voice shouted at me, breaking through my thoughts. Just hearing his accent made my arm hairs stand on ends still and my heart to beat faster. He was a new person. Happy, relaxed and full of love for life. I rushed into the living room of my flat and put the popcorn down on the coffee table that had once held a memorable glass of juice. The magazine no longer lived there either, it was filed away in a 'Memories' box, like so much else.

'Where are you?' I shouted, looking around for him. He appeared from the hallway in lounge pants and a T-shirt. It still made me smile seeing him in casual clothes, especially when he kept trying to put his hands in pockets that didn't exist. It had taken me a couple weeks to get him into them and now, I couldn't get him out again. I grinned at him and his splendour. He was the most wonderful man I had ever seen, and I was pretty sure that opinion would never change. His dark skin and dark eyes beamed back at me with delight.

'I can't get over how small this flat is,' he announced, pacing around in giant steps. I laughed at him, throwing a piece of popcorn his way. He held his arms out to touch each wall. 'Seriously, how have you managed to live here for so long and not been crushed to death?' I shook my head at his sarcasm, laughing with pretend insult, as he dropped himself onto the sofa beside me and pulled me in close to kiss my forehead. He smelt divine and I closed my eyes, storing the smell in my memories, praying I'd never have to live without him again. He threw some popcorn into his mouth and picked up the remote control. He pulled me closely again, glancing down at me through his thick, black eyelashes.

'What?' I asked, brushing my lips for popcorn crumbs. He smiled with those amazing dimples, gently pulling my hand away from my mouth.

'You're perfect,' he said, quietly as I blushed and laughed at him. He kept on smiling though, keeping my eyes locked with his and ever reading my soul. He whispered it again, more tenderly, before kissing me. 'Perfecta.'

ABOUT THE AUTHOR

Gemma is a Scottish wife and mother of two, who lives in Aberdeen. When she's not parenting or dog walking, she's reading or writing. She loves nothing more than to disappear into other worlds via novels, and so when it comes to writing books, she's in her element.
Simplified to a few words, Gemma loves - chocolate, her family, God, and a good-old, happily ever after.

Printed in Poland
by Amazon Fulfillment
Poland Sp. z o.o., Wrocław